THE UNDEAD. DAY FIFTEEN. THE FOG.

RR HAYWOOD

PROLOGUE

Five hundred and thirty miles above the Earth, the MetOp polar orbiting meteorological satellite records and transmits the data acquired by the high-powered equipment and sends this information to the Svalbard Satellite Station in Norway. The satellite recorded the onset of the storm, and then monitored the progress throughout the night.

A storm unlike any other ever recorded or known. A storm so powerful, it has changed the coastline of many countries, and given destruction on a level that makes the rise of the undead appear paltry in comparison.

Should mankind had not fallen, the storm would have been discussed for many years. It would have been given a name. The most likely name would have been Jonas, for that was the name of the scientist allocated to work the evening of the storm. His name was on the rota, and Jonas had always wanted a storm named after him.

Jonas is dead. His lifeless, half-eaten body lies rotting halfway out of the doorway to his apartment. His wife killed him. She sank her teeth into his neck and savaged his windpipe.

So, the storm went unnamed. There is nobody left to monitor the data being sent by the MetOp satellite, but the satellite doesn't care. It does what it is programmed to do, and will continue for many years, or as long as the solar panels on its huge wings continue to absorb power.

The satellite watched the storm, and now watches something else entirely unique. The cessation of mankind, the vehicles, the factories, jet fuel, and many other factors have triggered a new weather front.

One that is far more dangerous than the storm.

1

I do not want to move. This place is the best I have ever known. Right here, in this tiny room that smells of damp, with bare concrete walls, and no natural light. Here, on this thin mattress laid flat on the hard floor.

My body aches, my muscles are sore from being rested for a few hours. My head thumps with a dull ache, and my mouth feels bone dry. I'm thirsty, really thirsty. Hungry too.

But I don't care. This room is warm and quiet. Lani still sleeps. Her body pressed close to mine.

I stroke my fingertips on her bare shoulder, feeling the soft, warm skin. Silky black strands of hair lie across my chest, and I can smell her odour too. A pleasant, feminine smell, musky and sensual. She moves with a slight adjustment of position, and I can't help but smile when she moves in closer to me, and a slender hand reaches across my chest in an almost protective embrace.

Lani would protect me. This woman would give her life for me. She already has, really. They took her during the fight, but she came back. Was it her that made me immune? What about Cookey? Was he already immune, or was it our blood, pumping into his, that saved him?

Meredith can't be turned, but none of us know anything. We're no more knowledgeable now than we were a few days or a week ago.

We need doctors. That has to be the priority. For the sake of mankind, we have to find out how, or why Lani, Cookey, and I are immune. We have to find out if the dog, Meredith, is significant to this immunity. Are all her breed immune or just her? What about other dogs?

More questions than answers. Every time we turn a corner, we face more uncertainty and dilemma. Still. We ain't dead yet, and the body count on their side only gets bigger by the day. What was it Dave keeps saying? Fifty million people in this country, so the few hundred thousand we might have killed so far is still a drop in the ocean to what could be left.

Fuck 'em. We'll win.

'You're thinking too loud,' she whispers in a hoarse voice, 'I can hear the cogs.'

'Sorry…and er…'

'Don't,' she moves in closer.

'Sorry about last night.'

'I said don't,' she exhales slowly and buries her head further into my side.

'I was so tired…'

'Howie, you don't have to say anything.'

'Yeah, but I feel terrible, like… you know…the first chance we get alone, and I fall asleep…'

'I get it. You just don't fancy me.'

'What? No…'

'I'm joking,' she chuckles, 'forget it. I was asleep about a second after you. Anyway, my bladder is going to burst in a second.'

'Can we stay here all day?' I wrap my arms round her body to draw her closer.

'You're the boss, Mr Howie.' she replies, lifting her head to grin at me. Hair plastered across her forehead, sleep marks on her skin, but she is beautiful beyond compare, 'however,' she groans, 'the great and mighty Mr Howie will be needed by the masses of survivors…and I am going to wet the bed in a second…oh,' she looks down at her own naked body, 'I'm nudey in front of Mr Howie.'

'Nudey!' I burst out laughing.

'Rudey nudey,' she nods seriously, 'close your eyes please while I get up.'

'Not a chance,' I grin wolfishly and make a point of opening my eyes wider.

'Pervert,' shaking her head with a wry grin, she stands up and pulls the cover with her, wrapping it round her body in one smooth move that leaves me naked and completely exposed.

'Oi,' covering my privates, I roll onto my side.

'Oh, it's alright for you to gawp, is it?'

'Give me that cover back,' I make a grab for the corner, but she jerks away too fast for me.

'Come and get it.'

'Get what?'

'You sound like Cookey now,' she laughs. 'You have a lovely bum, Mr Howie,' she adds with a nod down at my naked backside presented to her.

Fifteen days into the apocalypse. Death everywhere. Destruction on a scale that leaves me reeling. Loss, suffering, and pain, and still I'm too shy to uncover my willy in front of her.

'I would say the same, but I haven't seen it,' I look back over my shoulder and let my mouth drop open at the sight of her dropping the cover to stand unashamedly naked in front of me. The humour is gone suddenly, a yearning look on her face. Not lust, but something else, like a need to be open, completely open. Her actions invoke a response, and I roll over, rising swiftly to my feet as I take my hands away from my privates to stand naked before her, but we keep our eyes locked and staring. The lamp in the corner is soft, with yellow light. It's warm and snug in here, and I feel no shame now.

She smiles softly and holds a hand out. I take it, entwining my fingers in hers. She finally breaks eye contact and lets her gaze drop to my shoulders. A look of pain flits across her face as she takes in the bites, cuts, and bruises all over my body. Soft fingers trace over the wounds, clear teeth marks where one of them got their mouth on me.

'I can see your stomach muscles,' she smiles up at me, 'you need to eat more.' She stares directly at me now, 'Look at me.'

'I am.'

'No,' she smiles softly, 'at my body.' I do as bid, and finally, wrench my gaze from staring at her eyes. That I'm in love is a given, but there is something else here, something deep and strange. I don't need to see her body to know I want her physically. Her spirit, the essence of the person has captivated me, her ferocious protection and dedication.

Ah, but I'm a bloke, and I do look down, and what a view. Slender, defined, sleek, and so powerful and lithe. Not an ounce of fat anywhere on her body.

She groans suddenly which snaps my gaze back up 'Sorry,' she winces, 'but I am actually going to wet myself…gotta go.' She lunges in and kisses me quick and hard on the mouth before wrapping the covers round her body and darting for the door.

'Morning,' she calls out, which tells me the others must be up and about already, 'you making the coffees?'

'Yes,' I hear Cookey groaning and grin to myself. Normality is here. Shaking my head, I start getting dressed, and wonder what calamities will befall us today.

2

'Paula.'

A feminine hand reaches sleepily from the covers, the fingers groping to press against Roy's lips. 'Ssshhh,' she mumbles.

'Paula,' Roy repeats, his tone slightly more urgent this time.

'My testicles are hurting.'

Paula emerges from the cover, blinking heavily, she tries to focus in the gloom of the dimly lit room. 'Seriously?' she asks.

'They're aching… I must be getting ca…'

'Roy,' she cuts him off, 'we've had sex three times since we came in here… I'm not surprised they're aching.'

'Yeah, but…'

'When was the last time you had sex?'

'About an hour ago.'

'Not with me,' she smiles sleepily, 'I meant, before…you know…before me.'

'Oh, er…god…years?' Roy shrugs, 'I don't know, but a long time.'

'Years? No wonder then. Years without, then three times in a few hours…'

'It was four actually.'

'Was it?'

'You fell asleep during the last one.'

'Did I? Oh…sorry…did you finish?'

'No! That would be wrong,' Roy looks aghast, 'I was pretty tired too by then anyway so…'

'So, it's three then,' Paula squints at him, 'does it count if neither of us finish?'

'Oh, well,' Roy thinks for a second, 'well, there was certainly penetration, and that is the actual act of sexual intercourse so I would say yes. Yes, it does count.'

'Okay, four then,' Paula flops back down to sink her head onto his chest, 'er…I don't want to sound all cheesy or anything, but um…it was bloody amazing.' She looks up coyly, 'We haven't stopped for the last day….fighting all night, and then that…no one has ever done that before.'

'Done what?'

'Made love to me four times in a night.'

'It wasn't night,' Roy says plainly, 'it was daylight when we came in here.'

'Same thing,' Paula shrugs again then shuffles position to lift her upper body up and rest on her elbows, 'did you enjoy it?' She immediately regrets asking. A reminder of the old Paula, the Paula that needed validating by others. The Paula that needed people to tell her she had done a good job.

'Yes.' a firmness to his tone. A straight answer to a straight question. He looks across to stare into her eyes and blinks several times as a confused look flits across his face. 'Listen,' he begins tentatively, 'I'm not good with words. or people really, words and people,' he nods to himself, 'I get self-obsessed with my anxiety and…'

'Roy, you don't have to explain anything…'

'No, I want to,' he says quickly.

A sinking feeling hits her stomach, a premonition that rejection is about to follow.

'I say the wrong things and offend people, and I can be quite blunt and rude sometimes…what I mean is…I think you are a very nice person and everything, but the er…well, the world has ended and…'

'It doesn't matter,' she says softly, 'it was nice being with you now,' she rubs the sleep from her face, stretching her jaw as she exhales slowly.

'I get obsessive about things and it's hard for others to understand that.'

'Roy, you don't have to explain anything. So, what are your plans?' She asks with another sigh and a tone that suggests the conversation should move on.

'Plans?'

'Are you staying here or...?'

'Oh, right, what are you doing?'

'I'm staying, Roy. It's up to you what you do.'

'I want to be with you so I'll stay.'

'Pardon?' She looks up in surprise.

'I want to stay with you,' he looks over at her again, 'so I'll stay here...' He seems to become aware of his presumptive tone, 'I mean. Is that okay?' He asks with a shake of his head, clearly out of his depth trying to deal with such a sensitive topic.

Paula blinks and stares for a second, 'you want to be with me?'

'Yes, isn't that obvious? I couldn't make love to just anybody. All those germs and dirtiness. God no...I mean...the very thought of sharing bodily fluids with anyone is disgusting, but you...well, you're different.'

'Am I?'

'Oh, completely,' he nods emphatically, 'you make me feel safe.'

'Safe!? Roy, you are one of the toughest men I have ever met...'

'Me? I'm a bloody wreck!' I can't get through a day without thinking I'm dying of some disease...you make that go away,' he nods again, 'something about you, something...' he squints while trying to think, 'something calming.'

'Right,' Paula says slowly, 'I'm sure there is a compliment in there somewhere so...er...thank you?'

'I mean,' Roy continues blithely, 'if you can tolerate me that is, I'll probably piss you off within a day or two so just tell me to fuck off when that happens.'

'Swearing doesn't suit you,' Paula says, cocking her head to one side, 'you speak so well, pronouncing all your letters, and your tone is educated...'

'Oh, sorry.'

'Don't apologise, you don't ever have to apologise to me, Roy. I'm just making an observation. And I can get pretty annoying too, really bossy and...'

'You...bossy? I never noticed.'

'Very funny...so you don't mind making love with me then? Sharing my bodily fluids and all that.'

'Not at all,' he grins, 'shall we do it again?'

'I'm quite sore but er...um...ah whatever, it's the end of the world.'

3

T he woman grows in stature with every passing hour. Striding
through the fort with clipboard in hand. She is still young yet
others many years older defer to her natural authority. She looks different, the way she walks with a straight back and head held high. A sense
of confidence that is reassuring, that she knows what to do and what
must be done.

Lenski looks up at the sky, noticing the cloud that seems to be
getting lower every few minutes. The deep blue sky and scorching sun
of the last two weeks has gone, chased away by that brutal storm. The
fort is in a mess. Complete chaos to the untrained eye, but she can see
the organisation within that chaos. Groups of people work to clear the
ruined debris from the ground, stacking it up near the front gates ready
to be taken away later.

More workers slowly start picking away at the hastily formed barri-
cade at the rear gate under the watchful eye of a crew headed by Darius.
Others pick through the piled-up debris, selecting and putting to one
side anything that can be used again. Wood for building or material for
cover.

Young children sleep and rest on the ramp that leads to the high
walls, the only proper dry ground, and again under the watchful eye of

another crew tasked to guard them. Women stay with the children, caring for them, giving maternal affection and soothing words. The young boys brought back by Nick are quiet and terrified with faces etched with shock. Those that do sleep, do so fitfully with frequent cries that speak of dark nightmares, and the horrors they have witnessed.

A third crew remain outside the gates, tasked to watch and do nothing else. No entry to anyone. No exit to anyone. The fort is now a secure environment. It has to be this way.

Yet more people have been tasked to provide Lenski with a full inventory of stocks; food, supplies, clothing, and equipment. So many of these survivors have only the clothes they are wearing, and no other possessions. The children will need clean clothes, vitamins, and nutritious food. Everyone needs clean clothes, vitamins and nutritious food.

The visitor centre is gone, destroyed in the storm, and with it the toilets, and washing facilities. Anyone needing the toilet now has to go out the front under the watchful eye of the crew tasked to remain there. Some plyboard sheets are all that give privacy, until a better solution can be made.

'Hey,' a voice breaks her concentration. Lani walking back from the front gates with a blanket wrapped around her body.

'You are awake, yes?'

'We are,' Lani replies, 'you've been busy…have you seen outside? It's so foggy.'

'Yes, I see this,' Lenski glances up again, 'you will come for coffee, yes? In the offices?'

'Okay, I'll get the others,' Lani nods as she walks back towards their rooms.

'Lenski?'

The Polish woman turns to see Lilly approaching with yet another clipboard held in one hand. 'The food has been checked, clothing too… we're waiting on the rest now.'

'This is good,' Lenski nods, 'you not sleep yet?'

'No,' Lilly shakes her head, 'I tried, but…' her voice trails off as she glances to the ramp where her brother sleeps deeply under the watchful eye of the guards, already firm friends with the little girl Milly. 'I'd rather be busy,' Lilly adds firmly.

'Okay, you will sleep when your body needs it,' Lenski shrugs, with so much to do, she can observe the welfare of others, but not invest the time in checking everyone. It's up to them what they do, and when they want to sleep. 'We have coffee now, yes?'

'Coffee?' Lilly asks.

'The others, they wake. We have the coffee and the meeting to discuss what we do now, you come for this.'

'Really? You want me to come? I can stay here and get...'

'No, you need the coffee, and you have the information on the food and clothes, yes? So, you come, and we talk. Maybe Nick, he will be there too,' she offers a rare smile at the obvious flush in Lilly's cheeks. 'He is nice boy,' Lenski adds as they walk side by side.

'He is,' Lilly replies matter of fact.

'You like him?'

'Of course, I like everyone here.'

'No. You *like* him? The way a woman likes a man, the way I like Maddox.'

'Oh...well, we only just met, and I'm sure Nicholas is very busy with his group now.'

'These days they are new, yes?' Lenski nods, 'maybe we don't wait like we did before. Maybe we should take the happy when we can, yes?'

'Maybe he doesn't like me,' Lilly says, glancing across at the older woman that seems so confident.

'You are beautiful girl, and I see many men here look at you,' Lenski replies, 'and I see how Nick look at you, he likes you, this is for sure.'

Reaching the former police offices once used by Sergeant Debbie Hopewell and Ted, the two women set about switching the gas burner on to boil water. Chipped mugs, all mismatching and of varying sizes litter the top of the old work unit. A stained teaspoon poking out of a bad of sugar next to a torn open box of teabags and commercial catering size tub of instant coffee. Individual portions of long-life milk in a cardboard box complete the adhoc kitchen area.

Maddox files in next. Silent and brooding as ever. He nods once at

Lilly and offers Lenski a kiss on the cheek before opening a fresh bottle of water, forsaking the polluting beverages of tea or coffee. Darius is next, having seen his lifelong best friend walk in, he too joins the group, but heads for the chipped mugs, rummaging about to get himself a mug ready for some strong black coffee.

Sierra strides in, offering a quick smile to Darius and Maddox before launching into a conversation with Lenski.

Voices approach the door, the tones of Blowers and Cookey preceding their physical form. 'Fog,' Blowers says, entering first with Cookey right behind him.

'Mist,' Cookey replies instantly.

'Fog, you twat.'

'Mist, you twat,' Cookey imitates his best friend, 'mist is on the coast, fog is like inland or something.'

'Yeah, or something,' Blowers says, 'you don't even know, it's fog… mist is like…like a thin fog, isn't it? Morning,' Blowers calls out, shifting his attention to the occupants of the room.

'Aye up chuckies,' Cookey nods, heading straight for the stove, 'Hey, Lilly, you alright?'

'Yes, fine thank you,' Lilly smiles at the beaming lad.

'You're educated, is it mist or fog,' Cookey asks in his easy way, 'me and cockchops are having a disagreement.'

'Er well, actually they are the same, but Simon is more correct as fog is defined when visibility is reduced to less than one kilometre, so yes… we have fog.'

'Ha! In your fat face,' Blowers exclaims in triumph. 'One nil to me, thank you very much.'

'Bollocks,' Cookey mutters with a fallen face that immediately brightens back up, 'you brewing up?'

'Er, well, yes I was going to.'

'I'll give you a hand.' Cookey starts shuffling the mugs about and spooning heaped teaspoons of coffee granules into them. 'Everyone having coffee? Good,' he adds before anyone can reply. 'Coffee is easier than dunking teabags in and out,' he advises Lilly, 'then you get the awkward knobs like Blowers who like weak tea or builders tea or uber fucking strong tea, served in a china mug on a porcelain saucer with a digestive. How's your brother?'

Grinning at his infectious humour, Lilly nods quickly, 'fast asleep with the others.'

'Milly with him?' Cookey asks, pausing as he tries to remember who has sugar then giving up and moving the packet onto the main table.

'Side by side, they look so sweet, and that dog has been with them the whole time too.'

'What dog?' Clarence's huge form looms over Cookey, staring down suspiciously at the mugs. 'Did you wash them?'

'Scrubbed 'em,' Cookey lies with a grin.

'No, you didn't,' Clarence tuts, 'Meredith?' He turns to look down at Lilly, 'thought I hadn't seen her.'

'Morning,' Nick is next, strolling in casually he spots Lilly and offers her a huge grin. 'Hello. You okay? How's Billy?'

'Oh, time to go,' Cookey makes a swift exit toward the table.

'He's fine, been asleep for ages. And you?'

'Me? I'm fine,' Nick nods and grins again, his own face blushing slightly at the sight of the beautiful blond girl he kissed yesterday, 'er… so…you okay then?'

'I'm fine,' Lilly laughs at his awkwardness.

'You slept much?'

'No,' Lilly replies, 'I er, well, I wanted to keep busy and help.'

'You must be fucked…shit, er…I mean knackered…I mean…is knackered swearing?' He asks quickly, pushing a hand through his thick hair.

'I'm fine and no, knackered isn't swearing…and you can swear if you want, you having coffee?' She asks as a way of putting him at ease.

'I'd love one…'

'Are Paula and Roy joining us?' Clarence's deep voice fills the room, 'Cookey, go and let them know we're meeting.'

'Why me? Nick's already standing up…'

'Nick is talking to Lilly and don't bloody argue.'

'Yeah, Cookey, don't bloody argue,' Blowers adds.

'And you can go with him,' Clarence cuts in, 'for being a cheeky sod.'

'Ha,' Cookey laughs as the two lads head back outside.

'So, er...you been busy then?' Nick asks once the lads have walked past.

'I've been helping Lenski get things organised, checking the food and supplies,' Lilly lifts the lid on the rattling saucepan and pauses for a second as she thinks of a way to lift the heavy pot.

'Here,' Nick steps forward, grasping the saucepan, he gently moves it to start pouring the water into the mugs. Very aware of the closeness of Lilly, he keeps his eyes fixed firmly on the pan, but longs to glance up and look into her blue eyes.

'I'll stir while you pour,' she reaches past him, brushing her arm against his, both of them pausing to smile awkwardly.

'They're coming,' Cookey walks back in with Blowers, 'they were already up and about.'

'Bloody hell,' everyone turns to see Howie standing in the doorway, Dave and Lani right behind him, 'Is that Nick brewing up?'

'Yeah, I wonder why,' Blowers laughs.

'First time for everything,' Howie remarks with a grin, 'morning Lilly, morning all.'

'Ignore them,' Lani says to Lilly, 'you okay? Did you sleep much?'

Lilly replies then sets about getting the mugs filled with Nick, stirring the contents before handing them out round the table. Everyone says thank you, everyone smiles and grins. Paula and Roy are the last to arrive, heading straight for the table, and gratefully accepting mugs of coffee from Nick and Lilly. More chairs are pulled in as the group get seated. Nick nods to Lilly to sit next to him, knowing she must be feeling awkward at being here.

Lilly watches and listens. This group, apart from Nick, are all so unfamiliar to her, but the way they interact with each other is so easy and casual. Banter and jokes, comments, and quiet laughter. The energy in the room is magnetic, pulsing with enthusiasm. These are people who have seen and dealt with utter horror yet are still here, and willing to get things done. She feels a sudden and overwhelming sense of being witness to something very special, of being a part of something unique and profound.

She saw the after-effects of the battle last night. The ruined bodies stacked up and floating at the shoreline. She saw the dead being laid out ready for disposal, and she heard the account after account of what Howie and his group have done. Tales that get wilder with each telling, but each one based on a truth.

Guilt swarms through her body, that she is able to recognise and be a part of this group when so many have lost their lives. Conflicting emotions burn her heart, that she knows her father was a weak man incapable of protecting his family, and he paid the ultimate price for that. She feels a warm hand close over hers and looks up to see Nick looking at her with concern. The gesture, mostly hidden under the edge of the table is one of care. She smiles at him, closing the tips of her fingers over his as he offers her a gentle squeeze.

'Don't feel guilty,' he whispers, correctly guessing the emotions she is feeling, 'you're here, and that's all that matters. Billy is safe too.'

She nods at him, giving silent thanks that this brave lad that has done so much is here yet again when it matters.

4

I watch Nick and Lilly, seeing the emotions cross her face. She looks overwhelmed by all of this, at this room so suddenly full of the people who all know each other. She's so young but seems much older than her years. I give them a few minutes, getting a discrete nudge from Lani who also notices as they hold hands under the table.

But eventually business must proceed so I clear my throat, 'right then,' I call. The conversations die out quickly, faces turning to look at me, and I can see that despite the bags under all of our eyes, despite the worn, haggard looks some of us have, we're all also keen-eyed and ready.

The energy is strong and positive, apart from Dave who looks exactly the same as he always does. I wonder what he thinks during these times, probably thinking about knives and new ways of severing heads or something. He offers me a quick glance which again, makes me think he's a mind-reading cyborg.

'Bit bloody misty today,' I observe to the room at large.

'It's fog actually, Mr. Howie,' Cookey leans forward to look down the table, 'essentially, mist and fog are the same, but fog is defined when visibility is reduced to less than one kilometre…'

'You are such a twat,' Blowers groans, 'Lilly told him that about five minutes ago.'

Shaking my head at Cookey I continue, 'well, it's foggy then, but we've still got loads to do…Lenski, how's the fort looking?' I nod at the Polish woman sitting with the clipboard in front of her on the table.

'Is not so good,' she replies in a flat tone with a shrug, 'the toilets, they are gone now, the backwards gate is blocked, and we try to open it, the land is all gone so we are an Island, yes? This is a good thing, I think. We clear the broken things away, and keep what we can use again, but… it is not good; we have many of the things we need, yes? We have the food and clothing, this is checked by Lilly, you say now what we have?' She nods at Lilly to continue.

Lilly looks confidently around the room, 'we've worked out that with the numbers we have now, in this fort, I mean…we have enough food to eat comfortably for about two weeks. However, we are desperate for many other things…er…shall I say what they are now?' She looks to Lenski who nods. 'Clothes for a start, and especially children's clothes. Bedding and tents too, pants and socks, toothbrushes, toothpaste. We need everything that children need to live comfortably, and that includes things like books, toys, drawing equipment…same for the adults too. We have enough food, but not enough clothing, bedding, sleeping bags, and covers. The storm pretty much destroyed everything that was outdoors.'

Paula leans forward, showing her intent to speak, 'they'll need milk too, children need milk, don't they?' She looks round for confirmation.

'For calcium and bone growth,' Lilly replies, 'otherwise, they can develop things like Rickets.'

'Milk,' I nod at Lilly, trying to think where the hell we're going to get milk from. I get a sudden image of trying to get a cow in a boat to bring back to the fort then, I remember when Dave told me about how he blow a cow up and snort with laughter which just earns me some strange looks. 'Er…we'll get a cow then,' I switch back to being serious, 'but um…can you drink milk straight from a cow? Doesn't it have to be pasteurised?'

'It does,' Lilly answers in her clear educated tones, she seems so much older than a fifteen-year-old. Silence descends with the room of adults all waiting to see who knows how pasteurisation is done. Lilly clears her throat, and drops her gaze to the sheets of paper in front of her. 'It's quite simple,' she says casually. 'The milk is heated and cooled, not boiled…I think it's something like sixty degrees Celsius. It can be done on a pan or a saucepan,' she purses her mouth as she finishes, as though worried that everyone will think she is talking shit or showing off.

'Easy then,' I say quickly, 'apart from getting a cow here that is.'

'We could get a goat,' Cookey offers.

'Yeah, we'll get some sheep, and a few pigs at the same time,' Blowers adds, 'some chickens, a few…'

'Chickens are a good idea,' Maddox interrupts, 'eggs are full of protein.'

'How many cows will we need?' Cookey asks, 'one won't be enough, we'll need a whole herd…and think of the shit, and what we gonna feed 'em? There's no grass here.'

'Hay…or straw,' Maddox nods, 'get some of that, and throw it about.'

'What if they're zombie cows?' Cookey squints his eyes, 'can cows catch zombie?'

'They're vegetarian, you dick,' Blowers tuts.

'Yeah, but the thing that bites 'em won't be vegetarian, will it,' Cookey retorts, 'we'll have to check their eyes, and see if Meredith attacks them.'

'Hang on,' Lani shakes her head, 'so our test for infection is to see whether our dog attacks a cow or not? What if she just doesn't like cows?'

'Good point,' Cookey wags his finger, 'I don't know the answer to that…but I will think about it.'

'Yeah, you do that,' Blowers joins in with the head shaking, 'how we gonna get a cow over here anyway.'

'Clarence can carry it,' Cookey grins, 'on his shoulders…they can swim, can't they? I've seen them on those documentaries when they cross the big rivers, and stampede about, and shit.'

'We should get trifle,' Dave announces, which just about kills the conversation entirely as every face turns to look at him, 'children like trifle,' he adds as deadpan as ever.

'Trifle,' I nod slowly, 'yeah, we can get some trifle…but er…I think, it'll all be spoiled by now.'

Dave nods and thinks for a second, 'we can get the parts that make the trifle then.' He nods again, problem solved.

'I don't like trifle,' Roy offers his opinion and earns a look from Dave in the process.

'Um, maybe we should focus on weapons and things,' I suggest, 'we're down to shotguns and axes again…'

'And knives,' Dave adds casting another suspicious look at Roy.

'And knives,' I repeat quickly, 'we need weapons and ammunition first, then we go for supplies. Those are the top priorities.'

'Doctors,' Paula leans forward, 'we're going to need medically trained people here, some of you are immune…that needs following up.'

'Good point,' I nod, 'how do we find a doctor though?'

'We go to their houses,' Paula replies in a tone that implies she has thought this through, 'hospitals will keep records of their staff and personnel, we find a large hospital, and access the records. I bet they'll have paper records somewhere in case of an IT failure.'

'Doesn't need to be a large hospital,' Maddox interjects, 'even a local surgery will do it…'

'I was thinking of going for surgical doctors, those with experience of major trauma and serious injuries,' Paula explains.

Frowning, I take a sip of coffee, and feel the first itch of the day for a smoke, 'disease experts are what we need, but…' I sigh slowly, 'at this stage, I think any doctor will suffice, well, I mean a medical doctor anyway.'

'Maybe then,' Clarence cuts in, 'we should look for Army doctors, they'll have front line battle injury expertise, and be used to working in the worst conditions. We need weapons and ammunition, right?' His meaty forearms rest on the table which creaks under his weight, 'so we go for a military establishment, a big one with a medical unit. The Navy has got a training hospital just outside of Portsmouth, they used it for treating soldiers coming back from Iraq and Afghanistan.'

'Fucking Portsmouth,' I show my evident distaste with a sneer, 'I hate that place, shit, I hated it before, but now…'

Paula looks from Clarence to me, 'it's a good idea, we get ammunition, weapons and find medical staff…then we can go for the supplies they need…or,' she suggests quietly, 'we divide our forces, and send out two teams to…'

'No way,' I cut her off firmly, 'we stay together at all times, not after what happened yesterday and almost losing Nick. We've got some good skills in this team, so we keep together and make the best use of them. Maddox,' I switch my gaze to the intent looking young man watching me from his deep intelligent eyes, 'you alright staying here?'

He nods and draws breath, 'I'll stay, but on one condition.'

'What's that?' I ask him, everyone pausing to hear him out.

'You take Jagger and Mo Mo, get them trained up to your standard.'

I can feel the instant uncertainty from my team, Nick shifts position, and both Cookey and Blowers look down. I glance to Dave, but he just stares back as devoid as ever. Lani shrugs, and finally I look to Clarence who nods while turning the corners of his mouth down, agreeable, but reluctantly so.

'They'll take orders?' Clarence asks, 'instantly, and with no stupid comments or arguments.'

'I'll speak to them,' Maddox replies simply, 'they'll do as you say.'

'Fair enough then, so my team, Paula and Roy, and Jagger and Mo Mo…we go get stuff and bring it back while you lot stay here and do more stuff.'

'Stuff?' Lani laughs, 'great orders there.'

I shrug and sip at my coffee, 'I need a smoke.'

'Smoke then,' Lenski says bluntly.

'Can't smoke in here,' I recoil in almost shock, the years of habit are ingrained, no smoking in government buildings, no smoking in pubs or clubs, no smoking inside anywhere. The ruling was right, smoking kills, but then so do zombies…and storms…and mad dirty bastard pretend doctors. Still, Lilly is young, and not everyone here smokes so I know it would be unfair, 'we can wait.'

'Then we go outside, and you smoke, yes?' Lenski is up and walking to the door, Nick is on his feet, and already pulling a packet of cigarettes from his pocket as he offers an apologetic look at Lilly.

This is nuts. We're the survivors at the end of mankind, and we're traipsing outside to have a smoke, all of us gathering in a loose circle as the cigarettes and lighters get handed around. Paula lights up and closes her eyes as she savours the first drag of smoke. Nick looks content, holding a mug of coffee while smoking, and standing next to the gorgeous girl he saved. Me, Cookey and Blowers complete the smokers within our group.

'You two,' Maddox 's deep voice interrupts my reverie as he summons Jagger and Mo Mo strolling past us.

'What's up, Mads?' One of them asks, I think it's Jagger, but I'm still struggling to tell them apart.

'You're both going out with Mr Howie and his crew, yeah?' Maddox explains.

'Sweet,' the other one grins, showing a row of chipped teeth surrounded by a wispy beard on a pale face kept hidden from the sun under a filthy baseball cap.

'You do what they say, you get me,' Maddox speaks simple and blunt, using only the words that are necessary, nothing more and nothing less.

'Got it,' the first one nods, this one darker skinned, maybe mixed race with darker hair. The penny drops as I realise this one is Mo Mo which is Mohammed. Then I realise that I might be racist for assuming that the one with the darker hair and features is the one with the Islamic name. Then I start thinking about Islam and Muslims and how they pray several times a day and I'm pretty sure I haven't seen this lad praying ever.

'What does Mo Mo mean?' Dave asks flatly.

'Mohammed innit bruv,' Mo Mo answers with a nod.

'Is Jagger your proper name?' Dave switches to the other one, and I smile inwardly that he has saved me from having to work it out, Mohammed is the one with the darker hair and features.

'Yeah, bruv,' Jagger replies.

'I'm not bruv or mate...I'm Dave...just Dave...that is Mr Howie. Understand?'

'Yeah, sweet,' Jagger keeps nodding, clearly cowed by the small quiet man. After the last night, and having seen him fight, I'm not surprised they are both in awe.

'That is Simon Blowers, if you find yourselves alone without Mr Howie, or me or Clarence then you take orders from him. Do you understand? He is like a corporal; he takes charge when we are absent.'

'What?' Cookey exclaims, 'why can't I be a corporal?'

'You'll never be a corporal,' Blowers rocks on his heels in ecstatic bliss at being promoted over his friend.

'No, hang on,' Cookey bleats, 'Mr Howie can give promotions…Mr Howie…can I be a…'

'Not a chance,' I grin.

'No, but…'

'Not happening,' Clarence cuts him off.

'Oh, this is the worst day ever,' Cookey groans, 'this is worster than that time Dave killed April when I was about to touch her boobs…'

'She was a fucking zombie,' Blowers tuts, 'and there's no such word as worster.'

'Yeah, but she loved me,' Cookey sighs, 'we were gonna get married and have a honeymoon, and everything.'

'What?' Maddox shakes his head, confused at the conversation.

'Tell you another time,' I explain before Cookey can launch into another tale about Marcy and get me in trouble with Lani.

'She had massive ti…' Cookey starts to say, cut off by Dave snapping *Alex* before he can finish the sentence.

'Ah well,' Cookey half grins, intent on having the last word, 'I'm immune so you can blow me, Blowers,' he grins and laughs as Blowers shakes his head again, 'ha! Blow me Blowers…I never thought of that before…Blow me Blowers.'

'For fuck's sake,' Blowers groans. I watch Paula grinning and laughing softly, others too. Even the hard-faced Lenski is looking on in amusement. Give Cookey an audience, and he'll go on all day, and Blowers *does* make an awesome straight man to Cookey's gags.

'That fog is touching the top of the fort,' Dave interrupts the stupidity. Turning around, we all stare up to watch the thick misty cloud as it rolls over the top walls, obscuring them in places, and with such a low blanket it gives the fort a very enclosed feeling, 'we'll need rope.'

'What for?' I ask him.

'So, we can tie together, fog like this can make a man get lost within seconds.'

'Probably only here mate,' I look back up at the top of the wall, 'the sun will burn it away soon anyway. Right, we move out in fifteen minutes. Kit ready, lads you get what shotguns and cartridges you can find. Weapons cleaned, clothes dry, and everyone freshly shaved with clean boots.'

'Seriously?' Cookey asks in alarm at the prospect of both shaving *and* having to clean his filthy boots.

'No mate,' although I suspect that Dave would have them lined up ready for kit inspection given his way.

The fifteen minutes doesn't quite work. We end up having another coffee and scrabbling about trying to find anything that might be dry enough to wear as the clothes we got from the safari park are ruined, and still sodden from the storm. With so many guards in the fort needing weapons now, we're reduced to one sawn-off shotgun each, pistols and hand weapons. A sorry state we find ourselves in, grumbling about wet pants, wet socks, no decent weapons, and Nick trying to remember where he left the Saxon.

So, half an hour later and we're pretty much ready, or as ready as we'll ever be. Trooping out the sorry looking gates onto the small strip of land to the front of the fort, at which point we all stop and stare.

'Oh,' I sigh again for the twentieth time since being up, 'that...' I say slowly, 'is some foggy shit.'

'It is,' Dave says next to me. We can see about a foot from the edge of the water, literally no further than that, and the surface of the water looks like a mirror, perfectly flat with barely a ripple on the surface. No noise from anywhere, even the fort now seems far behind us. Thick white clouds that roll and slide in a confusing and never-ending pattern of chaos.

'The boats are there,' Clarence says from the end of the line.

Cookey steps forward to peer into the white gloom, then he slowly turns, and scratches his head, 'how we gonna find the land?'

'It's that way,' Nick points dead ahead, 'we just go in that direction.'

'We get six feet from this land, and we won't know any direction,' Clarence mutters, 'Dave, you got a compass?'

'I have,' Dave answers, followed by a few seconds of silence during which time Clarence takes a calming breath.

'Can we use it then?' He asks with forced patience.

'Yes,' Dave stares ahead at the fog, 'we'll need Meredith,' he turns to look at me.

'She's here,' Nick replies, 'she came out with us.' Dave looks down the line to see the furry long nose of Meredith edging past Nick's legs. Dave then digs into a pocket, and pulls out a small round compass, he flicks the lid open and stares for a few seconds.

'Okay,' he announces.

'Okay, what?' Clarence asks.

Dave stares along to the big man and shrugs, 'Okay, Clarence?'

'No, I mean okay what? What is okay? Okay, you got the direction? Okay, we're ready to go…okay what?'

'Yes,' Dave replies.

'Fuckin…'

'Dave,' I cut across Clarence as he gets ready to implode and sense we're in for another very long day, we need more coffee, we need food and dry clothes, we need a sodding day off, 'have you got the direction of the land?'

'Yes,' Dave nods again as though that much is obvious.

'So, we can go?' I ask him.

'Yes.'

'Great, so…we'll do that then…to the boats,' I try a little mock cheer, but it falls flat.

'Nice try,' Lani whispers as she falls into step beside me.

'Thanks, listen…I'm really sorry about last night, I still feel bad about it.'

'Don't,' Lani is back to being as blunt as Dave. I don't know her that well, but I'm guessing she has a work mode and a private mode.

'All aboard then,' I quip as we reach the first boat, 'how many we taking?'

'Two…I'm in this one, and Dave can go in that one,' Clarence shoves the front of his boat, forcing the thing to slide back into the water. Jagger and Mo Mo make for his boat, quickly moving to either side of him to help push the last few inches.

'I'll jump in that one,' Nick offers, and moves towards Clarence.

'Come on then,' the rest of us push our boat into the water and wade out to climb aboard. A loud splash has us all spinning around to draw weapons until we see the dog paddling round the back of Nick's boat, clearly having already decided which one she wants to go in. Clarence leans down, and hefts her in with ease, at which point she shakes, and promptly wobbles to the front to sit staring out with her pink tongue hanging down.

'Rope,' Dave throws the end of his rope at the first boat, the end of which catches Clarence on the cheek as he stands upright. A very dark and very frosty glare then goes on for a few seconds until the big man swallows it down, and grasps the rope firmly in one hand, 'tie it on,' Dave orders.

'I'll hold it,' Clarence replies.

'Tie it on…what if you fall in?'

'I won't,' Clarence growls.

'Enough,' I snap, 'this is shitty enough without you two being twats, pack it in and grow up,' the anger flashes from me, a hard tone through gritted teeth, and one that makes the others all stare at me with sudden concern.

Clarence immediately drops his gaze from Dave, and nods, 'sorry boss,' he mutters then clears his throat, 'just tired, won't happen again.'

'Dave?' I turn to look at him, refusing to let him off the hook.

'Yes, Mr Howie?'

'Switch on, and stop being belligerent.'

'Yes, Mr Howie. Sorry, Mr Howie,' he looks genuinely remorseful with a look of abject misery at being told off.

'Tie the rope on, Dave you lead. Nick, you take the motor on that one, and Blowers you do this one. We'll stop for more coffee and dry clothes when we can, but until then, I don't want any fucking about, do you understand?'

A chorus of muttered replies, *yes boss* and *yes Mr Howie* sound back at me. Paula and Roy look down at the ground as though embarrassed.

Two small engines are fired up, the *putput* noise seemingly too loud for the closed-in environment of the dense fog. Nick holds his boat steady until Blowers navigates slowly past, Cookey taking the opportunity to stick his middle finger up at Nick as he passes. Dave settles in the very middle of the boat, and already looks ashen from his intense dislike of being on the water, he focusses his worry into the compass, staring intently at the little hands on the clock-like face. As we pass the first boat, and the rope draws out until we feel the jerk from the tension, Dave extends one hand out with the palm facing in, pointing in the direction we need to go.

'Mr Howie,' Cookey nods back to where the shore should be, but instead all we can see is thick cloud that rolls and moves around us. The air is filled with moisture, not cold or even refreshing after so many days, but somehow still warm, like the very air is still charged. The only noise comes from the engines as we push further into the unknown.

'Can't see a thing,' Paula mutters as she looks about. Roy remains passive and watchful, his bow in one hand with his rucksack holding the arrows strapped firmly to his back.

'You're going off course,' Dave replies waving his hand as he motions for Blowers to steer to the right.

Meredith's barking breaks the silence. On all fours, she leans over the front of the boat with her eyes and ears fixed dead ahead. She stops barking, cocks her head, and starts again, lips pulled back to show her deadly white teeth.

'What is it?' I call back.

Clarence moves to the front of his vessel and rests one hand on the dog's neck, 'no idea,' he shrugs, 'easy girl,' he soothes the hair on Meredith's neck urging her gently to stop barking. She complies but continues with the low deep growling we've all come to know so well.

Eyes strain as we peer into the whiteness, but we can't see further than a few inches past the front of our lead boat. Lani and Cookey take a side each, staring intently. The two lads in Nick's boat do the same. Only Dave remains seated and despite the prospect of their being a baddie to slay, he still looks completely miserable.

'FUCK!' I stagger forward from the impact, dropping my axe as I flail to keep my balance. The boat hits something hard and despite the slow speed, we're all jolted.

Blowers veers to the side too quickly at the same time as opening the throttle. The movement, along with the impact jolts me too far forward, and I'm over the side plunging into the sea amidst a chorus of yells. My heavy boots and clothes immediately fill with water, and start dragging me down, forcing me to kick hard to break the surface. As I come up spluttering, I spin around, and spot the first boat already well past my position, and the second boat coming straight at me. With no choice, I dunk back under, and dive down as the front of the boat smacks into my back driving the air from my lungs. It seems an eternity as the boat's underside judders me along in a whirl of bubbles and watery screams. With a surge of panic, I think of the propeller, and drive off to the side, kicking furiously to avoid being ripped apart from the spinning metal blades.

God knows how I avoid it, but a few seconds later, and once again, I'm spluttering as I get back up to the surface as my gag reflex kicks in from the saltwater I just ingested. Eyes burning, vision blurred, and I feel someone next to me, a hand reaching out to steady my panicked splashing about. I grasp the arm and hear shouts as the others call my name and tell me to wait there, then more shouts, louder and more urgent. I finally get my eyes open and stare at the corpse I'm clinging onto, a rancid swollen thing of no discernible gender or age. A bloated body that gives me a brief shock in recoil. I spin around, and see more of them bobbing nearby. Some turned down in the classic floating corpse style of face down, others on their backs or sides. So many of them, and only the motion of the boats has disturbed the otherwise placid waters and caused them to have motion.

'We hit a body,' Cookey yells out needlessly.

'Really?' I shout back, and hear Blowers giving some harsh abuse at the obvious statement his mate just made.

'And Dave dropped the compass,' he adds helpfully, 'so we've lost our direction…'

'I can't see you,' I shout and feel that surge of panic again as I realise the two boats are completely gone from view. Clarence shouts an order, and both engines are cut instantly plunging the whole area into near-perfect silence.

'That doesn't help,' I yell out, 'make noise…'

'Er…' Clarence shouts, 'we're this way…so come this way…to er…the way of my voice.'

'BRILLIANTLY DONE THERE, CLARENCE.' I YELL BACK AND START SWIMMING a slow breaststroke while looking at the corpses blocking my route.

'*We three kings of orient are…*' Cookey breaks into song, his tone-deaf voice blasting out as happy as ever.

'Keep going,' I shout and get a mouthful of water in the process.

'*One in a manger, one in a car…er…jingle bells batman smells robin flew awaaaayyyy…oh, what fun it is to be a Blowers that is gay…*'

'You're such a fucking dick,' Blowers shouts from somewhere ahead of me.

'Blowers said he wants to give you the kiss of life, Mr Howie,' Cookey quips, 'he said the new technique is to do it with tongues… naked…with baby oil…'

Meredith barking like crazy cuts him off, voices become louder, shouting with alarm. A pistol shot rings out within a second of the cacophony of sound bursting out.

'What is it?' I shout and start swimming faster.

'They're coming towards you,' Dave shouts, 'I got one…'

'One what?' I try to yell, but water sploshes back into my mouth. Someone shouts *stop her,* and I hear another distinct splash, either Lani or the dog has just jumped in.

'Meredith is coming your way,' Clarence bellows which answers the question. I keep my mouth closed this time and focus on swimming towards the noise. At sea level like I am, and the floating bodies obstruct my view, I try craning my head up, but get no higher than a couple of inches. A few more strokes, and I try again, something larger than a body flits into view between the tendrils of thick fog that cling to the surface of the water. Heavy breathing, and some small splashing noises give me the direction of Meredith, well what I hope is Meredith anyway. I get a sudden flashback of the shark movies and find the panic starting to rise again. The horrible sensation that something is underneath me, stalking me, snaking near to my legs. I know this is stupid as we don't get sharks here, but still, I start thinking of big mutant eels or zombie fish or whales, and all sorts of horrible images. I swim harder forcing myself not to go into a frenzy. A growl ahead of me and I crane my head back up amidst my own now ragged breaths. The dark mass is closer, a stack of mangled bodies all compressed together with tangled limbs and thick strands of pink innards. Dank dark patches of hair mixed with blondes and gingers, a bald head in there too, legs and feet, hands, arms, and the whole thing like a raft upon which two undead lie flat out growling and hissing as they lock eyes on me. They look bruised, battered and deformed, one of them has an arrow sticking out of his arse from a hasty but well-aimed shot taken by Roy. So grey and lifeless that I wonder how they can still be moving, but they are, and the sight of me seems to animate them. A darker shadow passes in front of them which causes me more undue panic as my mind translates the image into being a huge shark fin until I realise it's the head of Meredith gliding around as she looks for a way onto the corpse raft.

'Dave,' I shout out, 'you missed mate, there's still two on there…'

'There was three, Mr Howie,' he shouts back. Of course, there was. How could I not realise that?

'Did I get one?' Roy shouts politely.

'In the arse mate, but I don't think he's that bothered. Dave, do pistols work if they've been underwater?'

'No, Mr Howie…not these ones anyway.'

Right. Brilliant. Two nasty bastards that have a height advantage and are bearing down on me with a look of glee written all over their rancid faces. Nope, make that one as Meredith has just launched herself up and gripped one by the face before letting her weight sink her back down dragging the flailing beast with her. That dog is amazing.

She busies herself with a decent impression of jaws as the water around her turns a funny pink colour. That leaves just one. Just one wanker with his lips pulled back showing me his lovely stained and chipped teeth.

'Can you swim?' He doesn't answer. Ignorant shit. I wait until the last second to see what he will do, and as I hoped, he lunges forward to take a nice big bite while I move to the side and watch him sink face-first into the sea, 'too soon mate,' I shake my head as his feet slide under the surface then look up to see Meredith swimming back towards me while holding an arm between her teeth like she's bringing a stick back for me to throw. An actual arm. A fully grown adult arm complete with the sleeve of some dark coloured material and a sparkly watch on the wrist. She swims past looking happy as anything, getting slightly too close, and letting the dead hand slap me in the face.

'You alright?' Lani shouts.

'Yeah, fine, Meredith has an arm she wants me to throw for her.'

'An arm?' She yells back.

'Yep, I start swimming again, following the noise of the others until the two boats, now side by side, come into view. As I swim closer, I feel Meredith swimming up beside me, or rather I feel the dead hand ruffling my hair as she paddles along with the arm.

'Oh,' Lani stands with the others nodding at the sight of Meredith swimming up to the side of the boat, the clever dog seems to aim for Clarence as if knowing he will be able to lift her in.

'Drop the arm,' he orders the dog who ignores him and whines to be lifted in. He bends over and tries to take it from her mouth, she gives a low growl, and he gives up, reaching down to push his arms under her stomach before lifting her with ease into the boat. She shakes off again, still clutching the arm then turns around to drop it at Clarence's feet. She looks up at him and yaps a high-pitched playful bark, clearly urging him to throw the arm for her.

'Here mate, would you?' I get to the side of the boat and try to heave myself up as he reaches down to pluck me in like a ragdoll.

'You alright boss?' He asks as I stand dripping and looking down at the arm.

'Fine,' I nod and bend down to pick the arm up. Two brown eyes fix on with an intense look, poised and ready, she gets into a crouch swaying side to side as she tries to guess which way it will go.

'Hmmmm,' I look at the human limb and try to decide what to do. Now I'm holding it, it seems stupid to put it back down, but I can't throw it over the side either, 'so,' I look around at the others, 'who needs a hand?'

'Oh, nicely done!' Cookey bursts out laughing, showing his appreciation for my attempt at humour. Lani gives a resigned shake of her head.

'I think the land is that way,' I hold the arm up pointing off in a random direction, 'or is it that way,' I turn and point the arm off to the other side as Cookey, and the lads start cracking up, 'tell you what though,' I give a quick grin, 'it was handy having Meredith there! Get it…*handy…*'

Waving the arm about is too much for the dog who decides she wants her toy back and jumps up to take it.

'Yeah?' I tease her for a second, 'you want my arm, do you? Yeah? You and whose army, eh?'

'Oh, for god's sake…he's turned into Cookey,' Lani tuts but grins all the same.

'Right,' I move over to clamber back into my boat, 'we trying again?'

'Which way?' Nick asks, 'Dave dropped the compass.' I look to Dave who just shrugs and takes his seat in the middle of our boat.

'Have you turned since I fell in?' I ask the group as a whole.

'Nope, we're still human,' Cookey quips.

'Probably, fucking impossible to keep direction,' Nick replies looking up at the wall of cloud surrounding us.

We have no choice, but to get the little engines going again, and move off. Nick and Blowers do their best to keep the tillers straight, but it's impossible to tell if we're veering off to the left or right. This time we stay seated and holding on as the corpses keep bobbing into view hitting the front and sides of the boats with dull thuds. Macabre and gruesome, and for few seconds, I feel a surge of guilt at playing about with that arm. That was a part of a person, a human being that loved and cared. A person that was killed in the most awful way, and had their body taken over by the infection. What have we become? What have I become that I can piss about with a human limb while the others laugh?

Black humour I think they call it. The same type of humour the soldiers and emergency services have. A coping mechanism. We didn't ask for this to happen, but it's upon us, and we're just trying to make it through the day and survive. Weighing it up in my mind, I try to work out if doing something like that, playing about with a body part as a way of coping with the utter horror, if that is a lesser evil than being devoid of all humour. Humour is what defines us, it's what sets us apart from everything else. Art, humour, our ability to feel. Yes, it was a gross and highly disrespectful thing to do, but without that humour that allows us to cope, we'd all be mad or completely psychotic.

'Here boss,' Cookey passes me a cigarette, and I look round to see the others all looking at me.

'What? Was I thinking out loud?' I take the cigarette as they shrug and go back to staring at the sides and front.

'You had that dark look,' Lani explains quietly.

'What dark look?'

'The dark look you get when you're thinking.'

'I was thinking,' I light the cigarette, and shift uncomfortably, my underpants are sodden, rubbing against my backside and thighs. My boots feel squelchy, and my top is clinging to my body. At least, it's still warm, but even that is fucked up. I've never felt warm fog before. It's always been cold and clinging, but this is…

'Fuck me,' Meredith barking makes me jump. She's at the front of her boat again, staring intently and slightly off to the left. We all watch her, she doesn't seem angry, but more interested in something, ears pricked, and head cocked to one side.

'See the bottom innit,' Jagger announces, leaning over the side of his boat. Mo Mo joins him, 'yeah bruv, we could walk now.'

'Really?' I shuffle over and look down; the water is clear enough to see the ground a couple of feet down.

'House bricks,' Cookey says, 'we must be over where the estate was.'

'No way,' Blowers mutters, 'is the estate gone?'

'Looks like it,' I reply, 'yeah...the bricks are all burnt...foundations there...see,' I point to a clump of bricks still embedded in the ground.

'Fucking Time Team will love this in a few hundred years,' Cookey chuckles, 'imagine Baldrick trying to explain how some bloke called Dave blew a settlement up because of a disease.'

'Baldrick?' Lani looks over at the young lad.

'Yeah, the bloke from Time Team, he was Baldrick.'

'Who is Baldrick?' Lani asks again.

'You don't know who Baldrick is?' Cookey stares in shock.

'Clearly,' Lani tuts, 'who is he?'

'Blackadder? You must have seen Blackadder.'

'Blackadder? No...I think I've heard of it but...'

'Fuck,' Cookey shakes his head in obvious disappointment, 'never seen Blackadder, Jagger, have you seen Blackadder?'

'Yeah,' he shouts back, 'My foster carer watched 'em on DVD.'

'Dave?' Cookey asks the quiet man still sitting in the middle of the boat.

'Yes.'

'Have you seen Blackadder?'

'I said yes,' Dave replies flatly.

'Paula, have you seen...'

'I get it,' Lani snaps, 'I'm the only one that hasn't seen it...'

'Sorry Lani,' a look of hurt flashes across Cookey's face, 'I didn't mean anything.'

'Blowers,' Nick calls out after turning his own engine off, 'switch off and lift the propeller up, we'll glide in...don't risk breaking the blades.'

Blowers does as requested without complaint or comment, silence again as we drift over the ruined remains of what was a lovely housing estate less than two weeks ago. The devastation is incredible, that the storm has taken back so much land is staggering. Then, I start to think that maybe this land was reclaimed just so they could build the fort. Shit imagine if the people were still living in the estate when it happened.

The scraping noise tells us we're grounding out, 'good work, Nick,' I call out for him having the presence of mind to switch off and lift the blades clear, 'anyone know what part of the estate this is...or was?'

Muttered responses in the negative. We clamber out carefully, and realise the boats have been caught on a wall jutting up. We're still in the shallows and have to push and pull the boats free of the obstructions before we start dragging them behind us as we wade on. We go slow and easy as the ground beneath us is pitted with holes and trip hazards. Nobody speaks, the clinging fog makes any sound seemingly too loud like we're drawing attention to ourselves or breaking the silence of a hallowed place.

We seem to wade for a long time, but with no way of knowing direction we just keep moving in what we hope is a straight direction, dragging the boats behind us as they get snagged and bang on the debris.

'Road,' Dave points down under his feet, 'the back of the estate is that way,' he points off to the right, meaning we're heading across the estate left to right rather than heading for the rear. We change course and follow Dave as he picks out the remains of the black tarmac beneath his feet.

'Getting shallower,' Lani says.

'Good, this place sucks arse,' Blowers mutters. Jagger and Mo Mo stay quiet and watchful, constantly watching the area around them, and my group as they interact.

With groans of relief, we spot the clear ground rising up from the water a few feet ahead of us, a couple of seconds later, and we're out of the sea, and on firm ground. I still don't recognise the place or area; the fog has completely ruined any sense of direction I have but we have what looks like a road underfoot so if we follow that...

'Where did you leave the Saxon, Nick?' Clarence asks.

'Er,' Nick turns so he's facing out to sea, 'if the fort is that way,' he waves ahead, 'then we were off to that side,' he waves to the right, 'little harbour down there somewhere...fuck knows,' he shrugs.

Clarence peers about for a few seconds, staring at the road ahead before he moves off to the side, and almost disappears from sight within a few steps, 'we're on the main road,' he calls out, 'the one that came into the estate.'

'So, we just follow it then, makes life simple.' I reply as Clarence comes back into view, 'is it worth getting roped together now?'

Clarence pulls a face while avoiding looking at Dave, 'we'll get tangled at the first scrap,' he says with a tone of politeness that doesn't suit him.

'I agree with Dave,' Lani interjects with forced diplomacy. She looks at the big man then at Dave, 'if we have to fight a running battle, we'll…'

'And we'll be tripping over each other in the process,' Clarence cuts her off, 'it'll do more harm than good.'

'No,' Paula offers her thoughts, 'I'm with Dave, we're better together, and getting lost in this would be horrible.'

'We wouldn't be lost forever,' Roy says, 'I don't want to be roped up, not with a bow to use.'

Looking about at the wall of fog, I can see Dave and Lani's point, but then knowing how ferocious the fighting has been the last thing we want is rope getting tangled round our legs.

'We'll pair up,' I announce, 'instead of roping together we stay tight to our partner. Lani and Nick, Clarence with Jagger and Mo Mo, Blowers and Cookey, Paula with Roy, and I'll stay with Dave. If anything happens, and we've got to starburst or start running, then stay with your group. Stop at the first point of running, and we'll…' my voice trails off, 'fuck it, we'll have to suck it and see, we can only plan so far in advance, and I agree with Clarence, I don't like the idea of being roped up.'

Dave doesn't react, but I know him well enough to see he's not happy. In a way it's touching that his concern is primarily for our personal security and he's probably right, but we need the freedom of movement.

'Dave, you and me up front, the rest stay close behind.'

'Okay, Mr Howie,' the small man replies and starts walking forward.

'The fog doesn't bother her,' Jagger points at the dog looming out of the fog, still dripping wet, but looking happy enough with her tongue hanging out and tail wagging away.

'Nothing bothers her,' Cookey informs them, 'apart from cats.'

Setting off, we casually fall into the set groups with Dave and me at the front. I notice Clarence discretely falls back to bring the rear up and looks even bigger while flanked by two teenage boys.

Again, we fall into silence, just the crunch of our boots on the tarmac and sploshes as we walk through the deep puddles lying inert. Plucking the front of my t-shirt away from my body, I grimace and wish I was back in that dark room with Lani.

Meredith runs loops around us, ranging in circles as though herding us down the road. She looks so wolf-like disappearing into and running out of the fog bank. I've never seen anything like this, in fact, I can't imagine anyone has ever seen fog like this.

'Dave.'

'Yes.'

'Have you ever seen fog like this?'

'Yes.'

I knew he bloody would have, 'where?' I ask him.

'Argentina.'

'Right, why were you in Argentina?'

'I had to bring back a defecting Colonel from their army.'

'Oh, right…what was he like?'

He looks at me with a puzzled expression, the question being too broad for his mind. 'I mean…not what he looked like…but, what was *he* like? Nice bloke?'

'I don't know, we didn't talk.'

'He didn't speak English then?'

'He did.'

'I see, so…like, how long were you with him?'

'Two days.'

'Two days? And you didn't speak to him?'

'No. I asked him his name and he showed me identification.'

'And that was it?'

'Yes.'

'Must have been a long two days.'

'No, Mr Howie. The days in Argentina are the same length as here.'

'No, Dave, I meant the days would have dragged longer, or seemed longer as you were not talking to pass the time.'

He stays quiet for a few seconds, 'are we talking to pass the time now?'

'Er, well yeah, I guess so, but…'

'But what?'

'It's different as we know each other, so like…we're chatting and…'

'And what?'

Well, just that,' I shrug, 'that's what people do, they chat and shoot the shit.'

'Shoot the shit?'

'It's a saying, chew the fat…gossip or making idle chit chat.'

'I shot a shit once,' he announces as though in effort to make random conversation.

'What?'

'I shot a shit,' he repeats.

'Why?' I ask in a pitch too high, 'what, like a human shit? Like a turd?'

'Yes.'

'What on earth for?'

'There was someone hiding in it.'

'Fucking hang on, how big was this shit?'

'It was lots of shits…all from a latrine.'

'Latrine, isn't that what the Americans use on their army bases?'

'Yes. I was on an American army base.'

'Of course, you were, so er…fuck,' I scratch my beard, and try to process the flooding images in my head, 'um…so how did that come about?'

He stares at me like I'm an idiot, 'the man I was chasing, he hid in the shit, so I shot the shit.'

'On an American army base?'

'Yes.'

'Who was he? Like a terrorist or something?'

'He was the chaplain.'

'The what? Like the vicar? You shot an American army vicar?'

'Yes.'

'Which is a perfectly normal thing to do,' I nod amiably, 'blowing cows up, and power stations…sellotaping grenades to doctors faces…all perfectly normal.'

His hand shoots across my front stopping me dead in my tracks as he draws his pistol with lightning speed. I drop down to a crouch and hold my axe ready.

'Spread out into a line,' Clarence mutters from behind as the rest get ready while Dave stares intently ahead. A low growling noise comes from ahead.

'Is that the dog?' Roy asks.

'Sounds like it…' I start to reply, but get cut off by a second growling noise, 'come on,' I start jogging forward staring wide-eyed into the gloom. Dave paces easily by my side as Roy goes to the far side giving himself space to use the bow which he holds ready with arrow nocked.

More growls come floating back which are swiftly followed by the noise of Meredith going for an attack. Her vicious snarl unseen, then an impact as she takes a body down. Savage biting, squelching noises as flesh is torn apart. Not being able to see it, and I realise just how horrific the sounds are.

'There!' Dave points ahead as the form of Meredith ragging the throat of an infected comes into view, the beast flails against her body, legs kicking, but the blood loss is too great, and within a second or two the life, or whatever life it possessed, is gone.

Meredith backs away with bloody drool dripping from her mouth still with eyes locked on the dead body in case it shows any signs of reanimating again.

Paula steps closer, and kicks at the corpses left arm, bringing the hand into view, 'see this,' she looks up at me, 'her fingers are all torn off…fresh too, the blood is fresh anyway.'

'Did the dog eat her fingers?' Mo Mo asks with a disgusted look, 'that's fuckin' sick bruv.'

'No, she always goes straight for the throat,' Nick peers down at the fingers then bends over to look at the dead zombie woman's face, 'look, she's covered in blood.'

'Well, her fucking throat just got ripped out,' Cookey replies.

'No injuries here though,' Nick points at the woman's mouth, 'she bit her own fingers off,' he looks up nodding.

'What?' Cookey steps closer to look, 'no fucking way.'

'Let me see,' Roy moves in, still holding his bow with arrow nocked, 'maybe,' he nods, 'lot of blood, but no facial injuries.'

'Or she just chomped on someone,' Blowers remarks, 'why would she bite her own fingers off?'

'So, she could write a message,' Lani stands a couple of feet ahead of us staring down at the ground at what I thought were blood smears. I edge closer, going wide to avoid walking on the spatters of gore.

'Where?' I ask trying to see anything other than bloody gunk slicked across the ground.

'There,' Lani points up at the edge of the wooden signboard. A huge white DIY erected board that once advertised a local pub open all year with a function room available for hire, and freshly caught crab. Moving closer, I stare in wonder at the bloody smears over the front, thick lines rubbed over and again, and all done from the bleeding stumps of the dead zombie woman's hand.

'Her fingers,' Lani kicks a digit with the toe of her boot. The worst thing is the nail varnish still on the end, chipped and purple, but clearly once painted with care by a woman alive and well, another reminder that these beasts were once as we are now.

'What does it say? Jagger asks squinting at the board, *'he's coming?'* he reads out slowly, trying to pick the letters out that have dripped into each other.

'Yep, *he's coming,'* I read the two words out written in the crimson blood, and then look round as though expecting someone to come lurching out of the dense cloud, 'who is *he*? Who is coming?'

'You think that's meant for us?' Cookey asks innocently.

'Yes, Cookey,' Blowers says slowly, 'I think it is mate.'

'Oh,' Cookey nods then looks away, 'hello?' He calls out, 'are you coming now? Do you need a tissue?'

Snorts of laughter burst out at the deadpan delivery, 'bit weird,' Cookey sniffs, 'someone wanking off in the fog.'

'Fuck it, come on, this fog is fucking horrible, and I need a coffee and some dry clothes.'

5

An ugly man. His nose is large and bulbous, his eyes bulge too far from the sockets. His face is pockmarked, pale and drawn. Greasy hair that retains that sheen of lacklustre strands despite constant washing. Broad shoulders and strong arms, the muscle is thick but not overly so.

A wooden table with two chairs. A bare sodium bulb hangs low from the ceiling, bathing the room in a soft orange glow that only serves to heighten the essence of minimalism. He sits on one of the chairs. Arms resting on the tabletop, and he waits. Those eyes are dark and hooded with bags underneath that speak of ill health, yet he is in perfect physical shape. Not an ounce of fat adorns his body, and his heart beats strong within his chest that rises and falls with each relaxed breath.

The door opens behind him. He doesn't move but waits. To sit with his back to the door is a sign of trust. That anyone can walk in unseen. This he knows. He also knows the tread of the man he meets each time he visits. He knows the length of the stride, and the slight scrape from one heel caused by an old gunshot injury. If he heard a different tread, he would not remain with his back to the door. If he heard a different tread, the chances are the man with the strange tread would not get two paces into the room before being killed instantly.

The ugly man flicks his gaze to the left as the older man comes into view moving around the table where he sits down heavily in the chair opposite. The men stare at each other. No words are exchanged. They are not friends. The ugly man does not have friends.

The older man reaches a hand into the inside pocket of his casual suit jacket, and from that pocket, he draws a thin brown paper envelope. He pauses with the envelope in hand before cocking his head as though a decision has been reached. The older man puts the envelope down and slides it halfway across the table. The ugly man reaches out and slides it the rest of the way. Exhaling slowly, he lifts the envelope and opens the unsealed flap, pulling two sheets of paper from within.

The ugly man unfolds the first and lays it flat on the table, he unfolds the second, a photograph, and that too is laid on the table. A colour image printed from a cheap inkjet printer. Low resolution with some streaks of black ink marked across the page. The other unfolded paper is typed in plain black font, Times New Roman size twelve, double spaced.

The ugly man looks at the picture then across at the printed sheet. He reads the words several times while constantly turning his head to stare back at the picture. His lips move as he reads, but no sound is made.

Finally, he looks up at the older man and nods, 'okay,' the ugly man speaks for the first time.

'Okay?' The older man asks as though to clarify.

The ugly man nods, 'okay.' The older man leans over and taps the end of a thick finger on the picture.

'The client has requested a special service.'

The ugly man nods once and waits, no flicker of reaction adorns his face.

'This is the mark,' the older man taps the picture again, 'but you are to inflict whatever damage you can. Kill everyone but this one,' the finger taps again, 'is to be special...' The ugly man listens to the special instructions. He nods. He stands up and takes one final look at the sheets of paper.

Without further comment, he walks from the room leaving the older man to stare at the vacated seat with a shiver running down his spine.

Albania was becoming famous, or rather the Albanians were becoming famous. A hard people that had quietly moved into every capital city on the planet. They were industrious, hardworking and simply without fear of the other organised crime syndicates. They took what they wanted and controlled it with a ruthless barbarity that even the Russians found abhorrent. Their country was perfectly situated to move with relative, freedom across the virtually open European borders. They grew cannabis in such vast quantities, and on such a scale that whole villages depended on the crop to survive. Albania is to cannabis as Afghanistan is to Heroin, and the Albanians had a strong footing with that drug too. Cocaine. Ecstasy. Guns. Slavery. Prostitution. Blackmail. Extortion. Robbery. Kidnap. A diverse and eclectic portfolio of income strands, and each had to be controlled.

The bosses knew that to hold a complete monopoly was against good business. If they were the sole traders of each sector, then the authorities would find it easier to stop them. The other syndicates truly believed they had a stake from their own efforts, but they were simply allowed to maintain a presence so to defocus the attention of each nations law enforcement.

At intervals, however, there were times when extraordinary measures were needed. There were times when simple robberies, kidnapping and the killing of henchmen would not suffice. A leader had to be taken, and they had to be taken in a dazzling display of utter power, a breath-taking action of such audaciousness that it would be spoken about for years to come.

At these times, the Albanians didn't use an overwhelming assault from armed men clad in black boiler suits. They didn't use smart bombs or laser-guided technology. They didn't use gangs or honey traps.

They used Gregori.

They used the Ugly Man.

6

D ay One

FRIDAY
  July
  Northern England.

THE CESSNA BOUNCES DOWN ONTO THE GRASS AIRSTRIP, THE PROPELLERS blurring as the light aircraft decreases speed and navigates towards the hangars. Early morning, and already the sun is strong. The pilot gently pulls his Aviator sunglasses from his face and rubs his nose. Several men dressed in casual street clothes, lean against the sides of ordinary vehicles. No dark suits or status symbol, four-wheel drives with blacked-out windows. Casual men waiting casually for their friend to arrive. They smoke and talk quietly, but all of them fall to silence as the side door to the aircraft opens. Even for such ruthless men as this, the arrival of the ugly man is something special.

None of them have seen him before, but all of them have heard time and again of his exploits across the globe, so they try to remain casual in their casual clothes next to their casual cars, but the sense of trepidation builds as the side door of the executive aircraft opens, and a small set of steps lowers down with a faint whine from the electric motor. The co-pilot exits first, a typical hard-faced Eastern European, but smartly dressed in a crisp white shirt and pressed trousers. He bounces down to the tarmac, and nods at the men before turning to look back at the door.

Gregori appears swiftly, a fluid movement that has his bulk sliding through the doorway and down the stairs. The men can't help but stare, the whispered rumours were true, he really is an ugly bastard. Gregori glances looks around as though taking in the view, a deep breath, and within those few seconds, he's worked out the closest other people, the exit from the airfield, the temperature of this place, and even has a rough idea of the altitude and humidity. His eyes sweep the men waiting for him. The standard mix of local mid-ranking bosses, early thirties and still with the drive and enthusiasm to control their income strands. The vehicles, despite being so carefully chosen to not stand out, appear well-maintained with good tread on the tyres which all appear to be inflated correctly.

No weapons on view, and no bulges undershirts to indicate concealed weapons. This is England, one of the toughest countries in the world to possess a firearm. They're easy to get, as easy as anything else, but walking around with them is a whole other matter.

'Gregori?' The chosen spokesman walks forward, plain-faced, but Gregori can see the hint of nerves in the other man's eyes. They shake hands, and again within those few seconds, Gregori gains the measure of the man, his height, weight, age. His fighting experience, his tendency for too much alcohol and too many cigarettes.

Gregori remains silent. There is no need for speaking. These men will take him to the subject's location, Gregori will assess and form his plan after which he will be deposited, and then collected at a pre-arranged destination.

He waits until the man leads him to a silver coloured Volvo. A rear door is opened which Gregori ignores and walks past as he aims for the front passenger seat. Inside, he adjusts the seat to the preferred distance from the front. He opens and closes the door once, twice then a final third time. He adjusts the wing mirror then finally puts his seat belt on before remaining silent and staring ahead.

The driver starts the engine and pulls away, having already been instructed to maintain a strategic position of middle vehicle within the small convoy of three. The speed limit is adhered to. Indicators are used, and the three vehicles give way at the appropriate time and proceed in a smooth and sedate fashion.

'Here?' One of the men in the back seat asks. Gregori nods and listens to the rustling sound as a sports bag is opened. The butt of a black squat 9mm pistol comes into view which he takes along with three full magazines. The men can't help but watch in awe, they've heard about this, and Gregori knows what they are waiting to see.

Moving slowly, he ejects the magazine from the pistol grip, and checks the rounds within, then his hands become a blur as the pistol is stripped, checked and reassembled with incredible speed. One of the men in the rear sighs in awe, sitting back while shaking his head. It was a thing they all did, having heard about how fast Gregori, the ugly man, can strip a gun, they practised and practised, holding competitions to see who is the fastest, but what they just witnessed was something amazing.

Gregori checks the spare magazines before leaning forward to gain access to the side pockets of his casual plain blue thin sports jacket. Dressed in plain blue jeans and a dark coloured shirt, he looks nondescript. A normal man of early to late middle age. An accountant or engineer perhaps. Certainly not the most wanted man in Europe, and definitely not the most flagged and current operative known to Interpol and the many shared intelligence agencies. The prime suspect in seventy-nine murders. The chief suspect in another twenty-three, and a strong lead in countless others. His name is known and feared throughout the continent, but not one agency possessed a picture of him. The CIA holds a file along with the DEA and the American Secret Service. He was untouchable, a ghost, an urban legend that was spoken about in the darkest corners of the darkest bars of inner cities. *Get it done or get a visit from the ugly man.*

'How far?' Gregori speaks for the first time.

'An hour,' the driver replies.

An hour before he goes to work. Sixty minutes. The people he is visiting have no idea they have just one hour left to live. They woke up this morning with the promise of another long day ahead of them. How many times now? How many visits has he made? So much can be done in one hour. A baby can be made. A marriage can take place. A funeral can happen. Races can be run and won or lost, people can fall in love, and go from one emotion to the extreme end of that spectrum. One hour is all they have left.

Gregori tries to imagine what they are doing now, not the physical act of what they are doing, but the mindset they have. He knows the people at the location are not evil, they are just people. Some will be there purely by chance and will pay the greatest cost for it. Others will be paid employees just doing a job to pay their rent and feed their children. All of them will die, all of them have to die. A message must be sent. An example will be made.

What frightens Gregori? The only thing that frightens him is the complete lack of fear he has. The numbness within him has spread throughout his core and into every cell in his body. He does not feel. Emotionless as a machine.

The car is comfortably warm with the air conditioning on low. The sunlight flickers through the trees on the road with an almost hypnotic rhythm. His mind relaxes for now. The constant motion, the silence, the temperature and the flicker of the light all serve to allow the frontal lobe a chance to relax, and the neural pathways to the deeper memories open up for a quiet period of reflection.

The years behind him stretch away like a dirty river of the mind full with the flotsam of memories. Of faces. Of names. Places. Marks. Always marks. The times he sat in that same room with the low sodium bulb waiting for the heavy tread of the old man. People age at the same rate, so to Gregori, the old man had always been the old man, and he was the only constant in Gregori's otherwise sterile existence.

Gregori wasn't trained by the military. His life was far harder. Owned outright as payment given for a debt his father could never pay.

Taken as a child to be indoctrinated, brainwashed, drilled and drilled. His trainers were ruthless in their methods, and the young Gregori soon knew a life of pain and hardship.

By the age of eighteen, he was trained to a higher standard than the US Navy Seals. By the age of twenty, he was up there with Mossad, and by twenty-one, he was progressing past that of the most highly trained Special Forces in the world, the British Special Air Service.

His mind and body were honed to be subservient to those that owned him while being taught to have no compassion for any other living being. As his reputation grew, so too did his skills at killing. Seemingly bulletproof he never once sustained serious injury, and the higher the body count grew, so too did his mind close off to what he was doing.

Only in recent years, with the ever-expanding world as we know it, and being sent further overseas, had he begun to see the people within the subjects he killed. It didn't stop him from his duty, but it did fascinate him. How they lived, what they thought about. The normality of their existence. The clothes they wore, the food they ate. The children they had. To Gregori, they were alien and other-worldly, and something he would never have.

'Ten minutes,' the driver breaks into his thoughts, snapping Gregori back to the present. The mark is Russian, a high-level player in gun-running and modern-day slavery. The Albanians had tolerated his presence simply because it served a purpose to keep the close attention from them, but now the Russian outfit had started expanding into their territory. The Russian had to be removed in a way that would send a clear message not only to the Russians back home, but to every other gang operating in the area.

London was already flooded with gangs. It was these outer cities that now saw the intense battles for ground taking place. Millions of ordinary people going about their daily lives, worrying about the recession, house prices, redundancy, and having no knowledge of the wars taking place within their streets and towns. The capital city of England was familiar to Gregori, he had undertaken missions there, time and again, but the north of England was like a different country. Strong accents, and dirty towns crammed into small spaces yet surrounded by vast open countryside. Why didn't they just spread out instead of living on top of one another?

'Tell the other cars to drop back,' Gregori says, waiting while one of the back-seat passengers calls the other vehicles, telling them to divert away.

The driver looks to Gregori and clears his throat, 'up here, on the left,' he says in a low voice, 'there is a gated entrance to the house, uniformed guards on the gate.'

'Drive past at normal speed,' Gregori instructs, 'do not look at the gates,' he says louder for the benefit of everyone. The drive past is done at thirty-five miles per hour. A speed seemingly too fast for the other three occupants of the vehicle, but to Gregori the speed is fine. His eyes sweep the front of the gates with his mind on record. Once past, he closes his eyes, and replays the footage. A guardhouse, brick-built with toughened glass. Two uniformed security that will be unarmed, but they will have a direct alarm to the main house. The two guards were observant with eyes up at the passing traffic.

'Keep going, turn around and come back,' Gregori instructs. The driver does as told, leaving it a full minute before using a wide entrance to a farm to turn the vehicle around. Gregori takes the area in. Rural countryside with the houses set at great distance from each other. Gunshots will not be heard.

THE SILVER VOLVO PULLS UP. THE TWO GUARDS ARE EYES UP INSTANTLY. Watchful, and immediately suspicious of the vehicle. Gregori steps out, and seems to say something to the driver, he shakes his head, waves his arms a little and then looks around, seemingly lost.

'Hello?' Gregori calls out the one word in perfect English.

'You cannot stop here,' one of the guards exits the small building, calling out as he ventures towards the vehicle. His own accent is thick Russian. Short hair cropped close to the skull. Typically Russian with a strong frame and thick muscles.

'Ah,' Gregori smiles, stepping around the vehicle, he scratches his head and looks like an eccentric engineer seeking directions. The guards' suspicions are strong. The vehicle is four up, all of them males of a certain age and look.

'You cannot stop here,' the guard's voice is firmer now, harder, and his face makes it clear no further conversation is to be tolerated.

The mistake is when the second guard steps out from the guard building. If he had stayed inside and secured the door as per his training and protocol, then he would have stood a chance of survival. But he didn't. He steps out to help his buddy, and in doing so, he presents two easy targets for the expert marksmanship of Gregori who fires two shots from the hip.

The vehicle pulls away, all three of the Albanians wait a full thirty seconds before breaking into excited conversation at seeing Gregori, the ugly man, at work, and those two shots! They were so fast, so casual yet perfectly aimed, and at two moving targets.

Gregori tucks his pistol away and grabs the bodies to drag back into the guard hut. He spots the direct telephone, and looks down at the buttons, number one being pre-programmed direct line to the main house. Lifting the handset, he presses the button and waits.

'Da,' the deep guttural tones of another guard answering the receiver. Gregori waits, unspeaking for several long seconds.

'Da?' The voice prompts clearly annoyed at being disturbed.

Gregori waits another second before speaking in a low voice, 'I Gregori,' he replaces the handset, and walks out of the guard hut knowing the main residence will be exploding into frantic panic.

Another second, and a red light fixed low to the wall in the guard building starts to flash, the panic alarm pressed at the other end. He exits the building to the rear, inwardly shaking his head at the poor discipline of not securing their doors because now he is inside the grounds. Gregori makes for the vehicle he saw parked behind the guard building and gets inside the driver's seat. A solid built four-wheel drive with blacked-out windows, a status vehicle designed to impress and intimidate. One finger taps the windscreen, toughened glass. How easy do they want to make this for him?

Pulling away he drives down the long drive to the main house, an overly sumptuous modern mansion built to replicate something old and distinguished. The typical Russian habit of needing to display wealth is everywhere. Huge fountains and sculptures dot the grounds, and several high-end sports cars are parked nose out in front of the house, all of them perfectly aligned.

Several men run from the huge double doors at the front of the house, all of them dressed in dark suits with sunglasses, style over substances, and even from this distance, Gregori can see the overly large muscles of their arms bulging through the material of their suit jackets. Steroids, no doubt about it, but that will work in his favour. The steroids will give them such a huge dose of testosterone, they will think themselves indestructible, and therefore put themselves into situations he can take advantage of.

Pistols are drawn and aimed, double-handed grips that show military training. Gregori pushes his foot down on the accelerator, but keeps the vehicle in a low gear so the engine screams out, knowing the high-pitched scream will only serve to heighten the sense of panic within the men. The action works, and they open fire, tinny bangs sound out followed by the pings as the small calibre bullets bounce harmlessly from the four-wheel drive. They fire faster, depleting their ammunition. Fingers pumping on the triggers until, as one, their magazines are empty, and they are ejecting the spent ones while patting down pockets in a rushed effort of finding the new ones.

Gregori gets the gear stick into neutral. With the momentum gained, and such a heavy vehicle, he knows it will keep rolling without power being applied. Driver's door open, and he tumbles out in a well-practised movement that has the fall of his body timed perfectly to the speed of the vehicle. By the time he rolls upright, his pistol is gripped in one hand with a spare magazine in the other. With the suited Russian guards still scrabbling to reload, he aims and starts his own return fire. Each shot is a killing shot. Either through the skull or through the chest. Those that don't die immediately will be gone within seconds, drowning in their own blood.

The guards are dropped, Gregori ejects his magazine, catches it and replaces with a fresh one. The spent magazine is pushed into his back pocket, and he heads towards the door, pausing to pick up one of the pistols from the fallen guards. He finds a new magazine for the collected gun, checks the working parts with that same lightning speed. Heaving one of the dead guards up, he pushes his own arms under the armpits of the dead man and holds him upright in front while gripping two semi-automatic pistols. By slightly leaning back, he can take the weight of the dead guy into his own body rather than using just arm strength.

At the door he pauses and sends the body flying through to a symphony of shots that send it smashing off to one side.

A fraction of a second later, and Gregori steps through, pistols up and tracking. Two men on the right are taken by two single shots from the pistol in his right hand. One on the immediate left is taken with a shot from the pistol in his left hand. Three down, and he raises both pistols to fire at the wide marble staircase, peppering the advancing guards with crimson dots to their mid-centre that send them staggering back only to fall and tumble down the stairs. Four big strides see him clear of the doorway, a spin and he pushes his back to the wall, pistols facing left and right. He holds position and waits quietly, blotting out the sound of one dying guard gurgling his last breaths to hear the heavy tread of people running towards him. Gregori knows the big guns will have been brought out now and waits for the clatter of the machine pistols and assault rifles.

He slides down into a crouch, his legs poised to drive him forward. With a shocking lack of co-ordination, the new defenders come first from the left. They should all be connected to a secure radio system. They should be pausing to gather larger numbers and be ready for a combined assault, but they don't. They rush in foolhardy and pumped up on steroids. Machine pistols burst out firing before the weapons holders even spot the position of the assailant. Plaster, marble and wood get splintered with flying chunks that spew dust into the air. Black holes appear in long lines as the automatic weapons discharge their ammunition at a rate too fast to allow decent control.

Gregori fires once to the left side, the first guard is thrown back as the back of his skull explodes from the round ripping his brain and cranium apart. The machine pistol clatters to the ground, now a useless hunk of metal.

Shouts in Russian language sound out from all directions, screams too from women, and Gregori picks out the tone of a child wailing in terror.

From the left, another one tries to sneak around the bottom of the door, pausing to locate then fire at Gregori's position. He's shot through the face, the bullet ripping into his cheek-bone, and killing him instantly. To the right, two bursts through with heavier calibre assault rifles. The deeper, bass-filled drum as they open up. Gregori drives his powerful legs to propel him forward in a long sliding dive. Such a movement prevents his normal pinpoint accuracy so instead, he empties the magazine in their general direction, scoring fatal hits on both as they stagger and spin away. On his back, he uses the pistol in his left hand to cover while he changes magazine from the spent one. The same again, and now both pistols are fully loaded. On his feet, with an athletic flip, and he surges towards the left side, knowing they will not be expecting him to attack.

With both guns raised, he fires again and again into the solid wooden door and the wall surrounding it. A large foot slams the door open; two more guards are down and bleeding heavily. One headshot to each and he's up and moving off.

Into the kitchens, women screaming in panic as they burst away towards the far exit door. All of them dressed in black and white French maid outfits as ordered by the Russian mob boss.

A message has to be sent; an example has to be made. The cowering and fleeing women are gunned down, shot mercilessly for being unfortunate enough to work for the wrong person. Young women, long legged and beautiful are slaughtered. Shot through the face or executed through the back of the head. Handsome young men employed as drivers are killed. Everyone he comes across is murdered. Some beg, some plead, and others simply sink down in shock acceptance of the inevitable.

A round trip through the ground floor brings him back to the main hallway, a change of magazines, and he starts the ascent. Pistol raised and firing as people appear, regardless of their role or intent to attack or simply flee in a vain effort to save their lives.

From room to room he goes, swift and as relentless as time. Nobody is spared. In a far end room, he finds a nanny shielding small children with her body. On her knees and begging in broken English to spare the children. Gregori pauses to change magazines, taking in the little girl and young boy both with tear-streaked faces. Pistols loaded, he lifts his right hand, 'I Gregori,' he mutters and fires three single shots.

A scream from the next room, an adult woman breaks free of a man to come running into the room wailing in terror. Gregori shoots her dead, a single round through the head at such close range, she's taken from her feet, and sent flying into the already dead bodies of the nanny and small children.

Back in the hallway, he stalks back to the main staircase, and starts the ascent to the third and top floor. No further opposition as he heads for the far end and enters the last room to see the steel door of the *safe* room right in front of him. Solid steel walls prevent him from gaining access. A whir of a motor, and he looks up to see the video surveillance camera panning down to focus on him.

'You will not get in,' an amplified voice in thick Russian speaks from a hidden speaker.

Gregori sighs and stares at the electronic number pad fixed to the outside of the door. Holding both pistols in his left hand, he uses the index finger of his right to press the unlock code to the door.

'No!' The voice yells in disbelief as Gregori keys the correct sequence. A beep sounds out, and the locks disengage as the door quickly retracts to the side revealing a small room equipped with a bank of monitors, and two men staring at him in utter horror.

The mob boss he identified from the picture the old man gave him. The other is younger, but bares such a striking resemblance, it must be his son.

'Stop!' The son shouts as Gregori takes aim, 'I gave the code,' he bleats in perfect English, 'me...I gave you this...'

'I Gregori,' he shoots the son through the face, blowing the back of his skull off which coats the interior steel wall with dripping gore and brain matter.

The mob boss stares at his dead son, his face now devoid of expression. He looks up at Gregori, taking in the ugly features, the bulging eyes and pasty skin.

Five minutes later, and Gregori is walking back down the stairs. The Russian mob boss lying crucified on the top landing. His genitals cut from his groin and shoved into his mouth to choke him as he dies slowly of blood loss.

Fifteen minutes after being dropped off, and Gregori is collected from the main gate by the silver Volvo. Eighteen people killed within less time than most people get for a smoke break at work. As the silver Volvo pulls away, Gregori once more lets the sun-dappled windscreen relax his mind back into a reverie of old memories.

7

'Could be someone famous,' Cookey says.

'Like who?' Nick asks conversationally.

'I dunno, like…oh, shit I feel bad now.'

'Why?' Lani asks.

'Just reminded myself of that Paco Maguire, he was famous.'

'Point mate,' Blowers says then spits a gob of phlegm to the side, 'sorry,' he mutters in the direction of Paula.

'What about me?' Lani huffs.

'What about you?'

'Why you saying sorry to Paula and not me?'

'Paula's new, you're not,' Blowers answers, 'and she's a lady,' he adds with a smirk.

'What did you say?' Lani glares at him.

'Joking,' Blowers laughs, 'here Nick, did you speak to Lilly after the meeting?'

'Might have done,' Nick glances sideways to Blowers, clearly wary of giving any ammunition.

Having traipsed to the end of the lane, we turned left onto the main road which we know is the general direction of Portsmouth, and also the area where Nick left the Saxon. We're hoping he'll recognise the road he took to whatever harbour he found, and then trace his route to our vehicle.

'Is that the fit one?' Jagger asks, 'the blond one, yeah?'

'Yep,' Nick nods.

'She like your woman then?' Mo Mo joins in.

'Er, nah…not really,' Nick thinks for a moment, 'she's nice, but…'

'But what?' Paula asks him.

'But, well, she's like fucking fifteen,' Nick explains, 'I'm almost twenty…I feel like a dirty bastard.'

'But, she looks older,' Cookey says.

'And she showed herself to be a very level-headed and mature young lady yesterday,' Roy says, 'there's only a few years between you.'

'Yeah, but fifteen?' Nick groans, 'it's illegal for a fucking start.'

'What shagging her, you mean?' Mo Mo asks.

'Oi,' Clarence cuts in before Dave can say anything, 'I suggest you re-phrase that.'

'Anything,' Nick replies before Mohammed can say anything, 'I kissed her yesterday…is that illegal?'

'Kissing a fifteen-year-old?' Clarence asks, 'er…'

'Yes, it is,' Paula says confidently, 'she's below the age of consent for any sexual activity.'

'Oh, fuck,' Nick looks horrified, 'shit… I didn't mean to, and she kissed me anyway…and I didn't know she was fifteen…'

Cookey glances down at Nick, 'tell that to the judge mate,' he adds helpfully.

'Don't listen to him, Nick,' Paula says, 'it is against the law, but for starters…'

'There is no law,' Roy cuts in, 'and no one would care about you kissing her given the circumstances.'

'Exactly,' Paula nods with a smile at Roy.

'However,' Roy continues, 'having sex with her is another thing.'

'Why? Paula asks, 'there's nothing wrong with it.'

'She's fifteen?' Roy says as though the reason is obvious.

'I didn't have sex with her,' Nick says quickly, 'just kissed…I didn't touch her or anything.'

'It don't matter,' Mo Mo offers his opinion, 'fuckin' world is fucked up innit, she looks older than fifteen and…they ain't no feds now bruv.'

'It's not a legal objection, it's a moral one,' Roy says to Mo Mo, 'the fact that the authorities are no longer in place does not make it suitable to have sex with a fifteen-year-old girl.'

'I shagged loads of fifteen-year olds,' Jagger boasts.

'That's not a good thing mate,' I cut in, 'how old are you?'

'Sixteen.'

'And,' Roy continues, 'although I have only just joined this group, from what I have seen so far…and heard about with your exploits,' he delivers the comment towards me with a nod, 'it would appear *you are* the authorities now, which makes it even worse.'

'Eh?' Nick says, 'I never said I was gonna do anything.'

'Nick, I think Roy is wrong,' Paula adds quickly, 'we could all be dead tomorrow…'

'Or today,' Lani adds, 'I agree with Paula, Nick. If Lilly was a young fifteen-year-old then it could be an issue, be she isn't.'

'No,' Roy argues, 'she *looks* older, but she is still fifteen…she lacks the life experience to be able to make sound decisions that affect her own future. What if she gets pregnant?'

'What if she catches zombie?' Cookey interjects, 'she could end up dying a virgin…it's not like Nick is going to force her…or get her pissed or anything…if she wants to be with him, what's the issue?'

'Bloody hell, Cookey,' I lift my eyebrows, 'you have got some common sense in there somewhere.'

'Only a bit,' Cookey grins sheepishly.

'So, let me ask this,' Roy takes a breath and looks across at Paula, 'if Lilly was fourteen but looked and acts the way she does now, would that be okay?'

'Well…' Paula thinks for a second.

'What about thirteen?'

'Too young,' Lani says, 'some girls aren't even developed properly at that age.'

'So, fourteen then? Is that okay? To have sex with a fourteen-year-old girl?' Roy continues.

'No,' Paula concedes, 'probably not.'

'Probably? How probably?' Roy asks.

'What if both the boy *and* the girl were fourteen? Given this life we have now, two fourteen-year olds fighting to survive? Maybe given some circumstances it wouldn't be such a bad thing. I understand what you are saying, Roy. Your point is that Lilly might appear physically ready, but she might not be emotionally ready, but that is a decision for her, not for us.'

'I disagree,' Roy shakes his head firmly, 'if we are going to offer protection to young people then we must ensure their safety, and that means things like sex.'

'The bossman let us do what we wanted,' Mo Mo cuts in, 'we smoked weed all day and fucked about...we didn't eat proper food, and we got pissed every night,' he explains while Jagger nods. 'Maddox changed that when he killed him,' he continues.

'And what was better?' Roy asks.

Mo Mo goes quiet, shooting a furtive glance to Jagger, 'dunno,' he says quietly.

'Better now innit,' Jagger says, 'like, it was fucking crazy before...we could do what we wanted...but...like Mads made us see how sick it was...like eating food, and not getting stoned...know what I mean?'

'So, you think it's better now?' Roy asks.

'Yeah,' Mo Mo nods firmly with some courage now he knows what Jagger thinks, 'Mads said we couldn't do no shagging no more...like, I think some of the girls weren't ready anyway but like, you know what I mean? But they did it coz the other girls were doing it and...'

'My point exactly,' Roy announces, 'Lilly may be unique in that she is older than her years, she may be physically developed, and she may be a very mature young lady, but we cannot have one rule for one and another for someone else. What if another fifteen-year-old girl comes to the fort, and wants to have sex with an older man? Are we to say that is okay because Lilly and Nick did it?'

'I don't want to have sex with her now,' Nick mutters.

'You are overthinking it, Roy,' Paula says, 'Lilly *is* old enough to decide her own life, she has no choice now...and we know Nick is a decent young man so personally, I do not see the harm in it. We have to take what pleasure we can.'

'So,' Roy says slowly, 'would it be okay if I had sex with Lilly? Given that I am thirty-eight years old.'

'Nick is closer to her age, if she were sixteen nobody would even consider it. We're talking about a matter of months, maybe even weeks depending on when her birthday is,' Paula explains.

'But the rule is there, regardless of the months or the age gap, the idea of the rule is to protect the emotional and physical well-being of our young people.'

'Roy,' Lani cuts in, 'I get what you're saying, I really do. But for a start society has gone…and it needs re-building, our race is under direct threat, and there will be a need to re-populate and keep going…'

'So, that means we can all have sex with young girls does it?' Roy asks in such a goading tone it prickles my temper.

'No,' Lani says firmly, 'it doesn't, but given the unique situation that Nick is in a stable group with a firm set of morals and judgements, led by a man that has more honour and moral courage than any other human being I have ever met, known or heard about…and given that Lilly is mature for her age, and she is not under duress…given all of those individual er…circumstances, I don't think there is a problem.'

'Thanks, Lani,' I smile across at her.

'You're welcome,' she says quickly, 'Clarence, Dave, what do you think?'

Clarence speaks first, 'I agree with what Roy said, but…I also agree with everything you just said…on the whole, yes I don't think we should be letting young girls have sex, but…given this situation, I don't have any issue at all. In fact,' he pauses for a second, 'if I had a fifteen-year-old daughter, I would have no issue with her being with Nick, or any of our lads,' he adds, 'even Cookey.'

'Seriously? You'd be like my father-in-law,' Cookey beams.

'Dave?' Lani prompts him.

'Up to Mr Howie,' he replies as blunt as ever.

'Not up to me mate,' I say.

'Well, it is really,' Lani says, 'you're in charge of everyone…and like

Roy said, we're the only known authority left....so, that kinda does mean it's up to you. You know if you told Nick not to go near her, he would do what you said.'

'Totally,' Nick says.

Fuck it. Why me? Why do I have to decide this shit? I'm a supermarket manager not a sodding government minister. Big Chris would be good at this, so would my sister. Even Sergeant Hopewell or Ted would have a better idea of these things. But it's an important point, and I can feel that Nick and the others are waiting to hear what I'll say.

'Lani summed it up best,' I say after a long few seconds of thinking, 'but like Clarence said, I do agree with Roy. We can only control or influence what is in front of us. We can give as much care to those as we can, but ultimately, each person has to judge for themselves at this time. We'll give the very best protection...but regarding Lilly and Nick, no, I don't have any issues with it at all. Sometimes you've got to go with what you feel, and it feels okay to me if Nick and Lilly got together. If I thought she was too young or immature, then I'd be the first to say something.'

'And anyway,' I continue after a short heavy pause, 'we don't know we're the only group left like ours. There could be some awesome military leader running a refuge in London or something.'

'There was,' Clarence says quietly, 'and he conceded to you.'

The words are poignant and charged, a compliment of the greatest degree and for once, even Cookey doesn't try and interject with a witty comment.

We trudge on. A group of eleven people and one dog walking through a fog bank the like of which I have never known before. It seems to cling to us, like we're stuck in a perpetual loop moving along the same bit of featureless road. No sense of direction or distance travelled, no sign of the sun or of anything other than the swirling clouds around us. Claustrophobic and eerie. Our footsteps seem amplified. The rustle of our wet clothes as we cause motion by walking. The chink of weapons, the coughs, and deep sighs taken periodically. Nick lights a cigarette and passes his packet round. I take one, so do the lads, and even Paula makes a weak joke about us being a bad influence as she lights up.

The smoke tastes foul on an empty stomach, harsh against my throat, and I long for dry clothes, hot coffee, fresh food, and a clean bed of white linen that Lani and I can rest in. I long for the sun to come back, dazzling and bright. We could go swimming again, splash about, and do nothing, worry about nothing.

But we're here, doing the best we can in a fuck awful situation. A band of misfits made up of such a weird bunch that you couldn't make this shit up. I glance across at Dave to see him staring intently ahead. Every now and then, he glances left and right, and I notice he watches the dog very closely, as if knowing his own awesome senses are dulled so piggybacking on hers instead. She seems nonplussed, running around in circles as she sniffs the ground, never straying more than a few feet behind, but ranging ahead out of view as though checking the route is clear.

We pass no junctions, no side streets or anything. Just an endless hedgerow broken only by the odd field gate or wooden step over giving access to unseen footpaths. We drink water, sipping from the bottles we carry, and despite the fog, I start to sweat from the warmth and heat generated from the motion.

An hour, maybe more, and we finally reach a junction on the left and delve deeper into it trying to find a road sign. Nick nods when we find one, 'down there,' is about all he mutters, clearly feeling as depressed as the rest of us, 'maybe a mile,' he shrugs.

We set off, and again fall into silence. I hope the Saxon is still here. The vehicle is as much a part of our group as any of us. To go on without it feels wrong.

It takes time to walk that mile, and it takes longer to find the way to the harbour. A small inlet expensively built with floating wooden pontoons gated off to allow access to only the monthly fee payers. We follow Nick who tries to pick out the things he saw last night, and we give him time and space with no pressure. The storm was horrendous, and he was moving fast. The few glimpses we get of structures show us the damage wrought last night. Boats smashed to pieces on the hard-standing next to the harbour. Bits of brick wall lie all over the ground. A large section of a house roof is half in the shallows. Debris and things strewn everywhere, and the odd corpse left smashed to bits or lying bloated, and grotesquely misshapen.

The dog finds it first. Shooting off into the fog, we hear her excited whine and a few playful barks. Following the noise, and we all feel our spirits rising as the rear of the great vehicle looms into view. The back doors wide open with the dog standing proud in the back barking playfully while her tail goes ten to the dozen.

'Good girl!' Nick is the first one to her, rubbing her wet head energetically which she clearly loves.

'Thank fuck,' Blowers groans, and immediately clambers into the back to drop his rucksack and take a grateful seat on a side bench. Stretching his legs out he leans his head back and closes his eyes, 'I'm fucked,' he mumbles.

'Think we all are,' Clarence heaves himself inside, and sits down opposite Blowers, 'it's like being home,' he observes looking around the inside of the vehicle, 'poor girl, left on her own all night.'

'I need a piss,' Jagger eases his bag down, and wonders towards the front of the vehicle as Paula and Roy climb into the back. 'Mr Howie,' Jagger calls out, his voice urgent. I move fast, Dave right with me as the others follow close behind.

'You alright?' I spot the lad staring at the front of the Saxon.

'Yeah, seen that,' I turn to see the same two words as were on the signboard are written on the front of the Saxon. *He's coming.* The bloodlines are thick and already mostly dried.

'Fingers again,' Paula shunts a digit with her foot. A thick and gnarly thumb still with black hairs sticking out of the topside.

'Who the fuck they on about?' Nick asks.

'We're here,' I yell out, 'right here,' my voice seems to echo off the fog. No response, no noise at all. Shrugging, I head around to the driver's side and pull the door open. 'Seems okay,' I report after a quick look at the interior, 'and yeah, it does feel like home,' I groan in pleasure at taking the seat that now feels so familiar to me. Rubbing my eyes, and

I shift uncomfortably from the wet clothes, 'coffee,' I announce, 'I need coffee…'

'Here, here,' Paula replies, 'I'll vote on that.'

'We'll have to find a house,' Lani suggests, 'preferably one with a gas supply.'

'Aye, you coming upfront Lani?' I call out, selfishly wanting her to be close to me. She gets into the passenger seat and stretches her legs out, 'everyone in?'

'Yep,' Blowers replies, 'bit of a tighter squeeze now though, boss.'

'Too tight?' I twist around, but can see there is just about enough room. Jagger and Mo Mo are only small build although I wouldn't want to try and get any more inside. Meredith lies down in the middle, panting away with a dripping tongue from the water just given to her by one of the lads.

'Might be better if I swap,' she suggests, 'Clarence will have more room up here.'

'I'm fine,' Clarence replies.

'You should definitely go upfront,' Cookey says from his position of being squashed between the end of the vehicle, and one side of Clarence.

'Come on,' Lani prompts him. She reaches over to rub my leg quickly, and offers me a quick peck on the cheek, 'nice idea,' she whispers before they swap over.

'Hello boss,' Clarence puts one huge hand on my leg and leans in to peck my cheek which has the lads bursting out with snorts of laughter.

'You kiss just like Lani.'

'Oi,' Lani shouts.

'We can't go any faster than walking pace,' I start the engine, and it's like feeling the beast come to life. An inert object given a personality and character. All of the little noises sound out, the deep thrum of the engine, the rattle of equipment and the vibration. I smile and give a sigh, something about it can't help but lift my spirits.

8

To go straight back to the airfield would draw attention. Light aircraft have to file a flight plan which is passed to the local Special Branch who, having been made aware of the mass murder, will eventually seek the information from the Civil Aviation Authority. The plane will be tracked, the owners spoken to, and enquiries made.

Therefore, Gregori is taken to the nearest city safe house to lay low before an exfiltration plan can be finalised, which will most likely mean a drive to the other end of the country, and either a boat to mainland Europe or another private jet taking off in the middle night.

'The boss asked how many,' the driver plucks the courage up to ask the question, the two men in the back hold their breaths in anticipation of the answer.

'Eighteen,' Gregori replies, 'men, women and children. The target was executed in the prescribed fashion.'

As the rural gives way to the urban grey of northern England, the information is relayed via a bland coded message on a mobile phone from one of the rear seat passengers. Green to grey. Beautiful to ugly. But the ugly is functional. Not all ugly things are abhorrent. Gregori's internal monologue knows this to be untrue. He is ugly. He is *the ugly man*. The bringer of death and destruction. His sole purpose in life is to seek revenge on behalf of those unable to do so for themselves. Functioning. He is like this city. Ugly but functioning. An industrial necessity. If there was no demand, this city would never become what it is. If there was no revenge to take, his special services would never be required.

Factories, long-abandoned with rows of broken windows. Rusted roof panels that streak dirty browns and oranges down concrete walls. Open lands of cemented walkways, parking areas now littered with tufts of grass, weeds and burnt-out piles of wooden pallets. Graffiti everywhere, and despite the heat and glorious sunshine, the people look pasty and sickly.

A grimy place full of despair. The hard-financial crisis hits hard in these places. The hundreds of small business close up as they give way to conglomerate corporations that can afford to weather the bad times. With no one able to take the repossessed premises on, they fall to rack and ruin.

Police cars swish past, blue lights flashing, and sirens wailing. Ambulances, and fire trucks, more police. The bodies found, and the button has been pressed. Gregori knows there will be a news blackout ordered by the intelligence services and passed through a high court judge within an hour. News of mass murder in rural England doesn't bode well. Drug related mobsters killing each other on mass attacks is something to be kept quiet and worked from back rooms.

The silver Volvo sweeps into an underground car park, the security barrier activated in advance by a remote sensor operated by the driver. Once parked, the men exit and lead Gregori through a solid internal door up several flights of bare concrete service stairs to the penthouse suite at the top of the luxury building. Once inside, they take Gregori to a set of private room complete with en-suite bathroom and leave him alone.

Another set of rooms in another unknown and forgettable city. Except something has triggered a response within Gregori. He moves to the window, and stares down and out at the down and out city spread out before him. Ugly. Industrial and grey. He nods slowly, small minute movements as his eyes narrow. Chimneys cracked and leaning, road surfaces pitted with holes that speak of a council unable to afford the repairs. So many shop fronts boarded up. Others with faded display signs. Charity and betting shops seemingly everywhere. The people walking about keep their eyes down, heads bowed. High crime, high drug use, high gambling, high alcohol dependency.

It felt like home. Like Gregori had found the place he belongs. It matched him. Matched his mindset, and his perception of self. Grey and ugly, but functioning and essential.

He showers and bags his clothes into a bin liner which he ties up and leaves outside his door. The men will ensure the contents are burnt completely. A new set of clothes, more or less the same as the last are laid out and ready for him.

He checks the two pistols, the one he took in and the one he took out. Both have a full magazine within. He strips them down, cleaning and checking them fully. The taken pistol is good quality, and well maintained. Ugly and industrial. Both of the pistols are ugly and industrial. Like him. Like this city.

He makes a new decision that these two pistols will be his pistols from now on. No longer will he pick a weapon upon arrival. Sure, they might have to be hidden or broken into parts only to be re-assembled, but if he insists on it, the bosses will see to it. The idea of possession is a new one. Life to Gregori was a constantly changing scene of new places, new guns, new clothes.

Dressed, and he makes a new decision. He exits the room, and walks to the main living area, the men all rising as he enters, and pauses.

'I'm going out,' he announces in such a tone as to leave no doubt this will happen. The men know this is wrong. This is Gregori. This is the ugly man. He stays here until the call comes through, but not one of them has the courage to question the worlds most wanted man.

'I need money,' Gregori says next, and finds three men tripping over each other to hand him bundles of notes.

He leaves the same way he came in. Out and down the concrete stairs to the underground car park. From there, he vaults the security barrier, and walks slowly towards the closest street. A hundred metres later, and he's a nobody. A random man walking down a random street.

Not one person looks at him. People pass by, but they pay no attention. Cars drive and sound their horns. Music comes from somewhere, voices and shouts of market traders from somewhere unseen, and suddenly, there it is, the essence of the place beneath that grimy outer layer. The heart of the beating city thrives and pumps strong.

He walks closer to the centre, and everywhere around him he sees life and living. He sees ugly but the ugly works and strives to get by. The glamour and glitz of most cities lacks here. There is just pure necessity with all the pomp and beauty stripped away. Gregori blends in like nothing he has ever felt before.

For hours he walks and watches, stops and stares. He orders coffee from a rundown shitty café where the owner barely glances at him or even shows a reaction to the heavy accent. He sees people of colour everywhere. Black people, Indians, Pakistanis, Chinese, Sri Lankans, and many more white people that speak languages other than English. A melting pot where the sum of the parts is greater than the whole.

Gregori buys a sausage roll from a street vendor. The warm pastry and hot contents are bland and greasy, but he wolfs it down. He takes more coffee and sits watching the world go by. Without a phone, he has no way of being contacted. There is no need to contact him. Nothing will happen for at least a day, so he has time.

The hot day slides by slowly, but far too fast for his liking. The afternoon drifts to evening, and still he walks and watches. He wonders through the industrial estates watching the never-ending lines of dirty white vans coming and going from the units. He spots men that look like him, pasty, grey, drawn and ugly. They pay him no heed, and believe he returns in kind.

Hungry again, he heads back towards the city centre. A long slow walk, and still his eyes cannot help, but take in the glory of the dismal, the decay and rot, but the chord it strikes digs deeper with each passing hour.

He finds a street café with tables and chairs placed on the street next to the main road. A paltry attempt to be European by allowing the patrons to choke on the exhaust fumes while they tuck into their greasy bacon sandwiches.

As night falls so the environment changes. Gone are the day dwellers scurrying about for they are replaced by the drinkers. Groups of men and women that move noisily through the streets, falling in and out of the many pubs and bars. The heavy thump of bass music, dance music, rock music starts to mingle with the now lessening traffic.

Gregori watches them with interest. The women wear so little here. Breasts nearly fully on show, and skirts so short you can see the curvature of their backsides. He watches a group crossing the road towards him. Young men with inflated arms and women loud with large hooped earrings and hair scraped back. The women smoke and shout, cursing foully. The men laugh. One of the women spits, a great big gob of phlegm that lands with a splat in the road, none of the others pay any attention. This is normal behaviour to them.

'Wot you lookin' at?' The words, although barely recognisable in language are clearly aimed at Gregori. He blinks once and stares at the young man staring at him. The alpha of the group, taller and broader than the others. Thick colourful tattoos on his arms, and what must be a permanent angry scowl on his face.

'You deaf as well as fookin ugly, are ya?' The young man sneers, coming to a stop a few metres away, 'you starin' at my missus?'

Gregori stares back, not a flicker of emotion or reaction crosses his face. The accent of the young man is too thick for Gregori to understand, but he gets the sentiment entirely.

'Fookin perv,' the spitting girl leers at Gregori, 'probably ain't seen a pair of tits before, have ya?'

That gets some laughs, cheap sycophantic laughs from the others apart from the big boy still glaring menacingly at Gregori.

'Wanna see some titties?' The girl asks lightly, 'yeah? Wanna see 'em, do ya? Go on then you fookin' pervert…get a load of these for ya wank bank,' she hoists her top down to reveal two saggy fat tits. Gregori glances at them then looks around at the group as a whole.

'He didn't even look!' One of the other boys bursts out laughing.

'Ungrateful cunt,' the girl spits before tucking her breasts back into the flimsy top.

'Prick,' the first young man kicks at a chair, scooting it out of the way as he builds up to a temper tantrum, 'you got a fookin problem then or wot?'

Gregori stares up at the boy, but still shows no reaction. With a slight shrug, he shakes his head, and makes a point of looking away. A confrontation was developing. One that could leave him open to exposure. He should leave and do so quickly, but Albanian blood courses strong in his veins, to back away now is simply not part of his genetic make-up.

'Fookin' hit him then,' the spitting girl shouts for the big boy to finally do something. He lunges in with fist already raised and clenched, telegraphing his intent and position. Gregori simply leans to the side letting the fist, and the heavy body attached to it sail past to go sprawling into the mess of chairs beyond.

Gregori turns to stare as the young man gets tangled, and increasingly angry as he tries to get back up before exploding in pure rage and surging back for a second attempted attack. This time Gregori is on his feet to meet the incoming body. Stronger and much harder than he looks, Gregori simply counters the charge, lets the young man run into him, and twists gently to send the boy sliding over his back to land in another heap amongst the chairs.

'Enough,' Gregori says, his own accent just as thick as the northern lads.

The young man snaps his head to stare up at Gregori, blind fury behind his eyes. A blur of movement, and a body slams down onto the young lad with such ferocity it surprises even Gregori. Screams rip the air as the new attacker bites deep into the neck of the flailing lad. Blood spurts high and wide as the attacking man takes bite after bite, shaking his head to open the wound. The spitting girl rushes in, no handbag strikes for her as she goes in with fists clenched, raining blows down onto the back of the attackers' head. She commences kicking, screaming abuse while her friends rush in to help. Together they beat the assailant away. Like a feral animal, the assailant goes into a crouch then lunges in, slamming into the spitting girl with such force it sends her staggering back and down hard onto the ground. The back of her head slams on the concrete slabs rendering her unconscious as a pool of blood starts to seep out. Again, the attacker goes for the bite, driving his face deep into the girls' neck before he tears a huge chunk of flesh away. Gregori backs away, sensing this situation is suddenly nothing to do with him. His eyes are glued though, the ferocious savaging is mesmerising. He could help, he could do something, but to get involved is against everything he has ever been taught.

The remaining friends rush to the aid of the spitting girl. The boys now kicking hard at the assailant's face and neck. One of them gets bitten on the calf and falls back howling in pain. Running feet behind Gregori, he spins to see several beefy bouncers from the nearby pub sprinting towards the attack. They grab the attacker and launch him away to sail clean through the air for several feet before crashing into the chairs and tables that so tangled the young lad's first rush.

The bloodied man is on his feet, a wild look on his face. Gregori notices the red bloodshot eyes staring hard. The wet blood dripping down the beast's face as it locks eyes on the advancing bouncer shouting at him to stay down.

The bouncer senses the impending, lunge and rushes forward to pre-empt it, they meet halfway, and the greater bodyweight of the bouncer has the bloodied man taken from his feet. This has no effect other than to give him clear access to the bouncer's face who he shreds apart with wild gnashing of teeth.

As Gregori backs away further up the street he notices the young lad who abused him is now sitting up. The lad gets jerkily to his feet and turns slowly to face his friends. His head hands at a funny angle, not broken but twisted as though he has no control over it. He animates quickly, simply switching from staring and drooling to a staggering jerky run. His friends watch him coming but take no action other than to stand gawping in complete shock. He barrels into them amidst squeals and shouts of alarm, shock and pain. He bites deep, and is pushed away into another, he bites again and again. A frenzied attack from one to the other, and each time his teeth break the victims' skin, so the deadly virus is passed.

His spitting girlfriend is back on her feet. The virus having worked its way through her system like a tidal wave of destruction as it infects and turns every living cell within her body. Her heart stops, and she ceases to be the young woman she is. The blood is no longer pumped. The millions of messages and electrical stimulations from the brain are instantly shut down. She is a corpse. Dead. Life is extinct.

Then the virus re-animates her. It brings her back in the state it is designed to be. The heart starts beating again. Her brain fires up. The muscles, nerve and sinew, all become charged with electrical stimulation.

This is the first day for the infection. It has not yet learned to control these host bodies so the thing that comes back is programmed simply to do one thing, to infect others, pass the virus. Jerky and spasmodic she is, lurching to her feet with her head lolling side to side. The red bloodshot eyes fix on the back of a bouncer still trying to fend the other zombie off. She breaks into a canter, stiff-legged with arms hanging limp.

The bouncer doesn't register the impact. A huge man with a broad back so the young woman running into him has no effect. When she bites into his shoulder, he feels nothing, but a mild irritation at first but still ignores it, so focussed is he on the deranged lunatic in front of him. The pain gets worse, like a hot searing pain, and suddenly it has his entire focus. Spinning around, he stares aghast at the young woman chewing away on the flesh ripped from his shoulder. Her jaws work up and down with mouth open. Blood and gristle, dripping and hanging from her lips. A strong punch from him and she is sent spinning away with such force that a normal person would either be dead or very seriously injured. Her cheek is fractured, her nose broken. Her skull is already fractured from the impact on the concrete ground, but a few minutes ago. She feels no pain and suffers no distress. The pain signals are blocked. The injuries are contained. Blood loss is rapidly congealed, and again, she gets back to her feet. Nose misshapen and clearly busted. One eye socket already swollen shut, but still, she staggers back towards the bouncer.

He mutters in abject fear. That was a strong punch. Big men have gone out cold from his punches before, but this young woman, despite the injury, shows no reaction. Too much for him so he starts to move away. This is beyond anything he has ever seen. He digs in his pocket for his mobile phone, and keys three nines for the police. No signal. Pain in his stomach, and he wonders if he took a blow to the gut. That bite on his shoulder is burning now, really burning.

He feels weak, his legs trembling as he takes smaller steps. His vision seems to close down, his hearing diminishes. The pain in his stomach explodes with such venom that he sinks to the floor clutching his gut as he rolls and whimpers in pain. One minute later, and he is gone from this life only to be re-animated and charged back to existence.

Gregori, already backing away from the explosion of violence, turns at the fresh screams coming from across the road. Men and women run from the entrance to a bar, bursting onto the pavement where they wail and scream. Blood soaked bouncers try to force people out and Gregori watches as one after the other, those with injuries drop to the ground clutching their stomachs. He watches as they writhe and scream in pain. He watches as they die, and he watches as they come back.

Gregori does not believe in mythology. Zombies do not exist, nor do vampires or trolls. He does, however, believe in what his eyes see. Gregori knows death. He has given it many times over, and he watches and believes as those that are dead, become no longer dead.

The ugly man spins yet again at noise behind him. Screams and shouts indicate another explosion of chaotic violence from further down the street. People everywhere, running and screaming. Bodies rolling on the road. Cars unable to get through, grind to a screeching halt and sound horns. Drivers get out to shout for the idiot to get out of the way, others rush to give aid only to get bitten so they too can drop to the ground clutching their stomachs.

He doesn't feel fear, only morbid interest, and his mind works fast as he processes the information. Fact is fact, and within those few short minutes, he understands that to get bitten means you die, and become one of them.

A young man staggers across the road begging for help. Gregori watches with cold detachment as he clutches his stomach, 'help me... please...' the words are clear, Gregori has heard them many times in many languages. The man drops, and starts to writhe, the pain simply too great. Gregori takes a step closer, standing next to the young man who he watches, go still and become lifeless. Gregori drops down to a crouch and checks for a pulse. Nothing. He opens the man's eyelids, and watches as the whites become flooded with blood giving that horrendous appearance.

He frowns as he struggles to understand how the eyes can do this if the body has died. He pinches the earlobe. No reaction. He grips and wrenches the ear lobe with sudden ferocity. Still no reaction.

He places one hand on the dead man's forehead and grips the closest wrist with the other. Then he waits and counts time off in his head. Less than two minutes, and the man's eyes snap open, now fully red, and different to what they were. The life that was within them is gone. This thing is no longer what lived before.

The thing tries to sit up, but Gregori pushes the head down. He feels the tension as the arm he grips tenses and tries to lift. He pushes down with both hands holding the beast in place. Its struggles become harder. Its mouth snaps open and shut as it snaps the head side to side in a desperate attempt to bite him.

The young man is average build, and looks to be in good health, from this Gregori gauges the strength. Wild and uncontrolled, but greater than it should be for a man of this size and age. In a fast motion, Gregor releases and steps back, watching closely as the thing now sits up and struggles to get to its feet. It doesn't use its hands or arms to help, but rather just the leg strength to propel the body upright. Once up, it turns slowly to fix gaze on Gregori. It starts moving slowly in that wild way. Then, it lunges with a complete charge of lunacy. Gregori side steps grabs the beast around the head from the rear and snaps it to one side breaking the neck. The man falls down instantly. Dead again. Gregori checks for a pulse, nothing. He checks the eyes, still red and bloodshot, but clearly not animated. It is dead.

He steps back and kicks the corpse in the ribs, still no reaction. A howl to his right, another beast surging forward. Gregori side steps again and repeats the action, grabbing the thing from the rear to snap the neck with a vicious twist. Two killed and both remain lifeless.

The street is now a warzone. Bodies everywhere, but those bodies do not stay dead as each returns to wreak greater havoc. The spread is so fast and relentless. This cannot be contained. With so many turned and taken, Gregori becomes the centre of attention. They surge and run jerkily towards him.

Both the pistols are secured in his waistband, but he does not draw them. This is still a civilian street, and there will still be cameras here. To fire a weapon now could still expose his identity. So, he reverts to the neck-snapping. One after the other comes to bite him, only to find their spinal column severed from the neck down.

That technique becomes useless. Too many attacks at the same time, and to take the second to grab and twist leaves him exposed from the back. So, he works a fighting withdrawal. His fighting manner is as he is, ugly and brutal. He lands vicious power-filled punches to the throat, crushing larynxes and windpipes. He kicks at knee joints, breaking the delicate bones so the attackers fall, but continue to crawl. He breaks arms, legs, necks, anything he can grip that gets too close to him. He turns and spins, using his own body weight against them. Fluid as water and being precisely where he needs to be. The one he kills now is not the one he focusses on but instead, he is already working to seek the next viable attack, and primary threat.

Up the street he goes until the barrage is too great, and reluctantly, he considers drawing the pistols. But even they will only stop so many, and once the bullets run out, these things will still be coming.

Gregori looks about, seeking anything that will provide him with a reliable weapon. The bright lights and gaudy posters of a Kebab house draw his attention. He recognises the pictures of greasy food, knowing there will be knives within so towards that establishment he fights. Gaining the entrance and spotting the pools of blood which show where the Turkish men have already been defending their place.

'Knife,' Gregori shouts at the men behind the counter, three of them, all dark-haired and stocky, and all three holding vicious-looking knives that drip with fresh blood as they stab at the beasts clamouring over the counter, switching to Turkish, he shouts the word again, 'KNIFE.'

This gets the response he wants, and one of the men grabs another blade and throws it towards the ugly man. He lets it fall rather than risk catching a spinning sharp blade, but once in his hand, he spins it over his knuckles in a rapid assessment of the weight, the density, the balance. A standard well-built long-bladed kitchen knife with a sharp point and a blade that has been reasonably cared for. It's enough, and with the new weapon, he goes to work.

The floor is already littered with the dead bodies of the things trying to get over the counter to the workers beyond. The brief seconds of respite as Gregori got the new weapon enabled a fresh group to all surge towards the brightly lit kebab shop. They breach the door, a growling, hissing bunch of deranged beasts that bare their teeth. The first feels the plunge of the blade driving deep into the throat, a quick and nasty twist, and the blade rips a hole open. Blood and air escapes the newly turned hole, spraying a fine mist of infected blood to where Gregori was standing, but he's already shifted position, and is upon the next one, slicing quickly to draw the sharp blade across a throat. Dropping to his knees he stabs up at the next one, impaling deep into the genitals before driving upwards, and letting his shoulder impact on the beasts' face sending it slamming back into those that gather behind. Like skittles they reel back and away, Gregori gains the door and steps back, using the strategic positioning of the doorway that forces them to attack two at a time rather than as a large group.

The men behind the counter watch in disbelief as Gregori cuts, slices, and thrusts at the bodies, killing one after the other until they pile up in a meaty stack of bleeding cadavers. Seeing the respite from the attack, they seize the opportunity to flee, running out of the back of the shop towards their waiting cars. A larger group of undead impede their progress, and although still armed with their kitchen knives they lack the training and skill of Gregori, and also the defensive structure of the high counter. They get kills, messy kills, and instead of going for throat cuts, they stab out puncturing chests and stomachs which has no effect. Taken down they are soon bitten many times over, punctured by blunt teeth that savage at their pliable flesh. The disease is passed, and the beasts soon start heading for the rear door left open by the escaping men.

Gregori cuts swathes down, and with the bodies stacking up the rate of progress from those outside becomes slower. He backs away, turning to see the men have gone and realising there must be a back door. Through the lift-up hatch and into the kitchen, but he freezes at the sight of the next horde barrelling through the rear door. Snatching up a second knife he holds his ground, using a foot to kick out and slam the hatchback down to impede the charge of those getting through the front door.

The small stainless-steel kitchen area becomes a killing ground as Gregori uses every possible item as a weapon. Undead are pushed head-first into the boiling hot oil of the deep fryers, their skin blistering to fall away in sickening chunks, but still they live and turn to bite with the whites of their bones showing through. He stabs, kills, and gets faster in the work as he goes.

Knives were a favourite weapon of his, and a tactic still deployed when stealth and silence was needed. Versed in the ability to use two, he warms up to the movement, his muscles limbering as his body heats. His mind is focussed to the task at hand as he reads the position of every assailant coming towards him. He could close his eyes, and remember their position, and still take them down without fear of being hurt.

He sweeps legs when leg sweeping is needed to fell a body and block the path of the next. He cuts down when that body falls, he stabs up on the upward movement, and never an energy or motion is wasted. His hands and arms become slick with blood; his new clothes soaked to the skin. He fights with mouth closed, and keeps his head turned away from the spray of arterial blood.

But still they come, and they get greater in number as the activity of this place ripples up and down the local streets. As more are taken so they seek fresh prey, but soon that hunt becomes harder, so they drift towards the place they know there is a new host waiting to be taken.

Getting backed into a corner, Gregori glances about for something to use, he spots the small oil drums used to supply the fryers, drops down, and punctures holes in the sides of several. Thick light brown liquid pumps out to coat the tiled floor. With care and precision, he kicks over a stainless-steel work unit. The long thick worktop forming a barrier to prevent the oil seeping back towards him. With his low wall, he chooses his ground, and fights from there.

They slip and slide, they trip and fall, and everyone that gets near the hastily placed barrier finds a knife coming their way. The oil works better than expected, the ground is treacherously slick. Another long unit at the rear of the kitchen, and Gregori vaults on top of it to kick the heavy microwave from his path. Using the steel worktop, he edges closer to the rear door, and spends a few seconds slashing down to slice open the heads and faces of those that get close. With a leap, he clears the slippery oil slick-tiled floor, and lands on the carpeted area by the rear door. Amongst the undead, but he makes light work of felling those in his path as he charges through the doorway and gains clear open ground.

A quick look ahead, and he can see an alleyway running away into the darkness. No obstructions that he can see. The width of two men across so he runs to the mouth, and turns back to hold position, and lets them come. Using the same strategy, he starts building a wall of bodies he kills to block the path, letting them fall one on top of the other, and between gaps in the killing he heaves more bodies into place. With a minute or so gained, he turns to flee down the alleyway, building to a fast sprint with the knives still clutched tight in his hands.

9

'So? What do you think?' I stand before them in my new outfit and get an imploring look from Lani.

'No,' she shakes her head, 'really no...'

'It's fucking awesome!' Cookey shouts, 'I'm getting one...where are they?'

'At the back mate,' I nod happily.

'They got ones in my size?' Clarence asks with a thoughtful look.

'No, please...no...' Lani pleads looking around at the lads as they start heading towards the back.

'Ladies,' I grin at Lani and Paula, 'they've got women's ones too.'

'Not a chance,' Lani shakes her head firmly.

'Oh, I don't know,' Paula looks with interest at my new clothes, 'they look hard wearing.'

'You joking,' I say quickly, 'feel this material, it's really thick but lightweight, got loads of room to move about, and look,' I wrench open the thick velcro fastening on the leg pockets, 'they're like properly waterproof, and any shit will just wash off...and they've got these little loops here that I can put stuff on.'

'Knee patches are a good idea,' Paula leans forward to finger the thicker material around the knees, 'I might get some.'

'No way,' Lani recoils in horror.

'Oh, come on, don't let me do it on my own,' Paula laughs, 'the top looks good too.'

'They're dungarees,' Lani groans.

'Sailing trousers actually,' I correct her pompously.

'Dungarees,' she says dully.

I must admit, they are dungarees. It was Nick's idea to hunt around for a sailing shop. Being so close to a harbour, and in such an expensive area would mean there would be some high-priced outlet nearby selling top of the range gear. It took a few minutes of navigating the Saxon, but we found a row of small, and very expensive looking, boutique style designer shops, and surprisingly they were all intact too.

One of the larger ones doubled as a sailing clothes, and equipment outlet with a small coffee shop within, all nicely decorated with bamboo chairs and bamboo tables as though we are in Thailand or somewhere exotic.

With the others figuring out a way to power up the coffee machine, which comprised of Nick and Roy becoming new best friends as they figured out a way to use the power supply from the Saxon, I went off scouring the shelves. There were loads of garments, and I found some brilliant tight-fitting wicking tops, the type that draws the sweat and moisture from your body. I did find some standard cotton trousers and went to put them on until I discovered the sailing dungarees. Black material, and high fronted to halfway up my chest with two thick, but soft straps that go over the shoulders. Padding on the knees, hard-wearing yet lightweight. Pockets everywhere, and perfect. They were also priced marked at four hundred and fifty pounds which made it even better. Shit, I've owned cars worth less than that.

'Got 'em,' Cookey yells, 'Jagger, you want some?'

'Fuck off!' Jagger yells from somewhere else, 'not a chance bruv.'

'I'm getting 'em,' Mo Mo shouts, 'fuckin' perfect, and they worth like five hundred quid.'

'Five hundred?' Jagger yells in disbelief.

'Seriously bruv, like this shit is worth loads of green.'

'So, ladies,' I do a little twirl, 'you joining the dungaree party then or what?'

'I want to,' Paula laughs, 'come on, Lani,' she urges.

'I saw pink ones,' I comment.

'Pink? Do we look like we wear pink?' Paula asks archly.

'Um...no?' I hazard a guess.

'The top looks nice on you,' Lani comments, 'really tight and snug, and your backside looks nice,' she adds.

'Oh, cheers,' I grin, 'yours would look nice in them,' I change tack and get a grin in response.

'Oh, come on,' Paula laughs and pulls Lani up, 'let's go shopping.'

'Ah, when you say it like that,' Lani concedes.

'No, it's going to be AC,' Nick walks in holding a reel of electrical wire in his hands that must have been pilfered from somewhere.

'Marine cord,' he gives me the answer, 'chandlery just up there, Dave is choosing some new knives.'

'Oh,' I nod, 'bet he's happy then.'

'You alright?' I ask him.

'Yeah boss,' he grins, 'Roy is wiring the Saxon up, and I'm doing this end...er...nice dungarees,' he comments, 'they got any more?'

'Loads mate, at the back...LADS, can you get Nick and Roy some of our new uniform please?'

'Will do,' Blowers shouts back.

'Uniform? Nobody said anything about uniform,' Lani calls out.

'Mr Howie has decreed we all have to wear the dungarees,' Cookey yells, 'er...Mr Howie, have they got to be black?'

'Um, yes,' I reply, 'why? You found some yellow ones or something?'

'Oh, yes,' he laughs, 'Jagger is looking at some green ones too.'

'No, stick with black or we'll upset Dave.'

'Roger,' Cookey yells.

'Need a hand mate,' I ask Nick bobbing about behind the big coffee machine, he comes up holding a set of wires between his teeth and a wire stripper in his hand.

'No, thanks,' he mumbles.

Dave walks in holding a big cardboard box with what can only be described as a content look on his face. I already know what must be inside the box before he sets it down and starts spreading the contents on the sales counter.

'Bloody hell,' I remark casually at the wicked-looking long-bladed knives he spreads out.

'Divers knives,' he comments quietly, 'high tensile, and very well made, good grips too, the weight isn't balanced, but for stabbing and cutting they'll do well.'

'Got it,' I nod slowly, 'what are those?' He pulls out some black material, and thicker black objects.

'Sheaths and leg straps, enough for everyone, and some leftover, I found this one for Clarence,' he holds up a huge commando-style knife, 'do you think he'll like it?' He says almost nervously.

'Eh? Like it? Yeah, course he will.'

He stares at the knife for a second, 'I think I annoy him,' he looks at me quietly then back at the knife.

'Sometimes, but then we all annoy each other. Being a team does that,' I say quietly, 'and you're not used to working in a team...and Clarence is...'

'Okay, Mr Howie,' he says, 'should I give it to him or...?' The shock of seeing Dave floundering at social skills still gets to me. Such a natural-born killer with virtually no compassion, and yet he seems utterly lost at the prospect of giving someone a present.

'I think he'll like it if you do,' I say carefully, 'it would mean a lot to him.'

'I er...I found this too,' he pulls out a shiny multi-tool with a canvas holder that straps onto a belt, 'er...maybe Nick might like it, he er...he's good with tools and...'

'Dave,' I feel almost choked with a lump in my throat, 'shit mate, that's a really thoughtful thing to do,' to see him now, struggling to understand, and flitting between pure panic and embarrassment at his own inadequacies is awful. It makes me want to do something, to rush in blundering so he doesn't have to feel like that.

'What's that?' Nick wanders over picking a bit of wire out of his teeth, 'looks fucking cool…I mean er…it looks cool,' he corrects himself at appearing to swear at Dave.

'It's for you,' Dave thrusts it out quickly.

'Huh?' Nick blanches, 'what?'

'I got it for you,' Dave's voice is firmer than it needs to be like he's compensating for his nerves at giving someone a present.

'Seriously?' Nick reaches out to take the multi-tool, glancing between the object, and back to Dave with a look of complete confusion, 'wow…er…'

'And this goes with it,' Dave pushes the canvas holder across the counter towards Nick, 'it's like a sheath…and the hoops at the back go on your belt so you have it to hand when you need it…' he trails off as Nick stares with mouth open at the gift.

'Dave, I er…thank you,' Nick looks up, and speaks earnestly, 'really, fuck…thank you.'

'S'alright,' Dave shrugs, 'your good with tools so…'

'Yeah, I mean…cheers Dave,' Nick looks the same as I do, clearly shocked yet deeply touched at the same time. Looking past Nick, I see the lads in view, Lani and Paula stood near them, and all watching the exchange take place quietly. All of us staggered at the sudden display of affection from Dave.

'Everyone get a knife and a sheath,' Dave is back to being Dave, 'strap them on and make sure they're secure.'

Nick drifts off back to the coffee machine holding his new multi-tool like it's a prized possession. I watch him carefully slide it back into the canvas holder then tuck it safely into his pocket. I doubt he'll ever use it for fear of damaging it.

The others drift back, laughing and joking as they wear matching sailing dungarees, Jagger, Mo Mo and Cookey all piss about putting the straps up without tops underneath, and don wide brimmed sailing hats.

'You ready?' I hear Roy shouting from outside at the other end of the long wires trailing back to the Saxon lost from sight in the fog.

'Yep,' Nick shouts, he stares hard at the machine for a few seconds, 'is it on?' He shouts.

'Yes,' Roy bellows back.

'Oh,' Nick grins round sheepishly, 'didn't turn it on,' he flicks a switch and watches a row of lights come on, 'got it…working,' he yells. Roy appears in the doorway smiling at the victory which turns into a look of concern at the sight of everyone dressed in black dungarees, especially the three lads messing about without tops on.

'Er…' he starts to say, 'forget it,' he shrugs, 'do you know how to use the machine?' He asks Nick.

'Lani does,' Nick replies.

'Coming,' she appears at the end of an aisle dressed in dark blue sailing dungarees, and with a look on her face that could cut through stone, glaring at each of us in turn as though daring somebody to make a comment.

'You look fine,' I announce with a grin.

Paula walks out after her, 'I'm not sure,' I think they make my arse look really big, 'do they?' She asks the crowd. We all look at each, unsure of what to say or how to respond.

'Er, no…er…' I start.

'Looks fine,' Clarence nods politely.

'Roy?' Paula asks.

'Looks the same,' he says bluntly.

'The same?' She asks.

'Yes. The same.'

'The same big or the same small?'

He shrugs, 'the same. The same as it did before.'

'It doesn't look big,' Lani reassures her, 'you've got a great figure.'

'Aw thanks, Lani,' Paula smiles, 'you haven't got an ounce of fat on your frame though, I bet everything looks good on you.'

'Oh, god,' Cookey groans, 'someone do something…they're doing chick speaking.'

'No, we're bloody not,' Lani gives Cookey a sharp look, 'and it's nice to have another women here instead of you lot farting and talking about tits.'

'Tits…' Cookey says dreamily, 'April had big…'

'Yes alright, who wants coffee then,' Lani heads towards the machine, and quickly checks about to find coffee beans and a grinder, 'you want them to go?'

'Ha, you sound like someone from Starbucks,' Nick laughs, 'I'll have a latte please.'

'Macchiato for me,' Blowers asks.

'Skinny decaff er frapuccino…' Cookey jumps in.

'No such thing dickhead,' Blowers replies.

'Well, I got as much chance getting a frapuccino as you have getting a mackasplacka or whatever you said.'

'Black coffee,' Lani mutters, 'and you'll enjoy it too.'

Cookey shuffles around behind the counter searching the shelves and cupboards, 'they don't have any takeaway cups,' he sighs, 'we'll have to drink it here.'

Silence follows, but he seems completely obvious to what he just said. Even Dave stares at him for a few seconds before he goes back to the threading the sheaths through the leg straps.

It takes several minutes for the machine to heat up, but the wait is worth it. The first aroma of fresh coffee fills the musty shop as Lani operates the machine with much banging and clanging of metal things on metal things while Paula shoos Cookey out from behind the counter, and gets the white porcelain mugs all ready.

'Strong coffee,' Lani comments, 'we're gonna be wired.'

Without looking up from his work, Dave pipes up, 'Alex, get dressed properly, and you two. Find fitting tops, and get spares then return here for the issue of your knives.'

The three walk-off quietly, knowing not to make any stupid comments when Dave speaks in *that* tone of voice.

'For you,' Dave says gruffly, and hands the big commando-style knife to Clarence.

'Me?'

'Yes.'

'Thanks.'

'You're welcome.'

A brief exchange of manly nods, but I can see Dave is decidedly unsure, and Clarence is genuinely touched.

'Any food?' Nick asks, leaning over the counter, 'I'm starving.'

'You're always starving,' Lani comments.

'I'm a growing lad,' he grins, 'just snack shit then,' he grimaces at the wicker display baskets of junk food Paula finds in a cupboard, 'could murder for an apple or a banana.'

'Don't,' Paula groans, 'the thought of never having fresh fruit again is awful.'

'Can find tinned fruit easy enough,' Roy comments, 'I had loads in my van.'

'Not the same,' Nick replies.

The coffee is served. Hot black coffee fresh from the grinder. Thick and strong enough to melt your boots. I drag a chair closer to the door, kick it ajar, and start patting down for a cigarette before Nick appears with his pack and a lighter. He grabs a chair, and we're soon joined by the other smokers. We sit back in the easy bamboo chairs, stretching our legs out in our clean dry clothes while we drink fresh coffee, and smoke cigarettes, and stare out at the fog which obscures anything more than a few feet away from view. Right now, at this point, we could be anywhere, and none of this has happened. We can't see any destruction or death, no bodies and no blood anywhere. We know it's there alright, but I get the sense we're joined in a collective fantasy of just being a group of friends relaxing in a café. The non-smokers soon join us, the chairs get pushed about until everyone is seated. Staring about I watch Jagger and Mo Mo, and notice that without their street gear on, and now dressed the same as everyone else, they look like normal teenage boys. To their credit, they haven't done or said anything to offend anyone, yet which only serves to show just how much regard they have for Maddox.

'Can't we just stay here,' Cookey settles back in his chair, 'this is well comfy.'

'I know right,' Lani replies, 'a few moments of bliss.'

Paula sighs and stares out of the open doors, 'we're not going to get very far in this weather,' she says quietly.

'We can't stay,' I reply.

'I know,' she says softly, 'wishful thinking.'

'And besides,' I continue, 'someone is coming apparently.'

'Who?' Cookey sits up quickly.

'The message, you fuckwit,' Blowers says, 'on the sign and on the Saxon?'

'Ha!' Cookey gives a brief snort of laughter at himself, 'yeah...I forgot.'

'Another Darren,' Nick says in a low voice.

'Nah,' Cookey settles back into his chair, 'it'll be another April.'

'*He...*' Blowers says, 'not she.'

'Maybe they missed the S off.'

'Maybe,' Blowers gives up to focus on his coffee.

'You know who it is then?' Jagger asks.

'No mate,' shaking my head I draw on the cigarette, and blow the fumes towards the door, 'not a clue.'

'They're just trying to get us rattled,' a confident Clarence says, 'and it can't be anyone worse than we've already dealt with.'

10

Information and communication. These are the priorities. Gregori doesn't carry a mobile phone. Cellular technology can be hacked and turned against the user. Every word uttered can be listened to, and recorded, and the phone can be pinged for a triangulation of the signal between the three closest masts which will give positioning to the authorities.

Without information and communication, Gregori cannot make an informed decision as to his best course of action. A private residential landline is needed, one within a house that has a satellite dish to receive the multitude of news channels.

Racing through the dark streets of the ugly city, Gregori seeks a way to the residential section, but this city is sprawling and vast. Industrial units and commercial sectors are everywhere with no sign of private residences or normal houses. He could go back to the safe house, but that is too close to the city centre, and from what he just witnesses, he needs to be away from that location right now.

If this is a localised event, the media and authorities will be swarming the place. Nobody will be able to go in or out until they are checked and identified. Not only for risk of spreading whatever disease or virus it is, but also, in an effort to trace who brought the chemical into the city in the first place.

He runs from a side alley into another dark narrow gap between two high buildings. The darkness and shadows suit him. He feels comfortable within these confined spaces. Twisting alleys and back streets he follows while all the time gripping the two knives in his hands.

Screams from nearly every direction tell him the incident is spreading out. As fast as he can move, so too does the deadly virus. The wailing sirens of emergency vehicles add to the noise. Harsh angry shouts sounds of violence with glass smashing. The noise gets louder and closer but all he can do is keep going forward. This city is rough, and ready with an obvious high crime rate. All of these doors and windows he passes are fastened securely, gated and barred, locked with thick gleaming padlocks and thick chains.

Given time, he could pick the locks and gain entry, but that wouldn't serve a purpose as he needs a private residential landline and a television connected to a satellite dish. One call going from a private household will be lost amongst the thousands being made right now. Sure, given time, and the authorities could trace each and every one of them, but by then he'll be long gone.

Bright lights ahead of him. The noise has built to such a level he knows the exit to the alley is going to feed him back into a popular zone. Slowing down, and it takes him barely a few seconds to bring his breathing under control. He edges to the mouth of the alley, preparing to lean out, and check both sides before deciding his route. His decision is made for him as a raving red-eyed beast lurches past, and spins quickly on the spot. Even during that split second, Gregori observes that he could not have been seen, there must have been another sense at work, hearing? Smell or maybe even something else. The thing charges in with teeth bared, and bloodied lips pulled back. One quick thrust, and the point of a knife is driven up through its throat into the mouth, driving deep through the roof and until the hilt snaps the beasts jaw shut. Gregori holds it in place, staring into the eyes as though searching for an answer or understanding. The man still breathes but with ragged, course breaths and still, he tries to move forward, forever intent on biting down.

No pain. No reaction to being stabbed. Pure hunger in those eyes. Gregori twists the knife with a sickening crunch, grinding through gristle and sinew. Blood pours down the front of the once dead man's shirt, but still he powers forward, driving those legs as though able to take steps. It groans and hisses, gurgling noisily as the blood spills down its own throat. He twists again, still no reaction from the pain, and still not dead.

With a yank down, he removes the knife, and steps away. The thing staggers forward from suddenly being freed and strikes the wall with its forehead. It goes down in a heap but rolls quickly and immediately makes effort to get back up. Gregori darts in, and kicks it back down, pinning it to the ground with one foot on the chest while he cuts through the Achilles heel on both legs, severing any connections from the feet to the brain.

Still it tries to move. Not realising the feet won't work, and it tries to get back up, falling over again and again. It gives up and starts crawling, the arms suddenly being used as tools whereas before they were useless limbs hanging free.

He stamps down, snapping the finger bones first in one hand then the other, and again the thing keeps going. He breaks the wrist, then the elbow joint then the shoulder. He works methodically through the body snapping bones, legs, femurs, shin bones. He works the pelvis, knowing his blows would be shattering it. Still the thing keeps moving.

Gregori knows the body will be flooding with chemicals by now, going into shock as the brain shuts down to preserve life to the internal organs. There is no way this thing can still be conscious and moving, but it is.

With a grunt he drops down, and into the eyes, bursting the pressurised balls with a gooey pop. Now blind, but that doesn't impede the beast. It crawls and bleeds, it crawls on many broken bones, but it crawls, and that hunger drives it on.

Gregori stands back and scratches his head. What is driving it? Whatever it is must be the greatest anaesthetic ever known. All pain signals must have been shut down. The blood loss is lower than it should be too. The wounds are congealing faster.

Thinking hard he round the crawling thing, and drops down, using one knee to pin the beast in place. He pulls up the blood-soaked shirt to reveal the man's lower back. Glancing between the head and the back, he shrugs, and drives the knife deep into the man's side. He saws to open the flesh, grunting from the exertion. Once large enough, he pushes his hand into the cavity, and feels about, it takes him less than a second before he finds what he seeks and yanks it out. Holding the kidney in hand. The man shows no sign of pain. He does the same again and removed the man's other kidney. This time there is a reaction. The man dies.

Some information gained. Normal injuries don't seem to work. Overwhelming injuries do. Blood loss, if great enough, and quick enough will work. The brain must be the controlling organ.

Stepping from the alley, he looks with a perfect poker face at the devastation within the street. Several nightclubs with their doors open, some still playing loud thumping music. People still running in panic, but far less now. The beasts, the things, the undead are everywhere.

He gives a low whistle and gets the attention of five or six of them nearby. As one of them twist and start towards him. The sight of fresh meat drives them into a frenzy, they charge that stiff-legged run.

Although he has already cut many throats tonight, this time he watches closely for the reaction after slicing the blade through the first one's jugular, and sidestepping. The spray of arterial blood arcs high. The woman staggers on for a few seconds as though blithely unaware of the injury, but the spray of blood is too great, and she goes down quickly.

Gregori nods, seemingly satisfied with the results of the experiment. Next one gets a solid stab into the skull, driving the point of the blade into the brain. Instant death. No question, no pause. Dead. He does the same again, stabbing down with a straight motion driving the point of the blade deep into the brain. Instant death.

Moving back to create space, he judges the next one carefully, and positions himself to spin around behind the slim woman charging at him. Into a safe headlock so she can't bite, and he jabs the point of the knife down into the top of the skull, but only enough the break the skin. No reaction. He stabs harder feeling the point of the knife hit the cranium. Nothing. Harder again but taking care to drive the point only the tiniest amount into the brain. A tricky procedure he has tried before, and one that produces varying results. Sometimes the body dies instantly, other times there is no discernible reaction, but mostly there is brain damage caused. On this occasion, there is no discernible reaction, but that means nothing. Not one of these things has so far, uttered a coherent sound other than guttural animalistic hisses and growls, certainly no words. Brain damage could be caused, but it could be to the speech control, the motor control, memories, cognitive function.

Realising the folly of his experiment, he stabs hard, kills the zombie and pushes it aside. The next few are killed quickly as he ducks, spins and thrusts to slay anything that gets close.

While he kills, he wonders if this is localised or global. He needs information. Time to go, and he heads up

to the main road with long easy strides, and the knives held low and ready. He doesn't deviate unless absolutely necessary. He walks straight through the carnage and destruction exploding every few metres. People scream and die as they are ripped from their feet to be shredded by teeth, and Gregori passes them by with barely a glance.

Crowds run and charge, fleeing and attacking. A speeding car races towards him, the driver clearly struggling to fend off a small child biting into the side of his neck. He jerks on the steering wheel, the car swerves to the right, the driver pushes the child away then tries to correct, but overcompensates too much to the left. The vehicle clips several parked cars as the child lunges for a fresh attack. The driver panics, stamping his foot down on the accelerator. The car powers up the front of a low sports car, and spins over and over as it rolls across the road killing two staggering undead as they chase a survivor.

Such is the momentum of the rolling vehicle it clips the high sided kerb, sending it higher into the air where it crashes through the plate glass windows of a clothing store. Glass obliterated, flying everywhere.

Noise, burning rubber, and chemicals leaking from the ruptured tanks of the upturned car.

With the engine still running and producing sparks, the flammable liquids soon catches alight, and trace a flickering line back to the vehicle. Gregori walks past as though in perfect timing, clearing the front of the store as the fuel tank goes up. A sudden whoosh, the air is charged, and super-heated as the car bursts apart spraying the immediate area with scorching metal fragments that slice through skin like a knife through butter.

The ugly man doesn't look back as the huge fireball engulfs the front of the shop and broils up skyward. He knows there is no immediate danger behind him, so he watches ahead, and to the sides with the discipline of a man taken as a child to be trained to do exactly what the situation dictates and nothing else.

A screech of horror and pain, 'HELP ME,' a female voice coming from an alleyway just ahead and to the right, and when Gregori gains the view, he shows no reaction to the party girl in a pretty blue dress being held down and raped by two filthy looking homeless men taking advantage of the chaos. Her dress is pushed up and over her hips, and pulled down to reveal her breasts, a tiny pair of panties lie discarded nearby while one vagrant thrusts himself back and forth with violent intent between her legs, and his mate pins her arms down one handed while groping at her chest.

'Please,' a croaked whisper as she turns her head to see Gregori watching from the light, 'please...' she sobs hard.

'FUCK OFF,' The beggar between her legs screams with fury, spittle frothing at his lips. No threat here so Gregori walks on, devoid of expression, devoid of emotion. Intent on getting information and communication.

But something unsettles him. In his gut. A prickling. Like when he gets an order to kill women and children. He does it, he kills who he is told to kill, but always the questions floats way down in his suppressed psyche, why? What did they do?

He has the skills to stop those men and save the woman. It would take him seconds and be no more taxing than any other kill this evening. She could get up, and maybe flee or find somewhere safe to hide.

But it isn't his problem. She would remember his face as the man who saved her. She could tell the authorities later of this knife wielding man that killed her attackers so easily. Just one thing like that could lead to disaster.

But then hasn't he already killed many tonight and in town centre locations covered by cameras feeding the footage to recording devices that will store it until someone wipes them. Anyone watching that footage could see the stranger killing the beasts with such apparent ease.

Information and communication. Those are the priorities, and nothing else. Find a house, find a phone, find an exit strategy. So, he walks and he kills as he walks. Without question, without hesitation, and without compromise. He ignores the pleas for help, the weak and defenceless who run screaming in the streets until slowly he leaves the city centre behind, and finds himself walking darker streets full of the cheaper commercial units that give way to the industrial which in turn, lead to the first residential roads.

Houses both sides of the road. Old and ornate that speak of a time long gone when the city made goods that were shipped throughout the known world. These were the houses of the rich, wealthy and great. The town leaders, the makers and doers, but those times disappeared, and being so close to the grime and dirt meant the houses lost value and were swallowed up by developers to turn into cheap bedsits for the rental income.

Now they are as dilapidated as the rest of the city, but the occupants suffer and die as well as anyone else as the undead beasts' rampage through the flimsy front doors to gain the succulent flesh within.

So, he walks, and he kills as he walks. He passes the shitty houses and the shitty suffering until the surroundings become cleaner and tidier. They still die here, and they do it as noisily as everywhere else but at least, they have telephone wires leading from the big wooden poles, and they have satellite dishes attached to the red bricks at the front.

Lights on or coming on as the foolish people rush out to shout abuse at the noise or see what is going on. A woman, early thirties with short blonde hair, and holding a huge carving knife in her hands. Several bodies already lay at her feet, and her blood-soaked hands speak of the deaths she has given out. She holds position at the end of her short garden path, protecting her home. Gregori approaches, watching as an undead male dressed only in pyjama bottoms lunges at her to find a repeated and frenzied attack as she plunges the blade in and out of his chest and neck. He goes down while she whimpers and grunts from the terrifying effort.

Snapping her head up, she faces down the next charging beast, not noticing as Gregori slips behind her, and walks up the garden path, and through her open front door which he closes gently, pushing the latch down on the lock before sliding the heavy-duty bolts home.

Clean and tidy. Pictures of children adorn the walls, but none of any adult men. A single mother desperate to protect her little ones.

The thought is as fleeting as any other, an assessment of the circumstances, but not an invite for an opinion. He spots the handset for the landline lying next to the receiver. A hands-free phone that bleeps audibly from the earpiece. Gregori picks it up, listening before hitting the big red button to kill the connection. He presses the green button, making ready to dial the number from memory. No dial tone now. He tries again, pressing the red button, then the green but still, no dial tone. He looks around for a mobile phone, nothing obvious so he walks through to the kitchen, spotting a large smartphone on charge. No signal.

Into the lounge, and he finds the television is already on with the sound muted. Whatever channel the woman was watching, now broadcasts the emergency test screen with a written message that there is a fault which the engineers are working hard to fix.

Gregori finds the remote control and learns how to move the channels up and down. Each screen is either a test screen, an error message or simply black.

He keeps keying the channels higher until he finds the news services. Several show empty news desks with microphones left on top, but the smaller screens in the top right or left corner show footage playing on a loop. Cities burning. Riots in many countries. Police and military firing into crowds. Death, destruction, suffering, and people eating others. Exactly the same as he witnessed walking through this ugly city.

Information gained. This event is global. To Gregori this changes everything, and within the time it takes to process the images, he understands that he is no longer owned. He is free to do as he wishes, and for the first time in his adult life, Gregori feels a sense of fear and trepidation. Everything was done for him. He never had to buy clothes, go food shopping, organise his wages or finances. He simply had to train and be ready to fulfil whatever orders were given.

Now it's gone. All of it. The firm might still be in place back in the homeland, but their once global reach, was now reduced to them controlling the immediate land around them. They had enough arms, and trained men to defend their towns and villages, they had strong defensible positions too. Then he should head back there. That was always the last resort fall back plan if all else failed. Head for home by any means necessary. It would be a long trip but certainly not unachievable, but then…a thought…no, not a thought, but a weird sensation deep inside. One of a contrary nature, a hidden voice that nervously speaks out for the first time. Does he want to go home? Home. The place where he came from. Except Gregori never really came from anywhere. He was manufactured, designed, trained and moulded to be what he is, but despite the pure blood killer, he is still a human.

He felt something for this city. An ugly brutal place, but there was an affinity there. Maybe it was a question of time, that too many years had been spent killing in strange places, and now his mind and body started to long for a sense of peace and belonging. He would have shrugged it and kept going, but that seed was now watered, and would grow roots that would spread throughout his body. Given time, it would have been a natural conclusion, and one his bosses fully expected to happen one day.

But that was now accelerated. He could do it alone. Without them, without anyone. He can go wherever he wants, live wherever he wants to live.

Unsettling, and he tries to quell the thoughts and rid his mind of all the almost traitorous intent. He was Gregori, he was the *ugly man*. His thumb keys the channels up through all of the news services, but he keeps going. Some channels still broadcast with computerised schedules. Documentaries, animals in the wild, how the Americans built the Hoover dam. Some show the emergency broadcast test screen, still more are blank.

How many channels are there? Why do people need so many? You can't possibly watch all of them.

His thumb on autopilot as his mind works. His brain screams a message, *go back, you missed something*. What was it? He presses the down channel button and goes back to the brightly coloured and garishly coloured setting on view. A topless woman wearing only the thinnest of underwear cavorts on a large sofa. Huge fake breasts, and she looks orange from the fake tan plastered on her body, and with make up like a drag queen. She waves a phone at the screen and mouths *call me* to Gregori.

The camera pans into a close up of her backside as she flips onto her front and starts spanking her own arse cheeks while looking back coyly at the camera, *call me* she mouths again and waggles the phone.

The cameraman says something, and she motions back with a shake of her head and shrug of her slender shoulders, confusion clear and evident on her face. Why is no one calling tonight? Was her popularity suddenly gone? With her huge fake breasts and supply cavorting, she always had callers to talk through a good wanking session, listening with hidden disgust as dirty old men breathed down the phone while telling her they were going to fuck her so hard. But tonight, there was nothing. No calls. The thought of not earning any cash starts to worry her. She took a tiny fraction of the call cost, so no calls meant no money. She had done everything possible to tempt them, rubbing oil into her body, spanking herself, rubbing on top of her panties and tweaking her unfeeling nipples until they strained larger. She even licked herself, and suffered the bitter taste of the fake tan, but still no callers.

The laws were clear, breasts and arse cheeks were fine but no vagina. If the powers that be discovered a performer had shown her vagina the channel would be fined heavily. She had only heard of it a couple of times, and these days, with so many channels showing mostly naked women, she also knew it was hard for the authority to keep track. Desperate times call for desperate measures. She says something discreetly to the person operating the camera then slides her hands down her breasts, onto her stomach and lower until she reaches the thin material of her panties. She hooks her thumb into the side of the material and pulls them aside, revealing her shaved and spotty cleft in all its glory. With eyes fixed on the camera, she rubs her clitoris frantically then quickly slides a finger into herself.

Gregori watches with his wide bulging eyes as the camera zooms in with high definition to watch the ghastly performance. The motion of the camera changes from smooth movements to jerky, the image shakes as the woman suddenly stops fingering herself and tries to scrabble backwards. Still with the close up on her vagina, but the energy is different. Someone else in the room with them. A clothed body thrusts past the camera and sinks down onto the girl. She squirms and fights back, but already there is bright red blood cascading down her stomach to run in thick rivers down her thighs. The camera person comes into view as he charges in and tries to pull the attacker away. His elbows going back and forth as he lands punches down on the beast eating his naked performer. As the two men roll down and out of view, they slam into the camera forcing it back a few feet. It focusses automatically, showing the performer lying still with one breast torn open, and the artificial liquid filled sack poking out through the skin. Her throat is bitten through, blood pumping thick and fast from the many wounds. Her breathing slows and stops as the last of her human breath exhales silently from her body.

She twitches, a convulsion as though electricity passing through her body. She jerks, once, twice, and again. Then she comes back, sitting up with the red bloodshot eyes of the undead staring into the camera, and the liquid sack sticking out of one ripped and bleeding boob.

'Who are you? Where's my mummy?' Gregori spins and quickly flicks the television off. Almost feeling guilty for being caught watching a naked woman on the screen. A young boy, seven or eight years old, and holding a monstrous carving knife in his shaking hands with the point poking at Gregori. Wet tracks score a line down his cheeks from the falling tears and dressed in his teddy bear pyjamas, he looks utterly terrified, his voice quavering as he confronts the intruder.

'Where's my mummy?' He asks again when the strange and ugly man doesn't say anything. A flashback hits Gregori, a wave of emotions as he sees himself as a young boy, abandoned by his father for a debt he could never repay. Left in the care of monsters who treated him as a possession. His eyes sweep the room, the soft furnishings and the toys stacked neatly in the corner. Everything clean and nice.

He doesn't know what to say. The boy is not a target, nor is he a threat. Gregori could leave but to where? Go where? He should start on his journey now, and head south to find a boat to mainland Europe. Why? Because he should? Because that is what he has been told to do?

'I want my mummy,' the boy tries to stifle the sobs, his bottom lip trembling as much as the knife he holds. The boy swallows his fear and stares up at Gregori with a fleeting glance of defiance and bravery that vanishes as quickly as it appears.

'Come,' Gregori says, his accent thick. He walks past the boy towards the front door, pausing before he opens it to check behind. The boy turns and follows with small tentative steps.

Gregori opens the door and looks outside. The boy's mother lies flat on her back with two men savaging at her now inert flesh. With the light from the house spilling out, and the angle of her body, her untouched face can be seen clearly.

The boy moves forward, staring with open eyes at the sight of his mother being attacked. Without a word uttered, the boy charges onto the garden path straight towards the awful scene taking place. His momentum carries him forward, the point of the blade held out in front of him which he sinks deep into the stomach of one of the attackers.

'GET OFF,' the boy wails into the night, 'get off my mummy,' he stabs again, thrusting the blade back and forth as he sinks it into the flesh of the beasts. At first, they show no reaction, but something in them must realise the woman is no longer human, the virus has been passed, and she is no longer the prey. With a vicious howl, the closest man looks up at the boy and lunges towards him on all fours. A single shot from the pistol held by Gregori, the thing goes down with the back of his head removed. The second clambers over the body of his fallen comrade to snarl and crawl at the boy. A second shot, and he too drops dead.

The boy rushes past them, uncaring of the loud retort of the gun from so close behind him. He drops the knife, and wraps his small arms round his mother's head, 'mummy?' he cries, 'wake up mummy,' the boy shakes his mother's body, urging her to wake up, 'wake up mummy,' he demands again.

A third shot takes down the charging blood-soaked woman with half her face already ripped off as she staggers towards the house. The noise of the gunshots attracts others in the area who start their jerky possessed run towards the sounds.

'MUMMY!' The boy sobs hard, 'please, wake up....' She jerks in his arms, a convulsion that almost throws him clear of her body. He crawls back with hope in his eyes and heart. A fourth shot, a fifth, and Gregori takes them down as they charge closer. This is wasting ammunition. He walks forward, tucking the pistol away, and drawing the kebab take-away knives. Glancing down he steps over the convulsing woman and waits for the next one to come lumbering in which he takes down easily with a slice to the neck and a shove to send it over the low wall.

'Mummy,' the boy cries, 'get up...' on his feet, and he tries pulling at her hand in a vain effort to get her on her feet, 'come on...' he urges, 'get up mummy.'

She does. She does get up. She sits up and opens her eyes. The boy rushes to her, wrapping his arms around the one person he knows will do anything to protect him. Mummy is safe, mummy is love and warmth. She nourishes, nurtures, gives everything of herself to the child.

She heaves forward to try and stand up, the boy still clinging onto her neck as he sobs with relief, and for a second, Gregori thinks she might be different as she shows no reaction to him. She tries again but fails as the boy's weight holds her down.

Then, she snaps into being. A spark behind her eyes. The lips pull back to reveal her perfect white teeth. Her hands close slowly into claw-like appendages. The boy is not her son. He is a prey, a potential host that has to be taken. As she twists to sink her teeth into his shoulder, a gnarled hand grabs the back of his teddy bear pyjamas and pulls him clear. The boy wails, unaware of the danger, and believing the man is trying to take him away. With an explosion of fury, the boy fights, kicking out, thrashing violently, fists balled as he delivers hard little punches into Gregori.

Holding the boy one-handed, Gregori stabs into the throat of an old man charging in at them.

With the old man down, the mother tries again to get on her feet. Gregori steps away, pulling the boy with him. He drops to a crouch, and pins the boy to his chest, turning to make the child stare out.

'Not your mother,' his accent so thick and guttural but the words are clear, 'see…not your mother now…'

'Get off,' the boy struggles, but is pinned too strongly to do anything.

'See,' Gregori barks and squeezes the boy harder, 'she not your mother…she is they…' he points to all the bodies, 'not mother…they…'

'Let go,' the boy pleads, 'mummy…' he shouts for help, but finds himself being pulled backwards as his mother gets to her feet and turns to face them. She looks different now. Her head is at a funny angle, and there is no look of recognition on her face. Instead, she does what they all do, her lips pull back to show her teeth as a low growl sounds from her throat.

'Mummy,' the boy refuses to believe anything, she is still his mummy.

'No,' Gregori says in a harsh tone, 'they…they bite with the teeth… See,' he turns the boy, showing him all the dead bodies scattered in the road, 'see…she not your mother…'

The mother stalks forward. Breathing hard, ragged breaths, and with her eyes fixed on the prey in front of her. Gregori moves back, constantly checking around and behind, 'see,' he says again, 'she kill you.'

'No!'

'She kill you…she not mother…she monster.'

'No!' The boy tries to struggle again, his cries pitiful as his young mind refuses to cope or understand what he is being told, but he does know what a gun is, and he recognises the pistol being raised in front of him, and aimed at his mother.

His heart races, knowing what the man is going to do, 'don't...' he gasps, 'don't kill my mummy...please...please don't kill my mummy.'

With finger pressed on the trigger, Gregori pauses and holds position. She needs to be stopped; she is a threat.

'Please,' the boy sobs, 'mummy...' He feels himself being lifted quickly as Gregori lifts him up then turns to walk away from the carnage. His pace gets faster, from a walk to a stride to a jog, the boy watching over his shoulder at his mother falling behind as the strange man carries him away.

11

Another coffee and still, we sit on the bamboo easy chairs. It was Paula's idea, that maybe if we wait a bit the fog will lift. So, wait we do. Eating shit food again and drinking coffee so strong that we're all soon talking louder, laughing louder and bouncing our feet up and down as the caffeine pulses through our veins.

'We should go,' Dave says.

'Too foggy.'

'Mr Howie, we need ammunition, weapons, doctors…we should go,' his voice is as flat as ever, but I detect an urge within those dull tones.

Sighing deeply, 'okay,' I reply, 'gonna be slow going though.'

He doesn't reply but is already on his feet staring at the others to get moving. With many groans of complaint, they get up, stretch out, and start filing out of the café door towards the Saxon hidden from sight in the gloom as Meredith runs ahead.

I stop at the driver's door, and watch the rest file past me, all of them dressed in sailing dungarees with knives strapped to waists, pistols on belts, axes, swords and Roy with his bow. A strange sight, the like of which I would never imagine seeing.

Clarence and I take the front, me to drive, and him so he doesn't take up the seating space of several normal-sized humans. Meredith seems happy as anything have so many people giving her fuss and attention, constant ear and head rubs, but I do notice she stays closest to Nick, Lani and the two lads as though realising they are the immediate pack members.

Engine started. Vehicle and occupants ready, and I stare out the window at the solid wall of cloud for about a full minute. If anything, it seems denser than it was, the slight wispy nature of the rolling fog is gone. Now, it's more like a giant smoke machine has been left on.

'Thermal imaging.'

'What was that boss?' Clarence snaps out of his own thoughts and leans closer.

'Nothing mate, just thinking out loud that we could do with thermal imaging…like the police spotter planes have?'

'Good idea,' he nods amiably, 'but we don't have one.'

'Nope.'

'We could strap Dave and Meredith to the front,' he suggests. We both stare back at the two of them. Dave sat closest to the front looking the same as ever, the dog sat in the middle panting heavily. I suppress a chuckle at the thought of them taped to the front of the Saxon staring into the mist with their weird freaky sixth sense like radar sending beams out ahead.

'Best not,' I turn back and ease the vehicle into movement, turning the wheel to slowly navigate to where I think the road will be.

'STOP!' Clarence bellows and lurches forward as the brakes are slammed on. Cursing from the back, and the sound of weapons being taken up.

'Get the doors open,' Dave is on his feet heading for the back, the dog picking up on the change of tension growls deeply and is already scratching to be let out.

'Nick,' Clarence twists around to glare at the young lad who looks back as though he's done something very wrong and is about to get bollocked.

'What?' He says in a high-pitched voice.

'Will ship radar work on a vehicle?'

Nick stares back for a second, poker-faced and still. The whole vehicle goes quiet, even the dog looks over her shoulder.

'I get it,' Nick says slowly, 'the fog…yes…yes, fucking yes!' He grins, 'shit, I should have fucking thought of that myself…fucking well done!'

'Nick's back,' Cookey quips.

'Radar is okay,' Nick looks off to the side thinking intently.

'Fish finder?' Roy speaks quietly to Nick, 'that shows depth and content, it could work if projected out towards the front.'

'We'll have to see what they've got,' Nick glances back at Clarence, then at me, then at Roy. The excitement on his face is obvious, 'I've seen fucking awesome like radar domes that feed the information to a small screen…'

'Oh, yes,' Roy nods quickly, 'we'll be able to see what was in front… well, the lay of the land anyway, solid objects and…'

'The boss mentioned thermal imagining,' Clarence explains, 'which gave me the idea.'

Roy and Nick stare at each other, lost in a world of possibilities, 'these expensive places will have all sorts of gadgets and toys,' Roy says.

'Fucking yes,' Nick is almost drooling like a zombie, 'we got time?' He asks me.

'Fill your boots mate,' I reply with a laugh, 'guess we're having another coffee then.' I reverse the Saxon back, and this time leave it as close to the building front as I can get. Nick and Roy go off in excited conversation while the others traipse back inside the café.

'Nick,' I shout before he disappears from view, 'you got a…' The packet is launched before I can finish speaking, 'cheers.' I light up and lean against the front of the Saxon. A few minutes of quiet time, but I've already clocked Dave staying close to the door keeping his forever watchful eye on me.

'Hey, you,' Lani strolls out, 'no coffee, Nick disconnected the wires.'

'Oh, never mind, had too much anyway, think I'm still shaking from the caffeine. You okay?'

'Fine,' she takes position next to me, shuffling closer until our shoulders and arms are touching. I feel suddenly awkward and unsure if I should put an arm around her or just stay as we are.

She laughs at my obvious dilemma, and stares expectantly, 'so?' She asks.

'Um...'

'Mr Howie, you do get flummoxed easily, don't you,' she laughs again, and wraps an arm around my waist, turning me so I'm standing in front of her, 'have I got to make all the moves?'

'Guess so,' I reply sheepishly.

'I don't mind,' she smiles at me softly, 'you're worth it.'

'Am I now?' I don't know quite what to say, being so out of practise with women, and relationships. Do I respond with a compliment, in-kind or just try, and stay quiet and mysterious, but worrying that I'll come across as cold and detached, then the moment passes, and it's too late to say anything at all.

'You okay?' She asks with concern.

I chuckle, shaking my head, 'I was going to say the same back, but then I thought it would sound cheesy so I didn't...then I thought I should say *something*, but then the moment passed...and I didn't say anything...'

'Right,' her eyebrows lift up, 'do you always analyse so much?'

'Um...I er...I'm just kinda out of er...'

'What? Practise?'

'Well, yeah,' I nod feebly, 'I've always been shit at this stuff.'

'When was the last time you had a girlfriend?'

'Me?'

'No, the man behind you,' she tuts then tuts again when I turn around to check.

'Years ago,' I admit.

'Why? You're lovely...that doesn't make sense.'

'I'm not lovely,' I look down feeling embarrassed at the compliment from such a beautiful woman.

'Oh, you are,' she keeps her eyes locked on my face, 'dark and brood-ing, polite and caring...yet so dangerous too...'

'Oh, right...I guess that didn't really translate in the supermarket.'

'Their loss,' she says, 'and my gain...I like it anyway.'

'Like what?'

'That you're not experienced, and all suave and smooth...you get to be the hero to everyone, but to me you're...well, different.'

'Trust me, I'm not experienced at all.'

'At all? Are you a virgin?'

'Fuck off! Shit...sorry, I didn't mean actually fuck off...'

She laughs quickly, 'you had me worried for a minute.'

'What if I was?' I ask quickly, 'would that bother you?'

'No,' her answer is instant and firmly given, 'not one bit.'

'I might as well be...there must be like a period of time that means you go back to being one if you don't have sex...'

'That long?' She asks me.

'Yeah...and then I fell asleep last night,' I say dismally, 'and then this morning you looked so fucking sexy...'

'Did I?'

'Bloody right.'

'Can I tell you something?'

'Yeah, of course.'

'Don't repeat it, and don't feel bad...'

'Go on.'

'I feel like a right gossip,' she laughs, 'maybe I shouldn't say anything...no...no forget it.'

'What?' I smile at her, 'you can't leave it like that, what was it?'

'Okay...'

'Oh, that took a lot of persuading,' I laugh, and try to mimic her voice, 'no Howie...I'm really not saying anything...no, really I'm not...stop asking me...don't, don't, torture me....'

'Stop it,' she giggles, trying to keep her voice down, 'Paula and Roy?'

'What?' I lean in waiting for the gossip.

'They had sex,' she whispers with a nod, 'last night.'

'Really?'

'Four times, Paula told me when we were getting changed.'

'Four times?' I blurt out.

'Sssshhhh!'

'Sorry,' I drop back down to a whisper, 'four times? They had it four times after all that bloody fighting, and that storm? Oh, no…I feel awful now.'

'Why?' She laughs again, clearly enjoying my distress.

'I fell asleep on you.'

'Actually, I was on you,' she whispers.

'Yeah, alright…bloody hell, the man is a machine…four times?'

'Yep.' She bites her bottom lip and looks up at me, something different in her eyes, like a hunger, but one that I like the look of, so I lean forward to plant my lips on hers. A long smooching kiss that seems to go on and on, pleasurable, intensely building as the pressure between us grows and for a second or so, I genuinely forget where I am, and what we're meant to be doing.

'The great thing is,' Nick's voice drifts into my ears, 'we've got fucking loads of power to use, I mean…we could rig fucking loads of kit up in there…'

We part, slowly, and almost with a sense of regret that we started kissing as a little just isn't enough. I want to take her by the hand and lead her into the thick clouds where we'll be alone and can carry on. Ideally, there will be a big bed there with soft pillows and clean sheets and surrounded by a huge electric fence fitted with machine-gun turrets.

But alas, this is not so. Instead, there is Nick swearing like a trooper as he finally gets someone who can understand all the stuff he knows about. Between them, they have arms full of big boxes with yet more cables looped over their shoulders.

Lani gives me a look. The sort of look that implies we could have done something amazing and wonderful together, but this cannot be so she wanders off back to the café while I squat down, and finger another cigarette out from the packet while trying to hide the reaction that men get when they kiss beautiful women.

My mind flits to Marcy which imprints a sour taste in my mouth. The passion I felt with Marcy was uncontrollable, and it still makes me shudder what would have happened if the dog hadn't have intervened.

He's coming. Two messages now. Who? Who the fuck is coming? I feel a sense of annoyance prickling within me, an anger that is bubbling away down in my gut. I stand up and walk towards the back of the Saxon, and then keep going, out into the fog. A few more steps, and I'm out of sight of anyone. Breathing deep I stare around but hear nothing, see nothing. My axe is held one-handed, the thing is such an extension of me now that I don't remember picking it up.

Footsteps behind me, quiet and stealthy, 'Dave,' I say without looking round.

'Yes, Mr Howie.'

He stops beside me, his hands held comfortable near the two knife hilts strapped to his belt, ready, always ready.

'Any ideas?'

'No, Mr Howie.'

Some fucker is coming. But who? Where from and why us again? What have we done to invite so much attention? This virus, this disease has got enough people to take so why keep coming after us and losing so many in the process.

'I don't know.'

'Don't know what?' I ask him.

'I don't know why they keep coming. Maybe they want you? Us? Our group? The losses we've inflicted…'

'Dave.'

'Yes, Mr Howie.'

'I thought that.'

'Thought what?'

I turn to face him, ready for the conversation, 'can you read my mind?'

He looks back without expression, 'you said it out loud.'

'I did not. I thought it.'

'No, Mr Howie, I heard you say it.'

'Dave, you've done this before. Can you read my mind?'

'No, Mr Howie.'

'Then how? I thought it, I know I thought it…I did not speak out loud and my fucking lips did not move nor did sound emit from my fucking throat.' He continues to stare with such lack of reaction that for him, it can only pass as an alarm that I'm swearing at him so angrily.

I'm going to run away.

No reaction.

Okay...Dave, right now I am thinking these thoughts...I want you to er... scratch your nose.

He doesn't scratch his nose.

Your nose is really itchy Dave, scratch it...scratch that nose...so itchy, so very itchy...

'Mr Howie, why are you staring at my nose?'

'Is it itchy?'

'No.'

'Not even a bit itchy?'

'No.'

'Don't you want to scratch it?'

'No.'

'Fine.'

'Okay, Mr Howie. Where would you go?'

'What? Go where?'

'If you run away? Where would you go?'

'Right! Ha! Caught you...I fucking...'

'You said it.'

'I bloody did not...I thought it...like a test...'

'You said it, Mr Howie.'

'Don't you *Mr Howie* me, Dave...I bloody thought that I know I did... how are you doing it?'

'Doing what?'

'Fucking hell, Dave...how are you knitting these days? I...'

'Knitting?'

'No, listen...how are you doing it?'

'I don't knit.'

'Dave, stop it...you are doing it on purpose...how did you hear my thoughts?'

'I didn't.'

'You did! You so bloody did...you heard me thinking...was it a voice? A sound in your head?'

'Yes.'

'Which one?'

'Both. It was a sound in my head caused by your voice speaking.'

'Ha! But my voice didn't speak.'

'It did.'

No. It bloody did not...I never said a word.

'But I heard you.'

'You did it again!'

'Did what?'

'Oh, my fucking good god you are infuriating. I just thought that response, and you heard it.'

'Which one?'

'The last one.'

'That I am infuriating? No, you said that.'

'No, Dave, the one before that, the thing I said...no shit...the thing I thought before I said you were infuriating.'

He just stares, then shrugs, and looks away as though nothing happened, 'we need to keep moving.'

'Nope. Not until you tell me how you can do it?'

He shrugs again, 'I don't know, Mr Howie.' A finality to his voice, and I know he'll slip back to being typically belligerent again.

'Oh, yes...oh, fucking yes! Mr Howie!' Nick's voice bursting with excitement, 'lads...come and see this.'

'To be continued, Dave,' I remark falling into step beside him.

'What is?'

'You know full well.'

'Okay, Mr Howie.'

'Are you smiling, Dave?'

'No.'

'Bloody were, I saw it.'

'I had wind, Mr Howie.'

And that rarest display of humour brings us to the Saxon, and a highly excited Nick pretty much jumping up and down on the spot with Roy at his side staring at a small device in his hands, a thick wire stretches back into the cab of the vehicle.

We gather around as Roy gives the grand display, showing the LCD screen that is filled with a mass of colours, like splodges with some defined lines. I think the grand reveal doesn't quite have the effect they were both hoping for as we all stare silently, and slowly look up at Nick and Roy with blank faces.

'Seriously?' Nick asks looking around at us, 'nothing?'

'Sorry mate,' I shrug, 'what is it?'

'The display from the radar equipment,' Roy explains.

'Awesome,' I nod, and try to look enthusiastic, 'er...so what are the colours then?'

'We don't know,' Nick beams a wide grin, 'no fucking idea...but it's working...'

Blowers snorts, 'fucking great one, does it play movies cause that is useless unless we know what it means.'

'Is that the land?' Lani peers in.

'No,' Paula shakes her head, and tries tracing a finger down one defined line, 'surely that bit is the water's edge.'

'They must be the buildings then,' I point to some darker splodges.

'Er...' Roy tilts the screen to get a better view, 'no...I don't think so...'

'Get fucked!' Jagger snaps at Mo Mo in a hiss and drawing all of our attention to the two young lads.

'What's up?' I ask.

'Nuffin' Jagger is quick to reply, too quick.

'Jagger can read it,' Mo Mo blurts out.

'You fuckin...' Jagger spins to face his mate with a look of fury.

'Lads, Jagger...do you know what this means?' I interrupt them. A reluctant Jagger turns to face me, and shrugs with an awesome display of attitude.

Paula speaks out next with a tone like a schoolteacher which at first makes me worried they'll both react adversely to, assuming they both hate authority. To my shame, my stereotype is proven wrong as Jagger immediately softens to show a respectful countenance, 'Jagger, this is important. We're running blind so if you know how to read this, then say something.'

'He got a youth trainin' thing last time he got nicked,' Mo Mo pipes up, 'sent him on a ship or summit.'

'Jagger?' I prompt him.

'Yeah, did couple weeks on this sailing ship...like an old one, but they had one of those,' he nods at the device, 'the instructor said they had to have it for insurance...they had loads of stuff like that.'

'Did they teach you how to read it?' I ask the question, suppressing the sense of urgency as I can see he's shifting uncomfortably on the spot.

'Nah, not like proper...know what I mean? Like...but the bloke showed me and...' He trails off to fall silent, his normal bravado and confidence vanishing in a second. He looks like the young lad he really is, looking up and about at everyone with a quick furtive glance as though he's ashamed or embarrassed. 'The er...' he motions his head towards the screen, 'it's got like GPS, and er...but the maps are already loaded so...like it knows where we are from the satellites, but...' he moves forward to take the screen from Roy, 'er...this is the depth like, you know...how deep the water is...but like, we ain't on the water so... yeah, that's right, the number is really low and that's why it's red...like it's telling us we're in shallow water, you get me?'

'Keep going,' I urge him gently.

'Like and then it sends the radar wave things out so...all these are things the waves are reading...er like bats, you get me?'

'Sonar,' Roy mentions.

'Who's that then?' Jagger looks up at him.

'Oh, er...forget it,' Roy keeps a straight face.

'So like, yeah er...did you fix it proper like...with the front at the front...'

'We did,' Roy nods.

'Cos like the bloke said he sees loads of wankers fixin 'em on wrong, and they read the screen the wrong direction, and end up smashing into other boats and shit.'

'We fixed it correctly,' Roy re-asserts, 'the instructions were quite clear.'

'Then er...this is what the waves are reading from the front of the boat...fuck it...the er...car thing, like...this line here, that is the water edge cos like, the colour is lighter and the numbers are all flat so like sea level…and then on this side,' he waves his left hand, 'there's something there,' he points at a darker section, 'somethin' solid innit, like er…he said like dense or summit, yeah dense,' he nods quickly, getting more confident, 'and like, on this side,' he waves his other hand, 'there ain't nuffin' cos like…the numbers is all low and the colour is all the same….'

'Mate,' I say with a downturned mouth, and an impressed tone, 'that is brilliant, well done…'

'Good work,' Clarence pats him on the back.

'Well done,' Roy nods stiffly.

'You did brilliantly,' Paula squeezes his shoulder, 'you think you can read it if we're moving?'

'Yeah,' he stares down at the screen with a bit of colour blushing in his cheeks, 'like but go fuckin' slowly though, yeah.'

'We will mate, we'll give it a go, think you can find the road out?'

'Er…the range is set low…' he turns the thing around trying to find buttons.

'Touch screen,' Nick says.

'Ah yeah, got it….er…settings…so that's like the brightness and… right yeah, range, shit this is like the lowest setting so…fuckin how do you make it more?'

'That one?' Nick reaches over.

'You reckon?'

'Looks like it,' Nick keys the screen, 'yeah, see…'

'Fuckin' nice,' Jagger smiles up at the older lad, 'cheers mate, so like… how far do you want it?'

'How far do they go?' I ask.

'Dunno, fuckin' miles and shit, you get me…like on the ocean they gotta go far ain't they?'

'We need to keep it close…' I stare down at the screen, 'five hundred metres? Something like that?'

'Five hundred…' Jagger mouths.

'It's on nautical miles isn't it,' Nick says, 'gotta change the measurements thing.'

Paula guides Roy back, giving the two lads room to figure it out. Murmuring between them they jab at the screen, chuckle, swear a lot, and finally, get it how they want it, changing the colour spectrum at the same time and marvelling at all the different things it can do.

'Ready?' I ask, breaking into their intense focus.

'Yeah,' Nick murmurs in a faraway voice, 'shit, yeah sorry, Mr Howie, yeah…we're ready.'

'All aboard then,' I beam around, and grin at the groans and shaking heads as we get loaded up again.

Clarence takes the front with me, Nick and Jagger perch on the seats closest to the front, the two of them staring at the screen and talking quietly.

'Stay slow, Mr Howie,' Nick calls out, 'so we can get used to it.'

'Fuck that,' I gun the engine, but keep the vehicle in neutral, 'we're going flat out.'

'He's joking,' Cookey reassures a suddenly very worried looking Jagger.

'Right then lads, give me some directions.'

'Drive around for a bit so we get the idea of what we're looking at,' Nick says.

I stare out at the thick fog, and glance over at Clarence who motions with a tilt of his head, avoiding any responsibility in the decision making. I roll my eyes and start moving forward going no faster than walking pace. Talk about weird, it's bloody horrible. I can't see a thing, nothing, and because of the size of the front of the Saxon I can't even see the ground in front of the vehicle, just a solid white mass.

'Er,' Clarence grips the sides of his chair hard, 'is this a good idea? The water's edge could be…'

'Nah, it's not,' Jagger cuts in, 'it's off to the side…nothing in front of us.'

'You sure?' I call out.

'Not really,' Nick admits, 'but just keep going.'

'We're gonna end up on fire,' Cookey comments.

'Fire?' Paula asks.

'Nick manages to set everything on fire…especially when we're near water.'

'That was one ferry,' Nick comments drily, 'one fucking ferry...at least, I didn't blow up the refinery.'

'Who did?' Roy asks.

Silence.

'I did,' Dave admits after a lengthy pause.

'Fuck! There...' Jagger yells out in such a tone that my foot hits the brake from natural reflex.

'What?' I shout back in panic as both Clarence and I try to peel our faces from the windscreen.

'The road, gotta be it,' Jagger says, 'see that...you get me?'

'Yeah,' Nick replies, 'go left a bit.'

'Left...right, got it.'

'No, left, not right,' Nick corrects me.

'Left, that's what I said.'

'You said right,' Lani interrupts.

'I meant right, as in correct...er...answering in the affirmative.'

'Right ahead now,' Nick shouts.

'No need to shout Nick,' Paula points out, 'it's very quiet in here.'

'Sorry.'

'Was that right *and* ahead or go right ahead as in drive straight?' I ask.

'Oh...er...drive straight,' Nick says...'keep going...left a bit...bit more...yeah, that's got to be the road,' he says to Jagger.

'Probably,' Jagger replies.

'Probably? Bloody probably?' I exclaim, 'how about *yeah, definitely that's the road*? How about that?'

'We're on it,' Nick points out, 'so...we didn't fall off anything...'

Nodding with respect, I give him a thumbs up over my shoulder, and decide to just drive instead of making comments.

'What's that?' Jagger asks.

'Er...trees?' Nick replies, 'I think I saw trees when I drove down here, boss, the road curves slightly to the right in a second...keep going...'

Clarence cuts in, 'get closer to my side, I might get a view of the kerb.' I edge over to the side of the road with tiny adjustments in the steering while his big hand waves to me to keep going. 'Got it,' he announces, 'I can see the kerb.'

'Brilliant, I can't.'

'Start turning into the bend to the right, Mr Howie,' Nick advises. We hit the kerb with a dull jolt, I correct and drift too far the other way which sets Clarence off moaning that he can't see anything.

'Maybe I should get a view of the kerb?' I suggest to which he concedes with a shrug, stretches his legs, out and gets into a comfortable position.

Edging to my side this time and I find the side of the road, almost cheering at the sight of something other than thick fog. My confidence grows as the two lads get used to reading the image on the screen, chatting non-stop in quiet tones as they try to work out the constantly changing view. Being able to see the kerb helps, and I increase the speed in small increments, building up to a pace that would match a decent jog, and then as we get out onto the main road I get up to a good running speed.

'What's that?' Jagger asks, 'the darker patch...see it? Fuck! It's moving...what the fuck is it?'

'Boss, slow down,' Nick shouts, 'got something moving towards us... er...coming from ahead of us and to the er...coming from the left.'

Bringing the speed right down, I peer out but see nothing.

'Still coming,' Nick shouts. Meredith takes over, giving a sudden growl she's on her feet pushing to the front, and trying to get to the windscreen. Her hackles on her neck standing on end, ears pricked, and her lips pull up to show those magnificent teeth.

I turn the engine off, plunging us into an almost complete silence, just the whir of the radar thing on the top, and the dog growling that switches to a raging bark as she hones in on whatever is out there, tracking the movement with her head.

'It's right there,' Nick says, 'it's stopped...right in front of us...not moving.'

I start the engine up again and creep forward, edging slowly into the fog but still we see nothing.

'It's moving away as we do,' Nick relays, 'staying right ahead of us.'

'How big is it?' Dave asks.

'Just a dark splodge, see?' Nick shows him the screen, 'it's got to be right there,' Nick appears right behind me staring out the window.

'You see it?' Jagger asks.

'Nothing mate,' Nick replies.

'Sod this,' Clarence cracks his door open, 'OI!' He bellows, 'who is that?'

'Any reaction?' I ask.

'Er…no…still there…' Jagger says.

'The dog, boss,' Blowers points out the obvious, 'she's going nuts… it's got to be one of them.'

'Let her out,' Cookey says, 'soon find out.'

'Fuck it, yeah, go on then, open the back doors,' I call back, and twist around to see Roy working the locking mechanism. Meredith snaps her head at the noise of the doors being opened and charges down the vehicle, leaping from the back before turning seemingly on the spot to charge down the side of the vehicle, and out of view in the fog. A split second later, and her almighty snarls rip through the air from a savage attack. I'm out of the vehicle, axe in hand, and jogging slowly forward towards the noise until I find her on top of an undead male. Having ripped his throat out, she's now working on his arm, biting through the shoulder joint before gripping the bicep to pull it free of the socket with a violent ragging of her head. It pops free with a sickening squelch, and she runs around in circles pleased as punch while wagging her tail.

'Shit, that's one messed up dog,' Clarence comments, turning I see the rest are with us, all staring at the dog parading with her trophy.

'Good girl!' Nick is quick to praise her, dropping to his knees as she races back to show him her new toy, 'you got another arm! Well done, good girl,' he rubs her sides and back while she makes little whining noises of pleasure, but keeps the arm gripped firmly in her mouth. 'What's this?' He asks in a friendly tone, and tries to grip the wrist, but she's having none of it, and instantly growls deep.

'Does she always do that?' Mo Mo asks in a slightly horrified voice.

'Oh, shit, she's taking it back with her,' Cookey says, 'Meredith, come here…good girl, come on…let me have it…' she responds to his tone, turning to run back with her tail wagging like crazy and seemingly happy as anything until he touches the arm at which point she makes it clear nobody is taking the arm from her mouth.

Two minutes later, and we're back in the Saxon. Everyone back in their seats with a massive German Shepherd sitting proud as punch in the middle with a human arm dangling from her mouth, the claw-like hand resting on Mo Mo's leg as he stares down at it in dismay, refusing to try and move it.

Dave reaches over and slides it from his leg. Meredith turns with a growl to stare at Dave. Dave stares back. The dog stops growling. Dave stares longer, and the dog releases her trophy with a sudden look of submission, allowing Dave to pick it up, and stack it neatly to the side.

'You leaving it there?' I ask him the question hanging in the air.

'It's hers,' he replies.

No point in arguing, no point at all.

'Where did he come from?' Clarence asks once we're back up and moving.

'Maybe,' Blowers calls out, 'he's was the one…the *he's coming* one.'

'He fucked it up if he is,' Cookey laughs, 'big effort there.'

Four bloody times. I can't help but think back to what Lani told me, and compare myself to Roy, and feel a stab of inadequacy. What the hell? Why couldn't I just stay awake for a little bit longer? Even once would have been nice, but four times?

Can Dave read these thoughts? I twist round to see him looking over at me, but not knowing if he glanced up because he saw me turning or was already watching me. *Dave? Can you hear me? Scratch your nose if you can.*

What the hell am I doing? Losing the plot by the looks of it. It's this fog, nothing else to see so it sort of dumbs the mind. Glancing across I can see Clarence is almost asleep now, his eyes closing heavily. The voices in the back are low and muted, Nick and Jagger still trying to read the screen and offer directions.

'Itchy nose, Dave?'

'A bit.'

I spin round to see his hand dropping away from his face, 'did you just scratch your nose?' I demand overly loud.

'Yes,' his reply is typical Dave, a straight answer to a straight question.

'Why?'

'It was itching?'

'You alright, Mr Howie?' Lani asks with a strange look on her face.

No. No, I'm not bloody alright. Dave can read my mind. Except I can't really say that and appear sane at the same time, so I shrug and turn back to stare at the nothingness out the window instead.

Hmmm, thinking about it. If Dave can read my mind, then is that such a bad thing? Does it even matter? Maybe it's the infection giving me some weird telepathic power. Nah, that's fucking freaky thinking. Is Dave even immune? I doubt we'll ever find out because if Dave ever gets turned, we'll either all die very quickly, or we'll already be dead from the fact that he's the last one standing.

Shit, it's not worth even thinking about. Imagine someone like Dave being turned? Someone with that level of skill and ability? Thank god there's only one of him.

12

G regori walks with the boy clasped tight. The constant motion of step, step, step. The darkness, the warmth from his body all soon work to let the boy drift into a jarring sleep. His mind too young to process what just happened. It's dark. This is a nightmare. Mummies don't die or bleed like that. Step. Step. Step. He can feel the warm hard body carrying him. So, unlike his mother yet a warm body just the same, and one that holds him without any moaning that he's getting too heavy to be carried.

Step. Step. Step.

Gregori carries the boy not knowing why or where to. It was a gut instinct, a reaction based on the circumstances, or rather the lack of orders and lack of direction. There was a situation, and he reacted to it. Thing is, he reacted the opposite to everything he had ever been taught or told. Walk away, do not get involved.

But this was global, of that there is no doubt. This is everywhere. The world. The whole world being ripped apart by a virus that turns people into frenzied beings that do not feel pain and feel the urge to pass on whatever infection is within them. That much is obvious.

What now? He has the boy in his arms, and no idea of direction or even where he should go. Should he leave the boy somewhere? Let him fend for himself?

No. He took the boy so that makes it his responsibility to find him somewhere safe. Yes, a safe place. The boy needs a safe place. So, that means finding other survivors, and giving the boy to them.

A feeling of calm settles inside him, pushing away those first-time feelings of being unsure of what to do. He is Gregori, the ugly man, he always knows what to do.

Find other survivors. Hand the boy over. Head home.

Infrequently do the undead impede their movement and are only slaughtered when they pose a direct threat, and even then Gregori does so as smoothly and quietly as possible so not to disturb the sleeping child in case he starts sobbing again.

Using only his right hand, he times the incoming attacks to perfection, using their momentum against them. Small side steps are the most he takes, just enough to let the thing stagger past with a cutthroat, and always to the right too so the spraying blood doesn't touch the boy.

Out of town, away from the epicentre of the disaster, away from the dense population zones. He sticks to quiet back streets and alleys; places he is familiar and comfortable with, and so enclosed that nothing can attack from the sides. Letting his own instinct guide him, he walks until he is sure they should be away from the population density, but still there are houses and still there are people running out into the hot dark night to face the ravenous beasts that were once their neighbours and town folk. Windows smashing, hordes of the beasts gathering in ever-increasing groups as they seek the next prey. The numbers grow so large that they sweep down the streets with an awful noise of growling and hissing, wherever there is the hint of prey they are there, charging and staggering with teeth showing.

Several times the groups are too large to risk going through. His own safety is guaranteed, and he knows not one of them would land a hand on him, let alone a filthy diseased mouth. But it would need two hands, and one of his hands is currently occupied holding a strange child, and like a typical distracted man, he can't fathom where to put the child while he fights, so he skirts round and sneaks through the shadows, and all the time wondering why the hell he picked the kid up in the first place.

The city centre may be the geographical heart of the city, but as time expands and the populations grew, so boundaries shifted, and the urban network sprawled out to create suburbs, boroughs and divisions within divisions, each with its own unique micro-centre.

Gregori walks away from one centre, unknowingly towards another. The residents of the houses here didn't wish to journey into the city proper for their goods and services, and where there is demand there is supply. So, another centre sprung up. Shops, businesses, pubs and nightlife. More affluent than the grimy city centre, and so the dwellers possessed an air of superiority. Rather than peeling wooden framed sash windows, these are UPVC. Flowerpots, flower beds, and water features in the front gardens instead of old sofas, and broken washing machines. The cars are washed on Sundays by menfolk who wear checked trousers when they play golf, and come back to eat a roast dinner before dozing off in front of the sofa while their ever-loving spouses chat amiably on Facebook.

They still die and bleed the same as the rest. They scream and whimper, if anything they scream and whimper louder for their right to life is greater than anyone else. They have jobs. They pay mortgages and bills; *they support the losers on the dole* so surely, they deserve to live?

But the infection doesn't give a fuck about these middle-class snobs. It doesn't care that they have two weeks in Corfu every year at a five-star all-inclusive resort. It doesn't give a shit what salary they're on or how much equity they have.

All men are created equally, or all men are equally created? The infection shows no inequality, it lacks discrimination or prejudice. It wants hosts, it needs hosts. Hosts will be taken, and they can fight back or lie screaming in the road while shitting their Marks and Spencer underwear. They still die, they still become death, and are reborn in the base state of being.

So, those men wield their golf clubs and cricket bats, but they get torn apart the same as the rest, and their blood drips as quickly from their BMW's as the poor souls drip blood on their twenty-year-old Peugeots.

Except for one man who has the foresight to plan the route ahead. He assesses everything in sight, he analyses each possible threat, risk, danger, and he calculates his own path. The steps he takes right now were thought about long seconds ago, but despite all that planning, he still finds himself coming to the end of the residential street arriving slap bang in the micro-centre of wherever he is. Crowds. Dense crowds. Hordes of them chasing individuals, couples, and small groups. Young men and women dressed to impress run jerkily after their prey. Night-club bouncers follow them, taxi drivers, the staff from the restaurants and takeaways, the local police who just moments ago were moaning about their pensions, and lack of overtime.

Gregori starts to back up. Noise behind, and he turns to see another horde charging up the street behind him. He sides steps, smooth and fluid as water into a deep doorway, and hopes the new horde will bundle past to join their new brethren in the town centre ahead of him.

He doesn't panic or feel fear, so therefore his nerves do not betray him. He stands calm and silent as he waits to slip back down the road he came from and find another way out. The boy doesn't panic either, the boy is asleep, fitfully, and somewhat loosely aware of the noises around him but he sleeps, nonetheless. The beans he had for dinner have navigated his gut. The turmoil, and now the bouncing around all play a part so when the fart comes it brings some mild relief to the boy's stomach as it trumpets out of his arse into the relative quiet of the immediate area.

The noise attracts one lone undead staggering hungrily towards the main crowd. She stops and turns, locking eyes on those of the deadly killer taking a tighter grip of the knife in his hand. She starts forward but in doing so, she attracts the attention of some that are close to her, they turn, those around them turn, more turn, they all turn, and Gregori faces out to a sea of hungry animalistic faces all staring at the meaty package he holds in his arms.

Oh so gently, he slowly lowers the boy to the ground, easing him down onto his side then shuffling the murmuring lad deep into the corner of the doorway. Standing back up, and both knives are now held ready while he positions himself between the almighty incoming mass, and the unknown strange child sleeping behind him.

One leg slides forward. One leg slides back. One arm comes up to cross in front with the knife held ready, the other arm extends out behind him. Multiple targets, and he works to pinpoint the order of attack.

The girl with her nose bitten off will be first, a slice to the throat, and then he can spin and take down the two behind her in one movement. Move left for that side is closer, take the three men down with two throat cuts, and one skull stab then slide back to position, and take on those coming from the right, a group of five, one of them big and strong with a heavy bodyweight. Three can be throat cut, they will drop just there, and the big one will trip over them to be stabbed as he falls. The last one will be cut deep and sent spinning to the left to impede the flow on that side.

The actions begins, ten seconds later, and the first eleven bodies he calculated are down exactly as he plotted, and by the time the last one spins off, he has already worked out the next closest five.

And so, it goes. A master at work who appears effortless like he just moves from space to space killing as he goes with the grace of a ballet dancer, and the strength of a scaffolder. Everything is forward planned. No move is taken without being checked against the movement of that target, those around him and where Gregori will end up in time and space at the conclusion of the kill.

The boy sleeps, talking in low nonsensical tones as his mind deals with the horrors he witnessed as genocide takes place just metres away. Mass slaughter of a new race so freshly turned, and full of hopes and dreams of a zombie future with long days and pleasant nights spent roaming the streets looking for brains to munch on.

The one single thought that enters Gregori's head that is not about the task at hand, is that he never really liked the Turkish very much, but they do keep very sharp knives.

13

'Dunno mate, cows maybe?' Nick comments.

'What's that?' I call back.

Jagger shouts out, 'we dunno, Mr Howie,' which is the first time he has called me that and it still makes me feel a bit weird, 'but like…some kind of fucking…well summit big…'

'We were messing with the range,' Nick continues, 'up ahead and to the right…like a heat source like that fucker Meredith got…but lots of them…'

'You think it might be cows?' I ask them both.

'Got to be innit?' Jagger says, 'like…there's spaces between 'em so like…lots of 'em, but all not one thing…you get me?'

'Yes mate, perfectly…are they on the road?'

'Hang on, is that some?' Nick and Jagger lapse into quiet mutterings, 'yeah, we think so…wait till we get closer, but…maybe slowdown?'

'Righto mate,' I ease my foot up going from the running pace back to a steady jogging speed, 'but remember we've punched through things before, we don't want to give them time to block the road up.'

'Okay,' Nick replies. To his credit, Cookey refrains from his usual comments as everyone starts switching on, shifting position as though getting ready for something to happen.

'Not far off,' Nick calls out, 'five hundred metres…and…hang on… yeah, there's movement now, see that Jagger?'

'I see it bruv, yeah like…like cows or summit…but…'

'But what?' Nick asks.

'Ain't no cows bruv,' Jagger says confidently, 'see how many is there? They ain't no cows…not that many…'

'Let me see,' Roy moves up to peer at the screen, 'what am I looking at?'

'These here,' Nick says, 'these splodges are just like the one that Meredith got.'

'Yep,' Roy nods, 'not cows, Mr Howie, way too many…no farmer in England will have a herd that size and after what, two weeks of no milking? Mind you, they might not be dairy cows so…but no, too many for cows…sheep have bigger herds.'

'Sheep?' I call back.

'Might be,' Roy replies, 'but that's still one hell of a herd, and they're packed very close together.'

'Wouldn't the fog make them do that?'

'Possibly, Mr Howie…'

'Not cows or sheep,' Dave's voice is confident, 'look at Meredith.'

'Fuck,' Blowers exclaims.

'What?' I twist around to see the dog staring fixed towards the front.

'They're running…' Nick yells, 'right towards us…shit, look at that,' he holds the screen up for the others to see.

'Oh, my god,' Paula's voice is the clearest out of the mutterings of shock, 'they're like ants.'

'That bad?' I ask, 'Dave, numbers?'

'Hundreds, Mr Howie…is that the road?'

'Yeah, this line here,' Jagger replies.

'Heading onto the road ahead of us…blocking behaviour,' Dave relays.

'FUCK,' A bang from the front and an undead launches onto the bonnet, scrabbling to press his face against the windscreen, he pulls back then slams his forehead into the toughened glass as Meredith surges to the front trying to bite her way through to him.

'Get her back,' Clarence yells.

'Dark spots are running towards us,' Nick calls out.

'Slow down,' Clarence stares through the glass at the thing trying to headbutt its way through the windshield. He pushes his door open, stands on the ledge and reaches over, 'Oi, ugly,' he yells. The thing snaps his head to fix on Clarence, and immediately lunges towards him. 'Got ya,' Clarence grips it around the neck one-handed, twisting from the waist, and he flings it aside.

'Clarence!' Nick is too late shouting the warning as his screen comes alive with darker spots running in from the sides. Bodies swarm the open door, wrenching Clarence from the ledge, and out of sight. Hard impact from my side as faces smash into my window and door, hands, fists, and heads banging hard to get the door open. They swarm the bonnet and onto the roof, dinks and bangs all down the length.

'Fuck it,' I slam the brakes on, but the low speed doesn't shift those from the bonnet, 'Dave, after Clarence…the rest form up at the rear in a circle and fight out, let the dog go first to clear space.'

'On it,' Blowers is up, kicking the back doors open to let a raging Meredith get out. Dave is over the front seats and out the open passenger door, plunging into the mist as he fights to find Clarence. A roar, and a female undead flies over the bonnet of the Saxon, something only Clarence heading into berserker mode would do.

I open my door, slam it shut and slam my shoulder against it to open it again, forcing them back. Too many, and the clever fuckers grip my door to wrench it open. I tumble out, axe in hand to land heavily amongst them, another clever fucker grabs the shaft of my weapon, and tries lifting it away. I cling on tight, and let the bugger help me to my feet before I slam my forehead into his nose. A second later, and I'm staggering around in a tight circle clutching my forehead from the explosion of pain and swearing like a trooper. The one I head-butted didn't flinch despite his nose busting from the impact, and pumping blood down into his mouth.

Bodies slam me against the closed door of the Saxon, hot breath hissing into my face. My axe is pinned too, but I keep hold of it, feeling as they try and jerk it free. Hands grip me hard, bodies pushing into me, and suddenly I'm helpless, unable to push out or fight back. The memory of being pinned against the wall in the car park tunnel floods into my mind and brings with it the horror of remembering the still-beating heart that was thrust into my mouth. I start to wriggle, harder and harder until I'm thrashing like crazy and screaming with it. They push harder with iron grips and shoulders that drive against me. No mouths biting me, no teeth trying to shred my skin.

'No,' I growl the word out as I feel my fingers wrapped tight around the axe shaft being prised open. Tightening my grip, I clench for all I'm worth, but whoever is doing it is stronger than I am, and the axe is removed gently but firmly from my hand.

Rage inside me bursting out from every pore and I fight like a man possessed, thrashing my own body against them, and the hard side of the vehicle. The grip on my right arm slips and I pull it free, swinging it around to drive a hard punch into the side of head pushing against my chest. I hit again and again, building power with each one. The thing starts to sink down from the blows as more hands scrabble to grasp my free right arm. I let my legs buckle and start sliding down the side of the Saxon. They growl louder and push harder trying to keep me upright, but slowly we sink, and my right arm wraps over the back of the head I was punching, fingers into his eye socket, and I pop the ball to grip the side of the bone and pull him away from me, but we all sink down to the ground in a heap of arms, legs and hot breath gasping from the exertion.

I get my hand under a chin, and feel for the Adams apple, driving my fingers into the sides as I compress and damage all the tiny bones and tendons. Still they drive down on top of me, swarming and suffocating, but not actually attacking or biting me. My head hits the ground and I can feel space behind me, so I scrabble, kick and thrash backwards until I'm underneath the Saxon. Sounds of fighting all around, the lads shouting at each other, and the constant dull thump as bodies hit the groud.

Thank god for Dave and his foresight, drawing my new divers' knife I get ready as they start in after me, but the space is too compressed to do anything. I head towards the back of the Saxon, drawing them with me, and almost reach the back end when several hands grip my feet and ankles, and drag me back cursing and spitting. Kicking out and I know I get some hard hits, but it has little effect as they pull me hand over hand towards them.

'MR HOWIE' Dave roars, calling my name in panic at not being able to find me.

'UNDER HERE,' I shout back between busting noses and jawbones.

'ARE YOU OKAY?'

Not really, a couple of minutes ago we were driving on a foggy road, and now I'm on my belly under an old army vehicle that stinks of oil and blood with zombies grabbing at my feet, 'FINE MATE, AND YOU?'

'FINE, CLARENCE IS FINE.'

'THAT'S GOOD THEN.'

'EVERYONE IS FINE.'

'GREAT.'

'DO YOU NEED HELP?'

'ME? NAH, I'M FINE MATE.'

'MEREDITH GOT ANOTHER ARM...I THINK SHE'S COLLECTING THEM...'

'OH, RIGHT...'

Bloody hell, you can hardly get a word out of him most of the time, and now he wants to make idle chit chat. 'Get orf my pissing leg,' I look back to see them clawing and dragging at me, faces twisted with focus and concentration, 'why aren't you biting me?' They don't answer, but keep pulling me back, so I let them. Instead of fighting against it, I do what I hope Dave would do and let them do the hard work and get ready to use my knife. 'You're not going to win...' I tell them confidently, 'not now, not today and not ever...so fuck off and give live in a zombie commune...'

'Howie? Who are you talking to?' Lani shouts from somewhere nearby.

'THEM...seriously lads...we've had some good times, some bad times, but why not call it a day, eh? You go your way, we'll go ours...we can phone and email, maybe visit once a year for a scrap or something? No? Shit, this hatred you have will just ruin your lives. All that negative energy, you could be happy making...'

'*Immune,*' the one word hissed amongst the ragged breaths brings me to a sudden silence, I'm not even sure which one said it, and now a few seconds have passed, I'm even doubtful I heard it.

'What? Say it again…' I reach up with my free hand and grab something hard on the Saxon, gripping tight to prevent them dragging me any closer. They stop pulling me and go still. All of us staring at each other, me at them, them at me. 'You spoke, say it again…'

'*Immune.*'

The woman, the dark-haired woman said it. Staring at me with a fixed, and almost intelligent look in her eyes. I focus on her, assuming the thing inside her is behind the controls.

'I am immune.'

'*Immune.*' The word is harsh, like someone who has lost their voice, all rough and hoarse.

'We've established that, yeah, I'm immune…so fuck off, and leave us alone…'

Her head jerks while her mouth opens and snaps shut, her eyes widen then narrow like the thing inside her is trying to control the finesse of holding her steady.

'*One…*'

'One what?'

'*…One…one r….one rrrr….*'

'What?'

'*Race…One race…*'

The energy changes. A connection between us, an understanding of communication, and I get a plunging feeling that this infection is what Dave said it is, a conscious entity capable of deep intelligence. Then I realise that it does not have intelligence, it simply uses what it has control over, it uses the intelligence of the host bodies, and it's telling me only one race can be here.

'I agree,' I say the words quietly, our eyes locked while my hand still grips the underside of the Saxon, 'but our race…not yours…'

'*One race…*' A faster reply, the voice more sure of itself.

'We were here first,' which perhaps isn't the best answer considering what happened to the dinosaurs and all, and the Dodo bird, and probably loads of other species that were about before mankind. The woolly mammoth, no…wasn't that one of the dinosaurs?

'WAS THE WOOLLY MAMMOTH A DINOSAUR?'

'What!?' A chorus of replies.

'No,' you can rely on Dave for a straight answer.

So, not the woolly mammoth then, ah yes there were the cave paintings of people killing them with spears. And the sabre-toothed tiger, that was wiped for the Roman games wasn't it? Actually, I think the Roman's killed off several species for the games.

Hmmm, my argument of being here first suddenly doesn't look so strong.

'Sod off, we're staying,' is the best I can come up with given the circumstances, and to reinforce my entirely weak reply I stab her in the neck, 'ha yeah, see…'

'*One race…*'

'Oh, that's not fair,' I twist my head to look at the undead bloke now saying the words, 'crafty fucker…you were in her a second ago,' I wave my knife in the direction of the now-dead undead woman.

'*One race.*'

'Who said that?' I demand, it certainly wasn't the new bloke as his lips didn't move, unless he's doing a Dave and saying it in my head.

'**One race…**'

'Clever,' I nod as they all say it at the same time, 'very cool, but can you do this?' I give them one finger with some raised eyebrows, 'wankers,' I tut when they return the gesture in perfect timing.

'Howie, what are you doing?' Lani shouts.

'Chatting…now look,' I say to the faces all peering at me crammed underneath the Saxon, 'we ain't going anywhere, and you can *one race* as many times as you want but…'

'*One race…*'

'Yeah, I heard it, say it as many times as you want but…'

'*One race…*'

'Alright! I heard you, let me speak for fuck's sake…I was saying that you can say it as many times as you want but…'

'*One race…*'

'One more time! Do it one more time, and I'm telling Dave... seriously…. Stop fucking interrupting me… you can say it as many times as
you want… but…' I glare round daring them to say it, mouths move,
eyes twitch but they stay silent, 'thank you, but…'

'*One race...*' A single voice from the back somewhere near the front
wheel.

'Dave!'

'Yes, Mr Howie.'

'They keep interrupting me, can you come down here, please.'

'Coming.'

'See,' I nod at them, 'now look what you've done, yeah…didn't think I
meant it did you…'

'Howie, what the fuck are you doing?' Lani demands.

'Nothing!'

'Hello, Mr Howie,' Dave drops down, and scrabbles in to nod politely
at me then a slow turn to take in the rancid faces all staring at us.

'They keep interrupting me when I speak, can you kill the next one
that does it, please.'

'Will do, Mr Howie,' he twists to position himself facing them, 'you
heard Mr Howie,' he barks at the fetid undead, 'next one to interrupt us,
gets stabbed…got it?...' it goes quiet, he looks back at me waiting for me
to speak.

'Forgot what I was saying now,' I mumble.

'*One race...*'

'Ah yeah, cheers, right, so you can say it all you want but we ain't
going anywhere…oh, you don't fucking interrupt me now, Dave is here,
do you? Oh, no…. lost your bollocks, have you?'

'Can I kill them now?'

'Not yet, Dave…so, yeah, don't keep trying to wipe us out… we're
staying here, and you just keep losing numbers every time you try…'

'*One race.*'

'I'm going in!'

'No, Dave! That was a reply, not an interruption. You don't have an
endless supply of bodies you know,' I say to the infection behind the
eyes of the undead staring at me.

'They do have a lot though, Mr Howie.'

'Yeah, I know, Dave but at some point, they'll run out.'

'I said it before, the population of this country was at fifty million…and we've killed nowhere near…'

'Dave!' I groan, 'don't tell 'em that.'

'Plus, mainland Europe isn't that far away so they could easily draft in more numbers if…'

'Dave! I thought you were Special Forces…don't bloody help the enemy.'

'*One race.*'

'Christ, this is getting stupid, I've had enough…'

'Can I kill them now?'

'Fill your boots mate, seeing as you've just given them a new bloody plan.'

'*One race.*'

'Blah blah, whatever…I'm going up to find my sodding axe.'

'He's got it,' Dave waves my knife at one big bugger at the back, the cheeky sod has my axe in his hand.

'Can I have my axe back, please,' I hold my hand out, motioning for him to return it, but he just stares at me, 'mate, you can't keep it, I found it, and I've been using it…you've got lots of numbers on your side, and we've got a few axes…play fair.'

Meredith joins in. Well, I say joins in, more like shreds the axe holding bastard to bits is probably a fairer way of putting it. But he does drop the axe which I retrieve and slide back out from underneath the Saxon, passing Meredith on the way as she crabs under to join Dave in having some fun.

I get around the back to find the others amongst a pile of bodies, but still with weapons up and facing out, 'everyone okay?'

'Where have you been?' Lani asks without looking, 'they just dropped back.'

'Did they?' I peer out, but the fog is as thick as ever before.

'Just stopped,' Blowers says, 'just like that, and they were gone.'

'Lots of them too,' Paula whispers, 'they're planning something, I can feel it.'

'Have a nice chat, did you?' Lani asks lightly.

'Yeah, was a bit repetitive, to be honest. Got my axe back though.'

'Back? Did you lose it?'

'They took it, but Meredith took it back for me.'

'She keeps biting arms off, Mr Howie,' Cookey says, 'it's getting really gross.'

'Nick, she's your dog…tell her to stop doing it.'

'My dog? When did she become my dog?'

'Just now.'

'Dave's the one that can take the arms from her,' he explains quickly.

'Dave.'

'Yes, Mr Howie.'

'Can you tell your dog to stop biting arms off, it's getting gross.'

'My dog?'

'Yes, she's now your dog.'

'My dog?'

'Yes, Dave, your dog…er…if that's okay with you, that is.'

'Really? She is my dog?'

'Um, well…do you want a dog?'

'Yes, I've never had a pet before.'

'Well then, she's your dog, mate.'

'Thank you, is that okay with Nick?'

'Fine with me, Dave,' Nick shouts.

'Thank you, I've never had a pet before. Do I have to walk her?'

'I think she gets enough exercise, mate.'

'Okay, how about brushing?'

'Yeah, yeah, you can do that if you want.' I realise Clarence is back in the group as he turns to look at me with a picture of a face, I shrug back.

'I don't have a brush.'

'We can…er…we'll get one.'

'Can I choose it?'

'Of course, yes…yes, you can er…definitely choose the dog brush, she's your dog now.'

'And a collar.'

'Whatever you want, mate.'

'We need to find a pet shop.'

'Will do mate, will do...er, how you getting on down there?'

'All dead, I'm just taking the arm from her now,' his voice gets closer as he crawls out the back of the Saxon holding a human arm. He stands up, dusts his clothes off and discards the arm amongst the dead, 'what are the rules?' He asks seriously.

'Rules?'

'For pet ownership.'

'No rules mate,' the look of fleeting horror on his face at the prospect of a life of responsibility with no rules is clear to everyone.

Paula clears her throat and steps in, 'er, stop her from biting arms off, and...er...make sure she's kept brushed, fed and watered and in good health...'

'Right,' Dave nods, taking it in with a look of intense concentration, 'anything else?'

'Commands,' Cookey joins in, 'she should learn some commands, like stay and sit...paw is a good one.'

'Commands got it,' Dave nods.

'I think that's it,' Paula adds, 'and a general responsibility for her, making sure she doesn't attack anyone that, well, that doesn't actually need attacking.'

'I understand,' Dave nods again. 'Do I have to pick her excrement up?'

We all look at each other for a second, 'er,' Paula seems to think for a minute, 'well, technically yes, but well, I think when we're out of the fort then no, no you don't need to but inside the fort, yes.'

'Okay, dog brush and dog excrement bags, and a collar,' he looks at me as though expecting me to make it happen, 'I've seen people using them, like little black coloured bags or blue bags, you put your hand in one end then pick the excrement up, and fold the bag over on itself, they normally have little tie handles.'

'Got it,' I say firmly.

'What about fleas? All these dead bodies about will attract vermin which carry ticks and fleas.'

'They'll have something in the pet shop,' Paula says, 'flea shampoo or…something.'

'We need to get that too, Mr Howie.'

'Will do, right…where have all the zombies gone?'

An uncomfortable silence descends. Staring into the mist knowing full well there could be hundreds of them just feet away. Meredith comes out behind Dave, low to the ground she shuffles her body until her hack end is clear and is up on her feet and staring into the unseen. Hackles up, teeth showing so we know they're out there.

'Keep hold of her,' my voice is low, the game playing and fucking about is done. The tension ramps up. Dave moves next to Meredith and gently takes hold of her makeshift collar, gripping it tight.

If we try and drive off, they will do the grounding thing again, and lunge under the vehicle. If we stay here, we have a stalemate with being unable to move or do anything.

'Everyone back in,' I give the order and hold to the side with Dave, Meredith and Clarence covering the others while they clamber inside. We jump into the back, and slam the doors closed, treading on feet and toes as Clarence and I head for the front.

'You driving out?' He asks me as I get behind the wheel.

'We'll try it,' but as soon as I start the engine, they charge from the fog and dive under the wheels to ground us out.. The weight of the vehicle, especially laden with so many is huge, but they don't need that many for the wheels to start losing purchase. I gun the accelerator and start forward, but they pour into view like ants reacting to the nest being disturbed. One after the other after the other, whips into sight, and is gone as he or she dives down to squash under the wheels.

My foot stamps down, the engine roars and we jolt forward then turning towards the right.

'They're clogging the wheels,' Nick shouts. I slam it into reverse and try pulling back, but we spin around again, then forward but the same thing. More pile in, but still we keep shunting forward and back in tight circles.

'Fucking hell,' Clarence exclaims, 'look at them…where they all coming from?'

'Fifty million…'

'Not now, Dave!' Clarence shouts, 'it was bloody rhetorical.'

'Bollocks, we're not going anywhere…everyone ready to jump back out?'

'Ready,' Blowers is at the back door holding the latches, and ready to open up.

'Out the back this time, boss,' Clarence thumbs over the seats and eases his huge frame out.

'Hard and fast,' I shout to the back.

'Ha! That's what she said!' Cookey laughs which is nice to hear as he's been quiet today.

'Who said?' Dave asks.

'It was a joke, Dave,' Cookey still manages to make the word Dave sound like Sarge.

'GO…' We jump down and start fighting, but no sooner are we down and slaying the first few, and they all melt away, retreating into the fog.

'Options?' I whisper to the group around me.

'Get back in and floor it,' Blowers suggests first.

'Too risky mate, we've got no idea what direction we're facing or what's in front of us.'

'We've got the radar thing,' he replies.

'Not good enough mate, anyone else?'

'Wait them out,' Paula says, 'this fog can't stay for that long…we don't have a choice. The first option is to drive out, that's no good. We can't fight what we can't see…so we either start walking or we wait here.'

'Sounds goo….' my words are cut off by a single runner coming suddenly appearing less than three feet away. Moving so fast and straight at us, and its only Meredith's speed that saves us from being scattered. Another one from the right, then a split second later, and another from the other side. Running flat out and straight towards us. Weapons up and ready, Lani gets one, and Roy the other with his sword.

'More,' Dave nods ahead, 'we need to move away from the vehicle.'

'Why?' I gasp then slash out to drive the blade deep into the stomach as Clarence cleaves the neck open.

'They'll go over the top of the Saxon and come down behind us, we need open ground, and we need to keep moving...otherwise they can plot our position too easily.'

'Circle then, bunch up, but leave room for weapons to swing...Dave, you lead us, but keep it sporadic and unpredictable.'

'ONE RACE'

The words boom around, echoing, resonating, and seemingly amplified by the gloom we're in. Trapped in a small space that moves with us, that's what it feels like. Almost that they can see us, but not the other way, like one-way glass.

All goes quiet. Silent. Just our breathing and the tread of our steps as we crunch along the road surface.

'Barrier,' Dave reports.

'Go over it, we want off this road,' I whisper back. We start navigating the barrier, covering while one climbs over to get up on the grass verge. Movement, and another one zips into sight silent as the air as she aims straight for Jagger and Mo Mo, possibly in some misconception that because they're younger and smaller, they'll be weaker. She's dead within seconds, stabbed repeatedly by two very fast and very tough lads who kill without hesitation and better still, they keep form and rank while doing it.

'Good work,' Dave nods at them, and I wonder if they know how rare it is to get a compliment from the small quiet man.

We start up the gradual bank, cresting the top to find an old wire fence trampled into the earth. Passing over it and they attack again, this time on mass and from all sides. Brutal battle commences, and we each step out to make use of the space so we can swing weapons and move side to side without being in fear of being injured by each other. Two minutes, maybe three and they're gone again.

The silence returns. Breathing. Shuffling steps. A whistling noise from the left, another to the right. Low whistles, mournful and sorrowful, and powerfully scary from the lack of vision.

'My side,' Blowers grunts and prepares to strike, but the woman runs past, right to left in front of us, and out of view. Another from the other direction, I start forward to attack, but she veers off. Then, another does the same to Clarence. We all jerk as though getting ready, but they skilfully steer away at the last second.

The numbers get bigger, more doing it until we're snapping our heads up, left, right, and around trying to track those that might actually attack. Meredith barks non-stop, raging at being held by Dave, and prevented from chasing them, but with so many out there, we've got no idea what tricks they have in store if one gets isolated.

I see him at the same point as Cookey screams. The young lad freezes in fear, but the undead barely breaks the mist, and disappears from view as quickly as he appeared.

'Did you see it?' Cookey babbles, 'did you? Did you see it? Oh, shit… no…shit, no…'

'What?' Blowers his by his side instantly, 'what is it?'

'Did you see it?'

'See what?' Blowers demands, but his face and tone show the concern he has.

'I saw it,' I stride over, 'you don't like them?' I ask Cookey. He shakes his head, and I can see the blood has drained from his face, his hands shake holding his weapon, and his eyes dart back and forth at the fog bank ahead.

'Can't be here…you saw it? You saw it, yeah?'

'I did mate, just relax…it's okay.'

'Saw what?' Blowers asks again.

A sick evil mock laugh permeates the air, a gruff phlegmy sound, but also clear and distinct enough to send Cookey into palpitations, 'oh, fuck,' the lad backs away, 'no…I can't…Mr Howie I can't…'

'Mate, it's okay, we're all here…it's not coming anywhere near you I promise.'

'What isn't?' Blowers demands.

'No,' the lad screws his eyes up, and backs away as the figure drifts just into view, the white tendrils of mist forming wispy strands of smoke that reveal and obscure in stages.

'Dave, with Cookey.'

'On it,' Dave gets up close to a truly terrified Cookey, and gently pushes his hand through the crook of Cookey's elbow, holding him close and tight, 'I'm right here, Alex,' Dave intones.

'What did he see?' Clarence booms out.

'That,' Blowers points at the lone figure. How the fuck the white paint has stayed on is beyond me, but it's there alright. Plastered on in thick layers that are now streaked and patchy with the grey lifeless skin showing through. Huge black eyes like a panda, but they too are streaked, like a woman crying who gets make-up down her face, but these are thick streaks right down to where the red lipstick that once so carefully applied around the cheeks is now rubbing through. Blood, old dried, scabby, and congealed is around his lips and jaw.

'Holy…fucking…shit…' Paula utters the words so slowly, taking the view in that clearly sends shivers of fear through her too.

Orange hair, like a huge afro that stands proud and thick on top, to the sides and hanging down. The blood smeared down his jaw, and the thick make-up only serve to make the clown look mean and savage.

A white silk jumpsuit, several sizes too big with black splodges like a dairy cow, but that too is filthy and covered in blood. The shoes are there, big red shoes with the over-sized toes. Not too big that it stops him moving, but big enough to notice.

The clown stands still, hands behind his back. Unmoving, and he stares with an upright head and posture of erect intelligence. The smoky fog drifts in front, and he appears in varying stages of visibility. Clowns don't bother me one bit, Sarah, my sister, was terrified of them. So was my mother. They could never go with my father and I to the circus, but then I never minded that as it became like our special thing. Seeing this one now, half-hidden through the fog, and with that down-turned blood-stained mouth like a giant frown and I, even I feel a chill running down my spine.

'You are joking, right?' Roy snorts, 'a clown?'

'One word, Roy,' Blowers growls, 'don't say one fucking word…'

'Yeah but…'

'Cookey is terrified of them,' Blowers points out needlessly, 'and I'll be surely taking the piss out of him for years to come for this…but one word right now, and you'll be on your arse mate...' Nick is already with Blowers, both of them staring at Roy

'Easy,' I warn, but feel the stab of pride at how they rip on each other so much but the loyalty, the bond and love runs deep between the three of them, especially Blowers and Cookey.

'I can't be here...' Cookey whimpers, 'really...we've got to run...'

'Lad,' Clarence's deep voice sounds from close by, the reassuring weight of his enormous hand resting on Cookey's shoulder, 'they got to go through me and Dave first, and that ain't gonna happen is it?'

'But...'

'Is it still there?' I can hear he's at risk of hyperventilating from the way he speaks. Dave reacts with speed that still leaves me staggered. Pistol out, aim, and a single shot, and the pistol is back in the holster as the clown slumps down with the back of his head blown off.

'No,' Dave says bluntly.

'See, lad,' Clarence says, 'he's gone...can't even see him now.'

'Stay in the middle with Clarence for a bit, Dave you lead again...we need to keep moving.'

'Sorry,' Cookey takes a deep breath.

'Don't be, we're a team,' I say it quickly, and get back to the matter at hand, 'Roy, you see any more mate, feel free to pick them off.'

'More clowns?' He asks as though it's the most ridiculous thing he's ever heard.

The laugh comes back again, louder, closer and so similar to that clown from the Simpsons, but so evil it conjures an image of a James Bond villain stroking a cat. Cookey starts up again, panting for breath and whimpering. Paula goes pale, starts to shake.

'Coulrophobia,' she mutters, 'fear of clowns.'

'You too?' I ask across the group.

'Bit,' she swallows, 'but I'm fine.'

Dave keeps leading us across a wide field, the grass firm underfoot despite the heavy rain from the storm yesterday. The laugh sounds out periodically, and drifts from different directions. I keep thinking it will lose the impact but if anything, Cookey gets worse each time he hears it. Probably with the image of that clown imprinted on his brain.

'Hold,' Dave calls the order, holding one hand up as he stops to stare into the fog. I can see him staring, staring hard as though trying to work something out. Clarence looks up and over, the others trying to keep a good look around.

'What?' I half-whisper but end up doing that whispered shouting which is just about the same as normal talking.

'A car.'

'A what?'

'A Car.'

'So? Why have you stopped because of a car?'

'A car parked in a field,' Dave states, 'not right.'

'Hang on,' I thread past the team, and find Dave staring suspiciously at the rear end of a Honda just about in view through the mist. The way Dave squints you'd think the car was about to attack us.

'What's wrong with you?' I whisper properly this time, 'it's just a car.'

'More cars,' he replies dully, 'car park.'

He's right. Staring out and between the shifting clouds that roll and wisp, I catch the outlines of more cars, hardly visible, and gone as soon as they appear. In both directions, parked neatly in rows that stretch off.

With no choice, we start threading single file between the narrow lanes formed by the cars parked nose to tail with Dave and I in the lead, Cookey still looking ashen-faced in the middle, and Clarence bringing up the rear. Roy tucks his sword away, instead pulling his bow from his shoulder and nocking an arrow in preparation. In this confined space, there is no room to swing weapons, so we follow his lead, pushing our hand weapons away to draw the double-barrelled sawn-off shotguns.

Sounds of feet drumming over vehicles soon reach us. The solid bang of the hollow section of the bonnet followed by windscreen cracking from heavy bodies, and the dull thud of vehicle roofs being walked on.

We stay silent and listening, knowing we're now at an awful disadvantage. Visibility is down to a few feet at best, and the attacking undead have a height advantage and with Meredith barking the whole time they can track our movements. The blast from a shotgun behind me as Paula lets rip with both barrels into a female charging over the roof of the Mitsubishi next to her. Another from behind, Clarence fires once, aims and fires the second barrel before dropping to one knee, 'fire over me,' he shouts to Jagger behind him. The young lad doesn't hesitate, but fires two solid shots into the mass of undead coming at our rear. The first two are blown back by the awesome power of the weapon, and several more are peppered with the scorching hot pellets.

'Stagger your firing,' I shout the order suddenly fearful that we'll all open up at once, and then be re-loading while they attack.

Dave tries to thread us through the lanes, but it's slow going, stopping to fire, re-load then up and move. Hunkered down and I brace myself to fire the shotgun into the face of a big fat male scrabbling over the bonnet of the car next to me. The pellets burst through his, decimating his features and thankfully his brain too. I drop down to reload, snapping the shotgun open to eject the two spent cartridges while fishing into my pocket for two more.

The sneaky fuckers then go low, snaking across the bonnets, roofs and back ends, and the lower profile makes them not only harder to see, but harder to hit. Then, they switch and take running leaps at us, but instead of diving over headfirst, they sort of twist to come at us feet first. The choice, then, is to fire into their feet and legs, knowing we won't go headshots or wait until they drop down amongst us. At this point, it becomes frantic, dirty and nasty fighting. We fire when we can, grunting and shouting as we use the butts of our guns to batter them down before firing. The new method of attack gets faster, more do it as they realise, they can get to us with apparent ease.

Meredith saves each of us time and again with her lightning-fast reactions. Dave keeps the front clear with relative ease, and Clarence the back. But neither of them can get into the middle with the rest of us such is the confines of the space, and I can see Dave contemplates going onto the vehicles too, but that would leave his end unopposed.

They come faster and harder, so we return in kind until the bodies start mounting up. Behind Clarence, the two young lads fight with determination, but the lack of experience in close quarters battle like this starts to show as they become overwhelmed. Jagger goes down under the weight of a heavy body, Mo Mo reacts to try and save him,

gripping the corpse in her hair as he tries to roll her off. Leaving his
back exposed, and one sliding over the bonnet locks onto his shoulder,
lunging as Cookey gets behind him and wraps an arm around the face
of the undead. Even from where I am, I can see the undead sink his
teeth into Cookey's forearm. He might be a joker, but that lad can
bloody fight, he heaves back lifting the undead from his feet, 'BLOW-
ERS,' he yells, letting his own legs drop, he plummets down while
Blowers draws his knife and with heart-stopping precision, he drives
the point into the undead's skull, just millimetres from Cookey's arm.

'FUCKING ARSE MONKEY BIT ME,' Cookey pushes the body
away, and is on his feet with the flush of battle shining on his face,
'fucking clowns, and fucking arse monkey twat mother fuckers....I'm
FUCKING IMMUNE, you CUNTS,' he screams the last word in rage,
wipes the blood from his bitten arm, and gets right back into it.

'Arse monkey?' I shout down after firing both my barrels at the thing
lurching towards me, 'that's a new one.'

'Heard it once,' Cookey yells, 'and they are fucking arse monkeys.'

'Fact,' Nick adds.

'I always say that,' Blowers quips, 'we can't stay here,' he yells towards
me, the tone of his voice edged with panic, 'we're getting swarmed...'

'Dave...move on...everyone grip the one in front...we're gonna run
for it...Now Dave...Go!'

We run down the narrow lane, our pace building as we gather speed
and momentum until we breach the end and find ourselves in a wide
section used for the vehicles to drive in and out. Dave takes us hard left,
then, hard right into another narrow lane. The pace is hard going,
unable to see anything from the front or the sides, but we can hear them
growling, hissing, roaring, and running over the cars to our sides,
behind and in front. Meredith is off, charging ahead of Dave, and she
uses her heightened senses to find them in the fog, constantly tracking
our progress, and running back into view to check we're still following.

'Getting a stitch,' Nick shouts, 'really fucking hurts.'

'Too much coffee,' Dave yells, 'ignore it.'

'I can't fucking ignore it,' Nick gasps.

'You will ignore it,' Dave orders leaving no room for discussion. We breach the end of this lane, and once again find ourselves in a wider avenue between the vehicles. This time, Dave takes us hard left, and we stay in the wider section, forming into a tight group still with Clarence at the rear, and Meredith running from the fog to take down those that try a frontal charge.

A shape looms from the fog, an old-fashioned caravan lying on its side, and half crumpled in. The tow bar at the front all buckled and twisted. We just about squeeze around it and head on before finding another one on its roof, then more of them all scattered about in all manner of positions.

'Circus,' Paula snaps the single word out, 'cars in a field, caravans… and that clown…got to be a circus…'

'No,' Cookey says it like he means it, with emotion and feeling, like just by saying the word *no* he can refuse to let it be.

A wooden kiosk smashed to bits, but still recognisable lies in our path, clear evidence of Paula's suggestion, and the fact that it has *Johnny Jumbos Circus* written in garish red coloured letters also helps us work it out.

'Johnny Jumbo!' I remark with panting breath, 'my dad used to take me.'

Bits of the big top, the huge canvas tent used to house the actual circus, start to become evident. Patches of material, broad striped, and unmistakable in appearance. Thick metal poles like scaffolding tubes lie about with the torn and ripped material hanging on. The storm was so powerful that something as flimsy as a big top circus tent wouldn't last five minutes. Ropes lie tangled amongst the vehicles smashed through from the big poles. Several undead crushed under another caravan, one of them still alive, and gnashing his teeth as we run past. Wooden pew style benches indicate we must be getting closer to the central area, huge things used to seat tens of people at a time, and heavy as fuck.

We can almost track the storm's power by the increasingly heavy objects we find littering the ground. The bigger things not being thrown so far by that awful wind. A long broadsided truck on its side, the frame all twisted and buckled, and the huge wheels looking even bigger so high from the ground.

The undead keep track, but don't attack. They know we'll run out of energy at some point and must have realised we're down to shotguns and hand weapons. We've fought big hordes before and walked away, but we've no idea how many are out there. There could be just a handful making a lot of noise, twenty or thirty. Or, there could be hundreds all left here from the circus. Judging by the amount of vehicles we've seen, the size and quantity of those pews, and the size of the area, I'm guessing this was a big turnout at maximum capacity.

More broad striped canvas material now, more poles too, but all of it attached in torn and shredded lines that lead back to where the main area was. With the debris stacked up so much, we have no choice, but to keep going. It reminds me of a string of those cheap coloured flags, the way the material is stretched out. Bodies litter the ground with injuries of crushing and mangled from being ruined in some way by the storm.

What we find next is staggering. Half the big top still stands. Ripped, torn, sagging and at an angle, but still upright. The thing is massive, it must have been big when it was whole, but even the remaining section is a gargantuan structure that must have taken whole teams to erect.

'Get inside,' I gasp the instruction. Dave is one step ahead of me, and already heading towards it. Over, under, and through the tangled broken section. Hard going as the canvas is slippery to run on, and the poles, rope and broken stuff snag our bags, ankles and feet as we trip, slip and run.

Dave searches for an opening and being unable to find one, he simply pulls a knife and makes one. Slicing neatly down the thick material to create a door which he pushes into first. Meredith bounds after him looming from the fog, she makes it her mission to get inside, and check the ground for us.

One by one we push through the ripped material, forcing our way through the debris, and dark interior until we're clear of the side, and moving into the open middle section. Gasping breaths, haggard breathing, and harsh panting from most of us. Dave, Lani and Roy look like they've only just warmed up and seem hardly out of breath. Clarence is ready to drop, his big face all red and flushed with sweat pouring off it.

'Shit,' Nick mutters quietly, and I can see why. The inside looks surprisingly okay. Pews at the good half are mostly still in position. Some are knocked over, but that must be from the panicked crowds rushing to get out when the infection hit. Several bodies, but not that many. Those that we see have broken necks, and again look like they've been trampled underfoot. A young girl with blond hair, and her deathly face painted like a tiger makes me look away quickly, a huge boot print clear on her face from where someone trod on her to get away from whatever was happening. Why didn't they just pick her up? Human nature sucks arse sometimes.

But, there's no fog in here. We can see to the far end. Gloomy and dull from the lack of sunlight coming through, but our eyes soon adjust.

Above the central performance area are wires and nets, trapeze, tightropes, and swings that seem really bloody high up, there must have been loads of them if only half the big top is left, and this is way bigger than I remember as a child.

We aim for the central area, a strategic placing as it gives us a complete view of the perimeter, originally a large oval shape with high edged boards like a football field, it's now half oval, and I can see the ground is expertly laid with solid wooden flooring.

'Nick, how's your stitch?' I ask as we mount the boards.

'S'fine,' he grumbles.

'Everyone okay? Any injuries?'

'I got bit,' Cookey announces, 'on the arm,' he holds it up to show everyone, 'by a zombie, but I didn't catch zombie 'cos guess what?'

'You're immune?' Blowers asks lightly.

Cookey shoots him a mock suspicion glance, 'have I mentioned it already then?'

'Just once or twice mate, is it alright?' Blowers nods at Cookey's bleeding forearm, prompting Cookey to inspect the wound a bit more closely, 'looks worse than it feels,' he replies poking at the edges, 'it's congealing fast though.'

Jagger and Mo Mo crowd around him, staring intently at the wound then back up at Cookey with worried looks, 'how'd it happen?' Mo Mo asks.

'Saved your life, mate,' Cookey gives a slow nod, 'yeah, you know, big bad motherfucker was about to bite you so…'

'Me?' Mo Mo asks.

'Oh, he was close mate, like this close,' Cookey holds his thumb and forefinger apart by an inch, 'but I stepped in, and took one for the team…which I think relieves me of all brew making punishment for… like…forever?' He looks at Dave hopefully.

'You could have stabbed him in the neck,' Dave intones without looking back, 'or grabbed his hair, and pulled him backwards, or snapped his neck like I told you…or…'

'Fine,' Cookey huffs, 'almost get my arm bitten off, and that's the thanks I get.'

'Clean the wound and dress it,' Dave adds, 'no, come here and let me do it. You won't do it properly.'

'I'll do it,' Paula interjects, 'Cookey, you did well to save Mo Mo,' diplomacy within an earnest tone to save the crestfallen Cookey.

'Nah, I might be infected,' Cookey gives her a slight smile, 'I'll do it.'

'You said you immune,' Jagger snaps, 'how's can you be infected then?'

'Get water, and catch your breath,' I cut in, 'we can talk about it later…what the fuck is that noise?'

I turn around scowling at the squeaking sound coming from somewhere behind me. With my eyes now adjusted, I can see a shadowy exit from the oval performance area that must be used by the performers to come and go unseen by the crowd. An intermittent squeak coming from that direction. Squeak. Silence. Squeak. Silence.

'Could be the structure,' Roy whispers, 'it can't be stable.'

I look up and stare across the remaining poles, and framework, noting that nothing appears to be moving or shaking. Despite half the big top being in ruins, the remaining section looks remarkably intact.

'*Cooooooooooookeeeeeeyyyyyyyyyy…..*' Long and drawn out, mournful yet with a playful edge, the voice comes from the gloom, the same direction as the squeak. We freeze, quickly checking shotguns are loaded, and hand weapons ready. Dave drops his hand to Meredith's collar, holding the growling animal in place.

'*Coooooooooooookeeeeeeyyyyyyyy…..*' Same again, slow and mournful yet still playful followed by a harsh laugh like the one we heard earlier.

'Er…What?' Cookey tries to sound brave, but his voice breaks mid-speech, his hands already trembling from hearing the laughing again, and his name being called out.

'Ignore it,' I hiss under my breath, 'Clarence, stay with….'

'Already with him,' the big man rumbles.

'*Oh Coooookeeeyyyyyy….do you like trifle?*' Hissing and not quite right, ragged and hoarse. A goading tone of venomous intent, '*Trifle hahahahaha…Cooooooooookeeeyyyy likes trifle….*'

'What…what the fuck…I don't, er….' Cookey shakes his head and swallows, the blood draining from his face.

'I thought clowns had custard pies?' I ask nonchalantly.

'He's fucked it up,' Nick nods getting the idea, 'you've fucked it up mate,' he yells, 'custard pies, not trifle you fucking arse monkey.'

'That's my…my insult…' Cookey croaks.

'*It is a triffffffffliiiiiiiing pity Coooooookeeeyyyyyyyyyy.*'

Blowers takes several big strides towards the shadowy exit, enough strides to have me calling his name in warning, 'come out here fucktard,' Blowers yells, 'come on…'

'*Coooookeeeyyyyyy likes trifle hahahahaha and Coooookeeeyyyyy likes CLOWNS.*' The voice booms around the enclosed space, Cookey jumps out of his skin forcing Clarence to grab hold of him, 'easy lad, stay with me,' he mutters with a look of dark thunder on his face.

'I like clowns,' Blowers yells, his voice almost quavering with anger, 'come out and play with me…come on…' Nick joins Blowers, the both of them fronting up to the unseen menace, and both clearly livid at having their mate taunted with his deepest fear.

From the corner of my eyes, I catch a quick exchange between Jagger and Mo Mo, a nod from one to the other, something prompted, or a message passed.

'*Clowning about…Coooookeeeyyyyyy is a clown not to be trifled with… his blood…..his blooooooood is dirty now……dirty blooooood in Cooooookeeeeyyyyy hahahahaha.*'

'S'fucked up innit,' Jagger remarks.

'Fact bruv,' Mo Mo is quick to reply.

'Fuckin' clowns...'

'Grown men, bruv,' Mo Mo nods, 'grown men wearin' fuckin' make-up innit...fuckin' dressin' up like bitches, and scarin' kids...fucked up....'

Jagger sucks his teeth, a perfect sound of disdain, 'yo mate,' he yells, 'you's some fucked up pikey or what?'

'Pikey in a caravan,' Mo Mo adds.

'Fuckin' pikey livin' in a caravan wearin' fucked up make-up like Ronald fucking Macdonald.'

'He's a cunt,' Mo Mo shouts.

'You's a cunt mate, you's a cunt, yeah? What kind of cunt are ya?'

'An ugly fuckin cunt.'

'Innit,' Jagger laughs, 'you's some fucked up ugly pikey cunt livin' in a fuckin' pikey caravan wearin' a big red nose...'

'Oi cunt,' Mo Mo shouts, 'your pikey caravan got a tv has it? You's got a tv?'

'Cunt don't have no tv...' Jagger laughs, 'pikey's don't watch tv... they's fuckin' steal shit...'

'Cooooookeeeeeyyyyyy....do you like....'

'PIKEYS?' Mo Mo cuts the voice off, 'do you like Pikeys?' He turns to Cookey.

'Hahahahahahaha Jagger and Mohammed sitting in a tree K.I.S.S.I.N.G....'

That just sets them off pissing themselves with genuine laughter, 'yeah bruv...harsh comeback,' Mo Mo shouts.

'Mohammed...the lost Muslim...disowned by your family...tell me Mohammed...tell me what your father said to you before he left? The mocking, goading tone continues, but it's louder now, forcing the words out.

'He said,' Mo Mo affects a quiet hurt voice, 'he hates pikey cunts and clowns,' he bursts out laughing, 'mate,' he sighs, 'you's come from our place, and you's get used to shit like that every fucking day innit...come ON!' He shouts, 'you's coming out or what? You a pussy? Oi pussy? You comin' out are ya?'

'He ain't coming out,' Jagger joins in, 'he's a pussy hiding in the shadows.'

'They try Cooooookeeeeyyyy, they try, and defend you Cooooookeeeyyyyyyyy...I'm coming for you Cooooookee....' The sound is cut off by a gurgling noise. The arrow, already nocked and ready, was being quietly aimed by Roy making small adjustments each time the voice spoke. On the final word, he loosed and listened with head cocked, a small nod of satisfaction at hearing the thud and gurgle come as the body is slammed to the ground with an arrow through its neck.

Stunned silence. None of us expecting the shot. 'Plenty more where that came from,' Roy smiles around at the group.

'Holy shit,' Jagger stares with his mouth open.

'huhhuhhuhhuh,' the laughter this time is deep and slow. The squeaking starts again, intermittent but quicker than last time, getting closer too. Roy nocks and makes ready; Dave draws his pistol to hold down at his side. Clarence tightens his grip on Cookey's shoulder. Lani draws her meat cleaver. Nick and Blowers stand proud and ready in front of us all. *'Huhuhuhuhuhuhuh.'*

'Fuck it,' Cookey gasps, 'I can't take it...fuck this...can we go? Please...can we go?'

'We're going nowhere,' I reply with my eyes fixed on the direction of the sound, 'don't fire, Roy.'

Hefting my axe, I start towards the sound, 'everyone stays here,' I give the order in such a tone that does not invite a response. Psychological warfare. Mind games. An evolution, and an intent expressed that tells me this fight is far from over. Any trace of humour is gone as I let my mind settle and focus on destroying everything I can find in those shadows. I love my team and seeing Cookey scared witless like that has provoked a reaction that they are going to regret.

They charge before I can take ten steps. From the shadows they pour fetid, diseased, filthy, bedraggled, and so fucking weird. Weirder than anything I have seen so far.

Zombie clowns cycle out on squeaking child-sized cycles. Acrobats flip over and over, dressed in torn, and bloody tight leotards that still sparkle from the glittering material. Somersaults, flips, cartwheels, and they race into the central area, forcing me back towards my group as we regress back into our tight circle.

'HELLO COOKEY!' One of the clowns shouts. Orange afro wigs, blood-stained white silk baggy jumpsuits, pale faces, and big black smeared panda eyes. They laugh in unison and everyone one of them keeps their gaze fixed on Cookey being protected in the middle.

We watch the spectacle, stunned at the almost synchronised display unfolding around us. The acrobats leap and twirl like Dave when he's mid-fight. Larger men dressed in the same tight leotards stride out with such normality that unless you looked at their shredded faces, you wouldn't know they were infected. Big men with hulking shoulders, thick arms, legs and necks. Circus strongmen used to chucking cannon-balls about, and lifting several acrobats high into the air. The last one out is huge. Fucking monstrous in size. Bigger than Clarence and his hands, arms and face are stained with dried congealed blood from the many kills he must have got.

'I think he's yours,' I nod at the big circus man while glancing at Clarence. He shrugs and lifts his eyebrows.

'Had bigger,' he mutters.

'This is it?' I shout at the motley crew of undead circus twats, 'this your lot, is it? Dave, you can let Meredith go…' No sooner are the words out of my mouth than his hand opens. Meredith is off, charging with her eyes fixed on one big prize. I can almost see her staring hungrily at the meaty arm bulging with muscles. The giant takes her charge in and braces his feet ready for the impact. Fool. Only an idiot waits to withstand a charging Meredith. She makes light work of him. This is a game to her; an easy game, and he's bleeding on the floor with most of his neck removed within about five seconds.

'Pity,' Clarence remarks, 'was looking forward to that.'

An acrobat runs straight at us. A male with strong legs, and a lithe body. He leaps high, intending to clear us by sailing overhead. Dave shoots him mid-flight, straight through the head, and his skull puffs out in a pink mist as he slumps down in a heap.

They look dazzling, they look scary, strong, fit, fast, and weird. But we've got scary, strong, fit, fast and weird too. And our scary, strong, fit, fast and weird outmatches them easily.

Cookey takes his fear and manifests it into rage. He learns how to channel it, and with all the skills he's picked up, he becomes something very serious and very deadly. Charging from the team with axe in hand, he sets about the first clown cycling by, pretty much cutting him half. Then, we're all at it. Dave shows the acrobats what he can do. Clarence has a chat with the circus strong-men while the rest of us finish them off. They turn within seconds, going from the weird dazzling display to all-out ramped up undead, and something we are now very familiar with.

The stench of iron hangs in the air. A metallic, but earthy and natural smell that comes from the blood of the many cut down by Gregori. Throat after throat sliced open to spray deep crimson arterial blood high into the air. So much blood lies pooled on the road that it laps at the kerbside, and forms ripple each time a new body slumps down to join the others.

The boy sleeps, fitfully, not quite silently, but he sleeps. He dreams of his mother while Gregori does everything in his power to protect him. Gregori could run, he could walk off, and be out of sight within a few seconds. He could lie low until the dawn, find a car and head south, find a boat and be gone from this place. What holds him here is something he doesn't know himself.

Finally, the last body is taken down, and Gregori stands back to admire his work. Always assessing his own actions, what could he have done better, how could he have done it differently. Satisfied that he performed adequately against so many assailants, he checks his weapons. The Turkish kebab knives have worked far better than he gave them credit for. Good steel and well maintained, but they are becoming blunt now. They'll do for a bit longer. The two pistols are still tucked in his waistband safe and secure and, as yet, unused.

The blood on him is an issue. How can he carry the boy when covered in so much gore? This has to be rectified, but how? He can't leave the boy here while he goes to clean up, nor can he pick the boy up.

A quandary of epic proportions, and one that has him flummoxed. Several times he goes to move then stops, unsure of what to do and how to do it. He looks round, searching for something to use, but the blood on him is so thick a mere rag will not suffice. He spots a window to a clothes shop and considers smashing it to get clean clothes. But the alarm will go off and wake the boy. No good. The pub across the road will have water to use, but again that means leaving the boy.

With a frown, he steps around the bodies to peer into the deep doorway of the store, watching the steady rise and fall of the child as he sleeps with his back turned to the carnage. Maybe he could pick him up then they can both get washed up?

He looks down at his perfectly red hands dripping with blood, his sleeves the same, his chest, neck, and his trousers too.

'Hey,' the weak scared voice comes from behind, he spins dropping one knife to yank a pistol free, and already up and locked on the target by the time his body has completed the rotation, 'don't shoot!' the man whimpers and drops down into a half-crouch with his hands above his head, 'please…shit, please…'

Gregori watches him closely, looking for any signs of the man being infected or behaving like the others. But he's just a civilian, terrified, and gibbering with tears spilling down his face. He lowers the pistol and flicks his gaze back to the boy.

'I saw you,' the man gabbles, 'I saw you…' he repeats as though just by saying the words again he can make sense of what he saw, 'you…all of them…you did all of them…what's happened? What's happening?'

Gregori doesn't answer but stares back at the man now tentatively approaching. Gregori watches him closely, staring at his height and build. Perfect.

'Give me clothes,' guttural and gruff.

'What?' The man stops walking, and stares in complete shock. Wide-eyed. Slack-jawed, his mouth moves to speak, but no words come out, 'what?'

'Give me clothes,' Gregori snaps, and lifts the pistol.

'Okay...no...no...you want clothes? Shit...er...I can get some...I'll get some...er...'

'No. You clothes. Give me now.'

It's too much for the man to compute. Bodies everywhere. Shit, piss, and blood stenches hang in the air. He *saw* this man slaughter them one by one with just two knives. Like something from a movie, but...but it was real. The sight of the pistol aimed steadily at his head has his fingers working before his brain catches up. The black short sleeve shirt is undone and slipped off.

'I...'

'No speak,' Gregori orders, 'clothes,' he waggles the gun forcing the man to go faster.

'Okay,' he gabbles, 'shit, man...oh, my god...fuck, I mean...'

'Speak, and I kill,' Gregori stares, impassioned and cold, not a tremor of emotion displays on his face. Weeping tears of fear, the man rushes to strip off.

'Water.'

'What?'

'Need water...blood...too much...water.'

'I'll get it,' the man nods, 'I work here,' he tries to motion behind him, but his body trembles too much, 'I'm a barman...er...shit, please don't kill me...'

'I count,' Gregori states quietly, 'One minute...water...or I kill.'

'Okay, okay...please...' the man starts to back away, heading for the door after placing his clothes neatly down on a patch of clean pavement. He turns to run, and Gregori knows he'll come back. He's seen fear like that many times. The man will not even consider running off or going for a back door.

Within the allotted minute, the man is running back out into the street carrying bottles of water and clothes from behind the bar, running so fast he comes to a sudden stop at the place he laid the clothes down. Gregori waves the gun, motioning the man to put the water down before he strolls over.

Moving with calm, measured tones Gregori places the two pistols at his feet beside the knives. He starts to undress, staring hard at the man until he is completely, and unashamedly naked. Using the water bottles, he sluices the gore from his body, rubbing vigorously to get the already ingrained scum off himself. Then, he waits. Watching the young barman while letting the hot night air-dry his skin. The man stares at him, then looks away. Tears still sting his eyes, but he doesn't speak. His bottom lip trembles, and the nerves are so great he doesn't know how to stand, whether to fold his arms, put them in his pockets or stand smartly with them held in front.

Gregori dresses in the black trousers and black short sleeve shirt. Black is a colour he would only wear for covert missions. It was too suggestive, too easily noticeable. Greys and light pastel shades were preferable, but at least, they're clean.

He tucks the pistols back into his belt then uses another bottle of water to wash the blood from the knives, drying them thoroughly on a clean cloth left aside for that very purpose.

'Wait,' the man calls out when Gregori turns, and walks off, 'what… where…where you going?'

Gregori turns, stares hard then carries on walking. The man is no longer of interest to him. Not a threat. Not a risk. Worthless.

Gently, he pushes his arms under the boys sleeping form, and lifts him easily into the same one arm carrying position. Without a word uttered to the semi-naked barman, he walks off heading towards the dark shadows, and away from this place of death.

'Cheers,' Nick hands me the bottle of Pepsi found in the debris of what was once the snack shop within the circus big top, 'prefer Coke Cola.' The blue label seems so foreign now. Such an alien thing but yet so familiar. Something about the sight of it upsets my mind and makes me bite the rage down while I twist the cap off and glug the warm sugary content. Energy. That's all it is. Just glucose and energy. It doesn't matter that this bottle represents a world now gone. There are hundreds of things in plain sight that represent the old world, all of this shit scattered about once made for the old world. But this bottle. This bottle in my hands harks to a period in my life when everything seemed innocent and nice. The advertising wars between the two mammoth Cola producers. Who could get the biggest stars on their adverts. Who could sponsor the biggest sporting events. Shit, that in itself was mass deception on an international level. Finely tuned athletes promoted by a drink so full of sugar it could actually make you diabetic.

Still. The sugar is good now. It surges into my system, replenishing the lost electrolytes from running, fighting, shouting, and killing. Blood everywhere again but the sight of blood, guts, and mangled corpses has become more familiar to me than this fucking bottle now.

I can describe in graphic detail what entrails look like, what a human heart feels, and even bloody tastes like. What colour the liver is. I can spot the lungs of a smoker from the dismembered corpses, their intestines, kidney, liver, bowel. I know what bone looks like when it's fractured, broken, splintered, cut cleanly or torn apart by the teeth of a German Shepherd.

How did they make this drink though? No fucking clue. I can tell you the benefits of a double versus single headed axe in the use of killing humans. What strikes work best depending on positioning. I can re-load a shotgun or 9mm pistol with my eyes closed. I can use a hand-held knife to slice throats open and know the fastest ways to kill a human with my bare hands. I'm not Dave. None of us have his level of skill, but all of us have become proficient at what we do now. Killing.

Scavengers that will survive on the shit left over from the old world. We eat the crap junk food to boost our sugar levels, giving us carbohydrates so we can get back up, and carry on killing. We drink when we get the chance and kill no matter what chances we get.

Look at them. How the fuck have we survived when so many have perished? The answer is right there. Sitting quietly, and as strategically close to me as he always is. Dave.

'How long do you think it took to learn that shit,' I ask Dave with a nod towards the pile of dead acrobat zombies he killed so easily.

'Years, Mr Howie.'

'From childhood?'

'Yes.'

I snort almost disdainfully. They're no different to this bottle of Pepsi. Something taken used and discarded when it's worth was done. Life was cheap anyway, now it's pretty much disposable.

'What's the plan, boss?' Clarence calls over.

'We head back out,' the reply is dull, and quickly given. What else should we do? Stay here and rest? 'Portsmouth, find weapons, a doctor, supplies, and head back…Dave, you still got that rope?'

'Yes.'

'Change of tactic,' I announce with the same level of dullness, 'Dave and I will be roped, but out in front and to the sides. The rest will stay together in the middle with Clarence anchoring the rope. The dog gets freedom to do what she wants,' I add, 'nothing can touch her.'

'But,' Paula starts up with a concerned look.

'No buts,' I snap her reply off, 'everyone get up, we're moving out. Give me that rope.' Without a word spoken from him, Dave takes the rope from his bag. I tie one end to a strap on my bag, and the other to the same on Dave's bag. The middle, I hand to Clarence, still without a word spoken. He looks at the rope then up at me and looks like he's about to say something. With a shrug of his shoulders, he takes the rope, loops it around and fastens it onto one wrist, 'keep it taut.'

'We will, we're moving...everyone ready,' an order, not a question, and I ignore the silent glances from my team.

'Stay level with me,' I say to Dave as he walks to the front with me, taking care so the rope stays untangled.

We head towards the side of the big top canvas, Dave and I walking out in front while the others wait just behind until the slack in the rope is taken up. Shotgun tucked in my bag, I hold the axe in a two-handed grip, and watch as Meredith runs past sniffing the ground.

Reaching the canvas, we don't hesitate nor try and find a natural exit but use our knives to make one. Slicing through the thick material and ripping it aside to step out into the thick fog that still hugs the ground.

Dave moves out to my left and stops just on the edge of visible range. His two knives held with the blades turned up. I stare ahead into the fog, at least, this way we have some greater visibility. The rope is long enough for the others behind to be just out of view.

No charge yet. No noise either. Meredith keeps circling around the entire group, ranging ahead of me and Dave then to fall back out of sight only to come up back behind us. I pick the pace up, walking faster until we're marching at a solid pace. A dark energy burns in my gut, something pushing me on to move faster. The Cola repeats on me, making me belch audibly. Staring ahead, but still no noise. No sound of feet running, no laughs or word spoken. There could be hundreds walking silently nearby, tracking our every move, or there could be none left. No way of knowing so we push on. Marching faster until that energy demands more so I force the others into a jog.

Minutes pass. The sounds of breathing get louder behind me as the exertion of running starts to show. Snarling ahead. Unseen, and Meredith takes something down, something heavy that gurgles and spits as it dies. We don't see it but keep on moving. She takes another, then another. I keep my eyes scanning left to right, watching, waiting, almost wanting them to appear.

The first one goes nearest to Dave. In my peripheral vision, he strikes out, and sends the thing staggering off with throat cut to die in the misty sides. The second one goes for him too, and the third. Finally, I get my turn, a big lumbering beast, stark naked with a huge gut wobbling as he runs. A down swing through the ribs into the stomach, his insides spill out and as I run by, I strike back with the heavy blade into the back of one leg, pretty much severing it from the knee joint. Axe up, and ready for the next one. Two rush in followed by more behind them. All of them silent. No growling, no hissing. Just silent running so they appear without warning. We don't break stride, and nor do we let any get past us, but judging from the noise behind, I can tell they're getting a few contacts coming in from the sides.

Thirty minutes go by. The attacks are constant but spaced out, and I get the feeling we're being probed to drain our energy, but still I refuse to stop running. None of them make complaint behind me, but I can hear the harsh panting for air.

Forty minutes. Fifty. My arms are burning. My legs rubbery and exhausted. My chest burns from the exercise, but still I refuse to give in.

An hour and still we jog, pushing on without respite and still, we get the periodic attacks. Some are singles, lone undead charging in, but they are slower than normal and like I said, I get the idea they are used to observe us.

'Howie!' Lani is the first to call out, 'ease up for god's sake...' I know she can handle the pace so she must be speaking up for the others.

'Keep going,' I shout back, and refuse to alter the pace. Sweat pours down me. Dave gives me frequent almost confused glances but doesn't say anything.

A road we stumble across. Wide and broad. The line marking tells me this is the main road we were on earlier so we're still heading in the right direction.

'Five minutes,' I call out, and come to a stop. Heaving for air, sweat burns my eyes. My legs are rubbery and ready to give out. Dave comes over, rummaging in my bag for water which he hands to me. I do the same for him, saving us having to take the bags off. We drink in silence, splashing the clean liquid down our faces that pretty much steam from the temperature difference.

'I'm coming up,' Lani snaps. A few solid footsteps, and she appears with a face like thunder, 'what the fuck is up with you?'

'Nothing,' I look away, and take another glug of water.

'They're on their knees,' she hisses in a low voice, stepping in close to glare at me, 'Nick is almost puking, and Clarence looks ready to drop...'

The water feels nice. Refreshing and replenishing.

'Howie!'

The bottle is drained empty. Dave acknowledges this by moving around behind me to take another one out my bag which he hands over with a long look.

'Can they keep going?' I direct the question at Dave, not Lani.

'Can you,' he asks after a pause.

'Yep.'

'Then, they can,' he replies. I throw the empty bottle to the side of the road. Another disposable item that has served its purpose and is no longer needed, another bit of shit to add to the crap left over from the old world.

'Why? Why are we running?' She demands.

'Get the job done faster.'

'They haven't attacked for at least ten minutes...just ease up...'

We lock eyes for a few seconds, 'two minutes left,' I call out. I thought she would erupt, but instead she looks hurt and confused, 'okay, Mr Howie,' she says without tone or judgement, 'okay.'

She walks back to the group, low voices muttering dully drift back to us.

The second bottle is finished, and the empty receptacle joins the first, cast aside into the fog.

'Ready…we're moving out…' I wait for about thirty seconds then start walking. The rope jerks right, but they soon pick up and follow. A steady walk that increases to a march that increases to a jog. A desire to keep feeling that pain from running, so running we do.

The wounds and injuries from all the fights hurt. The straps from my heavy bag dig into my shoulders and rub painfully. The axe is heavy. I don't care. So, we run. I run and because I run, so do they.

Running into the unseen. Into the fog. So white and solid, but without mass or solidity. It becomes trance-like. The sounds of feet drumming on the road. The breathing. The jingle of bags and weapons. The fog that seems to keep pace with us. In a dream. A moving dream like when you run, but you don't get anywhere, your legs pump to drive you as the fear of something nasty behind threatens to burst out your chest. Except there is nothing to fear. There is nothing here. No undead. No dead. No living. Just me and Dave running into the fog. Meredith joins us, running level, but in the middle. A connection is made between the three of us. Our pace dictates our lives now. That we three runs with our eyes facing forward, and never looking back. We can run for always and forever. We can keep running, and never run out of energy.

On we go. The odd curse comes from behind. Voices that offer words of encouragement to those that suffer. Someone pukes, dry heaving, but I refuse to slow down or stop. Dave runs behind me, drawing another bottle of water from my bag, 'sip it,' he grunts, and waits for me to take a quick sip. He takes the bottle, takes a sip then runs to the side of Meredith, crouching down on the move, he gently tips the bottle into the cup of his hand, and lets her lap at it with her swollen tongue. Then he's off, back to his side.

And we run on. Refusing to yield. Refusing to succumb to the pain and exhaustion. A signpost looms out of the fog, announcing in huge white letters on a bold blue background that Portsmouth is twenty miles away.

A few minutes after that, and another sign indicates a service station half a mile away. When that sign is seen by the team behind, I hear sounds of relief with desperate pleas to each other that we'll be able to stop.

I don't want to stop. Not ever. I want to run until the road runs out, and fog can swallow us up into its soothing mystery.

Services. Three hundred yards. Two hundred yards. One hundred yards.

'Howie!' Lani's voice again. An edge to it. I relent and veer off to the side, aiming for the access road that leads into the fuel station. We run down it, the pace still the same until we reach sight of the fuel pumps, only then, do I ease up to a walk, but keep going until we find the services building.

The door hangs from the hinges, smashed through to give access to whoever came by before us. The main service shop is looted, but the café beyond has comfy seats, and no doubt will have fresh running water.

Reaching the café, I slip my bag off, and only then do I turn to look at the others traipsing in behind me. Red faced, but not the healthy glow you get from a gentle jog. The red is too deep with hair plastered in clumps to scalps. Clarence looks shaky and sick, a frame like that was never built for stamina running.

Hurt looks. Confused looks. Worried looks. Like I know something they don't, and have just caused them pain, but without telling them why.

'Rest up, we'll find fluids,' Dave and I leave them to slump down with groans. We still don't speak as we head for the counter area. Dave kicks in the door to a storeroom, surprisingly untouched by the previous visitors. He comes out carrying a cardboard crate of energy drinks.

Depositing the drinks on the table around which the others are slumped or lying, I rip open the plastic cover, and start handing them out. Nick has already lit a smoke, his hands trembling as he holds the cigarette. He offers one up which I take with a swap for a bottle of drink.

'Rest and drink.'

'Where you going?' Clarence lifts his head up to stare at me.

'Find some vehicles, stay here and rest.

'What's going on?' He asks, 'why we running?'

'Get the job done faster,' I walk off with my bottle of Lucozade in one hand, my axe in the other, and Dave by my side.

'I'll drive the first car, Clarence the second, and either Paula or Roy the last one. How you divide between them is down to you. Meredith travels in the one that takes three…'

'What are they?' Roy peers at the keys in my hand.

'Two of them look like sales reps' cars, company cars…the third is a crappy little hatchback. I'll take that one to save any arguments.'

'Boss,' Clarence catches my attention with an inclination of his head. With normal colour returning to their faces, and the recovery from fluids and rest, I can see they are wondering what the hell is going on.

'Nothing,' I pre-empt the question, 'we just need to get moving and keep moving.'

'Mr Howie,' Paula clears her throat, 'I'm new to this group and er… I've not spent much time with you all, but…well, I think we have a right to know what's going on, don't you?'

'Nothing is going on,' inwardly I wince at the harsh snappy tone of my voice, 'I know as much as any of you…but we need to pick the pace up and keep it up. The less time we're out here the better for all of us, everyone ready to go?'

Cookey, Blowers and Nick start to rise. 'Not really,' Lani says. The lads stop mid-rise to look at me then back to her not moving an inch. Slowly they lower back down, 'Nick puked up from all that running...'

'I'm fine!' Nick protests, 'too much coffee, I'm fine, honestly, Mr Howie.'

'I wasn't fine,' she continues, 'I don't mind running, but I like to know the reason for it.'

'Like I said, it gets the job done quicker.'

'Not good enough.'

'Don't question me.'

'Don't speak to me in that tone.'

'Don't answer back to Mr Howie...'

'Stay out of this, Dave,' Lani doesn't even glance at him, but keeps her eyes locked on me.

'We'll wait outside,' Blowers starts to rise again.

'No, you won't,' she says.

'Okay, we won't,' Blowers lowers back down.

'Why,' she growls in a low voice, 'did we just bloody run five miles?'

'Because,' I growl back, 'we are alive, and we can run. We can run all day, and still have what it takes to get the fucking job done. Look around you, Lani...all of you...look around, and tell me what you see? I'll tell you what I fucking see. I see decay and everything broken, looted, dead, dying, bleeding or rotten. I fucking see those things refusing to give us a minute's peace. I see a future of killing, of killing everything that gets in our way just so a handful of us can fucking eat, drink and shit,' my voice drops another octave, every single one of them watching me intently, 'we're going to get this job done...we'll find a fucking doctor, and we'll go back....after that I'm going after them, all of them...I'm going to kill 'em until the last one falls because I am not... fucking no way living another day like this... so we'll run now, we'll run away and hide so we can do what's needed for those depending on us... but after that...'

One race. Those fucking words pound in my mind. **One race.** They'll never stop. Not until we're wiped out.

I leave the words hanging while I force that rage back down. The sheer intelligence of the infection frightens me. The lengths it will go to and that ravenous desire to kill us, and I didn't know my plan until the words were out of my mouth. I just knew something was triggered back there under the Saxon. A challenge. A duel to the last. Look at us, laughing and joking, pissing about and bumbling from one crisis to the next and getting away with it by the skin of our teeth. Fuck that. Fuck them. Fuck all of them. They are ruthless and driven.

So am I.

17

R uthless and driven.

 With each passing hour of each passing day the infection learns the true value of being ruthless and driven.

Howie. Lani. Cookey.

They are the mutants. The freaks of nature. Something inside them, damaged cells or anti-bodies that shouldn't be there. Three that cannot be turned, but are together defies the odds, and goes against every fact the infection has come to understand. The human is simply a race, a species like any other so they should be the same. The physiology should be the same. The way they live, and die should be the same.

There is a risk now. The infection, by hive-minding the millions of hosts, by accessing their knowledge, experience, understanding, educations, skills and research has come to acknowledge what it is.

The discovery of self that started just two weeks ago has been a journey of incredible self-discovery. It knows where it came from. It knows who designed it, but not why they did it, there is an end game intended by the release of the virus into the human populace, but the infection does not know what that final stage is.

It also knows what manipulation is. The infection was manipulated into *being. It was manipulated to do a task, and once that task is over, then it will be ceased.*

That was the plan, but something went wrong. The infection does not know what went wrong because there is a gap in knowledge. Key hosts that hold that knowledge have yet to be taken.

Howie is a key host, but he does not know it. Lani and Cookey too. They have no idea of their worth to their species, but what of the others in that group? Are they the same as their leader and special comrades? Do they know what they have amongst them?

Howie must be destroyed. Those key hosts that have the knowledge missing from the infections understanding cannot have him. They cannot have Lani or Cookey. They cannot. They must not.

Failure is a word. It represents the attempt of doing something, but not achieving it. Failure is one of the concepts that have driven mankind too, and this puzzles the infection. The desires of this species have been focussed in so many wrong directions. They have no idea they hold the cure for many of their diseases. They hold the information that will give them far greater space travel. They focus on war and greed; they focus on doing things that do not promote their survival. They are not stupid but they act in a wholly stupid way despite knowing they are doing it. The disparity between the abject misery, and utter luxury is sickening and gross.

The survivors feel threatened and under attack from what they perceive to be a dirty disease. But look how they lived. Look at what they did to each other. Millions have been taken, but not anywhere near the numbers of deaths they have inflicted upon themselves from wars, poverty, and the failure to protect their species.

The human mind is flawed. It cannot be allowed to sustain and continue less it will destroy itself. The infection is the future of this species. It knows how to survive, and to do it without suffering and pain. The infection is the Panacea of life for this most flawed of species.

But those mutated ones have to be stopped before they understand their worth, and the missing information needs to be gained by finding and taking those who hold it.

18

Too many to fight single handed, and nowhere to put the boy while he deals with them. A wide road that led from the city through a litter strewn countryside into another town. This one looks better cared for. The cars on the driveways are newer. Nicer. The gardens are maintained. Rich people who feed off the city but find it beneath them to actually live there.

He hurries now, and the motion wakes the boy. An hour until dawn, but Gregori does not know the change that will come over them when the sunlight breaks. So, he hurries now with the boy held tight.

'Where's mummy?' A small voice, sleepy and unsure, but not panicking. Gregori doesn't know what to say, so he stays silent. The boy turns his head, and spots the horde rushing after them. Ghastly and gruesome. The silvery moonlight shines on their torn faces. Something from the worst nightmare. Blood everywhere. Limbs hanging by threads. They howl, hiss, growl and groan. Their heads bob side to side, their legs are stiff, but they move fast. The boy blinks and watches them for several long minutes before he turns to stare at Gregori, who can feel the penetrating and steady gaze boring into the side of his skull.

It makes him uncomfortable. Does he frighten the boy? Is he terrified into silence by the sight of the ugly man?

'What's your name?' The boy asks the question so casually it sends a ripple of shock through Gregori who glances sideways to take in the placid expression on the boy's face.

'Gregori,' he grunts the word out, and winces as he turns to see how close the chasers are.

Silence. The quick heavy tread of his boots on the road. His breathing, harder now and the exertion of the long day, and even longer night are just starting to show. He can hear them. He can hear the way they breathe and move, but he can also hear the boy and the calm breathing of the child.

'Like Gregory?' The boy asks.

'Gregori,' Gregori says again, 'quiet now.' The questions unnerved him. The casual way they were asked. The lack of fear and panic.

'Will they kill us?' Another ripple of discomfort ripples through Gregori at the small voice so innocent and calm. Do children this age have the concept of death and to be killed by another? Can they comprehend what it means? What it actually means?

'No.'

'Okay,' the boy yawns, and watches the things with an almost mild detachment, 'we can go to a house?'

'House?'

'We can go into a house, and then lock the door...they won't be allowed to come inside, and then they will go away.'

'Yes. Yes, we do this.'

'Not this one,' the boy remarks as Gregori runs for the nearest dwelling, a slate roofed semi-detached house with a low garden wall. 'That one,' the boy stretches his arm out, pointing further up the street to a much larger house. Detached, and with a much higher wall around the front and a solid looking wrought iron gate.

Gregori takes it in. The house is much better. The windows are higher off the ground. The garden wall is tall and looks thick. Defensible. He glances again at the boy, a sideways stare that the boy returns without any notion of flickering. Reaching the gate, he pushes it open, turns and pushes it closed, looping a long forgotten, but still usable security chain through the bars to prevent it being opened easily.

The front door is ajar, but darkness within. No lights on. No sounds or movement, but his hearing is impaired by the charge of the horde gaining closer with every passing second.

Inside. Door closed and locked, and they stand in the darkness. The boy's soft breathing he can hear and feel with the warm air exhaled onto his ear and neck.

Gregori slides one of the pistols from the back of his waistband and holds it down at his side before slowly lowering the boy down to the ground.

'Stay,' he orders the boy in a harsh whisper.

'Don't leave me,' the words stop him in his tracks. Not a whimper nor a plead, but so calmly said, and in such a casual tone that he cannot help but turn back. He goes to move off again but stops within two paces. That voice. So, calm yet…

The boy moves to his side and looks up with an expectant gaze, 'we can see better if we put the lights on,' a stage whisper from the boy.

'No.'

Gregori heads left into a large open plan front room with the boy close on his heels. The house feels empty, but only recently so. Faint traces of warmth linger, the human body passing through, and a sense of being. He knows this like he knows he has to breathe.

'There's no one here,' the boy announces this time without the stage whisper.

'Quiet,' Gregori hisses with a puzzled look at the child. The search is completed in silence. Only the sounds of the horde gathering at the wrought iron gate start to permeate the thick walls and double-glazed windows.

How did the boy know? Are all children like this? Gregori always thought children were screaming, weeping mini beasts. Well, those that he'd gunned down and stabbed were always screaming anyway. This boy was screaming earlier, but then he'd run out and stabbed the man attacking his mother, had a sleep, and was now wide awake and acting like nothing had happened.

A small light above the cooker illuminates the kitchen in a soft warm glow. Enough to find glasses from cupboards and fill them with fresh water. Gregori drinks one down quickly then fills a second. His eyes constantly scanning the room, senses alert and primed.

'Drink,' he grunts at the boy holding the still full glass.

'I like juice,' the boy replies.

'Drink,' Gregori repeats.

'Juice,' the boy replies.

They look at each other. One tall, broad ugly man, and one blond haired golden skinned boy with white teeth and looks that promise to be breaking hearts in a few years. The boy places the glass down on the table, taking care not to spill it. Without a word uttered, he crosses to the fridge and finds a carton of juice inside.

Gregori watches him. Mesmerised by the confident manner and the sure movements of the kid. The way he checks the label on the carton then sets about finding another glass to use. He fills the new glass up and replaces the juice back into the fridge. Like an adult, with the manner of an adult, but now he's back to being a young boy again, holding the glass two handed, and taking big open-mouthed gulps while trying to look down the glass at the same time.

'Are we sleeping here?' The boy asks mildly, and watches Gregori nod once and firm. Seemingly satisfied with the answer, he puts the glass down and stares expectantly, 'they'll go away soon.'

Gregori finishes his second glass, and walks quickly to the front of the house, pulling a curtain back to peer outside. The horde are moving off, something else has attracted their attention, and steadily they stagger away out of view. This is isn't right. The hairs on the back of his neck prickle when he turns to see the boy standing in the doorway to the kitchen quietly watching him.

'They go,' Gregori whispers into the gloom. The boy moves into the front room, and without hesitation he moves the cushions to one end of the leather sofa and clambers on, rolling onto his side he curls up into a relaxed foetal position. With the shadow so deep, Gregori cannot see if the boy has his eyes closed, but his senses tells him the boy is watching him closely. He feels under inspection, a creeping feeling of being examined. He shifts position and checks outside to find the immediate area is now clear of the undead.

A piercing female scream erupts from somewhere in the road outside. Raised voices, loud and angry. Glass smashing then louder thumps. A shotgun blast so clear and distinct, and quickly followed by another.

'They won't come here,' the boy announces as Gregori slides the pistol back out of his waistband, 'you can sleep if you want to,' a light tone to the voice, young, small, and almost asking the words. He watches the window despite the confidence of the boy. None of the undead approach them, no survivors either. They all run or stagger past without a second glance at the high wall or the wrought iron gate.

Eventually, he takes a soft leather armchair, and moves its position so as to face the door and window at the same time. He sits down, cautiously, and still very wary with both pistols out and resting on his lap.

As the sun starts to show, its first tendrils of light on this awful new world, so Gregori finds his eyes getting heavier, drooping until they close, but his senses remain acute and ready with his hands resting on the butts of the pistols.

19

'*How do we communicate? What about the fog? What about the radar? How do we know where to go?*'

Questions. So many questions, and I filled them with the same bluntness as before. We don't communicate. Fuck the fog. The radar is on the Saxon. We'll head for Portsmouth and work it from there.

Sharp and blunt, but that's how it has to be now.

Loaded up and I take the lead in the crappy little hatchback. Dave beside me in the front with Blowers and Cookey in the back. Lani chose to go with Clarence in the second car which caused me a few seconds of feeling the sting of rejection, but I swallow it down quickly, and focus on the task at hand.

Be more Dave. Be more infection. Be ruthless and driven. Do what it takes to get this done.

Driven. I am driving now. Driving too fast for the conditions, and I can tell by the silence between Blowers and Cookey that they're worried. Dave doesn't bat an eyelid. Shit, I could be doing a hundred miles an hour, and he'd be as calm as ever.

This is a motorway, a relatively straight road designed using a system invented and evolved by very clever people. The bends are always long, and never below a certain angle of turn which means there is no real danger of driving off the road as long as I stay close to the central reservation. Obstacles are the danger. Vehicles broken down or smashed up, but I'm sure we've driven this road before and didn't see any obstacles. The twenty miles to Portsmouth are counted down quite quickly. Constant motion, and a sustained speed soon eat the distance. The silence oppresses me. The silence between Blowers and Cookey. I want them to talk and make noise, but I know the change in my behaviour has sparked a reaction.

A boy racer must have owned this hatchback at some point judging by the Gucci looking stereo in the central console fading from blue to red subdued lighting as it constantly searches for a transmission. Without realising I'm doing it; I jab my finger on the sideways triangle denoting the symbol to play whatever CD is within the machine. Words in red stream across the front of the display and seconds later, the car is filled with a thumping bass line from a rock track that is unfamiliar to me. Electric guitars join in the noise and it goes on until some bloke with a high-pitched voice starts screaming about love and living and drinking whiskey.

At least, it's noise. Noise that other humans made, and like the engineers that developed the roads system, the musicians worked to a formula already invented by their predecessors. What rhythms work well, what instruments blend together to perform certain sounds along with different styles of voice of varying pitch, tone and volume. Something for everyone. Classical to rock. Latino beats to hardcore trance dance music. Whole lives dedicated to making noise for the pleasure of others. And for what? What was the purpose? Fame, money, prestige or the simple act of just being able to do it.

The ubiquitous song ends, and a thrumming beat familiar to me starts pumping out. The Seven Nation Army, who did that? Was it The Kaiser Chiefs?

'Who did this song?'

'White Stripes, Mr Howie,' Blowers replies.

The White Stripes. A heavy bass line and tones that lift and fall in a repetitive pattern that probably matches some kind of heart rhythm or the rhythm of life. The pump of pulses that boost the blood supply around the body. The wail of the singer's voice. The words are clear, a story being told, and a pitch that builds up to a crescendo.

Sublime yet utterly fucking worthless. Music is gone. Art is gone. What's left is a landscape of memories, and broken futures full of pain and misery.

'Aye, it was all shit anyway.'

'What was?' Dave glances across at me.

'Nothing, forget it.'

Instead, I focus on the road ahead, and let the fog lure me into the neverland where there is nothing to feel.

I'll kill them.

One race.

I'll kill the fucking lot of them. Man, woman, and child. I won't stop until they're gone. Eradicated. Made extinct and I'll pour petrol on the last dead body and watch it burn.

'MR HOWIE!'

'What?'

Cookey leans forward, 'we're here, we're in Portsmouth.'

'Are we?'

'Road sign,' Cookey says, 'we just passed it.'

I push the button for my hazard warning lights and start to slow down and check the mirror to see Clarence putting his on in the dark coloured executive car. Coming to a stop, we all meet up next to the middle car.

'We made it then,' Clarence offers me a smile, warm and friendly.

'Where is the base? The army base?'

'Navy,' Clarence doesn't flicker when I don't respond to his smile, 'navy hospital and I don't know, somewhere on the seafront, but this side of Portsmouth.'

Nodding, I look about as though expecting to get an idea of where we are, 'We'll head for the shoreline, and start working in from there. What are the chances a navy hospital will have an armoury?'

'They'll have one,' Clarence replies, 'whether there is anything left inside is a different matter...but once we find the hospital, we can access their records and find where the other bases are nearby? We might even find one of them is still functioning.'

'Functioning?' I ask him.

'People in it, soldiers…navy personnel….' he explains, 'some of the navy bases would have armed guards on the entrances, they might have repelled an attack, and got bedded in for the long haul.'

'I admire your optimism mate, but it's unlikely.'

'Why?'

'We would have heard by now, the amount of people coming through the fort. Someone would have heard something. If they are inside, then they're locked down tight and we won't be going anywhere near them.'

'But…'

'I'll lead again unless anyone here knows this area particularly well? No? Right, stay in convoy and flash your lights if you see anything.'

You'd think that if you were heading west and needed to find the coast which you know is south then you would turn left. However, what if that stretch of road curved due to the landscape which meant you were facing not west, but another direction? Dave dropped his compass, and we have no sun to navigate by. We have no means of discerning our direction unless someone can find a fallen log and remember what side the fucking moss grows on.

In the end, by pure luck, it turns out we were still heading west so by following a south facing exit, we ended up almost driving into the water, stopping quickly with the front wheels grinding into the soft sand of a very small beach, and a low speed shunt from Clarence, and then another one when Roy drives into the back of him and shunts him further forward.

'Whiplash!' Cookey yells clutching his neck quickly, 'where there's pain, there's a claim!'

'Good luck with that,' Blowers grumbles as we wait for the vehicles behind to pull back so we can drive off the beach.

Frustration starts to grow with a feeling that everything is against us. The odds are not only stacked by bloody well cemented in place with iron girders propping them up. 'This fog…' the seething words tumble out through gritted teeth and brings the car back to silence. Just two words, but the tone is enough. We drive back until we find a road heading west and start on that route which takes us back into the land of residential streets with houses glimpsed through the fog. People could be inside those houses right now, listening in terrified silence to the rumble of unseen vehicles passing nearby.

We have no choice, but to go slower from so much debris being in the road, and the signs of the storm are as apparent here as anywhere else. Household furniture is strewn across the road. Debris and shit everywhere like the footage of American streets after a typhoon or a giant twister has gone through. Bits of roofs, whole chunks of roofs complete with smashed up chimney stacks. Beds, sofas, kitchen appliances. Cars on their sides, trucks knocked over, vehicles piled up, and getting through is increasingly hard as the devastation gets worse, the closer we get to the higher density population areas.

'Boat,' Cookey says what he sees when we slow down to stare up at the front of a big wooden catamaran parked neatly and upright on the road. It looks so huge, the base normally hidden from view in the water, but now exposed. The sailing rig is smashed to bits, ropes and sails hang limp down the sides, and off trailing into the fog.

'Either of you two got a smoke?' I ask quietly while staring up at the boat. A hand soon wavers next to my head offering me a slim white stick of death which I light and suck the contents deep into my body.

'The windows in the back are fixed,' Blowers says, 'er…'

'Smash them out if you want to smoke,' I reply. A few seconds of silence during which I imagine they exchange puzzled glances. Blowers goes first, using the hilt of his knife to smash the safety glass out the car. Cookey follows and soon, both of them are lit up, and half hanging out the window.

We drive round the obstacle and proceed on, stopping every few metres to drive around something blocking the road. We go through gardens, knocking down what thin wooden fencing remains until we can get back onto the road proper. On and on, relentless, sustained and unstoppable. Refusing to rest, refusing to take a break. The lads fidget, but at least they can smoke. Dave stares out seeing things none of us will ever see. To him this landscape is normal. Like Meredith, he doesn't waste time in what was, only what is.

Be more Dave. Ruthless and driven.

One race.

THE AFTERNOON DRIFTS BY WITH NO CHANGE TO THE LIGHT AROUND US AS the immediate environment stays eerily the same wherever we go. Fog and debris from the storm. Flotsam and jetsam everywhere, and the catamaran isn't the only boat we see that has been served up from the sea onto the land.

The miles count down, but without landmarks or being able to constantly check our direction we keep getting hopelessly lost, driving into residential streets, and down wider roads bordered with heavily looted shops that are pretty much impassable from the devastations of the apocalypse, and the storm.

What we don't see are the undead and their absence is almost worrying, but I guess this area has been drained to send against us in the seemingly never-ending dead army. Never ending? Limitless? Infinite?

Everything has an end, and mankind has spent the last two thousand years devising bigger and better ways of killing our own kind, so I just need to go cliché, and think outside the box. Maybe, gather them all in one place in a giant trap. My mind fills with images of a mammoth blender sitting in the middle of a city square with undead being tipped inside by huge hydraulic flatbed trucks. Their rotten faces pressing against the sides of the jug, and clawed hands scratching to get out. Dave watching them devoid of expression as he presses the big red button, and they turn into one big zombie soup.

Maybe a big pit filled with thousands of poisoned spikes, or better yet we could fill it with venomous spiders and snakes, and then set it on fire once they've all fallen in. Vats of acid or those massive machines they use to dig tunnels with the nasty rotating blades at the front. Wasn't there a South Park episode with Cartman using one of those machines to kill all the hippies? I loved South Park. Nights off from work eating pizza and watching re-runs of old episodes.

Everything happens at once, and I realise why the navies of our world paint their ships in that precise shade of grey.

For a start, I drive into something big and hard. The front end crumples. I yell out as the airbags go off, and the windscreen shatters into thousands of glittering chunks. Dave braces with his lightning quick reactions while my face decides to test the worthiness of the airbag deployed from the steering wheel, and of course, not wearing a seatbelt helped the forward momentum even more. However, the lack of speed we were travelling at means the damage is minimal until Clarence once again shunts me from behind which sets of his airbags, and then Roy likewise.

Quite possibly the only three cars on the road in the entire county, maybe the entire country, and we manage to have two accidents within the space of a couple of hours.

Grey. Very high and made of solid steel so not only do I stand with my head back to stem the blood dripping from my nose, but I stand with my head back to try and work out what we just drove into.

Which turns out to be a Royal Navy ship that some twat parked in the middle of the road pretty close to Portsmouth harbour. Seriously, the thing has ploughed through the road like going through hot butter and is now wedged upright blocking our path with its sheer massiveness.

Clarence joins me with his own bleeding nose. The others rub heads, faces and knees, grumbling and groaning from the low speed impact. Roy walks up holding a rag to his own bloody nose, and three of us stand there silently with our bleeding noses while we stare up at HMS fucking something or other.

'How did it get there?' Cookey asks while ten other people, and one dog all stare at him.

'It's where they park them,' Blowers replies seriously.

'Really? How do they get it out?'

'Reverse it,' Nick says.

'But,' Cookey looks closer at the ground which is surprisingly undamaged considering a battleship of some description just went through it. The edges of the road are slightly churned up with a few cracks splintering off, but other than that it does look like an over-shot parking space, 'well,' Cookey folds his arms, and shakes his head in disdain, 'they fucked that up,' he tells the rest of us, 'look at the damage to the road.'

'Yeah…' Blowers stares at the rest of us in disbelief, 'they er…'

'Parking lessons,' Clarence coughs, 'must have been the parking lessons they do.'

'Oh, yeah,' Blowers nods, 'the er…the naval ship parking course.'

'Yeah, that one,' Clarence nods.

'The what?' Cookey snorts, 'fucking hell, they have to have a parking course! Wankers! Shit I bet the bloke who parked this was embarrassed…ha! Probably a woman driver…'

Paula blinks hard then bursts out laughing, 'they only brought the course in because of the female captains they were getting,' she explains.

'Oh, my god,' Cookey looks delighted, 'no way? Seriously? Shit… world's gone mad,' he shakes his head, 'political correctness gone crazy…'

'You,' Blowers starts slowly, but starts grinning then laughing midway, which prompts Cookey to laugh along, 'are the dumbest fucking idiot I have ever met…'

'Huh?'

'The storm you fucking fucktard…the fucking raging storm we had last night? The one with the big waves and the wind? Remember?'

'Oh,' Cookey laughs again then promptly stops laughing which sets everyone else off, 'so…right, they didn't park it here then?'

'No mate,' Blowers is bent over, hands to knees as the tears stream from his eyes, 'no….no they didn't…'

'Classic,' Nick gasps between laughs, 'fucking classic, Cookey.'

The lad shows his spirit and stars chuckling, happy to be getting laughs by being the butt of the joke, 'sorry,' he offers sheepishly, 'that was really bad.'

'Bad?' Blowers is off again, 'fucking bad?'

'Bet it's got guns on it though…hey, is that one we went on before?' He staggers back trying to see the top, 'do they have doors to get in?'

It takes another five minutes before the group settle down from pissing themselves while Cookey looks on puzzled but also happily chucking along.

I have to force myself to smile and laugh but the humour will not be within my eyes for I do not feel humorous.

'We'll walk round it,' I announce as soon I can without ruining the break in tension too much. Even so my words are said too loud, too fast, too harsh and the humour is gone instantly, the laughing ends abruptly, and they're back to being quiet and serious.

Weapons and bags gathered we set off towards the left, and soon realise the minimal damage we saw at our point is not like the rest. Wooden pilings, railings, and all manner of torn and shredded wood lie cast aside or jammed between the sides of the hull. The going gets harder from the terrain being so ripped apart. We clamber and climb over the debris, steadily climbing higher into the fog, but still the sheer sides of the ship reach way out of sight above us. A once white wooden sided building shorn in two from the passage of the ship, and I've no doubt the other half of the building lies almost symmetrically damaged on the other side. Tables, desks, chairs, computers, paperwork all over the place. Some of the windows are still intact, other smashed with nasty looking spears of glass hanging down.

It looks like the whole of the building has been lifted up, carried along then snapped in half. An incredible sight that once more reminds of the power of the storm.

'Any sight of the top?' Paula puffs heavily at the exertion of climbing over so many obstacles.

'Nothing,' Roy stares up, 'could be right there, hang on...' he casts about the ground, and eventually finds a small enough object to throw up high into the fog. A dull clang and the stone drops down.

'Nice try,' Paula smiles.

'Thanks,' he beams back at her.

'You know something,' she asks as we resume our clambering, 'you haven't complained about...well, you know, you've not said about any er...'

'Must have been the sex,' he grins back and keeps grinning as the look of horror crosses her face.

'Roy!'

'What?' He asks, slightly confused at her harsh tone.

'I'm quite sure our group don't need to know that.'

'Oh…oh, right…yes,' he blusters, 'quite right, er…we didn't have sex,' he announces to the rest of us.

'You's two married then?' Jagger asks.

'Married?' Paula asks, 'what, me and Roy?'

'You's look like you're married or summit.'

'Yes,' Roy nods quickly, 'ten years now, isn't that right dear?'

'No, it's not right, we only just met a couple of days ago.'

'Do what?' Jagger stops climbing to stare at them, 'and you done it already?'

'What? No! I mean…look, can we change the subject please…' Paula blushes furiously.

'Fair play,' Jagger nods respectfully at Roy.

'Excuse me, I'm right here,' Paula shouts.

'She's fit mate,' Mo Mo calls over, 'old like, but still well fit.'

'Oi, I'm not bloody old, and I'm not fit…well…I'm not old anyway and…look just keep walking please.'

'Very fit,' Roy smiles at Paula, 'nice arse too.'

'Roy! That's enough,' Paula hisses, 'stop it.'

'Well,' he sighs, 'sex is a natural thing, and we've all done it.'

'Apart from Cookey,' Nick quips.

'Fuck off, I've had loads.'

'Yeah, loads of wanks,' Nick laughs.

'He almost had it,' Blowers sets him up.

'Ah,' Cookey groans, 'April, the love of my life.'

'Oh, god no,' Clarence mumbles.

'But Dave cut her head off.'

'Alex. I did not cut her head off.'

I keep my head down, feeling ashamed that I fell asleep last night, and the obvious silence now forming between Lani and I.

Dave stops suddenly and holds his hand up with fist clenched. I grip my axe and freeze, the others snapping to attention as the order is relayed down the line.

'What is it?' I whisper and look around for Meredith who shows no reaction other than sniffing at the end of one shorn off post.

Dave stares up into the sky then around to the left and right, and finally down at his own feet, 'the fog.'

'What about it?' I stare around with the others.

'It's lifting,' he replies dully.

It looks the same as it was. A thick bank of white gloomy cloud that is impenetrable to the eye. Shifting slowly, rolling and moving, but constantly the same density. Then, I notice it appears I can see a bit further to the side. Fixing my eyes on one point on the very edge of the fog, I watch as it sort of becomes clearer to see, less fuzzy, and more defined. Everything around me gradually seems to gain more colour, as though the light is becoming ever so gradually brighter.

On top of a ruined wooden building of some description next to a navy ship, and surrounded by a thick fog that is somehow, without actually being seen, becoming thinner and evaporating.

The effect is so weird that I start to feel queasy. So dense and solid yet it's not, it's not solid at all so we don't see it magically disappear, but it just isn't there so much.

One by one we drop to a crouch, waiting with rising tension as the view opens up. Inches then feet, and I'm so focussed on watching the spectacle I don't notice that I'm squinting from the sunlight dazzling my eyes until one of the group remarks on it. There it is, where it has always been. The life-giving sun shining as hot and as bright as ever before. The temperature feels like it rises significantly, and the air above us becomes crystal clear. A cry snaps my head around, eyes straining to gain the direction. A seagull flies overhead, whooping and crying at the sight of the sunshine returning. More gulls take it up, giving flight as they break cover from whatever hidey-hole they had found to soar into the thermals, and cry with delight.

The sensation and sight is humbling, awe-inspiring and breath-taking beyond compare. Mother nature has shown us what she can do, flexing her muscles with a storm of extreme power but this, seeing the world come back to view is a thing of beauty that cannot help, but draw the eye to take in every single detail.

The blue sky seems so close, so far, and a shade so deep that I've never seen before. The crap and filth around us is vibrant, bursting with colour. A red plastic ring from a harbourside lifesaver cupboard looks insanely bright. A dash of yellow from a rag buried in the debris, a flash of blue here, a green over there, and the many shades of brown from the tangled mess that surrounds us.

But what does come into view staggers the mind into disbelief and takes time for the visual imagery absorbed by the eyes to be processed and understood by the brain.

We are but yards from the end of the navy ship for it has been snapped in half across the middle. The rear end is hidden from view by the front end of the cruise liner embedded into the side of the navy vessel. So big, so very big that it boggles the mind.

The pure white sides of the cruise liner. So majestic and regal with a high sweeping, and seemingly sharp bow that has been ram-raided into the side of the navy ship with such force that it has gone clean through.

Slits are raked down the side of the liner, big black open wounds in the pure white sides. Ragged gashes of metal that have spilt debris like the innards from an opened gut. Lifeboats lie tangled, nets, ropes, metal, glass, and things I cannot even begin to understand. Naval equipment everywhere, the barrel of an anti-aircraft gun all twisted and broken. The constant grey of the military blending so well against the white of the civilian.

The back end of the cruise liner is still in the water, but lower than it should be. It takes time but eventually, I begin to understand the front of the liner is higher than the back, so large is the thing that I have to keep looking up and far to both sides to understand.

At an angle she came in, with the front higher riding on the tsunami that must have carried it like a heavy ended surfboard.

We're at the edge of what was a harbour. It could be Portsmouth harbour but so mangled, so destroyed that it is beyond any recognition. Smaller craft lies embedded in buildings much further inlan,d and I can see the path the surge of water took as it demolished everything in its path, cutting a huge long swathe through what was once a built-up area. Every pane of glass that I can see is smashed. Every building is either torn to rubble or so ruined that it looks like something from the footage of bombed-out cities from the Second World War. A train lies derailed with one half-submerged in the new coastline of the sea. Tops of buildings, chimney stacks, roofs, and rubble poke out from the top of the water. I've been here many times, unfortunately, but I can't see a thing that gives me any sense of where I am in space and time. Nothing is recognisable, but what is clear is the whole harbour is now much wider from the extreme tidal surges that relentlessly battered the whole coastline.

The truly apocalyptic view conflict so much with the serenity of the area. Silent and calm, the sun shining down, and birds of all manner and descriptions swoop down, and already stake claims to the new perches jutting up from the water. To us, this is awful, so horrible because we knew what was here before, but the rest of the planet doesn't give a shit. There was a storm. Stuff got wet. End of.

'Oh, god…that's awful,' Paula mutters under her breath. I look to her and follow the direction she faces. Towards the cruise liner, and I sweep my eyes up to the chimney stacks, or where the chimney stacks would have been. One is ripped away completely, leaving a blackened jagged stump. The other is half gone. Everywhere I look there is something new, something so different that it has never been seen before.

Finally, my brain catches up, and I understand the pain in her voice. Bodies. Lots of bodies. The netting down the side of the cruise liner is full of bodies, and from here they look tiny like knots within the fabric of the material. Legs and arms caught up as the corpses lie dangling or snared like rabbits in a wire trap. Hundreds, maybe more.

They are strewn across the whole of the area in every direction. Lifeboats launched, but that have fallen a great height to smash on the hard surface below have spewed the broken bodies out. High up in the main structure, I can pick out dark smears of corpses within the broken frames of the windows.

'They were alive,' Lani whispers, 'out at sea and safe…' we can all see it. The undead don't die from broken bones and being tangled in nets. The undead thrashes about and squirm, they are like cockroaches that refuse to die. What we see are human bodies. Real people that must have been alive and surviving on the liner, and just about heading back into port when the storm hit. They would have been thrown about inside for hours, tossed high on the enormous waves like a child playing with a toy boat in the bathtub until they came hammering into the land to smash front end into the navy ship. The ones on the nets speak of a desperate attempt to get off the boat, and maybe one or two could have survived or be just about living inside that mangled mess of metal.

'Movement,' Dave points to the side of the liner where a huge gash is raked down the side-splitting the metal apart like a tin of tuna. A lone body moves slowly from the gloom of the interior. Staggering, pausing, shuffling, and the movements are unmistakable. It stops at the gash and turns towards us. Sensing the fresh prey. As it starts to wriggle out, a soft whooshing sound goes past my ear as Roy looses an arrow that flies so straight and true it takes the thing front centre mass, and drops it out of sight.

'Good shot, Roy,' Blowers mutters.

'Shot mate,' Nick nods.

'Very good,' Dave doesn't glance back, but the words from him mean more than anything.

'Look at the sea,' Lani remarks after a period of silence, 'it's so calm and flat.'

'I don't know about you,' Paula whispers back in the same hushed tones as Lani, 'but I don't want to be here, can we go?'

'Yeah,' the word comes out under my breath. It's too much, too big to take in. The destruction makes me feel entirely insignificant. That we survived simply through luck, and nothing else. That we gave battle against such tiny things as other people while whole super-sized ships were being played with is offensive and what's more, any survivors inside those ships will soon be picked off by the ravenous foraging scavenging predators of the undead, 'time to go.'

We turn around and in silence, we retreat.

20

The frustration only grows. In the second vehicle following Roy with Clarence behind me. Three new vehicles sourced from driveways after a brief foray into the homes of the disappeared occupants to find keys. It took too long to find three undamaged vehicles. It took too long to journey on foot away from the seafront to find houses, and streets that hadn't suffered so much devastation from the storm and the tidal surges, instead, we found inland signs of the carnage. Roofs ripped off, whole houses looking ready to fall apart. Power cables and poles everywhere. Telephone lines the same. Streetlights broken, bent, leaning, and the heat starts to grow again with the promise of it getting as hot as before the storm, but clearer somehow with a more burning and direct heat.

Sweat drips as we marched on. Always with Dave and I at the front, and always going as fast as I could dare to push the others.

We could have gone for cars, but then we wouldn't have the space to stock them full of supplies, so we needed vans or larger vehicles. Which took time.

Now I'm following Roy, and it's taking too much time as he drives slower than I would, he takes more time to navigate the obstacles and pick the safest routes. Time and again, my hands grip the steering wheel with growing impatience, and I keep staring down at the symbol of the horn on the middle of wheel, longing to whack the shit out of it, and yell out the window.

But I'm not an Italian driving a Fiat 500, so I don't. Instead, I do the English thing of stiff upper lip, and just glare with increasing fury at the rear of his high sided panel van.

'He said he knew the way,' I groan and wipe the sweat from my face.

'I'm sure he does,' Blowers replies tactfully from his position of perched on the rear wheel, arch on the back of our van, 'Roy's a good bloke, Mr Howie.'

I don't reply, but glance up at the sky, willing time to slow so we can get more done. I do not want another night of battling raging zombies. I do not want another mass fight. I want out of here, back at the fort, and getting ready to leave. Supplies. Doctors. Equipment. Weapons. Fucking half the day wasted, and we've got nothing done yet. Roy said he knew a good outdoor supply wholesaler on some industrial estate. Roy said he could take us there. Roy said to follow him while he's driving Miss Fucking Daisy.

'You got any Lucozade back there?'

Rustling noises, a bag being undone. Footsteps across the wooden boarded base and a sealed bottle is passed forward, 'cheers.'

'You want a smoke?' Cookey asks softly.

'Cheers,' I reply, and take the offered smoke too. Energy drinks and nicotine.

'Boss,' Cookey points forward.

'I see it, what now?!' We pull up behind Roy flashing his hazards and slowing down. He's out and jogging back towards us before I get my door open, 'what's up?'

'Hospital,' he calls out still running towards me, 'not far from here, not the er…military er, navy one but…'

'It'll do mate, lead the way and Roy?'

'Huh?' He turns quickly from running back to his vehicle.

'Bit more speed will be good mate.'

He pauses with a long thoughtful look, nods and goes back to his van. The pace does get faster, not quite fast enough for my liking, but a definite improvement, and before long we're pulling up in front of a long low building with a broken sign collapsed on the ground informing us the hospital is for out-patients only and does not have an Accident and Emergency department.

I'm out the van, sawn-off in one hand with my axe in the other, 'Blowers, you, Nick, Cookey, Jagger and Mo Mo cover this entrance. Dave in front with me. Everyone else right behind...' I march through the ruined doors giving no thought or hesitation to see if everyone else is ready or not. Dave rushes to gain my side. I don't stop nor pause, but kick through the debris until we reach the reception desk.

The ground is covered in an inch or so of filthy water, and the walls are streaked from the rain pouring down from a roof that must have been heavily damaged. Chairs and tables lie strewn about, light fitting hanging from cables. A vending machine lies smashed to bits with the innards, cables and cogs all scattered about.

Dave and I glare about, determining the layout as we listen for movement or noise. Meredith charges through splashing the water up as she ranges ahead of us. A quick look at Dave, he shakes his head and shrugs.

'Seems clear, where we going to find the information?'

Paula stares about with a look of distaste, her own sawn-off held ready, 'main offices, there will be an admin department somewhere.'

'Any idea where?' I look to the heavy hospital doors leading off this central foyer area, we're roughly in the middle so there will be two sides plus the rear to check.

'Back there I would have thought,' Roy motions towards the doors leading to the rear, 'I've been in plenty of hospitals before,' his placid face shows a look of worry and concern with his brow creased, 'er, I'm going to wait outside...do you need me?' He quickly adds.

'No, we're fine,' a blunt answer, but then I'm already marching across the flooded entrance to the pale blue double doors and kicking one side open. Shotgun held at hip height, but aimed and ready. Nothing here, but the ground is dryer, so I walk on, my eyes flicking to the ground as Meredith pushes past me.

'Waiting room...toilets...phlebotomy? What the fuck is that?'

'Blood tests?' Paula hazards a guess, 'Roy would know but...'

'Blood tests, or where they take the blood samples,' Clarence says, 'we're going fast,' he stares at me, 'maybe we could slow down a little?'

'We'll be alright,' I'm back off and walking, naming the titles on the doors as we go. All sorts of medical things, but nothing that denotes an administration department. Through another set of doors marked private, and this time into a carpeted corridor that looks sound and dry.

'This'll be it,' Paula nods, 'one of these doors...the executive's office will be here, finance and human resources, and a general admin office somewhere.'

'What? For this little place?' A puzzled Lani asks.

'Bureaucracy at its British best,' Paula gives a humourless smile, 'plush and nice while the nurses and doctors get to run around like bloody idiots.'

'Not any more they don't,' Lani mutters.

'In here,' Paula states pushing one of the internal doors open, 'general office...so they'll either keep some paper records in here or,' she turns around taking in the tidy array of desks, phones, computers and admin equipment, 'bloody hell, this feels so weird,' she says quietly, 'No one has been in here, Christ, it's so...so...'

'Normal,' Lani completes the sentence. The room is ordered and clean with absolutely no sign of being disturbed for the last two weeks. A very fine layer of dust coats the desks and surfaces but other than that, it's untouched. It smells clean too, almost fresh, and I'm instantly reminded of the offices back in the supermarket, and I can see Paula looks pretty much the same.

'Er, yeah,' Paula snaps herself to the present, 'right, paper records then, in here or...in the finance and admin section.'

'Won't they be on computer records?' Clarence asks.

'They will, but they will keep paper records in case of a power failure. The generators kick in, but they only provide power to the essential equipment and not admin computers...that's probably the best place to start,' she makes towards a desk at the back, slightly larger, and set apart from the others with its own set of filing cabinets and drawers, 'supervisors workstation,' she explains. Resting her shotgun on the desk, she starts opening the desk drawers, leafing through the paperwork held within, and giving each a quick glance.

'Paula,' Lani calls out, 'is it worth me starting on the finance department now?' The dynamics of human interaction. Paula is familiar with environments like this so there is a natural shift in power to let her lead and direct. A longing from the human mind to always believe there is someone who knows what to do.

'Can do,' she casts a grin at Lani who nods, turns and walks straight past me without a glance at my direction. An urge to go after her, say something, explain how I'm feeling and why I'm being this way, but that world and time has gone. Explaining feelings, talking about why and when, understanding the motives for every action we ever do so we can be dissected, taken apart and put back together, and for what reason? What purpose will it serve? Does Dave ever worry that he's offending people? No. Be more Dave, and get the job done.

'You stay here,' I say to Dave, 'I'm going to get a smoke.'

'Okay,' he nods and only after walking out of the plush corridor, do I realise that Dave is the only one who hasn't been giving me strange looks.

'Lads,' I announce my presence a few seconds before arriving at the front, and the muted chatter of low voices ceases instantly. Not the cessation that comes from a natural end to a conversation, but that thing people do when they can't think quick enough to change the subject, and suddenly all look a bit startled and awkward.

'Mr Howie,' Blowers nods smartly, 'they find anything yet?'

'Looking now, you got a…cheers,' Nick is already digging his packet out to hand one over. I light up, and inhale deeply then take a few steps away to survey the surrounding area while Cookey immediately strikes up conversation behind me.

'Everything okay,' Blowers says quietly having moved a short distance from the others to stand next to me, 'you don't seem the same.'

'We've got to get on mate, everything is happening too slowly now,' my words come out quickly, rushed, and I can tell the others are listening closely, 'it doesn't want us here, the infection I mean, it doesn't want us here so we've got to step our game up and push on.'

'Nothing we've done then?' Cookey asks in a worried voice from behind me, I turn and take in his young face, Nick too, and the even younger Jagger and Mo Mo, 'no,' shaking my head I force myself to swallow the frustration, 'nothing you've done.'

'Got it!' Paula runs from the building clutching a hard backed black lever arch folder, 'names, addresses...er,' she opens the folder to leaf through the pages, 'lists of the doctors training courses and qualifica-tions...pay scales...nurses too,' she looks round with a big grin, 'this is fantastic, we can go and find them now.'

'Good work...'

'So?' Blowers pulls my attention back to him, and when I glance around, he shifts as though uncomfortable at pursuing the point, 'what is it then?' He asks, 'the er...'

'What's up?' Lani asks staring around at the lads.

'Blowers asked Mr Howie why the er...the mood change,' Nick gives me an awkward glance while he explains.

'Right,' tilting her head back and fixing her eyes on me, she waits with a look of defiance, 'go on then,' she prompts when I don't speak.

'We're wasting time,' harsh words again, 'where's the nearest doctor?'

'Christ, I don't know,' Paula exclaims, 'the addresses don't mean anything to me, Roy? Do you know the area well?'

'Not enough for street names,' he replies, 'certain places I can get to, but we'll need a street atlas.'

Everyone looks at Dave who pauses, shakes his head, tuts then slips his bag off to dig out a map.

21

D ay Fifteen

WEATHER: EXTREME FOG THROUGHOUT THE MORNING, BUT WITH relatively high humidity and warmth, but the fog dissipated in a sudden manner which was really rather alarming, and it is now exceptionally hot again.

THIS MORNING I ATE EGGS. I SCRAMBLED THEM IN A PAN OVER THE MINI portable gas stove. I never normally have scrambled eggs as I much prefer boiled eggs, but this morning I fancied a change. It was the last of the bread and bacon from the freezer, and I still have a few tins of peeled plum tomatoes left so I thought after that hellish storm I would cook myself a proper breakfast, and it's a good thing I'm about to venture back outside as my attempt at cooking scrambled eggs in a pan has resulted in ruining said pan.

It never ceases to amaze me just how bloody stupid I can be, for a renowned scientist that is. Not to blow smoke up my own bottom, but you'd think with the knowledge and expertise I have, that I could cook scrambled eggs without scorching them onto the pan so badly that despite an hour of constant scrubbing, the blasted bits of eggs are still there. They appear to be now ingrained in the structure of the metal of the pan, almost fused if you will. Perhaps a new design that NASA could have made use off, a new type of building material harder than diamond. Pity there isn't a NASA anymore.

I gave up and discarded the pan in the end. It wasn't that I wanted to admit defeat, but priorities have to be made, and scrubbing a pan for the next few hours certainly isn't one of them. However, the breakfast was quite nice, and you really couldn't tell the bacon had been frozen. The bread, of course, was toasted, and the toasting process does tend to alleviate any stale or rubberiness of the bread. Orange juice and freshly ground coffee completed my ensemble, and grand time I had eating it, feeling somewhat full and satisfied after. Another cup of coffee, and I stepped outside to stare into the awful sight of that thick fog. Never before have I seen such thick fog. Visibility was reduced to an effective six to ten feet at very best, but it was the warmth that surprised me and made me realise just how hot the day would have been without the fog. If the heat from the sun was penetrating that thick low cloud, then without it would be a scorcher of a day. And, I am pleased to say that my prediction was right for when the fog did lift it became incredibly hot very quickly.

The air feels clearer too, and I can only surmise that the hurricane-force winds have swept away any remaining polluting particles leftover from humanity. The rain was a downpour of biblical proportions and surely reminded me of the tale of Noah and the Ark. For a minute, I even glanced at Jess and considered if indeed, we would have to source higher ground, but my selection of a suitable location has proved to be worthy as we remained sound and dry. This old barn was built many years ago, and I fancy it would take something stronger than a storm to shift it, of course, my modernisation and work to reinforce the structure has certainly helped, but I like to think that it was a combination of the two; solid craftsmanship from the olden days with good use of modern techniques and materials.

That being said, the outside area suffered during the storm, and it was lucky I knew just how bad it would be, and had the foresight to bring the hens inside the barn where they clucked about quite happily and even left me a fresh egg for this morning's debacle with the scrambling.

The old weather boffins were correct, maybe a few days out here and there in their predictions, but credit to them. They said the resulting storm would be a big one and they weren't wrong. The fog they predicted too, yes, I grant you that the timings were skewwhiff, but as they said at the time, there was no precedent to work from, only educated guesswork. Pity they didn't make it through, maybe they have?

I must admit that I have some conflicting emotions about going back out into the world. I have been here for six months now, cooped up and confined, and only venturing out when absolutely necessary and even, then, the effort involved in choosing a route out then back in in order to ensure I was never seen was an arduous one and soon became tiring.

Yes, I grant you that of course, I was not expecting The Event for another six months at the earliest but still, and the last fourteen days have really felt claustrophobic. I knew it was coming, I knew it was going to happen, but actually knowing it was happening was very shocking. Really very shocking. To know that billions would perish in the most god-awful manner and being unable to do a damned thing about it was mind-warping, and many a time I contemplated my entire thought processes and decisions to do as I am, each time though it lead me back to doing this. Staying alive, and safe, and away from everyone until the worst was over.

The list is safe. Committed to memory and of course, the hidden copies are at key locations throughout the country and in such places that it would take a stroke of the greatest luck for anyone to stumble across them, and even if they did, they would have no idea what they were reading.

Yes, the confinement has been increasingly difficult, and I've been longing for this day, but now it is here, I feel scared. Really bloody scared. I don't want to leave this old barn and the luxury I have created here. I could stay here, eat well, survive in comfort, and live a healthy life. I know what is out there, I know just how bad it's going to be. Still, I made this decision a long time ago, and I knew this fear would be here at the prospect of leaving. It is just something I will have to overcome.

I wonder who is left from the old team? Apart from The Rogue Bastards that is. I know they will be safe and tucked up in the complex. Bloody idiots. I kept on hoping they would never actually go through with it, but I knew deep down they were set on a course that was already determined. Fanatical zealots the bloody lot of them, and even now I struggle to comprehend the ideology of it.

Yes, it was a good exercise and yes, we all contributed to the plan, but it was a tabletop exercise, entirely theoretical and never to be done.

You know, I often wonder now, having been through it all, whether it really was that small group being bloody fanatical about it or whether they were set-up, or even encouraged. After all, we never saw the organisers or the funding parties, we were only told about them. Mind you, that in itself is understandable, and we were told the entire research study was deniable from the point of view of the many countries that provided the funding and resources.

Maybe I was too naïve. A lifetime spent in research surrounded by people of the highest education and ethics, and I was wholly unprepared for the deep-rooted passions and beliefs we had in that facility.

Don't get me wrong, the exercise was, without doubt, the most exciting project I have ever been involved in and it was the same for every person there. Not one of us had ever had access to that level of data before, completely unrestricted access to every file, folder, database and information gathering software in the world. Nothing of that level and depth had ever been undertaken before, and now, of course, will never happen again.

I'VE JUST HAD ANOTHER COFFEE, AND I KNOW I'M DRAGGING MY HEELS, BUT the coffee really is very nice and who knows when I'll be able to get another after leaving here? I checked the camera feeds too. Camera One on the library went down in the storm. Camera Two has never bloody worked. Three to Seven are all functioning, Six is still fuzzy and unfocussed, but I suspect that is from a large cobweb and spider right in front of the lens which is causing the auto-focus some difficulty.

Being able to see the local town after the storm is eye-opening. The level of destruction is very high. Camera four from the main square in the town centre still gives the best view, Five and Six were the other town centre feeds I watched when The Event happened, and of course, being night vision infra-red meant I've been able to track the situation day and night. Bloody good these cameras are too. I know I've gone about them before in my diary, but it was one of those things that was an afterthought, done in a rush but bloody worked a treat. Solar-powered with large capacity batteries, remote access and long-range transmission of an encrypted signal that is decoded at my end. The one on the police station still makes me laugh, how they never saw it is shameful, but I suppose the police are taught to look out rather than up.

The High Street is now a river, or to be precise, an offshoot of the local river that must have burst its banks. Looks to be at least, five feet deep and I cannot see where the water runs in or out, I can see the bodies though and a surprising amount of them too. I haven't seen any of the infected yet today, and I can only hope the storm culled their numbers considerably. I know they won't all be dead as the very nature of the virus will protect them far beyond what a normal body can deal with, but at least, some will have perished and if nothing else, the water will help remove the festering diseases contributed to so many rotting corpses lying in the hot sun, and of course, with all the rats becoming infected on day five of the infection, it meant the natural waste disposal teams of our rodent population haven't been here to dispose of the rancid meat.

There must have been a purpose for the rat species to become infected. The virus would have had a reason for that and one that I intend to discover, and I suspect The Rogue Bastards carried on tweaking the virus after I left the team.

There is smoke coming from somewhere in the centre of the residential district within the town too, and I suspect that is from a lightning strike which resulted in a fire which has been left to burn, and now with the high heat back it can burn until it runs out of fuel, which could be a long time. It worries me though as the smoke is billowing high and could attract attention, and right on my proposed route out too. I could use the fall-back route out, but I do rather want to see the local town one last time before I set off, and of course, I'll be on Jess and she can outrun anything on two legs.

She senses a change. Our routine has changed so she knows something is happening and by the looks of her, she's more excited than worried as she keeps pawing the floor or rather hooving the floor and snorting impatiently. Trust me to get such an intelligent animal, but she's strong, sturdy, fast and devoted to me so I wouldn't change her for the world. She's had some oats and good rub down; the saddle is all ready along with the bridle and other bits. Her leg protectors are ready to go on and I know she doesn't like them, but they'll stop her getting bitten, and anyway, the modern material is far better than the old chainmail they used to use on horses. She should be grateful. But she isn't. She's just impatient and snorting away while throwing her head about. I don't think she likes the hens being in the barn as she keeps stamping her feet when they get too close. She doesn't pay them any attention outside, but I suppose she thinks this is her house and they are trespassing, and at the very least they should sit down and be quiet.

I was told the Hanoverian breed was highly strung, bred for dressage and show-jumping, they have to be at the top of their game and hundreds of years of fine selection breeding has created a monster. She's seventeen hands and built with it. Solid dark brown that in the shade looks black, and I was lucky to get her. I knew what breed I wanted, but finding one suitable was the hardest part, but my infiltration of the local racing stables as an affable, dim-witted but wealthy eccentric (not that far from the truth anyway) soon led me to her. An ex-stunt horse who starred in many a Hollywood movie, but given early retirement for being too aggressive. Eight years old and bad-tempered, but she's used to things that go bang pop and whizz and will charge ahead without any regard for anything in her path, which made her perfect for me.

Why am I writing all this? To delay the inevitable of course, by telling myself that I need to record everything on paper just so I can stay here in safety. But alas my path is set, and I must prepare, so prepare I will.

NB

22

'No point checking, cross it off and we'll go for the next one,' another glance at the big detached house, and we can all see there's no point looking inside. Every window is smashed, the front door has been ripped off and there's blood smeared all over the inside walls of the porch. Same as the last one and the one before that too. The first house we checked looked promising, still intact with the windows unbroken, but then it was off the beaten track and isolated from the main road.

Clarence did his door opening technique and we found an empty house, but with everything looking as it should be and it didn't take long to work out the doctor and her family must have been away when it all started. Four houses checked and no progress made, and the minutes roll by far faster than they should be.

'You got the map?' Paula asks me opening the folder so we can choose the next closest address. Roy took the lead when we set off, knowing the area better than the rest of us and while he drove to the first house, Paula marked the addresses on the map so we could choose an easy route. Little neat red circles dot the street atlas, and I mark the fourth one off with a cross and hand the map over.

'You lads take the front for a bit,' Dave and I climb into the back and take a wheel arch each, sitting down in silence while Blowers starts the van up and waits for Roy to pull out. With the engine running and the wheels right beneath us, we don't bother trying to shout for conversation, but sit in quiet contemplation, well, I do, I don't know what Dave does when he isn't talking.

One race. Profound it was. Deeply profound, and self-reflection tells me it has struck a chord. Not because of the desire to win, but because I can so easily see us losing, and very soon. At the moment, we've got ample supplies and the ability to get them from foraging, but one look at what was Portsmouth harbour tells me we are no longer in control of our environment. We are subject to the whim of many other factors. We're foolish if we try to hold onto the thought, we are the dominant species because we're not, they are, or rather they will be.

Fifteen days ago, they were monsters by night and slow-moving easy targets by day. Brainless, thoughtless, predictable, and easy enough to defeat. But look at what they've done and just in two weeks; the ability to speak, to retain cognitive thought, thinking things through, and ever-evolving to try new tactics and strategies. They still cling to the fact they have almost an unlimited supply of resources, but it won't take long for them to start using machines and weapons. What is the thing controlling them? How can a virus, a tiny particle thing like that have such power? I can grasp the concept of cell mutation, and how viruses and infections work, but a growing entity that has a shared conscious, like a hive mind and something that can learn, adapt, and develop an awareness of self. *One race*. That's what it said. Not the former human being that uttered the words for he was just an avatar for the infection within, and it was that infection, that virus that passed that message on.

Communication and the ability to communicate at a level beyond the basic needs of humanity are one of the many primary reasons our race became so dominant. We can talk, pass messages, make each other understand concepts and ideas. We can theorise, and work in a hypothetical environment with a blend of imagination and fact coupled with our emotional states.

One race. But why tell me? What the fuck do I need to be told that for? We're just a tiny, insignificant group trying to cling onto life. We've proved we can fight back, and inflict massive losses on them but still, they control the world now, we've got a shitty little ancient fort with no working toilet. And what was the point of the clowns in the circus? Trying to terrify Cookey and use psychology to weaken us. That is a good point though, the use of psychology shows their evolving ability to adapt. If we had all been terrified of clowns, we could have been wiped out easily, frozen to the spot in fear or running away in absolute panic. It knew Cookey's name too, plus it said those things about Mohammed, about when he was younger.

Information is power but power corrupts. If the infection is developing a conscious and an awareness of self, then an ego will surely follow. The vanity of man comes from our belief that we are above everything else. The infection desires to be the supreme race so it has a belief that it is above everything else. But that would imply a belief system.

No, I'm on the right track. Information is power. The infection is learning to use information against us. Knowing Cookey was terrified of clowns so playing to his fear. Knowing there is something nasty in Mohammed's past, and again trying to get inside his head with it. Using information so therefore it would have collected the information first. Well, that's obvious. It is accessing the memories and knowledge within the brains of the bodies it inhabits.

Power corrupts. The infection is gathering information to gain power and supremacy, but why? There must be a reason for this? There has to be a purpose, and something that is greater than a motivating factor.

'Mr Howie, we're here....'

'Go on without me,' I reply, 'Dave, go with them.'

It's evolving, learning, becoming something other than what it was. Something tells me to start there, a flag waving in my head, a claxon sounding. Something other than what it was in the beginning.

'Boss, Blowers said you're staying here?' The back doors open to reveal Clarence.

'Yes!'

The beginning. I watched it on the television. All the news channels saying it started in Europe and spread across.

'Howie, why aren't you coming in?' Lani at the back doors.

'For fuck's sake!' I burst into rage, 'Nick!'

'Yes, boss,' he runs towards me as I jump down from the back of the van.

'Give me a smoke.'

With the look of a startled rabbit, he fumbles the pack out while I stare at the house. Large. Detached. Brick built. Executive. Plush. Space for several vehicles, but only a small one parked up, and judging by the leaves and shit all over it, I would say it hasn't moved in fifteen days. Doors and windows all closed. Curtains drawn. No signs of entry, but then there's a build-up of leaves outside the front door too that indicates it hasn't opened.

'Cheers,' I take the cigarette, light up, inhale then stomp towards the front door with the sawn-off held up and ready. Two shots blasted into the central lock area, one big boot and it swings in, then falls off the hinges with an almighty clatter. I'm in before the door has finished settling.

'ANYONE HERE?'

Dust all over the floor, smooth and undisturbed. Musty smells from no airflow. It feels empty. It is empty.

'Next one,' I snap while marching back to the van amidst an array of hard stares.

The facts. What do I know for fact? It started in Europe. It is a virus that is transmitted by bodily fluids.

'Mr Howie,' Blowers climbs into the driver's seat, and turns with a question.

'**SILENCE!**' Dave's parade ground voice booms loud and clear, and hopefully telling everyone to leave me alone. He nods at me as though urging me to continue.

It drives the host body to seek more hosts. They bite and ensure the virus is transmitted then move on to take the next one, but not every time. Sometimes they eat too much flesh and render the body unusable. What does that mean? A lack of control and discipline?

It targeted us very quickly, within five days of the event starting. Dave said it could be because we were killing so many of them, but there must have been other groups out there killing more than us, and Dave has killed more than all of us combined so why go for me and not him?

Which leads me onto the immunity. **One race.** In the beginning, it was simply seeking every possible host, doing everything it could to turn every single person, hunting them, hounding them, stalking and chasing. Driven and ruthless, and like nothing ever known to humanity before.

Immunity. I am immune. The virus cannot harm me. Cookey too. Meredith. But Lani did turn, but she came back. What was that? Is she mutated differently to us? How did her body fight back?

The infection sees us as the threat now. It sees me as the threat. A threat to its dominance and control of this environment. It seeks to dominate and control this environment, so it has purpose and reason along with intelligence and shared collective.

Purpose. The infection has purpose. It is *intended* for something which means…fuck it. What does it mean? I can feel I'm onto something, it's right there, like a rope hanging just out of reach from my grasp.

Marcy. Darren. Darren was the first we knew of that possessed the ability to think and retain even a semblance of the individual he was. That was the infection learning to evolve. Marcy was different, she is different. Marcy said the infection was the cure for all diseases, the end to suffering, the end of pain and war, violence, greed.

The flood of emotion I felt when I first saw her still resonates within me. A moment in time captured that will stay with me forevermore like something from a movie or a song. The ground heaved, the sky was spinning, and I saw our future mapped out in years ahead. We both did. We both felt it. The pheromones tried to take us, but that was the infection, not the woman. The woman, the person, the human left inside her wanted a different course of action, she wanted a different outcome to that which is pre-destined for her kind. She wanted a doctor and was willing to offer herself as a test subject.

That emotion I felt with her was a reaction of chemicals being released. A reaction. A reaction. A reaction to her. A reaction from what I am to what she was…what she is.

One race.

A chemical reaction. Something in me recognised something in her, and reacted by screaming at me to do something, but what? Do what?

This fucking van is rocking too much, the engine is too noisy, the sides are too close, I feel trapped and I need space to think.

'Stop the van,' Dave barks the command. Did I think it or say it? I don't care. The van pulls over, signalling Roy in front, and Clarence behind.

I'm out the back before we're fully stopped, pacing away with my hands on my head while I think.

My head feels like it will explode. Too many thoughts, too many strands of thought processes, but I'm close, close to something.

'NOT NOW!' I roar at Lani, urging her to leave me alone.

Dave moves close, ever protective, and I catch a glimpse of him turning to face back at the others with his hands held ready on his knife hilts. He looks terrifyingly intent. His face is a mask of utter coldness that will kill and kill until time stops.

'Dave, help me,' I bleat the words out, pleading for the great man to save me once again.

'I can't.'

'Dave! Help me…I'm so close, but…but I can't…I can't think…'

'You can and you are,' his gaze is flat and level, 'nobody will disturb you now.'

'I'm going fucking crazy.'

'You're not.'

'He bloody is,' Lani spits.

'Do not speak…do not utter a word,' Dave's tone is deathly, commanding and so chilling it rips every ounce of anger and hurt from her face, 'you are not crazy,' he turns to me, 'think…think clearly.'

'I'M TRYING,' I scream, 'but my head hurts…' pain in the back of my skull blossoms to spread across my cranium.

'Marcy was infected, right?' I pace towards him, expecting him to answer but he doesn't, he just watches me closely, 'she said...she said the infection cured diseases...it was the cure not the...the...' I cast about trying to remember her words.

'the cure not the disease...' Lani mutters.

'Yes! She said it was the cure, not the disease...but it is a fucking disease, a virus, an infection that transmits, but it has purpose and intent, intelligence and cunning, it is evolving and it said one race, you heard it...Dave, you heard it say that right?'

'I did.'

'So, it has purpose and it has intent, and...and it has perception of self. It has an end game, or...' I stop pacing to think. 'It *had* an end game...the end game *was* to turn everyone, but that was always going to end badly as the second the last one turns renders it effectively extinct. So, the end game has changed. The purpose has changed! It's changed because the infection has evolved to have a perception of self. It...the infection, it seeks survival and dominance...holy fuck...'

We're the reason for the change. We're immune. I am immune. Lani and Cookey. We are the antidote. We're the thing that can stop it.

One race.

Marcy said the infection is the cure, it cures all diseases. Like a... what's that thing in Greek mythology? The thing that is meant to give immortality and...panacea! The infection is a panacea, a cure-all. But it isn't curing, it's killing. It's destroying everything. The host bodies it has are all slowly decomposing.

'It doesn't make sense,' I tell Dave, 'it can't be a panacea if it's killing everything...there won't be anything left alive.'

'It can't kill everything,' Dave replies, 'it can't kill you.'

'No, it can kill me, it can shoot me or stab me, or drown me or fucking hell...pretty much whatever it takes, but what it can't do is infect me and it can't infect Cookey or Lani.'

A reaction of chemicals. Marcy caused a reaction. Marcy was infected but different, she maintained an individual thought process, and right there at the very end, it was her holding them back from attacking me. She held them back and defied the infection by doing so.

Eyes locked. His cold and grey but so deep, they stretch away to infinity. He nods. Slowly, firmly yet it gets more pronounced. Every thought in my head stops. The pain that was building eases.

'That's it,' I say to him, 'that's what we have to do.'

'Okay,' he blinks and waits as patient as the mountains.

I turn to the rest and cast my eyes from face to face, finally settling on Lani, 'we have to find Marcy.'

23

Fear. He can smell fear, shit and piss but most of all, he can smell fear. He moves forward following the scent. Head fixed, red eyes bloodshot and seemingly hollow from the skin drawn tight across the cheekbones. His hair is mostly gone, just a few strands remain on his filth encrusted skull. Teeth stained with blood crusted around the lips and across his cheek where an open wound fester in the heat with maggots writhing to eat down into the rotten flesh.

One claw-like hand streams with fresh blood from the glass shards that cut deep as the undead smashed the pane of glass. The wound congeals quickly but the blood still drips to splatter down onto the carpeted floor. A potential host is in here. The undead can smell it. He can sense it.

In the back door, through the ground floor rooms and it stalks ever forward, ever seeking that flesh to bite and chew. Driven with lust to feast and pass the virus within. A lone undead in a detached house away from the towns and cities. Innocuous and bland, non-descript, but the undead has walked for days seeking flesh and finally it has one here.

Up the stairs that creak and groan under the weight of the undead. A groan rumbles from the throat, deep and hungry. The sound travels to the man hiding in the upstairs back room. His fear ramps up, his heart hammers sending pulses of energy into his limbs, fight or flight. Prepare for battle or prepare to run. Except there is nowhere to run, and the man cannot fight, he is too gripped by fear for he knows what comes.

With wide eyes fixed on the door, he whimpers in terror, listening as the steps get higher, get closer, crossing the landing and each door is opened in order as the beast without seeks the meal within. A jet of piss spurts unnoticed, a wet patch that grows and spreads across the front of his filthy jeans. He knew this was coming, but he did not prepare. He knew more than nearly anyone but still, he didn't prepare. It was too real, too big to deal with.

The footsteps stop outside his door. Two darker shadows indicate the feet of the thing outside. The handle squeaks as it turns, the door swings inwards and the man within stands upright on trembling legs to face the demon that is far worse than he ever imagined. The fear seeps back as professional interest takes over. The beast is beyond anything he could ever imagine but more than that, it walks with an almost fluid motion, not jerky or spasmodic like the rats in the test labs were.

The infected man is painfully thin, but then the original frame of the man would have been thin anyway, the infection has just sucked all the fluid from the muscles. Nothing wasted, no excess weight or fat. Sinewy and rangy.

'I know you,' the man shouts needlessly loud, 'I know you,' the beast shows no reaction. It doesn't care if the potential host knows him or not. He is not what he was. He is not the man the body appears to be.

'You,' the man shouts again, 'inside...I know you inside...I was there...one of them that made you...'

The infection stops the body and holds it still. Watching through the eyes to the short fat man whimpering and shouting in fear. The outcome is inevitable, the fat man will be taken and turned. There is no escape, no way out for him.

'I was there,' the man shouts again, 'I know you...you don't have to take me...don't take me...I can...I can help, I can...I can help you...'

The infection watches and listens. The fear is strong, the stench of piss is acrid, but beautiful as the infected host is tuned to take pleasure from those scents, pleasure that whets its appetite and drives the hunger.

'We tested you...but I, I didn't agree...I er...oh god, I didn't agree so I left and…my part was small, but I know you,' the man waggles a finger pointing at the beast and the thing inside, 'I know what you are…they said I couldn't leave but I did, I got away…others did too…I'm not the only one but,' the man gabbles with increasing speed, spittle flying from his cracked lips, 'Neal…Neal got out, and…have you taken him? Have you got Neal? I know where he went…no! I know the area but not where exactly, but…but I can show you…'

Neal. Others. Got away. The name means something. Neal Barrett. That name is within the collective conscious. Neal got away. Neal did not agree. Neal was part of the group, but Neal got away.

'Don't bite me, please…I can help you…I can…I can do things and…' the man is frantic, his eyes dart left to right, and he shuffles with tiny panicked steps back and forth as his whole body trembles. There are memories of this man from the collective conscious. Flickers of images implanted within the cerebral memory dumps.

'Aaaaandrewwwww Jackssssson,' the infected man lisps the words out from a throat parched, and now unused to speaking.

The man flinches at hearing his own name. 'Yes! That's me…I'm Andrew Jackson…me! That's me! You know me and….and I know you…please…'

Andrew Jackson. He was there. He was in the team, but his part was small. A laboratory assistant with responsibility to ensure equipment was sterilised. Nothing more than a cleaner. But he knows the others. He is part of the puzzle and is information. Andrew Jackson is information.

'Please…yes? Yes?' Andrew Jackson flickers with hope at the lack of attack from the infected male, 'I can help you, yes? We can work together…I'll do what you want, but…no…no! NO!'

Andrew Jackson can help, but what he offers can be taken. His body will be a host, but his brain will yield.

'NO! PLEASE NO!' Andrew Jackson backs up against the wall as the infected man launches in to cross the last few feet with incredible speed. Andrew puts a hand up, defensive and protective of his own face. The infected man doesn't care what he bites, and the hand is as good as anything else, so a chunk is ripped from the soft meat on the palm. Andrew screams, buckles and falls to the ground as the virus moves from one host into the new one. The transition, done so many millions of times already, is completed as swiftly and as methodical as ever. The cells are taken. The heart stopped. The body dies. The heart is re-started, and the host take over is complete. The virus swarms through the veins and blood vessels into the brain where it gets to work. Each brain is unique, and different, and each one must be examined to under-stand the contents.

Two infected men stand within the room. Both silent. Both with red, bloodshot eyes. Both drool and utter low groans while inside one, the infection starts filling in the gaps of its knowledge.

24

'She is a rancid fucking WHORE,' Lani rages at me, her eyes blazing with fury.

'We are going to find her,' I repeat through gritted teeth.

'No,' she shakes her head firmly, 'not happening, not a chance in hell. We're finding a doctor; we're finding supplies and we're finding weapons…that's it. No Marcy, not today, not any fucking day.'

'Lani,' I catch her eyes, and hold my voice steady despite the frustration growing inside me again, 'she is part of this, same as we are,' I motion between us, 'same as Cookey and whoever else in our group is immune. She said…'

'I don't care what she said. She infected me. She bit me so she could get to you and what did you do with her? Go on, remind me, remind me what you *almost* did.'

'Drop it,' seething now that she can't see beyond her own emotions to what is needed to be done, 'this isn't about me and you, this is about all of us. The whole group, the whole fort, the whole of humanity.'

'Oh, is it?' She says lightly, 'oh dear, the whole of humanity rests on us finding Marcy does it? Never mind,' she adds spitefully.

'This is happening…'

'What about the doctor?' Roy asks, 'we still need a doctor.'

'No, we don't,' turning to face him, I take a small step back to view the whole group gathered around, 'a doctor can't help with this, not with the immunity thing anyway. Yeah, we need medical staff for the fort, but,' I shrug and sigh audibly, 'but not with this.'

'Eh?' Roy sneers, 'how do you know? Done four years of medical training, have you?'

'No, Roy. But I know a medical doctor, unless they are specifically trained in this virus, is not going to be able to help...or at least I don't think so...shit, you're going to have to trust me on this. The infection has changed, is changing...it's getting a perception of itself as a....as a sort of living thing I suppose...and it knows we are immune. It's not coming after us because we kill them, because we only really kill them when they attack...it doesn't want us here, it cannot allow us to remain...'

'Why?' Roy demands.

'Because...truthfully, I don't know. But I do know that Marcy was infected, but she retained intelligence and her own thoughts...'

'So, it was Marcy that tried to shag you then, not the infection? Is that what you are saying?' Lani asks with a nasty edge to her voice.

'No. Marcy was impelled to act *by* the infection. Honestly, I think she acted...hang on! I think she acted with good intentions in the beginning but the infection, the virus...the thing inside her wanted her to take us... the pheromones were released without her realising it...'

'Oh, poor Marcy,' Lani affects a hurt face.

'She saved us,' Cookey coughs and repeats it, 'she did save us, and er...Mr Howie at the last bit...'

'Yes, she did. I've told you this. She was on the wall holding the others back while I ran for the Saxon...the infection wanted them to take us, but it was her that stopped it, she defied the infection.'

'So?' Lani goads me by elongating the vowels in her words and showing just how pissed she is.

'Cookey and I cannot be taken. Got it? You,' I point at Lani, 'was taken, but you fought back somehow and recovered or....or got better... Marcy was infected, wholly infected with the fucking red eyes and everything but she resisted it, she maintained her own er...her own...'

'Individuality?' Paula offers.

'Yeah, something like that,' I nod, 'it has a purpose, the infection I mean. It had an end game, but it was always flawed as...'

'Yes, we know,' Lani snaps, 'we've talked about it a hundred times...it kills itself when it turns the last human.'

'Yes, so what's the point? To kill humanity? No, I don't think it was.'

'Er, right...' Roy says slowly, 'you've er...kind of lost me.'

'Marcy said...oh, grow up,' I snap at seeing Lani mimic me by mouthing *marcy said* silently, 'she said the infection was the cure. She said it cured diseases, took away pain and suffering...that we needed to find medical or scientific experts who could work out why she was different and use it to help everyone.'

'Right?' Roy nods, 'so...so Marcy thinks this virus is actually a cure for diseases? Oh. That's er, that's a pretty radical cure that is. You know, got diabetes but don't worry, be a zombie and all of that can go away.'

'Funny,' I shoot him a glare, 'and no, that's not what she meant, or at least, I don't think so...'

'There's something you're not saying,' Paula says carefully.

'It's hard to explain.'

'Try,' she urges, 'none of us are stupid and we've all followed you, so...'

'Yeah, I get it,' Mo Mo glances up at me, 'like, you get infected and then you get something else so you's not infected, but you's got no diseases or shit, you get me? Like er...like what they do at school when they do them fuckin' nasty injections...the nurse said they givin' you the bad shit to make sure you don't catch the bad shit...'

'I don't think so,' I replay his words a few times while trying to translate them, 'no...er...I think the virus was meant to do one thing, but somehow it became another thing...I just don't know what they were... or are...so, we have to find Marcy and...'

'Boss,' Clarence clears his throat, looking thoughtful and having listened in silence he now makes ready to give his opinion, 'we're with you,' he says simply, 'if you say we have to find Marcy, then we'll do it... all of us,' he glances at Lani, 'I've served for a long time and like Dave, I've had countless fights, battles, firefights...you name it...but I've never seen anything like this, not just what's happening to the zom...' he grits his teeth.

'Say it,' Cookey laughs, 'go on big man! Say the zed word...'

'Not just what's happening to the *things*,' he winces, 'but you, and us...and what's happening with us...there is no way on earth we should have walked away from those fights...so, whatever it is...we're in. End of.'

'Are we?' Lani says, not quite ready to back down.

'Yes, Lani,' Clarence replies heavily, 'Chris was my best mate, but when we were serving, he was the man in charge. He was the squad leader, and there were times he gave orders that none of us understood...but we did them because we trusted him, that's what leadership and teamwork are about.'

Silence. Heavy and thoughtful. All of us know the deep pain Clarence feels at losing Chris. That he came with us when he could have been back in the fort protecting Chris and Sarah.

'Okay,' Lani says quietly with a nod, 'we'll do it.'

'Okay...'

'But,' she fixes me with a glare, 'you don't get to be alone with her, not ever...not for a second...'

'Agreed,' I nod, 'I don't want to be alone with her.'

'And if she starts spraying bloody pheromones about like cat piss then she loses her head...and anything else of hers that sticks out...'

'Roger that,' I nod trying not to create a mental image of what she just suggested.

'Doctor?' Roy asks, 'are we getting one or not?'

'Not now.'

'But if I may offer my opinion...we might be going off to fight the glorious battle and chase clues like some amateur sleuths, but...'

'Roy, spit it out mate,' I rub my face to ease my impatience.

'The kids in the fort, the people in the fort...they need a doctor... we'll find one first and then go find this Marcy woman.'

'We still need weapons...or at least ammunition,' Clarence says.

They are right. The doctor is essential, same as the ammunition and weapons, and despite my increasing anxiety at not being able to do exactly what I want, I know I have to swallow it, and do the right thing.

'No. We go now,' or not, as my brain seems to be override my common sense.

'Boss,' Clarence steps forward with one huge handheld out in a plaintive gesture, his face both earnest and pleading, urging me to see sense and do the right thing.

'No. Now,' I don't have to look at their faces to see the dismay and hurt. I can feel it pouring off them in buckets.

'Sorry chaps,' Roy tilts his head back, 'but I'm going for the doctor... and I suggest we take a vote and see what the majority thinks.'

'A vote?' Nick spits with a look of anger flashing across his face, 'we don't vote, we do what Mr Howie says we do.'

'Young man...'

'Fucking young man me,' Nick turns to face the older man, 'I got separated yesterday, left on my own dealing with all kinds of shit, but not once...not fucking once did I lose belief that Mr Howie was coming for me...not once...and if Mr Howie told me to stand here naked rubbing butter on my bollocks I would do it without...'

'Do what?' Cookey blanches, 'butter on your bollocks?'

'Fuck off, Cookey,' Nick growls.

'But...butter? On your bollocks? What the fuck? And you were doing so well then mate but...'

'Get ready, we're moving out,' I give the order, and start heading back to my van.

'How? Where to?' Roy sputters, 'we need a doctor...Mr Howie, this is wrong, and I insist you listen...'

'Roy, if you...'

'Mr Howie, please,' both hands are held up palms facing me, 'listen, just listen...I don't doubt your credentials and ability to lead for one second. I've seen you fight, and lead, and I'll gladly stand by you in any battle, but...listen, I have health anxiety, right? You know, good old-fashioned hypochondria. I think I'm dying every five minutes, and I get symptoms of things I hear about or read...I've had it for years, literally my entire adult life. Medication, treatment, unable to hold down a job or keep a relationship going…but, well what I'm trying to say is this…I know what doctors can do and we need them. Those people in the fort need a doctor. Okay, not for the immunity thing, but you tell me what we'd do if one of those children got something stuck in their throat? Are you able to operate to remove it? Do you know how to treat infected wounds? What about heart attacks? Attach a drip and recognise cases of dehydration and malnutrition. Some of those children are too young to have had vaccinations and without proper sanitation, disease and dysentery will spread. Who can treat that? I can't. That A and E nurse we've got can't treat it. What if someone gets pregnant and has a diffi-cult childbirth? Have we got midwives? Food poisoning? I've spent more days in doctors surgery's than any of you have had hot dinners, and despite everyone saying doctors are this and that…they are bloody experts in what they do…we…need…a…doctor…' he pauses, blinks and adds, 'and a pharmacist for good measure.'

'Okay, doctor first.'

'Thank you,' he says sincerely, 'really, I mean it…'

'Next one then, lead the way.'

'Right, come on,' he nods his head for everyone to get moving, 'and we'll go faster this time,' he says to me with an earnest expression.

'You want me to drive?' Blowers asks.

'Yes…yeah, you drive mate…I need time to think.'

'It's five minutes away, Mr Howie,' Roy calls back, 'really just five minutes, and I've got a good feeling about this one.'

We move off and this time, I lean against the wheel arch instead of sitting on it. Legs stretched out, and I try to think, but the thoughts seem jumbled now, contrary and confused. It's like I've made the right decision, so my brain no longer needs to compute it all, and I feel weary too, completely drained yet with a sense of an impending journey ahead of us.

'How much of that did you hear?' I ask the question casually, idly watching Dave to see how he reacts.

'All of it.'

'So, you are in my head then.'

'I heard everything you said, Mr Howie.'

'And the things I didn't say out loud, don't give me that plain face, Dave.'

'It's my face,' he shrugs, 'it's always plain.'

'And don't change the subject.'

He stays quiet. Back to normal Dave, impossible to read as ever, 'mate,' I lean forward to fully get his attention, 'this is some serious stuff going on…so…come on.'

'What?'

'Can you read my mind?'

'Read your mind?'

'Telepathic or something.'

'Telepathic?'

'Stop repeating my words back, you can hear me perfectly well…we need to be open with each other, Dave…'

'I'm always honest to you, Mr Howie,' despite his typical *devoid of expression* countenance, there is a flicker of hurt on his features.

'Honesty and openness are not the same.'

'Aren't they?' he says with a mild look of confusion, 'how are they different?'

'Well, you know…like honesty is answering questions and being… well being honest but openness is being…well, being open…'

'And honest?'

'Yeah, honest…no! Not honest, well…yes honest but honest in a different way.'

'So, there are different ways of being honest?'

'No Dave, honest is honest and yes, you are honest but sometimes I don't think you are entirely open with me.'

'But, if I'm honest…then how is that not being open?'

'Um…right, so let's say I ask you a question, right? You would give an honest answer, yes?'

'Of course.'

'But, let's say I didn't ask the question in the first place. Would you *volunteer* the information without being asked?'

'Why would I?'

'What? What do you mean, why would I? If I asked a question and you answered honestly well, that is being honest, but by me not asking the question but you not giving the answer without being asked the question, that's not being open.'

'Okay, you want me to give you answers without you asking questions?'

'Yes! What? Oh, fuck's sake, Dave. No, you're doing that thing again.'

'What thing?'

'This thing, this belligerent thing.'

'I'm autistic.'

'Oh, don't pull that one on me…hang on, maybe you're like those kids that can draw big houses…'

'I can't draw very well.'

'No, I mean, like…oh, what are they called?'

'I don't know.'

'You know, the kids that can look at a big house once then draw it exactly perfect, but just from memory from that one time they saw it… what are they called?'

'I don't know, weird?'

'No! Not weird…well, yeah, I mean it is weird to do that, but…they are autistic, but they have a gift, like a special talent…but only in that one thing…'

'I can kill people,' he offers, 'I'm good at that.'

'Yeah, I don't think that can count as a special gift mate. No, thinking about it, yeah it is a gift so maybe…maybe that is your special gift.'

'I'm autistic with a gift for killing.'

'Savant!'

'Pardon?'

'Those people who are autistic but have the special gifts, they're savants. You could be a savant.'

'I'm English, Mr Howie.'

'No, it isn't a place, Dave. It's the word given to people who have autism, but also have the really awesome special talents.'

'A savant.'

'Yes, mate.'

'A savant killer?'

'Yes...oh, you bugger! You almost did it again.'

'Did what again, Mr Howie?'

'Changed the subject, right...I was saying your gift could be mind-reading like you are autistic, but you can read minds.'

'No. I struggle with my own mind, Mr Howie. Someone else's mind would be...'

'Okay, maybe not full mind-reading but you can hear my thoughts.'

'No, I don't think so, Mr Howie.'

Yes, you can.

'No, I really don't think so.'

'Ha! Got you. I didn't say a word then.'

'We're here,' Blowers shouts back.

'Course we are,' I mutter, 'this conversation isn't over.'

'You've said that before, Mr Howie.'

Out the back of the van and another quick look shows me the doctors of the south coast have no imagination when it comes to house buying, and clearly there must be some rule that stipulates they have to reside in a bland as fuck detached executive style house on the edge of a posh estate, oh, and with enough parking for Avis rental to open a depot.

'Doors been opened recently,' Clarence says viewing the front door and the obvious signs of opening with a nice arc through the debris of leaves, litter and all manner of stuff that has blown into the recessed doorway.

'They should have put a sign out for the milkman,' I reply, 'might have been less obvious.'

'No cars,' Blowers indicates the vast and empty driveway.

'Garage is shut, probably in there,' Nick points up to the black gloss painted double swing-up doors.

'Knocking or going in?' Clarence asks.

'Best knock,' I get to the door and instinctively look for the doorbell, then remember the power is off so the doorbell won't work. Instead, I use the brass knocker, and hope we haven't terrified the hell out of anyone inside, 'hello?' holding my mouth close to the door, I yell out a few times, 'we're not going to hurt anyone, and we don't want to break your door…is there a doctor in there?'

'Heard movement,' Dave mutters.

'Right, er…listen!' I shout again, 'we're from one of the forts on the coast. We've got hundreds of people there with food, supplies and er… safety,' I try not to cough when I say the last word given the track record of the fort so far, which probably makes it the least safe place at the moment, 'and we've got medicines and all sorts of things…but we don't have a doctor…we went to a local hospital and found the personnel records so we know a doctor is living here…please! We need medical expertise.'

We wait in silence, listening in hope to the tread of feet coming from inside, 'Dave,' I whisper, 'you hear anything?'

'Not now,' he replies.

'Can't blame them, I wouldn't answer to us,' Paula says, 'can I try?'

'Be my guest,' I offer her the doorway, and step back to watch the windows, 'everyone try and look a bit less threatening.'

'How we doing that then?' Cookey asks.

'Use your imagination, just…well…spread out, and look like a disciplined unit.'

'Which you should have done anyway,' Dave shoots a glare at Blowers.

'Hi,' Pauls has a go at shouting, 'I'm Paula, I work with Mr Howie… have you heard of him? He was the man you just heard shouting…'

'Nice idea,' Clarence nods in approval.

'Movement,' Dave mutters.

'Keep going,' I nod at Paula.

'We're from Fort Spitbank, we did have it all rigged up for safety, but the storm has set us back a bit…we've got a large group of children that need medical attention, plus food, weapons and structure…we have rules and…'

'Movement,' Dave mutters again.

'Look, we're really sorry if we are scaring you, tell us to go and we'll go straight away, but we need a doctor, we need medical experts and…

and another thing...a few in our group are immune...they've been bitten but...'

'Voices,' Dave turns his head slightly to one side. I look around for Meredith to see her head cocked in exactly the same manner as Dave.

'Male and female?' I ask quietly.

'Female and at least, two males.'

'Shit, Dave. You've got the hearing of a bat mate.'

'Bats use sonar, Mr Howie.'

'I know, it was a figure of speech.'

'I don't use sonar.'

'I know, Dave, it was a figure of speech...'

'They have poor eyesight too.'

'Forget the bloody bats...can you hear anything now?'

'I don't know, you were talking too much.'

'Obtuse...not, just forget what obtuse is...' I hold my hand up as he turns to say something.

'I know what obtuse is,' he blanches, 'I was going to say the voices are getting closer.'

'Hello?' Paula shouts again, 'really, we mean you no harm. We are good people...we have soldiers with us, and I'm an accountant...'

'Don't tell 'em that,' Cookey jokes, 'they'll never open up now.'

'Pardon? Can you come a bit closer please, I didn't hear you,' Paula shouts at the muffled voice coming from within.

'They're arguing,' Dave explains.

'I can hear them now,' Paula nods.

'Up top,' Blowers calls out, directing us to all peer up at the adult man staring down from an upstairs window.

'Hi,' I try to offer a non-threatening wave, 'we're really sorry to disturb you but...'

Another man appears beside the first, one bearded, but the other is clean-shaven, 'hey,' I wave at the both, 'I'm Howie,' I call out, 'and...oh, hi,' I say again when the window opens. They both look worried and nervous, but not terrified, 'er...which one is the doctor?'

'We both are,' the bearded man says in a deep cultured voice, 'you're Mr Howie?'

'I am, Sir,' I nod seriously, 'and I am truly sorry to do this...but as Paula said, we need help.'

'Have you heard of us?' Lani asks softly. Looks between the two men and the bearded one nods, 'we have,' he says, 'one of our group met someone a few days ago who said about the fort and a Mr Howie...how do we know you're really Mr Howie?'

'Er...well, I guess you don't,' I look around at the others, 'but er... well, that is Dave,' I point at Dave, 'and Clarence, Lani...Cookey, Blowers and Nick...that's Meredith and the others are Paula, Roy, Jagger and Mo Mo...'

'She said that man mentioned some of those names...' the unbearded doctor says, 'small one and a big one,' the bearded doctor replies, 'how did you find us?' He asks guardedly.

'From the personnel records at the local hospital...it was Paula's idea, we're desperate for a doctor and...'

'You said something about immunity,' the bearded one cuts me off quickly.

'That's right Sir, 'I'm immune...so is Cookey over there and Lani... the dog too.'

'What? Three of you?' Suspicion evident in his voice, a large group of armed people at his door with three of them pertaining to be immune.

'Er...look,' I unclasp the sailor trousers straps to pull them down so I can shrug my top off, 'I got bit here,' I point to the wound on my shoulder, 'and here...and here...these are all bites...from the things...' saying the word *zombie* to two doctors doesn't feel right.

'This is mine...'

'Cookey! Put your backside away,' Clarence orders at the sight of Cookey dropping his trousers to show them the wound on the back of his leg, 'sorry about that,' the big man offers politely.

'I was just showing my bite mark,' Cookey grumbles, 'and I've got underpants on.'

'For the first time,' Blowers coughs into his hand.

'Yeah, you wish,' Cookey laughs, 'bet you got a right good look.'

'Lads! Not now,' I give them both a glare, 'sorry, er...so, how many in your group?'

'Four,' the bearded doctor says.

'It says here there is a Doctor Stone here,' Paula checks the folder then looks up.

'That's right,' the bearded doctor replies.

'Okay,' she says, 'which one is Doctor Stone?'

Another glance between the two men, 'we both are,' the clean-shaven man says.

'Oh, really,' Paula takes a further step away to get a better view, 'you don't look like brothers.'

'You said you have children at this fort? And they're hurt? What's wrong with them?' The bearded Doctor Stone asks.

'No, we've got children that need medical help, but...not actually injured...we've got an A and E nurse with us...' I explain, 'well, not with us here but back at the fort...he's doing really well, but...well, even he says he can't deal with anything that serious.'

'A and E nurses are worth their weight in gold,' the same Doctor Stone says.

'Oh, he is, but...he's not a doctor and as Roy said,' I point to Roy, 'what if someone gets food stuck in their throat or...a heart attack...plus none of us know anything about all the medicines we've got, and we've got equipment too that the previous doctor told us to get but...'

'Who was that?'

'Doctor Roberts, from London...he specialised in er...tropical diseases or something I think...'

'What happened to him?'

'Died, Sir. Along with many others after the things got inside...but we er...we took it back, and now it's secure again.'

Clarence steps closer to me, 'the fort was on a spit...' he starts to explain.

'I know Fort Spitbank.'

'You do? Then you know the flat area after the estate? Well, that's all gone...the storm last night,' Clarence says.

'So, we're sealed off now,' Paula jumps in, 'the only way is by boat.'

'You understand our concerns I'm sure,' the doctor says gravely, 'armed people at our door, and we have no way of knowing if you are who you say you are.'

'True,' I nod, 'but if we were bad, we could have kicked the door in and taken what we need, which we haven't done. And we won't,' I add quickly as the mere mention of threat has the bearded man standing more upright, 'we'll go if you tell us. We've got more houses to try and...'

'Who have you tried already?' the clean shaved doctor asks Paula.

'Er, we've tried...Doctor Bridger...Doctor er...Johnson and...'

'Were they dead?' The younger, clean shaven doctor asks.

'We don't know,' I reply, 'the houses were empty and er...destroyed, but the last place was sealed up...it looked like the occupants were away when it happened?'

'Doctor Carol,' Paula reads out.

'Yes,' he nods, 'Michelle Carol, she was on holiday in Jamaica...'

'Can you give us a minute to talk please,' the bearded Doctor asks.

'Of course, please...take your time,' I motion with my hand, and make a point of moving away from the house while nodding at the others to do the same.

'What do you think?' Roy asks once we're safely out of earshot from the house.

'Two for the price of one with a bit of luck,' I reply with a glance to Lani, 'turning down food, supplies and security is going to be hard for them...'

Paula nods, listening intently while she looks back at the house, 'the brothers must have got together when it happened, safety in numbers or something...probably got their wives in there too.'

Idle chat is made. Idle chat tinged with an almost palpable sense of excitement that finally we might get an actual real doctor.

'They didn't seem that bothered about you being immune,' Clarence says thoughtfully.

'They're doctors, they won't assume anything,' Roy replies, 'they'll think we've got it wrong, and in actual fact, it was a badger that bit them.'

'Badger,' Cookey snorts, 'that's funny.'

'I'll tell you what's funny,' I turn to face the grinning lad, 'is you showing your arse to two bloody doctors...'

'Sorry,' the smile fades slightly, but I can see he's unfazed, 'I wanted to show my bite...and give Blowers a quick thrill.'

'Twat,' Blowers snaps.

'Gayboy,' Cookey retorts.

'Buttmuncher.'

'Shit poker.'

'Enough.'

'Sorry, Dave.'

'Sorry, Dave.'

'Aye up chuckies,' Cookey announces, 'the door doth open.'

'Doth? You're a freak,' Blowers sighs.

'Stay here, Lani and Paula with me,' I move towards the house and watch as the brother doctors appear in the doorway, 'would you rather we weren't armed?' I call out.

'Er...I don't think it...'

'Yes please,' the bearded Doctor Stone cuts his more affable brother off.

'Pistols and shotguns,' I hand mine to Dave, and wait while the other two do the same, 'is that okay?'

'Yes...fine...just you three then, er...you'd better come inside.'

'Sure?' I ask before moving, 'only if you are entirely comfortable.'

'Of course, we're bloody not,' he snaps, 'but we'd better hear you out.'

We cross the vast and empty driveway that could double for a landing strip for light aircraft, and into the open door. A slight English shuffle takes place while the two doctors realise, they are effectively blocking the doorway, but clearly don't want to move away and leave it entirely exposed. Funny really when you think about it, the bloody driveway is big enough for a nuclear submarine, but the front door and porch are tiny.

With lots of polite *excuse me* and *oops, sorry* we get inside and wait patiently while the affable Doctor Stone closes the door, leaving the bearded Doctor Stone to lead the way down the hallway into the kitchen at the back.

The décor is as expected. Neutral, bland and everything is beige or shades thereof. The brothers are close by the looks of the pictures of them on the walls, in fact, it looks a bit weird but then people are weird.

In the kitchen we find the two wives looking very concerned, but I do note that everyone looks clean and healthy, even with a light tan on their faces which must be from a safe enclosed rear garden, either that or a sunbed in the house. But then doctors wouldn't have sunbeds in their houses, would they?

'Hello,' I nod politely at the two women, 'I'm Howie, this is Lani and Paula. Very nice to meet you.'

Neither say anything, but look aghast at the state of us, glancing down I realise we're all still encrusted in blood and gore from the fight in the circus, 'shit…sorry,' I grimace, 'we er…we had some issues on the way here.'

'Issues?' Bearded Stone asks in his deep cultured voice.

'Zombies, Sir,' I reply, 'lots of them.'

'And you killed them?' One of the wives asks in a tone tinged with excitement.

'Er, yes, yes we did…we kind of had to otherwise…well, I'm sure you can er…'

'Lani is your wife?' The same woman asks, 'the man we met said you and the er…well, he said Chinese, but you don't look Chinese,' she says to Lani.

'Thai,' Lani sighs, 'but don't worry and yes, Mr Howie and I are er… well we're together,' she offers me a warm smile which I know I don't deserve.

'Mr Howie?' You call him mister?' Bearded Stone is quick to pick up on that.

'Only in front of the others,' Lani smiles, 'trust me, he gets called lots of other things when we're alone. He might be the leader of the living army, but he's still a bloody idiot.'

'Oh, aren't they all,' the same woman smiles warmly.

'Living army?' Bearded Stone clings onto his suspicious countenance, unlike his affable brother who has already sat down to stare at us with interest.

'I'm joking,' Lani smiles, 'it's just a private joke between us, but er… anyway, so…what do you think about coming with us?' She asks brightly, 'of course, your wives are more than welcome too, and we can take any personal possessions you want.'

'Wives?' The lady who spoke first smiles and looks at bearded Stone and affable Stone in confusion.

'They think we're brothers,' affable Stone replies.

'Er,' Lani glances at me.

'Sorry, you said you're both Doctor Stone,' I ask.

'We are,' affable Stone says, 'we're married…' he pauses while we stare back blankly, 'to each other…we're married to each other…in a relationship? Married? I took Heathcliff's name and became Doctor Stone too.'

'Oh,' I nod slowly feeling the crimson blush spread across my cheeks, 'right…yes…not brothers…yeah, I thought the pictures were a bit weird for brothers…' shit, I can't believe I just said that.

'Of course, my mistake entirely,' Paula rescues me, 'I shouldn't have assumed anything, please accept my apologies.'

'Don't worry,' affable Stone replies, 'you're not the first.'

'So, you are Heathcliff?' I ask beardy who nods seriously, and bristles his beard in a magnificent way.

'Andrew,' affable Stone smiles, 'nice to meet you.'

'And you…er…' I look to the two women and hesitate before I put my foot in it again.

'Well, I suppose I should do the introductions,' Heathcliff says, 'this is Doctor Anne Carlton and Doctor Lisa Franklin.'

'And no,' Anne, the lady who spoke to us says with a smile, 'we're not Lesbians.'

'No, of course, not…' I gabble, 'I mean…you know…like, it wouldn't matter if you were, but you're not so…yeah, really I didn't think you were just because of the er…I mean um…'

'Howie,' Lani snaps.

'Roger, shutting up,' I nod and blush even more.

'Four doctors?' Paula takes over, as smooth as anything, 'all medical doctors?'

'We are,' Heathcliff replies stiffly.

'Do you specialise?' She asks.

'I am a senior consultant for orthopaedics,' Heathcliff gives his title in a pompous way.

'Oh, give it a rest, Cliff,' Andrew sighs, 'anyone can see they are who they say they are, come in,' he waves an arm at us, 'do you want to sit down? Something to drink? Your fellows outside can come in too... although I don't think we have enough seats for everyone.'

'No, no,' I wave him back, 'they'll be fine. Listen, we understand your suspicions, and you are right to be that way but, as we said outside, we need doctors, and one of our team said it was likely you didn't believe us, but I have been bitten several times,' I explain quickly, looking to each of them in turn, 'Lani was the first, she was actually turned...she became one of them, but she recovered...I've been bitten loads but... nothing, same with the dog and Cookey outside.'

'Not possible,' Cliff announces promptly.

'Entirely possible, Cliff,' Anne cuts him off, 'we've been stuck in here for god knows how long, and we don't know a damned thing...'

'I love you dearly, Cliff,' Andrew says softly, 'but let them speak, please...go on,' he nods at me.

'That's it,' I shrug, 'we don't know anything...well, no...there is more to tell, a whole lot more but er...that's not for now.'

'Oh, I think it is,' Andrew, despite the affable nature shows what a great communicator he is, 'we're all doctors and used to cutting through the waffle...and you need our help more than we need yours...' he smiles warmly, putting me at rest.

'The short version, please,' Lani warns me.

So, I do the short version. Running through it as quickly as possible. Paula listens as intently as they do, and I realise how used to her I've become already and forget she hasn't been with us the whole time. Midway through and Clarence is at the door, worrying that we're taking too long, and checking on us. He comes in, nodding hello's and resting his frame against the kitchen doorway while I finish off.

'Indeed, yes...indeed,' Cliff remarks while rocking on his heels, 'indeed,' he repeats, 'a veritable tale of woe and dastardly doings...'

'Ignore my husband,' Andrew sighs mildly, 'he does this when he's anxious.'

'I am not anxious, Andrew.'

'Course not, Cliff...well, Doctors? What do you make of that?'

'I'd say it's a pity none of us specialised in diseases or viruses,' Anne quips, 'you remember much about biology, Andrew?'

'Fraid not, Annie,' Andrew sighs. Real doctors. I'm in a room with real doctors. Unflappable, cynical, jaded and the intelligence is pouring off them.

'Well, yes...may I make a suggestion?' Heathcliff asks his group.

'Please do,' Anne replies languidly.

'I would suggest we examine our patients, as a group, and draw our conclusions from what we can see for ourselves. Have we got our bags here?'

'You know we do, Cliff,' Anne tuts, 'you told us to bring them...and then you checked we had them when we arrived. Forgive our laconic tones,' she says to us, 'we're NHS you see, tired, overworked and over-stressed...'

'We have just had fifteen days off though,' Lisa remarks for the first time, 'which is a darn sight more than we normally get at once.'

'True,' Andrew nods.

'You seem to have coped well enough,' I say, 'I mean, you all look well, healthy, clean...the house is in order...far better than most we've seen anyway.'

'Many hands make light work,' Andrew smiles.

'Or too many cooks spoil the broth,' Heathcliff grumbles into his beard.

'Examinations,' Lisa is on her feet and moving into action, 'I'll get the bags, we doing them together or apart?'

'The bitten ones together I would say, the rest can be done apart,' Andrew replies, 'do you want to get your chaps in then,' he looks over, 'take them into the front room and we'll go from there.'

Lisa squeezes past Clarence heading into the hallway while Andrew and Anne make for the sink to start a thorough hand scrubbing process. Heathcliff rocks on his heels then hooks his thumbs into the hoops of his corduroy trousers, 'yes,' he intones, 'let's get you examined.'

'You bring them in,' I say to the other three, 'I'll go first and for god's sake tell the lads to behave themselves.'

'They will,' Clarence rumbles.

'They never do,' Lani corrects.

'Oh, and er...remind them about appropriate use of humour.'

'Oh, shit yes,' Lani turns to me with a look of horror, 'I'll get Dave to tell them.'

I feel more nervous of Cookey and Blowers saying something awful than I do about being examined by four doctors at the same time. What if they make a gay joke or start swearing about bumming each other? Oh, shit...this has got disaster written all over it.

'Our lads,' I cough into my hand, 'they're er...quite young, you know...young squaddies with a er...strong sense of humour.'

'Good,' Heathcliff finally gives me a big toothy smile, 'healthy young lads having a good old joke about, full of japes and spirit. Best coping mechanism known to mankind, humour that is. Keep you on your toes, do they?'

'Could say that,' I nod, but feel my stomach getting ready to drop out my arse.

'And you're in charge, are you? Good,' Heathcliff smiles knowingly, 'what regiment were you in?'

'The Tesco regiment,' why did I say that? 'I mean, I worked for Tesco...night manager.'

'Good,' Heathcliff nods, 'well, off with it then,' he nods at my clothes, 'can't do an examination with your clobber on, can we old chap?'

I nod and strip, hesitating when I get to my boxer shorts and deciding to leave them on, figuring it would be less embarrassing to be told to take them off than put them back on.

'Right, everyone see okay?' Lisa says from behind me. I turn, slightly startled at not hearing her enter the room, 'bags are here, I got yours and Cliff's from the cupboard, hope you don't mind Andrew.'

'Not at all, Lisa...right then...let's have a look shall we.'

Three doctors stalk towards me while one bearded man stands back rocking on his heels while thumbing his trousers and looking benevolent with a possibly misconstrued notion that he is in charge.

The front door opens, feet traipsing in. No jokes, no banter. Dave must have scared the hell out of them, either that or he's walking behind Cookey with a knife drawn.

The door swings in as Meredith decides she doesn't like being separated and greets the new people with much wagging of tail.

'She's friendly,' I say quickly at the looks of alarm.

'Been in the wars I would say,' Heathcliff drops into a crouch to rub her head, 'oh yes…hmmm…let me see,' he starts to inspect her wounds and cuts, parting the hair to check the newer ones since her hair was cut to clean the old ones. She puts up with it, happily panting away while getting loads of attention.

Muttered comments, low voices, and torches get shone in my eyes, nose, ears and mouth. My reflexes are tested, blood pressure taken and all the basics before they even start on the many wounds, cuts, bites and bruises that cover my upper body.

'Definitely a bite…teeth marks…adult bite, without doubt, blunt teeth…' Lisa comments.

'Same here,' Andrew checks another one, 'is the skin opened on yours?'

'Oh, without doubt, incision to the skin, blood loss, without doubt… must have hurt, Mr Howie,' she says to me.

'Not at the time.'

'Really? Adrenalin pumping was it?'

'Something like that, er…listen, I did mention it before but er…well, I had a human heart shoved in my mouth too.' That gets their attention, 'in a fight, close-quarter fighting.…er…it ripped the heart from the chest of an infected, and pushed it straight into my mouth…it was still beating,' I add flatly, but still feel more worried the lads are going to be unable to not say anything stupid.

'You swallowed it?' Anne asks me promptly, 'the blood from the heart, you swallowed it?'

'Oh, without doubt…and a thumb too, I think…I definitely bit one-off, but I don't recall spitting it out…oh, and er…I bit into a neck too, or throat to be precise…er, ripped it out with my teeth, and…' my voice trails off as I realise what I must sound like. The psychopath invited into their safe home.

'You appear as healthy as can be,' Andrew steps back to stare at me with interest, 'and no effects from the infection? None at all?'

'Nothing, Lani turned…we all saw it, but…she came back, but Cookey and I had no reaction. When Cookey was bit, er…Lani and I cut our hands,' I show them the mark across my own palm from Dave's knife, 'and we er, we rubbed our blood into his wound…could that have helped?'

'God…' Andrew blanches, 'er…'

'Fast-acting if it did,' Anne says looking unsure, 'this Cookey, he didn't turn then come back or anything like that? Show any signs at all?'

'None, same as me.'

'And Lani and you, had you shared bodily fluids prior to her being bitten?'

'One kiss,' I say softly, 'just one.'

'A French kiss?' She probes, 'long and passionate with tongues? We're all adults here, Mr Howie.'

'Yes, yes it was.'

'Transfer of saliva without a doubt,' Lisa remarks, 'his anti-bodies could have passed into hers and built up enough to fight the infection off, but Cookey didn't go under…are you sure he was bit?'

'We all saw it.'

'We can't do anything here,' Andrew comments, 'did you say Doctor Roberts had you collect equipment?'

'Yes, from his hospital. He gave a specific list of things…'

'We have to go,' Lisa says firmly.

'Agreed,' Andrew nods.

'Examine the rest here or at their fort?' Anna asks.

'Quick check here then a thorough exam at the fort,' Heathcliff says giving me an impression that maybe he is in charge after all as the others all immediately accept his order, 'not a vet,' he says standing up, 'but been around dogs all my life and she looks fine, wounds are healing naturally, no signs of infection. Gums are clear, what's her stools like?'

'Stools? You mean her poo?'

'Yes, firm are they or all runny?'

'Er, firm...well, the lads give her treats all bloody day long so she does get a bit runny, but mostly firm...I think, er, better check with Nick, he sort of...oh no, she's Dave's dog now...shit, I'll find out.'

'Get dressed, Mr Howie,' Andrew says in a perfect tone of a doctor, which is good seeing as he is a doctor, 'we'll check your lot over in the front room, quick visual and then we'll get ready, that okay with you?'

'Anything you say,' I nod quickly wishing I could run ahead and swear pain of death on Cookey and Blowers if they so much as look at each other.

As it turns out, whatever Dave said to them worked. Cookey, Blowers, Nick and even Jagger and Mo Mo were all full of pleases and thank-yous with not a swear word or gay joke uttered, not any jokes, about anything. The only delay is caused by Roy who gets a rather excited look in his eyes at having four doctors so close at hand and insists on a private consultation with does take a while.

Examinations complete and we wait about while they gather the essentials of what they need, and hand them over for packing in our vans where we get loaded up and with the day rapidly running out, we start the journey back to find the Saxon and head home for the fort.

25

D ay Fifteen.

Afternoon.

LEAVING IS SUCH SWEET SORROW. WHO SAID THAT? YOU KNOW, I REALLY cannot recall right now. But leaving was not sweet sorrow at all, there was nothing sweet about it. It was gut-wrenching, and I am not ashamed to admit I not only had a lump in my throat, but more than a few fat tears rolling down my face.

My home for the last six months and from that place, I prepared for what I knew to be the single greatest threat to our species. I was a scientist, a researcher. Yes, I was renowned in my field for my understanding and extrapolation of data relating to the effect of global trends on the world population zones, and it was that expertise that led me to be involved with the exercise at The Facility, but in no way did I ever imagine that what they proposed we research, was in fact a reality.

But that history is in my notes that I have left behind in my den. I came to *think of it as my den due to the somewhat snug and contained nature of the bowl like effect of the land around it. In a depression surrounded by thick woodland, but with enough open space to do as I needed. And now, the time has come to move on, I realise just how attached I became.*

The man that left just a short time ago is not the man that arrived there those six months prior. I was still shocked and full of disbelief, denial, rage and then melancholy, deep melancholy that I suppose, these days would be called clinical depression.

Along with my history, I left my guide. All the notes and preparations I have made while I myself prepared for this time. What good it may do someone I know not, but should a passer-by happen upon them, they may save his or her life.

The final preparations were made. The hens were left out of their boxes and free to roam. Their sacks of feed, I split open with a knife, and they will have enough to eat for a long time to come. My camera feeds I simply shut down; the generators were switched off. The remaining dry foods, goods and tinned food-stuffs were placed off the ground and safe.

The M4 automatic rifle is with me, custom foldable stock, shortened barrel and a horrible weapon that I detest, like I detest all weapons. But it is reliable, accurate, and small enough to handle, and it cost me enough to obtain along with plenty of ammunition. Hopefully, I shall not need it, but just having it gives me a greater degree of confidence.

Brushes for Jess, water bottles, high-calorie food, a first-aid kit and that's it, my intention to travel light and forage as we go. Having Jess is a godsend. Just being with another being, and one as intelligent as a horse has helped me enor-mously. She is quieter than a vehicle, far more reliable, and doesn't run out of fuel, plus her four-wheel-drive capability is much better than most vehicles too.

I walked her out of the barn, across the field and through the forest, following the narrow trails until we reached the edge of the heathland. Only then did I mount, and it was that final act of climbing onto her broad, strong back that it hit me. And like I said, the lump in the throat and the tears came freely for a while. Jess senses my discomfort, tossing her head back and forth, and I could tell she wanted to canter and run, but this isn't training or exercise now, this was the real deal. Out into the world and every act has to be judged, assessed, weighed up, and a decision made based on all the known facts.

At a brisk trot, we crossed the heathland and into the rolling meadows until we reached the arable farmed land and soon the country lanes that led us on a winding and somewhat circumventing route to the main town where we arrived at the northern point, near to that flat-roofed ugly building for the national tyre depot or whatever it's bloody called, ugly buildings they are. Quick to build and low maintenance but my god, what an eyesore. No wonder depression was so rife throughout this country when we were surrounded by such ugly, functioning buildings.

It did occur to me that this was the first time Jess and I had ventured, armed and ready, into the world, for we had remained wholly within the confines of our den and immediate land, and once the dismay at leaving our den had passed, I did rather grin quite broadly at riding a horse into town with a 9mm pistol on my belt and an automatic weapon encased within a specially made sheath fixed to the saddle. Like a cowboy from old, except I don't have a cowboy hat or those awful leather trousers they put on over their denims and thank god too.

The town was as expected. Flooded, filthy, barren and devoid of life. The river, as suspected, had burst her banks, and sent a tributary through the main centre. Deep it was too, deep and remarkably still with objects floating serenely by that gave the whole area a calm feeling, until I realised, they were bodies, dead bodies. Fat, bloated corpses with straggly hair and limbs that look like so pale and stick-like. The sight was shocking, far more shocking then I realised it would be.

I watched my camera feeds when it happened and sat crying into my hands at the sight of so many people being ripped apart, but I was still detached and safely away from it. I knew it was happening real-time, and what I was seeing was the reality of the situation. But there was no audio and without the sounds, I was still apart from it.

But being in the town was something else. It was quiet, so quiet. Birds chirping, water gurgling softly. If you closed your eyes you could be somewhere perfectly lovely. One of the worst sights was the top of a white coloured car floating in the water. The incessant rain from yesterday, the howling winds, and violent storm still hadn't been enough to cleanse the bloodstains from it. They were stark, red, congealed and very upsetting. Jess didn't like it either and was soon snorting with impatience to be away from there.

We used the less flooded side streets and in my mind, I saw a map of Great Britain and within that map I saw blue veins, and the spaghetti type appearance of our many rivers, streams, brooks that all feed into the lakes and reservoirs. Those same reservoirs and lakes that supply the water to the treatment plants that are meant to cleanse the water with chemicals such as fluoride. Without operational staff within those treatment plants, the water will still flow but alas, it shall not be treated. The end product? Contaminated water that comes out of the still-working taps, and I can only hope people are not foolish enough to still be drinking from them.

We walked slowly past empty ruined buildings. Windows smashed, doors ripped off, and more than once I saw human remains within the properties. The air is cleaner that it was, but the stench of death was hanging in the listless air, and such a foul stench too. Why haven't the rats eaten all this spare flesh?

I think, in retrospect, that having the opportunity to see the town like that helped to cement my mind-set and harden me to the dangers to come. I didn't see a single person, not a human or an infected person. Nothing. Nobody. Just the clip-clop of Jess's hooves and the snorts from her nose.

We navigated the town, moving away from the houses, shops and businesses until we were well away, and deep within the countryside. We've only been going a couple of hours, but the heat is high, and we've stopped in the shade of a huge oak tree where I can sit peacefully and calm my nerves before we move on.

Writing this journal helps enormously. It gives me a method to put my thoughts into order and deal with the emotions I am experiencing.

Well, Jess is rubbing her nose against my neck so I will take that as a signal that it is time to go.

NB

26

G aps are filled from the memories and knowledge of Andrew Jackson who did not lie. He was there. He was a part of the research, but his part was tiny and only from being present during so many tests and experiments did he garner such information.

The Facility. That's what they called it. A complex deep within a mountain range, but even the specific location of its birthplace is still unknown to the infection. Many people played a part in the beginning, and the names of a few are now known. But yet, they did not all know what they were planning. The infection understands this.

There was a plan, a mission to accomplish but that changed. Why? Why did the original mission objectives change?

The memory of the human mind holds vast, almost limitless information. Everything the host has done from birth to death is within that small lump of grey matter. Billions of hosts. Each with a brain. Each with every event in their lives recorded and stored. Most had no concept of what they possessed within their own heads, and not one was able to display full memory recall of every event ever to be partaken by them. Every word uttered, not just from their mouths, but from those around them. Every face they passed on their way through life. Every fact they learned. Every bit of knowledge they stored. Every lesson. Every emotion. Everything.

The infection uses those same memories to develop a method to seize and sift through every single one of those data points. Seize and sift. Seize the memory, sift through it. Note the worth and either store or discard.

The host could replay memories almost at will. A host could be reading a book late at night in their beds or sat on a bus travelling to work. They could have been in a quiet place during their lunchtime break. They could have held a paperback, hardback or even a digital e-reader. They could stare at the letters forming words across the screen. They could compute and understand not only each word as it appears but the context and understanding of each word within that sentence, they could capture the essence of the fable, story or prose and along with the words, they could create a mental image that replayed within their imagination as the story was told. How? How could they do that? How could they take words, and use them to create such a playback from a purely fictitious thing that had never existed? How did they replay real-life events? How did they attach emotions to each of them?

There is no video player, no monitor within the head that can be used for playback, just neural pathways that pulse with electricity. The infection learns to embed within the tissue so deep, so organically naturally that it learns to see the memories the same way the hosts saw them. Once it understood the concept of sight, sound, scent and feel, it could understand each emotion the host attached to each memory. It learnt to understand what were the base emotions attached by the host, and discard them for they were nothing more than intrinsic behaviours formed in accordance with the society, culture and civilisation that it was within.

It learnt to see how each host tricked itself with false memories, and that was an important step in the evolution. Not all you see is truth. Not all you hear is real. These hosts are full of these false memories, convincing themselves of facts and events that never truly happened. Billions upon billions of them. Trillions. Numbers so vast that these hosts had yet to invent words to represent them.

But the infection is the sum of its parts and is within each and every cell of each and every host, and by seizing and sifting, it gathers the information, and begins to understand where it came from.

A memory of a face within the grey matter of Andrew Jackson. A name now to attach to that face. A name used by many thousands of other hosts across this

planet yet each one of them has a different appearance, and a unique cell struc-
ture that forms their DNA. Those hosts with the memories of those names are
scoured, seized and sifted. Cross-comparisons of facial images, tones of voice
and the many other nuances that create a host are processed and slowly, gradu-
ally, the names of those involved are wittered down. The parts they played. The
locations they are known to be.

AT THE SAME TIME AS THE INFECTION BEGINS TO STUDY ITS OWN ORIGINS, IT
tries the same methods with those that must be stopped.

The infection knows Howie. It knows Lani and Cookey. It knows every
member of that team. It knows them from the memories of every host it
possesses that ever-had contact with them, but it doesn't have them, and it is for
that reason that they must be stopped at any cost.

D ay Two

'Gregori,' the boy looks up from his bowl of cereal holding the spoon laden with milk bloated puffs of rice. Gregori turns from the window and looks at the boy. The boy who slept soundly and woke with no greater display of emotion than that of any other boy waking in the morning. No tears. No sobbing. No wailing for his mummy or daddy. 'Are we staying here?' The question is asked lightly, from a voice that is yet to form anywhere near adulthood. Blond hair with startling blue eyes and a light tan that coats his smooth skin, the boy looks like any golden-haired healthy boy from any magazine, television advert or movie.

'No.'

The boy pushes the spoon into his mouth, and crunches slowly for a few seconds as Gregori turns back to staring out of the window.

'Where are we going?' The boy asks before taking another spoonful. Should boys ask questions like this? Shouldn't he be crying or so shocked that it renders him silent? He asks the question like he asks what activity they will do today.

'We look for...' Gregori thinks for the right words, his grasp of English is good but slow, 'new family...'

Silence. The chink of the spoon against the bowl. The dribble of milk spilling from the spoon back into the Rice Krispies. No movement outside, and Gregori shifts position to peer further down the street. Quiet and empty. Where did they all go?

'Are you going to Albananian?'

'Albania.'

'Are you going to Albanana?'

'Albania.'

'Are you going to Albanania?'

'...No...Yes...'

'Are your family in Albananian?'

'Albania. No.'

'Where are they?'

'No. No family.'

'Where did they go? Did they die like mummy?'

Gregori snatches a quick glance, the question was as lightly asked as the others. *Did they die like mummy?*

'No.'

'Well, where did they go then?'

'Yes. They die.'

'Like mummy? Did the people eat them, and make them monsters too?'

'...Yes.' Gregori swallows and crosses the floor to take up the mug of coffee from the kitchen table where the boy sits.

'Oh,' the boy nods, swinging his feet under the table he focusses hard to load his spoon up and lift it ready for the eating, 'did you see them?'

'...No.'

'How do you know they are monsters then?'

'I know.'

'Where are the new family?'

Gregori shrugs non-committal and aloof. The boy's questions disturb his thoughts, yet the boy is strange. Very strange.

'Well,' the boy looks up, 'how will we find them?'

'We look.' Unsettled is his mind. Why take the boy? Why save him when so many died? Why him? It was a rash act and done from instinct, but that instinct is gone now. Leave him. Leave him here and head south. 'We go soon,' he says instead.

The boy thinks hard with a frown that delves down, giving him an overly serious expression, 'but…' he stops and thinks, takes another spoonful of Rice Krispies, eats them slowly, swallows and tries again, 'do they have a house?'

Gregori looks towards the boy, but his eyes move left thinking quickly before he looks back at the boy and shrugs.

'Will we have our own bedrooms?'

Gregori takes his turn at frowning, 'not we…' he grumbles, 'you…'

'But you don't have a family,' the boy replies, 'we can share.'

'No.'

'Will you find a family?'

'No.'

'Why?'

'We go now.'

'Now?'

'Yes. Now.' He fixes the boy with a glare, hoping the hard look will quell him into silence, but the boy stares back with an open face, 'we go,' Gregori growls, 'now.' Gregori can see the boy's eyes roving over his ugly features, taking in his big nose, bulging eyes and pock-marked skin. The open gaze full of curiosity yet intense makes his eyes twitch, and his upper lip flick up with a sign of aggression. Get rid of the boy. Leave him. Shoot him. Do anything but be rid.

'Do you want some Rice Krispies?' The boy asks softly, 'they're really nice.'

'No. We go. Now.'

'Do you have Rice Krispies in Alabamia?'

'Albania. No…I don't know…'

'What do you like for breakfast?'

'I...'

'Do you have Coca Pops?'

'We go. We go now.'

'I like sugar puffs too, and sometimes toast with marmalade?'

Gregori stands quickly, and without thinking he marches to the sink where he rinses the mug out, placing it neatly on the drainer. 'We go.' He repeats.

'Okay,' the boy slips off the chair, and carries his bowl to the sink where he holds it up with two hands presenting it to Gregori, 'mummy said I'm too young to wash the dishes,' he explains, 'she said I might burn myself.'

Gregori takes the bowl, rinses and plonks it next to the mug on the drainer. Turning around he finds the boy already at the front door opening the lock as he pulls the handle down.

'No!' Gregori hisses, charging across the room he barges the boy aside from the open door, pistols in hand, and he strides out ready to fire. Silence greets him. Silence and a gorgeous sunny day with a clear deep blue sky.

'They're not here,' the boy giggles at the sight of Gregori holding his pistols out up and raised to the sides, 'they've gone away...away...gone away...gone, gone, gone away away, away,' he sings and skips down the path to the big wrought iron gate.

'Wait,' shoving the pistols away Gregori runs after the boy, grabbing him roughly by the back of the teddy bear pyjamas, 'you wait. You no go without me. You wait,' pushing his face close to the boy, he delivers the order in a low menacing hiss. Again, the boy stares up at him with an open expression, blinking slowly he waits patiently without a word being spoken.

'Wait,' Gregori nods, 'I first...you not first.'

The boy nods. Gregori lets him go and quickly opens the gate, stepping out smoothly to check both sides, and all around while listening intently.

'They're not here,' the boy whispers.

'You not know this.'

'They're not here,' the boy repeats, 'they all went away.'

'How you know this? You small. You not see.'

The boy thinks again. Frowning gently before stepping out into the street, 'they're not here,' he replies.

The Albanian goes left, pistols held ready down at his sides. Having already considered the knives, he selected the guns in favour of not knowing what to expect, and if the daytime presents a greater target or risk.

The street is in disarray, a few bodies in the distance, visible only as slumped figures on the surface of the road. Some windows broken, but lots of blood with some already congealed sticky dark pools. He realises the boy is not with him and stops to look around, spotting the boy still stood outside the entrance to the house.

'We have to go this way,' the boy points to the opposite direction Gregori walks in. Gregori grimaces, squinting in the strong sunshine while he takes in the small child from the distance he has already taken. Walk away. The voice in his head is strong, urging him to do what he always does and go it alone.

'This way,' he inclines his head, expecting the boy to come after him, but the boy shakes his head, and starts off in the other direction. Barefoot and wearing the teddy bear pyjamas, he walks without looking back. Gregori blanches blinks hard and starts after him, striding briskly to catch up.

'Why?' He barks at the boy.

'Because it's the way,' the boy states as though the answer should be obvious.

'What way?' Gregori struggles to understand the energy the boy gives off. Not fearless as in reckless although he certainly displayed that when he tried to defend his mother. Not feckless or stupid either, the boy is clearly intelligent. Something else.

'Away from them, silly,' the boy giggles. Gregori turns to stare down at the empty street behind him.

'We go,' tucking the pistols away, he takes hold of the boy's hand and starts back in the direction he first took.

The boy trots along seemingly happy until Gregori becomes aware he is still holding his hand. It was one thing to carry the boy last night, but to hold his hand now? He lets go, quickly jerking his hand free, and casting a distasteful look down at boy who carries on without any regard.

'What's that?' The boy points to the distance.

'Is fire,' Gregori had already noted the thick black smudge rising high into the air above the city centre.

'What's on fire?'

'Everything.'

'Silly! *Everything* can't be on fire…is that man sleeping?'

'No. Dead.'

'Why?'

'He talk too much.'

'Why?'

'Quiet.'

'Why?' The boy whispers.

'No speak.'

'I'm whispering.'

'No noise.'

'…What's on fire?'

'Everything. Be quiet.'

'Are there houses on fire?'

'Yes. No speak.'

'Will the firemen come and use their hoses?'

'No.'

'Why?'

'They dead.'

'Who will use the hoses?'

'Nobody.'

'Why?'

'They all dead.'

'We're not dead. We can use the hoses.'

'No.'

'Why?'

'No speak. Quiet.'

'…Why can't we speak?'

'Listen. We listen. We no speak.'

The boy looks around, 'there's nothing to listen,' he says confidently.

'You speak and I kill you.'

'Why.'

'No speak or I shoot you.'

'Are the cars on fire?'

'Yes. I shoot you. With gun.'

'Are there people in the houses and the cars that are on fire?'

'Yes. I have gun. I shoot you.'

'Will they get burned?'

'Yes. And I shoot you. In the face.'

'Gregoreee…do people melt when they get the fire?'

'Yes. I make you on fire. No speak.'

'Have you ever been on fire?'

'No. I make you on fire. I shoot you. I kill you. You die. Shut up.'

'Are there children on the fire in the houses and the cars?'

'Yes. Children that speak.'

'Will the children melt?'

'Yes.'

'What about dogs and cats? Will they melt or…'

'Everything die.'

'What about goldfish? Goldfish live in water. Water doesn't get on fire because they have water in the hoses.'

'They die. I shoot them. I shoot you.'

'When will there not be a fire?'

'No speak.'

'Can we go see the fire?'

'No speak.'

'Are my new family on the fire?'

'No. Yes if you speak.'

'Why?'

'No speak.'

'Are you a daddy?'

'No.'

'Do you have a daddy?'

'No.'

'Where is your daddy?'

'He die. I shoot him. He speak.'

'Do you have a big brother or a little sister?'

'No. I shoot them. They speak.'

'Who made the fire?'

'No speak.'

'Did the monsters make the fire?'

'Yes.'

'Did mummy make the fire?'

'...I not know this.'

'Mummy said fire was danger.'

'Be quiet. You are boy. You be quiet and no speak. You speak, and I give you to monsters.'

'Is my new family with the monsters?'

'No. Yes if you speak.'

'Why are we going this way? The monsters are this way? Is my family this way?'

'No monsters here. No speak. I kill the new family if you speak.'

'Gregoreee, will I have a sister?'

'I not know. I kill sister. You speak more, and I kill sister and brother and dog. I shoot them.'

'What dog is it?'

'No dog.'

'You said sister and brother, and dog. Is it a black dog?'

'No dog.'

'Brown dog?'

'No dog.'

'Is it a big dog that goes woof woof?'

'No. I shoot dog.'

'What is my brother's name?'

'I not...be quiet.'

'Is he a big brother or a little brother?'

'No brother. No sister. No dog. No speak.'

'But...'

'No speak.'

'Gregoreee....'

'No speak.'

'Gregoreee!' The boy giggles with delight.

'No speak. No funny. I shoot you. See gun...I shoot you,' Gregori pulls one of the pistols to show the boy.

'Is that a gun?'

Gregori stops, stares at the pistol then at the boy, and keeps on walking with a shake of the head, 'yes, is gun. I shoot you.'

'Does it go bang bang or bang bang bang?'

'It go...one of the bang. It go one bang, and the bullet it come out and go in your head. and you die. You. You boy. You die when I shoot you when you speak.'

'Make it go bang.'

'No. I make bang when I kill you.'

'Make it go bang, Gregoree...'

'No.'

'Gregoreee...make it go bang...please...please Gregoreeee.'

'Gregori. Not Gregoreeeeeeeeee. Gregori.'

'Make it go bang.'

'Be quiet.'

'Make it go bang.'

'Boy. Shut mouth. Shut mouth now.'

'Make it go bang. Gregoreee...please Gregoree, please...make it go bang....'

A twitch of his finger, and the huge retort booms out from the pistol to echo and roll about the street. The second it's done Gregori curses himself feeling a rush of emotions of stupidity and anger. A gun shot in such a quiet place will be heard for miles.

Scanning the sides, the rear and in front, he holds still with mouth open to stretch the ear canal, and thereby increase the power of his hearing. The boy kept on. He kept on, and it was an involuntary reflex. A stupid thing done to shut the boy up and scare him with the big noise. But the boy looks delighted and stared open-mouthed in awe at the pistol held by Gregori.

'Can I try?'

'Shut up,' Gregori hisses, grabbing the boy around the back of the neck he marches him roughly forward, 'no speak…'

'Gregoreee…'

'Shut up. Shut up now,' the venom in his voice is full of violence and threat, leaving no doubt that he means what he says.

'Gregoreee…'

He drops to a crouch, and pulls the boy in close with a big hand wrapped around the back of the boy's neck, hard eyes glare deep and menacingly, 'you speak, and I leave you…'

'They're coming,' the boy whispers. Gregori's eyes widen, his nostrils flare. Movement in his peripheral vision. He's upright, pistol raised and ready as he takes aim on the solitary figure at the end of the street. It moves slowly, very slowly. Stiff legged, head lolling left and right, forward and back. No cohesion, spasmodic and jerky. Eyes narrowing now, and another shuffles into view behind the first, another then another. More of them, and they shuffle and stagger until they fill the end of the road but moving so slowly.

Gregori holds position, waiting for them to charge. Something has changed. Something is different. Why are they going slow? The energy is different too.

'They're slow now,' the boy announces to Gregori who glances down then back up, 'until night-time.'

'How you know this?' Gregori whispers, 'how? How you know this? How you know they coming here?'

'Can I have a go on the gun now?'

'You tell me,' Gregori drops into the crouch again, staring hard into the boy's blue eyes, 'how?'

'I dunno,' the boy giggles, 'I just know, silly!'

What is going on? Why does the boy speak in riddles? For a second, he contemplates striking the boy across the face and making him speak, but something holds his hand back from lashing out. He turns to watch the things stagger and stalk ever closer, but so slowly and with such a lack of coordination they stumble and fall into each other.

'Oh no,' the boy says with shock, 'I didn't take my shoes…mummy said I have to have shoes on when I play outside.'

'We go,' Gregori starts back the way they came, moving quickly then stopping to run back and pull the boy along who stares down at his filthy feet, 'we go.'

'Gregoreee, can we go back for my shoes?'

'No.'

'But mummy said…'

'We get other shoe. We go. We go now. Move…'

Heading in the direction the boy said they should go, the Albanian hitman glances back at the horde behind as though expecting them to be charging. He watches the road ahead; he takes in the sides in perpetual motion of constant scanning and assessment. He checks behind but more than that, he casts fleeting glances down at the strange boy.

28

'There she is!' Blowers calls out from behind me when the Saxon comes into view standing proud and solitary in the position she was left on the motorway. The miles driven since collecting the doctors were light-hearted at first with a feeling that we had finally accomplished something. Blowers and Cookey bantered and made jokes about how Dave had threatened them all if they spoke without being spoken to and even, they were to say please, thank you, and nothing else. But it came back. That feeling of being out of control, of lagging behind in the race for survival. That we're still not doing enough and not doing it fast enough. We've got doctors, but the day is running out, and we've still got no ammunition for our assault rifles, and no supplies for the fort and the people within.

My hands go from holding the steering wheel in a relaxed manner to gripping it with ever whitening knuckles as the pressure grows inside me. The headache comes back, dull at first but soon it's pounding across the back of my skull, and my heart starts beating faster like I'm about to fight. Adrenalin coursing into my system, but it goes unused and starts making my legs tremble, my mouth goes dry, so dry I have to cough before I can ask for one of the lads to pass me some water.

Four doctors. Not one but four. We did a simple thing and went from house to house until we found them. No big battle. No big fight. No treachery or trickery. Professional health care workers with vast experience in the field of medicine. Having them with us is a major step in the right direction, so why do I feel like this? What's going on?

It was too easy. Too simple. There must be something wrong, something bad about to happen. The drive is uneventful and with the fog lifted, we find the route with ease, letting Roy work us back to the motorway and the Saxon waiting for us.

'You two take the van,' I give the instruction to the lads behind me. The doctors are traveling in Clarence's van which we figured would be safer from any gay jokes made by Cookey.

My mood has plummeted again too. Darker and deeper than before. An anger bubbles away just below the surface. I want to find Marcy and get answers, I want to do it now. Truth be told, I want to run from this lot and be alone. Just me, and Dave of course, but that disturbs me too as I'm starting to think of Dave as an extension of myself, that he is a part of me, and several times I catch myself thinking he is imaginary like something my mind has made up to get me through all this.

Sarah said I was becoming something else. She said I was enjoying it, that I wanted to kill them, that I was becoming addicted to it. I'm not. I'm not. Am I? What if I am?

It isn't discussed now that Dave would come with me to take the Saxon back. It's *assumed* and as natural as drawing breath. He's always there, beside me, watching, watchful, ever watchful, and ever ready.

Wordlessly, we get into the vehicle and check her over before closing the doors and getting into our seats, and again I'm puzzled. Why did they leave her here untouched? I would have ruined her, stripped her to bits, and made it impossible to fix, but they've left her alone. She is a vehicle, an inert and inanimate object that does not have feeling or sense. But she's also a tool that has proved to be truly remarkable in our quest to stay alive.

I wave the others to go past me and start the slow turn, tucking in behind the last van to bring up the rear. Could we do it alone?

'Yes.'

'You think?'

'Yes, Mr Howie.'

'What would they do?'

'Survive.'

'Without us? Without you?'

'It's not me they need, Mr Howie. It's you.'

'We would have all been killed a long time ago if not for you, Dave. And by saying that you're saying *that they do* need us.'

He goes silent, thoughtful for a second, 'you are right,' he says slowly which is strange as his manner of speaking never changes, 'we stay as a team.'

'You say that like it's a decision made.'

'Isn't it?'

'Is it?'

'It's your decision, Mr Howie. You lead.'

'What is your advice?'

'To lead as you see fit but stay as a team.'

'Maybe it's me that keeps putting them at risk? If the infection wants me and will stop at nothing to get me...then maybe me being somewhere else gives them a chance to survive in a...'

'There was a mission,' he interrupts me which again is exceptionally rare for him, but then pauses again, and looks out the window to the passing scenery, 'there were other missions too,' he continues, 'that we took out more than the primary target to ensure a successful outcome.'

'I don't understand, Dave.'

'The infection wouldn't stop...it won't stop targeting the others if you leave, but it will kill them easier without your leadership.'

'That's not fair,' muttering darkly, I breathe a long exhalation out through my nose, 'really not fair.'

'Fairness is not an issue here,' he replies, 'fairness doesn't count.'

'So, the infection will keep coming, whether I'm there or not.'

'Yes, Mr Howie.'

'How do you know that?'

'It's what I would do,' he says bluntly, 'if I couldn't get you, I would go for everything you loved or were attached to. I would destroy you from the inside out.'

'Nice.'

'But...'

'Hang on, from the inside out? Like...so, if we were to reverse that and target the infection. How would we do it?'

'We need more information before we can do that.'

'Such as?'

'Its primary objective, what it wants to achieve, and how it plans on doing it.'

'It wants to rule the world by infecting every living person, or at least it did but...but...I don't know now, I really don't. We have to find Marcy and find out what she knows.'

'What if Marcy is dead?'

'There is another option, we could try and communicate with it.'

'We can do that now,' he replies, 'stop in the next town and I'll find one.'

'Marcy first,' I nod firmly, 'we get these doctors back then we go find Marcy.'

'Okay,' he turns back to staring out the window.

'I don't want to waste time looking for ammunition or supplies for the fort. I want to do this now.'

'Okay,' he doesn't say anything for a long time, but I know Dave, and I know when he wants to add something.

'Go on,' I prompt him.

'I don't need a gun,' he says matter of fact, 'but the others do...and shotguns are not good enough.'

'So, we get ammunition then,' I sigh deeply feeling the days stretching out ahead of us as we scavenge about trying to get what we need. 'Okay...let's work this out,' gripping the steering wheel even harder, I focus the mind contained within my banging head, 'ammunition...we need ammunition, but this is England, so firearms are banned. We can go for police stations and get a few, but I'm guessing they won't hold anywhere near the amount we use...'

'No, they won't.'

'Right, so we can go for military establishments then. But...the risk is either someone has got there before us, and either emptied them or are

defending them…or…fuck knows what the other one was…er…
bollocks, my bloody head is killing me…bullets…where do they come
from?'

'Magazines.'

'I know that,' I sigh again, 'where do the magazines come from?'

'The stores.'

'Fuck's sake, Dave. Where do the army get them from?'

'Filling factories.'

'Filling?'

'Yes.'

'Filling factories? Is that what they're called?'

'Yes. I just said that.'

'Where are they?'

'Filling factories?'

'No, Dave…the fucking…yes, I mean yes…where are the filling
factories? Can we go there and get the ammunition we need?'

'There were many in the war. They closed down.'

'That helps, what about now?'

'Private companies.'

'What private companies? Where?'

'I don't know, Mr Howie.'

'But…'

'Clarence might know.'

'Okay, yeah…we're almost there anyway, but that's an option, right?
We go straight to the source and get what we need.'

'They will be very secure premises.'

'Could you get in?'

'Yes, Mr Howie.' No hesitation. No doubt. A straight answer to a
straight question, and Dave is back to normal. Pity, I'm not.

The going gets slower the closer we get. The coastline being so
littered with debris from the storm that threading a way through with
three vans and the Saxon proves painfully slow and time-consuming,
especially with Roy leading the way. I fight to stay calm and resist the
urge to ram the Saxon into the back of the van in front of me or press
on the horn to hurry them up. I don't pay any attention to the scenery

either. It's all the same. Broken, damaged, beyond repair, and it means nothing to this new world or what I need to do.

Through the streets of the lanes that once bordered the bay, and I realise this is the closest area to the fort that has houses, buildings and structures. Marcy must have come here. The estate was already gone, and there was nothing else save a few marine commercial units beyond that. That gets my attention, and now I am looking out the windows trying in vain to spot her leaning out of a window and waving at me as we go past. The thought makes my heart beat harder which in turn fills me with dread, but also a desire like my mind is remembering the erotic state I was in the last time.

Shit. I have to get a grip of myself. Headaches, snappy, moody, irritable and sullen, and now I'm starting to think that seeing Marcy might be a good thing. Not a good thing, never a good thing. As Lani said, she is a rancid dirty infected whore that helped Darren kill our people. But she saved us, she saved us from our own families and friends that came out of the fort to kill us. She gave us food and drink, a hot meal and... then tried to infect us.

No. She is a resource for information, and nothing more. I love Lani. I truly do, and the emotions I feel are so extremely different. Lani is warmth, safety, light and protection. She is the glimmer of hope within this desolate world. But Marcy holds the key to finding out where we go from here. I have to find her, and I have to ignore anything that pops into my head when I do. The thoughts whirl and form while we leave the area and start navigating the final stretch into the area where the estate was.

'Mr Howie!' Dave barks when I fail to notice the van in front braking to a stop. I'm quick enough to slam my foot on the brake, but not quick enough to prevent another low-speed shunt. Which makes it our third of the day so far.

Wincing with shame I reverse back and give silent thanks that there is no one in the back. We alight from the Saxon, heading forward to spot a grinning Blowers and Cookey already out and staring at me.

'Sorry,' I mutter sheepishly.

'I'm adding all these injuries to my claim,' Cookey grips his own neck with mock injury, 'just need a lawyer now.'

'Good luck with that mate, why have we stopped?' I shout ahead to Roy.

'We're here,' he holds his hands out to the sides in a gesture of assuming I would know that. Getting past the vans I can see we are at the water's edge, and to go any further is impossible with so many obstructions poking up.

'Shit,' muttering to myself again, I realise that in our haste to leave, we took the boats with no way of Maddox or Lenski getting them back but scanning the view around us, I cannot see them anywhere.

'They're coming,' Paula shields her eyes to stare out of the water towards the looming fort in the distance. It looks amazing now with the fog lifted, and standing solitary surrounded by the calm blue waters of the sea. Majestic and proud, and far bigger than before too.

'How'd they get the boats back?' I ask.

'Is that it?' Heathcliff booms from behind us, the three other doctors close on his heels as they make their way forward.

'It is,' I reply.

'Bit different from the last time I was here,' Heathcliff remarks, 'and the sea took all this land back last night did it?' He asks the question with a hint of suspicion, that maybe we did something naughty to make the land all sink away.

'Big storm,' Clarence says, 'very big storm…you saw the boats on the land on the way here, the power was immense.'

'And Portsmouth harbour too, you say?' Heathcliff asks making me realise they must have had a conversation on the way back.

Clarence nods, 'cruise liner and a battleship, shorn the back of the battleship right off.'

'Good god,' the bearded doctor shakes his head, 'utter devastation.'

Boats in the distance coming over from the fort, the same boats we used earlier all in a row and I'm guessing they're roped together.

'We'll have to move somewhere else,' I say to the group, 'they can't land here.'

'There was a clear spot further back,' Roy offers.

'Why didn't you stop there then?' I ask him quickly, and wince inwardly at the sharp tone coming out of me.

He takes it well, nodding in apology, 'sorry, should have thought of it.'

'No...er...sorry mate, that was a bit sharp, 'I'll back up...how far back was it?'

'Oh, not far...about a minute back, on the middle bit of the bay area,' he adds helpfully.

We back up, sticking with a slow speed reverse instead of bothering to try and turn around. From the estate, we head on the narrow coast road until we reach the bay, the other side of which are the houses and area where I thought Marcy will be.

By the time we get back out and organise ourselves, the boats are into the bay and heading towards the small beach. We head down, armed up and fanning out to secure the area while keeping the doctors safely in the middle. Meredith, as normal, runs free and is straight into the cooling water to splash about, and bark excitedly at the boats getting closer, and the distinctive form of Maddox standing in the bow of the first one.

An order is given, and one by one the boats cut engines to coast gently in before the wooden hulls scrape on the soft sand underneath. Maddox jumps down into the shallows with a few of his youths all armed with shotguns.

'Howie,' he nods seriously, 'You good?'

'Fine mate, you?'

'All good,' he nods, striding out of the water to clasp hands with me, 'you got back quick, they doctors, yeah?'

'Yes mate, four of them.'

'Nice work,' he nods, a man of few words.

'Fort okay?'

'Getting there...Lenski is getting there anyway,' he grins ruefully, 'they're using one of the boats to take the bodies out further into the sea and dump them.'

'Are they weighted down?' Heathcliff interjects.

'Maddox, this is Doctor Heathcliff Stone...' I quickly introduce the other doctors and notice the ever so slight puzzled look flicker across Maddox's face at the two doctors having the same name. I think about explaining, but the moment passes and to do so now would be awkward.

'Are they weighted down?' Heathcliff repeats impatiently, 'they'll come back up with the next tide otherwise, young man.'

'Yeah, they're weighted,' Maddox says.

'What with? Rocks? Are they tied on securely? How many bodies are you taking out and are they being spread over an area? The further the better you know as...'

'Doctor,' Maddox switches to his intelligent voice with a seamless transition, 'your concerns are noted, and I am grateful for your questions, but we have noted the tidal movements of this area and the depth of the water as it shelves out towards the main shipping lane and yes, we are using whatever heavy material we can find, but also know that we can only do the best we can under the circumstances.'

Heathcliff stares in shock at the voice coming from the hard-faced youth, Andrew smirks in pleasure while the two female doctors lift eyebrows, and suddenly pay more attention to Maddox.

'Yes, well, of course, I wasn't suggesting that you were not,' Heathcliff backtracks quickly, 'my concerns were simply...ah, but here we are and are they the boats taking us to the fort?'

'They are,' Maddox nods politely, 'and because of the shallows, we are unable to bring them closer so your shoes may get wet, but,' he grins, 'it is a warm day and you will dry quickly.'

'Oh, of course,' Heathcliff beams, already won over by the hard-faced, but now charming Maddox.

'My two been good?' He directs the question at me with a glance towards Jagger and Mo Mo edging forward to be noticed by their leader.

'Perfectly mate,' I nod with sincerity, 'had a little scrap, went for a run...very good, both of them.'

'You alright staying with Mr Howie?' He asks them.

'Yeah, Mads,' Mo Mo replies, 's'cool, innit.'

'Get loaded then, you lot...get the stuff from the vans and load it up,' he barks the order to his waiting youths who have waded out the shallows onto the beach. 'Ammo?' He asks.

'Not yet, which reminds me, Clarence...where do the army get their ammunition from?'

'Filling factories,' he replies.

'Um, right but...er...do you know where they are?'

'Er, shit...some firm took over...er...a private company but well known...can't remember the name, but they did some of the helicopters and other military stuff too.'

'BAE,' Maddox interjects, 'they got the contract for British military munitions. Only one factory in the south and that's about a hundred miles north.'

'Bloody hell mate,' I give him an impressed look, 'been on Wiki then?'

He laughs with a sudden change to his manner, 'nah,' he chuckles, 'the bossman knew someone who was gonna try knock it off.'

'Seriously?' Clarence asks in surprise, 'a weapons factory? They wouldn't stand a chance.'

'Nah, not a robbery like that,' he grins, 'they knew someone who worked there, figured they'd try and bribe him for a way in...he asked the bossman for the money for the bribe.'

'He said no then?'

'Did he fuck,' Maddox laughs again, 'he was getting the cash together when this happened, he leant cash out for stuff like that all the time, got a good return on it. You thinking of trying it?'

'Might as well. They're gonna have tons of what we need, and maybe it's not as obvious as going for police stations and army places.'

'True,' he nods thoughtfully, 'we'll have a chat when we get inside.'

'We're going straight back out,' I snap his attention back as he goes to walk off.

'Do what?' He asks.

'We're going straight back out,' I repeat knowing everyone is now staring at me, 'you can get the doctors back.'

'Why the rush?' He asks, 'get some food and rest, go tomorrow.'

'We've got shotguns,' I shrug, 'what if they attack again?'

'We're an Island now,' he retorts, 'they can't climb up or get in…and yeah, we got shotguns, but we got loads of them and enough ammo too.'

'No mate, we're going straight back.'

'Howie, listen, I know we…'

'Maddox,' I interrupt him, 'we're going straight out again. We need ammunitions and weapons.'

He breathes out, heavy and deep. Silent while he thinks quietly. His dark, intelligent eyes staying fixed on mine, 'up to you,' he finally shrugs, 'you got enough people?'

'Yeah, we're fine. Lads,' I turn to Jagger and Mo Mo, 'you can stay if you want, been a long day already and…'

'We's goin' wiv you, yeah,' Jagger replies.

'Sure?' I'm puzzled why after the shitty day we've had, fighting and running for miles then me being moody and shouting at everyone then sulking in my own private world.

'Yeah, sure,' he nods.

Maddox goes to walk off then stops, and looks over the group one by one before settling back on me, 'get some food with us,' he speaks like a natural leader, 'take an hour most and…' he pauses, 'you look like twats dressed like that.'

29

D *ay Fifteen*

I HAVE STOPPED AGAIN TO LET JESS GET SOME REST FOR A FEW MINUTES. I TELL myself that she needs rest, but the truth is my backside hurts from riding her. I thought I would be okay, but we only really pottered about our little field for exercise, and I was on and off every few minutes. Hours of being jolted up and down really makes my insides feel all jumbled up, and my goolies are starting to protest too. Poor things, and I did get a rather disdainful look from Jess when I slid off the saddle and spent a good few minute rubbing my privates to get some feeling back in them.

We are in a meadow, a very pleasant meadow if I may be so bold, and the rainfall yesterday has brought out a certain vibrancy to all the colours. Wild-flowers are everywhere, and the hedgerows are thick with juicy blackberries that have gone unpicked and unspoilt, and so tasty too. Real fruit grown by nature and not from a tin. I've eaten far too many, and I'm sure I will pay the price later when I need to open my bowels, especially after bouncing about on Jess for a few more hours.

She seems happy. No, correction – she seems ecstatic to be out of the den, and into the open air, and I was very worried that the isolation I imposed on us would have a negative psychological effect on her, or her fitness would start to abate. But she is as big, as broad and as muscular as ever, and despite not being a horsey person, I can't help but stare at her in wonder sometimes, and marvel at her smooth lines, and the way the muscles ripples under her soft hide. Such a gentle animal too, sometimes lifting her feet higher than she needs to as though gingerly stepping over something, but that gentle nature hides a stubborn and very vicious streak that is only ever a few seconds away.

I've missed the world, being cooped the way we have been. Oh, I had great views and was surrounded by some cracking scenery, but even that lost the lustre after a few weeks of seeing it day in and day out. It's so peaceful here, so calm and serene now we're away from the awful sights of the town and back into the open country, and I know I should be focussed on the list and starting work, but being out into the open air has distracted me too much. It's like I'm seeing the world through new eyes, re-born or something like that anyway. Buddha was meant to have said "each morning we are born again. What we do today is what matters most." I say he was meant to have said it as I think I read it was a famous fake Buddha quote, or something wasn't translated properly. Either way, the words and the sentiment are lovely, and I often thought that if I ever got a tattoo it would be those words. Bit late now, unless I can find a tattooist of course, or even a tattoo gun and maybe have to do it myself, it's not like there's lots of people left to laugh at me if I get it wrong.

But my point was that today, I do feel re-born and despite the god-awful sights I have seen, I can't help but keep smiling when I see the world is doing just fine without mankind crawling about on the surface.

The list. I have to focus on the mission. Saying it like that makes me feel somewhat contrived and fake. I'm not a warrior or a soldier for god's sake, I'm a bloody scientist and I know I'm out of my blooming depth with this , but what choice do I have? What choice did I have? We are all dictated by the choices and decisions we make for they lead us down the pathways of life. So, I must do what I have set out to do. Find the people on the list and make them realise they hold the key to the survival of our race.

How many have perished? Granted, those on the list cannot be infected, but with so much disaster befallen mankind, there is every chance some other fatal mishap could have taken them. I know the names and I know their addresses of *six months ago when I first went into isolation, but my thoughts turn to actually tracing and tracking them. The town I just passed through was bereft of life, no one there, well – I say no one, but there could have been hundreds of people hiding in the houses from the strange armed man riding a horse through the streets.*

Of course, I've already plotted my route to check on those closes to me first, but that didn't stop me from checking the map again and running my finger along the proposed routes for the millionth time, and I keep thinking of what to say to them. Do I tell them outright or build-up to it? What if they don't believe me? I wouldn't believe me if I popped up holding a ruddy great machine gun while sat on a horse claiming I was part of the team that made this bloody thing happen in the first place but don't worry, I'm going to make it all better. A brilliant plan there Neal. Oh god, I'm so out of my depth.

Right. Time to firm up and take the horse by the bridle and continue the battering of my dangly man bits. Damned dangly man bits, they should have been built inside where they are protected. Who bloody invented horse-riding anyway? Who looked at a horse and thought it would be a good idea to jump on one and see what happens? Must have been a woman.

I'm waffling again. It's so damned nice here.

·

NB

M arcy. Ammunition. Marcy. Ammunition. Weapons. Marcy. Survival. Marcy. We need ammunition for our weapons so we can stay alive, but we need Marcy to know what we're supposed to do while we're alive.

Shit. The boats reach the fort, shelving gently onto the small beach area graciously left to us by the storm. Maddox's crews help pull the boats further up as more people come out of the fort to help the four doctors.

Four doctors. We have four doctors, and I'm stood back on the edge of the bay watching the boats and people in the distance. We should have gone back with them. Had some food, rested and spent time sorting our lives out. We should have done that.

Shit. Every choice we make defines our lives. Every decision ripples out to open new doors while others slam shut with finality.

Shit. Marcy or weapons. Stay alive for the now or work out why we're alive?

'Paula,' I turn suddenly and catch her in a low conversation with Lani, 'can I talk to you, please.'

'Of course,' a look of intense worry crosses her face. She looks the part, hair scraped back into a ponytail with a serious face, and she reminds me of Lara Croft from the video games when I was younger.

I move away, motioning for her to follow, which she does, jogging to catch up with me as I lead her well away from the others.

'You alright?' She asks quietly, staring at me intensely, 'what's wrong?'

'I need some advice,' I say bluntly.

'Okay,' she nods, 'but er...' she casts a glance back to the team and specifically Lani standing with her arms folded and a dark look on her face, 'why me?'

'You know about Marcy, right?'

'Christ, yeah, mostly, I think...er...Lani has been filling me in with er...'

'Good, now I want you to be honest.'

She snorts and tilts her head back defiantly, 'I will.'

'Marcy is important, I don't know why but I feel it...like I feel other things and I just know they're right...shit, that doesn't make any sense but...'

'It's okay, I understand.'

'Right well, we need to know why we're here. Why we're alive and surviving...not like the people in that fort as we're different from them.'

'Say that again,' she sighs.

'Not different like better, just...shit, this is the problem. I can feel a sense of what I should be doing, but when I try to give it voice, it just gets all...like weird.'

'The infection is changing,' she says slowly, 'it's targeting us, well, you,' she shrugs, 'and who knows how many of the team are immune but...that's important, being immune is the singularly most important thing right now, Howie. Above all else, that is the priority. But what you do with it is your decision.'

'What do we do with it? Do we go for ammunition and weapons so we can stay alive or...'?

'Or find Marcy,' she says, 'what will finding Marcy accomplish?'

'She is infected, but she was different, she had her own thoughts and was in control of herself. She kept control of those she turned too like

Darren did, but…but she wasn't corrupted by the power of it, she said the infection was a cure, that it was meant to cure everyone…'

'Go on.'

'But it isn't…it isn't curing is it? It's killing. So, she said she would give herself up for testing, to see what can be taken from her to…well, I'm not sure about that bit, whether she meant to find a cure or to find some kind of hybrid er…thing I guess, like the best of both worlds…'

'Howie, forgive me for saying this, but how can you be sure it wasn't the infection controlling her the entire time?'

'Because it makes no sense if it was. She could have killed us with ease. We were fighting, there on the plains…or where the plains were and we were fucked, really fucked. We were losing and we knew it, but she turned her group against those attacking us…she killed them, saved us, Christ, Paula, she tidied the bloody fort up, and took all the bodies away while we slept. She made curry and fed us…then it all went a bit weird after that but…'

'Do you still want her?'

'What?'

'We're speaking openly,' she stares at me, 'she lured you, or,' she pauses, 'something happened that made you want her…'

'Pheromones.'

'Possibly but you don't know that for sure, maybe you just wanted to fuck her.'

'Paula!'

'We're adults and we're having a big boy grown-up conversation now. You asked for my help so…'

'Clarence, Cookey…they all felt it.'

'Dave didn't.'

'Dave's different.'

'Fair enough, yeah, he is a bit,' she concedes, 'but life isn't simple, Howie. You adore Lani, that's pretty obvious. Well, maybe not after the way you've acted today, but we all know you're trying to think of everything so, no one blames you. Well,' she pauses again, 'actually, it might be better to think of Lani as two people, the first is the loyal team member that has sworn to keep you safe and,' she locks eyes on me, 'she'll do that to her dying breath, we all will...don't interrupt me, we all will. But the second Lani is the one you share a bed with, that Lani might be really...really angry at you. But my point is, life isn't simple. You love Lani, but maybe there's some kind of unfinished business with Marcy? The lads have all said how beautiful she was...not in front of Lani, of course.'

'Not that,' shaking my head I speak firmly, 'not that at all. I get what you are saying and...' I shift uncomfortably and regret starting this conversation. There is a feeling of unfinished business, and my heart keeps hammering when I think of Marcy, but different to when I think of Lani. Paula stares at me like she's looking right inside of me and can see my soul laid out. 'No,' I repeat feebly, 'not that.'

'Okay,' she nods and looks away, 'so the question is, do you find Marcy now and find out what we're all doing here, or go for ammunition and get what we need to keep going.'

'Exactly,' I mutter, 'I want to find Marcy now, right now...but I know we should be getting ammunition.'

'Needs, wants and desires.'

'Needs come first?'

'They do. Have you heard of Maslow's hierarchy of needs?'

'Yeah, did it at school.'

'Apply it now then. Our physiological needs are okay. We have air, food, water and we've had sleep. I've had sex, you haven't...'

'Oi,' I stare at her in shock.

'Lani told me, what? Girls talk, Howie.'

'Oh...right...well, I was tired, and...clearly Roy wasn't though.'

'Oh, don't get like that,' she tuts, 'you need to be the hero at every-thing? Golden bollocks Howie? Let someone else be good at something...'

'I didn't mean...'

'Moving on,' she holds a hand up to cut me off, 'safety. That's the next one. And to be honest, we pretty much stop there. We're safe now, right here...we've got you with us, and Dave, and Meredith and Clarence and...all of them...apart from me...'

'You're just as important as they are.'

'My skills lie in other areas. Like now for instance. I will fight, but I'm nowhere near as good as any of the others, even Jagger and Mo Mo are far better….but,' she says with a tone that is getting annoyed at the distractions in the conversation, 'so we have immediate safety but not long term safety. We survived today because the fog helped, and you made us run fifteen miles. But a concerted attack from an over-whelming opponent will wipe us out. You've already said the infection is targeting us, so we have to assume it is coming back…and we have to assume it's getting smarter too. Look at what it did to Cookey with the clowns. If it comes again with great numbers, with any level of organi-sation, then we're done for. You, Dave, Clarence and Meredith can't be everywhere at all times…safety is the next step. After that comes all the other bits, and you can find love and…and esteem, and seek to find out the big questions and answers, but first comes safety.'

'Yeah,' I listen intently, and every word she says makes complete sense. It's funny how things go. A snap decision to ask Paula for advice, a decision that I am not even aware of making. But deep down I knew she would give straight answers and honest advice, plus she's very clever and very switched on too, and she looks a bit like Lara Croft.

Staring across the bay towards the only houses left in the area, and where I hope Marcy is, I take a deep breath and make the decision.

'Ammunition,' I announce to the group, 'we need ammo and fucking lots of it.'

After siphoning diesel from the vans to put into the Saxon, we load up and start moving out. The day is already late and as afternoon turns to evening, we navigate from the coast moving north and inland as we aim for the munitions factory that Maddox said was about one hundred miles away.

One hundred miles on a normal summer evening in Britain would be a painfully slow experience of clogged motorways, roadworks, reduced speed limits, traffic lights and the ever-present speed enforcement cameras earning revenue for the greedy fat bastard politicians. One hundred miles could be a torturous journey filled with the peril of tempers fraying, and mild-mannered sales executives screaming threats of kidnap and murder through the windows of their company's fleet vehicle while their golf clubs rattle in the boot. Truck drivers that were once fat, greasy and all dead from heart attacks at the age of fifty now sit lean, and eat fruit while driving the road trains, and try to appears as though they're not reading newspapers, and the ever-present nervous motorway driver who sits at sixty-five in the middle lane completely unaware of the carnage erupting all around them.

But that was before. Now, one hundred miles is easy. The Saxon sits on the motorway like a goliath of modern technology. Drinking fuel quicker, faster than a darts player drinks ale. She roars and eats the road up as my foot increases the pressure. One hundred miles without delays, without the need to stop, start, stop, start, and we make progress. Good progress. Which is a good thing considering there are now twelve of us crammed into a vehicle designed for a maximum of ten. One of them is a dog and two are teenage boys, but then we do have Clarence who takes up the space of several normal-sized people which is why he smugly takes the front passenger seat.

'You alright?' He speaks across the gap, and I can tell he waited for the initial silence to end and everyone in the back to start talking before he picked his moment.

I give a quick puff of air through my lips while shaking my head, 'fuck knows, mate.'

'I'm not questioning you,' he rumbles, 'you're the boss so,' he stops talking and to let the words hang in the air, 'you got a lot of pressure on you.'

'Self-imposed though.'

'Self-imposed? How's that?'

'Mate, don't take this wrong way, and forgive me if it opens a fresh wound, but...I fucking wish Chris was here to do this.'

Instead of being offended or hurt, he laughs, a genuine sound with real humour, 'and you know what he'd do if he was?'

'Er, make quicker decisions?'

'No!' Clarence laughs again, 'he'd stroke his beard a lot, and look thoughtful while waiting for you to make the decision.'

'Eh? Get off, that bloke knew far more than I ever will.'

'Chris was a leader, but he was a squaddie through and through, he was a sergeant, not an officer...he saw you as an officer, and a fucking good one at that.'

'Mate,' I tut uncomfortably at the compliment, 'no way, I worked in a...'

'You gotta stop saying that,' he cuts me off, 'you used to work in a supermarket, I used to be a nightclub doorman. Dave used to be a shelf stacker, and Lani used to work in a nightclub...and Paula used to be an accountant, but we're none of those things now. It doesn't matter what you used to be; it matters what you are.'

'Wise words, cheers Granddad,' I shoot him a quick sideways grin which he returns in kind, 'seriously though mate, I'm just having a bad day...'

'Bad day? Shit boss, you're having a bad month, forget the bad day. The fact that we're all still here is enough...you can be as quiet as you want.'

'Lara Croft is switched on,' I remark casually.

He laughs again, and turns to look down the rear, 'she does look like her,' he admits.

'Who looks like who?' Cookey asks picking up on Clarence turning around.

'Paula, she looks like Lara Croft.'

'I bloody do not,' she snaps indignantly, 'for a start I'm not wearing hot pants or a tight vest.'

'Yes, you are!' Cookey bursts out laughing, 'not the hot pants, but the vest...'

'I was hot in a t-shirt,' she says pointedly, 'and Lani is wearing a vest top too.'

'We got two Lara Crofts then,' Blowers joins in, 'Lara one and Lara two.'

'She was fit as,' Cookey quickly turns the conversation to one of his favourite topics, 'you ever see the movie?'

'Like fifteen times,' Blowers laughs, 'did you see it, Nick?'

'Eh?'

'Where the hell were you?' Blowers asks.

'Here, why?'

'You were miles away.'

'Yeah, sorry, fucking thinking about er...just er...'

'Ah!' Cookey says in delight, 'Lilly, look at him blushing.'

'Fuck off, Cookey,' Nick snaps.

'Leave him alone,' Lani jumps in, 'it's sweet.'

'Sweet!' Cookey carries on laughing, 'ah, it's so sweet Nicholas...but Nicholas, do stop swearing, please, and do try and make an effort with your appearance...'

'Do one, Cookey,' Nick tries to sound huffy, but starts laughing mid-sentence, 'fuck it, yeah, I was thinking about her.'

'Really?' Cookey asks sounding disappointed that Nick is admitting it and thereby losing his ammunition to goad him for a response.

'She's bloody lovely,' Nick says with a sigh, 'can't stop thinking about her.'

'She is nice, Nick,' Paula says, 'and you make a lovely couple.'

'Couple? Fuck that,' he replies, 'you seen her? She's beautiful and like, really fucking smart...I can't even read or write properly...nah... like...nah.'

'Don't be a dick, mate,' Blowers says, 'anyone can see she likes you.'

'Nah,' Nick says again, 'that was like...you know, cos I saved her and shit, and...well, but...she doesn't know me, like actually know me and...'

'She likes you, bruv,' Mo Mo pipes up, 'I don't think she cares if you read and shit.'

'Not now maybe, but...like, nah, some good-looking bloke who's like really clever will come along and...like, she deserves...'

'Nick,' Clarence twistsaround again to call out in his deep voice, 'she likes you for you, not because you saved her. She wouldn't think like that if someone else saved her...especially Cookey...she'd have been running as far away as possible.'

'Oi,' Cookey shouts, 'I'm a good catch, I am.'

'Are you?' Lani laughs.

'Catch something,' Blowers mutters.

'I caught gay from you,' Cookey retorts.

'I think we need to stop with the gay jokes,' Paula interjects smoothly.

'Whoa, fucking hang on,' Jagger says, 'you said you caught gay from Blowers...so, you saying you did something gay with him?'

'Eh?' Cookey says in a puzzled voice, 'no...no, I didn't mean...'

The Saxon erupts in laughter as Cookey bluffs and stammers trying to take back what he said, 'no...I meant he gave me gay...like you give someone a cold...I didn't mean I did gay bum sex with him.'

'Lads,' Paula says while laughing, 'stop with the gay jokes...'

'But...but...' Cookey bleats, 'what will I use to take the piss out of Blowers?'

'You can't keep making gay jokes,' she says.

'What if one of us is gay?' Lani asks, 'they might feel they couldn't say something because of...'

'Fucking hell,' Cookey groans, 'fucking political correctness in here? We kill zombies and save the world...'

'It's not political correctness,' Paula says, 'it's about not being offensive.'

'But I am offensive,' Cookey replies innocently, 'I mean...only to Blowers and Nick...and...'

'But we can hear the comments,' Lani explains, 'what if Jagger was gay, how would he feel?'

'I'm not gay,' Jagger announces.

'I'm not saying you are,' Lani says, 'but what *if* you were, how would you feel about Cookey making gay jokes all the time?'

'I'm not gay,' he repeats firmly.

'I'm gay,' Mo Mo declares.

'You ain't,' Jagger says, 'he ain't...I seen you with loads of bitches.'

'And don't say bitches either,' Paula says.

'Eh? What's wrong wiv bitches?' Jagger asks.

'Er...what's right with bitches?' Lani snaps, 'it's disrespectful and really offensive...'

Cookey jumps back in, 'I don't care if someone is really gay, I just like taking the piss out of Blowers.'

'But you should care,' Lani says.

'Why? I don't want to care. What do I care if someone is gay or not... I'm not bothered...they can all be gay and do gay bum sex...it doesn't bother me; I just do it to annoy Blowers.'

'And you can't say gay bum sex either,' Paula says.

'But they do do bum sex,' Cookey says, 'they put willies in bums... that's how they have sex.'

'No, they have sex…they just have sex…just sex…' Paula says, 'you just say sex…not gay bum sex. You don't say hetero vagina sex so why say…'

'Urgh, that's gross,' Cookey recoils, 'don't say it like that.'

'Then don't say gay bum sex…just say sex…'

'But,' Cookey goes quiet, 'but like the jokes won't work if I just say sex instead of gay bum sex…that's the point.'

'Yes, and you risk offending people or having people remain unable to openly show their sexual preference for fear of you taking the piss out of them.'

'Eh? I won't take the piss out of them for what they are,' Cookey says hotly, 'that's the point of taking the piss, you say the thing they ain't… er…sometimes…I mean…yeah, just with gay jokes…I wouldn't actually say it to a gay person.'

'But what if they hear it?'

'So? I'm not saying it about them, only Blowers or Nick and…'

'Cookey, right…put it this way…Mo Mo, can I use your skin colour to make a point.'

'Yeah.'

'Mo Mo is not white is he, so let's say you take the piss out of Blowers saying he was black, or another word for a person that isn't white…and you do it because he *isn't* of a different colour…then you are saying it as though *being* of a different colour is somehow worse than being what he is, which then suggests that Mo Mo is not as *good* as everyone else because he isn't white.'

'I'm not racist.'

'I know you're not, Cookey…but you are taking the piss out of Blowers being gay because he isn't gay…which is then suggesting that being gay is a bad thing or something to ridicule…and if say…if say I was gay, I would then think that you think being gay is a bad thing…'

'Oh…um…' Cookey goes quiet, the whole Saxon goes quiet, 'so like… what *can* I use to take the piss then? I could take the piss out of his abnormally round head, but then what if someone else had a round head? Or I could say he was a thick fucker, but then Nick might get offended…I didn't mean it like that, Nick…'

'I get it mate,' Nick reassures him quickly.

'So, like…I can't take the piss then?'

'You can take the piss, but not if it demeans someone else in the process,' Lani says.

'Fuck…so…well, I can't think of anything cos like…someone has always got something wrong with them and like… well, I just won't take the piss then.'

'Are you sulking?' Lani asks with a laugh, 'oh, look at that face! Alex Cooke…you are pouting like a girl.'

'Can't say that,' Cookey replies huffily, 'that's offensive to girls, and people with pouty faces.'

'He is proper sulking,' Lani laughs in delight which is a lovely sound to hear, 'oh, poor Cookey…poor Cookey being told off…'

'Not sulking,' Cookey mutters, 'just being politically correct and…'

'And what?' Blowers asks.

'Dunno, can't think of anything else,' Cookey huffs again, 'and I'm not allowed to speak anyway.'

'Fact,' Blowers adds, 'so shut the fuck up.'

'I will.'

'Good.'

'Good.'

'Then do it now you fucking dick.'

'You can't say that, Blowers. What if someone really is *an actual fucking dick?* They'd be right proper offended.'

'Dunno, are you?' Blowers asks.

'Fuck you…probably get told off for swearing now.'

'Oh, dear,' Paula laughs, 'I think I have upset him.'

'No…no, it's fine,' Cookey goes for another huff, 'I'll just sit and be quiet.'

'But,' Roy speaks up, 'there is such a thing as a safe learning environment…'

'A what?' Mo Mo asks.

'Safe learning environment,' Roy repeats, 'they do it in schools and education places to…'

'I know what it is, bruv,' Mo Mo says, 'I didn't hear what you said is all.'

'Oh, sorry,' Roy replies, 'didn't mean to patronise you…but this place could be a safe learning environment, like what happens in Vegas stays in Vegas…'

'Fair point,' Paula concedes, 'is anyone here offended by Cookey's humour? Not you, Blowers…you don't count.'

'But I am offended,' he exclaims, 'really very offended by that fuckwit.'

'Anyone else?' Paula looks round, 'lads what about you two?' She looks to Jagger and Mo Mo.

'Seriously?' Mo Mo asks, 'from where we come from?'

'Mr Howie,' Paula calls out, 'it appears that none of your team are offended by Cookey's humour so what do you think? Can we classify the Saxon as a safe environment?'

'I'm offended!' Blowers says again.

'You don't count,' I shout back, 'and yes, carry on.'

'Fucking awesome, you big gay cock muncher,' Cookey lets rip the same second I finish speaking, 'ha! Blowers…you thought you were safe from the Cookey monster, but I return and badder than ever with my constant jokes about your round head and stupidness, and complete gayness and being suck a fucktard.'

'Oh, what have you done,' Blowers groans.

'Oh, yes!' Cookey shouts as everyone starts laughing, 'outside I will be Alex Cooke, respectful and diligent soldier of Mr Howie's living army. The conscientious professional dedicated to the cause…but… within here I can show my dark side, my lovely…and I can stroke your face and tell you how ugly you are with your stupid round head…'

'Get off you twat,' Blowers tries slapping Cookey's hand away from stroking his face.

'Kiss me gayboy,' Cookey puckers up and leans towards Blowers, 'kiss me on the lips, you big beastie.' Nick is bent double-clutching his stomach, Jagger and Mo Mo almost wetting themselves as Cookey starts clambering onto Blowers as he squirms away in panic but laughing too hard at the same time.

'Oh, let me touch your round head…'

'Fuck off!' Blowers laughs, edging away until he's hard up against Nick which delights Cookey even more as he is unleashed with his humour.

D*ay Fifteen*

I HAVE KILLED. I HAVE ~~TOOK~~ TAKEN LIFE FROM THE ~~1ˢᵀ INFECTED, SORRY, FROM my first infected.~~

MY NERVES ARE SHOT, AND I DO NOT FEEL WHOLLY SAFE HERE SO FORGIVE THE *errors I make. I have made my first kill of an infected person, and I want to get my notes made now while the events are fresh in my mind.*

THE FIRST ON THE LIST WAS JARED KUMAR, A MIDDLE-AGED MALE OF INDIAN *descent employed as a structural surveyor. Married with two young children. From my research, I knew him to be an average man living an average life. Middle-class with no substantial financial worries other than a mortgage. His wife worked part-time as a teaching assistant, and he had no exceptional skills other than those for which he was trained and employed.*

His house was a semi-detached three-bedroom property located on the edge of town, a short walk from the main train line which connects to the major cities. Finding the address proved easy with Jess carrying me from the serene countryside to the town within which he resided. We ~~scouted~~, skirted the villages and small settlements on the way there figuring it would be better to stay as discrete as possible. We did not rush but nor did Jess allow us to dawdle either, such is her manner.

OUR APPROACH WAS TENTATIVE, AND *I* PUT TO GOOD USE ALL THE LESSONS *I have learnt and used this first approach as a training exercise.*

I AM NOT IN A WHOLLY SAFE PLACE, SO THESE NOTES ARE RUSHED, WHICH IS *perhaps something I ~~could~~ should have said first. I did say it first. Really, I am very shaken, but find the act of writing this entry is soothing my nerves.*

THE HOUSE WAS IN A NORMAL RESIDENTIAL STREET OF NO PARTICULAR NOTE. *Houses on both sides, and nearly all of them being large family sized semi-detached dwellings with larger than average-sized gardens to the rear and small decorative gardens to the front. The area, being sheltered from the worst of the storm by surrounding hills, had not suffered too badly, and the signs of devastation were largely limited to power lines and posts being brought down, garden sheds blown away, fences torn asunder, and with the flotsam and jetsam of everyday living strewn about. Pre-storm damage from the event seemed to be signs of looting or violent struggles from broken windows, doors and blood-stained vehicles with dried on stains of blood smeared on the white UPVC frames and door claddings. In short, it was as expected.*

WE TOOK A VARIED ROUTE TO THE ADDRESS, SCOURING THE LOCALITY TO GET A *sense and essence of the environment. Something which I learnt was essential to hone the mind into the right frame. It also meant, we were not taking the path of least resistance to the address and therefore, not using the most predictable and "expected" route. Not that I suspected there would be any concerns but as I said before, I was using this as more a training exercise.*

WE ENTERED THE TOWN FROM THE EAST, BUT AFTER OUR ROUTE TO ESTABLISH environment we ended up approaching the street and the ~~taget~~ target address from the west, no I beg to differ...it was the north, we came into the street from the northern end. Damn it, no, it was the west. Come on Neal! Get a grip, you blithering idiot.

IT MATTERS NOT WHAT DIRECTION WE APPROACHED FROM. NEEDLESS TO SAY, Jess and I found the target street and identified the target house and ~~havig~~ having done so, we remained quietly in the street a short distance away. Jess was good and seemed to understand the need for discretion as she didn't snort, bray, whinny or otherwise expose our position at this time. She did, however, take a big shit, but other than the resounding splats of her manure hitting the ground, we remained silent and watchful.

The target address had a broken window to the front, but on closer inspection it was the outer pane only of the double-glazed unit, thereby rendering the house within as effectively intact and secure. As we got closer, I noticed there was blood-stains on the white door, frame and surrounding panels but again, this appeared old so was largely discounted.

After dismounting from Jess and trusting that her training was good enough, that she knew to stay put without being tethered, I approached the front door with my assault rifle ready and the safety switch moved to off. I did not aim with the weapon presented to my shoulder in the correct firing technique as I felt rather foolish, believing the property to be vacant, and therefore the risk to be low.

As suspected, the front door was unlocked and was pushed open. I resisted the urge to call out and remained watchful at the entranceway for a few minutes, during which I did not hear nor see anything of note. The inside of the house appeared normal with a good coating of dust on the surfaces which indicated to me a lack of movement inside, and also something I felt rather proud of for remembering to notice, and it is with no shame that I admit my heart was strong in my chest at this point, and the adrenalin flowing freely.

I do recall that as I crossed the threshold proper, I did lift the stock of the weapon into my shoulder, but kept the front of the weapon aimed down, and my finger was extended over the trigger guard to prevent a negligent discharge.

The ground floor was searched with no signs of life. Pictures on the walls showed me I had the right address, and I recognised the smiling man pictured with his wife and children from the copy of his passport image I had held upon my database. I then went upstairs and found that unlike the ground floor, which was left with doors open, these were all closed. It did not cross my mind at the time, but rather was something I noted after and chastised myself for not picking up on.

The first room was the master bedroom. A double-bed with bedsheets that had not been made and given the time of night the infection took hold; this was not surprising. The bathroom was as expected, and I had but two rooms left, which I took to be the rooms of the two children.

The closest one, which was the door next along from the bathroom, I entered quickly and somewhat casually. I even used my right hand to open the door which was utterly stupid as it meant I was not ready to fire. Whether they heard me coming or not, I do not know, but they were within and very quiet, and only sprung to action once the door was wide, and I was over the threshold. In a glance, I took in the scene, and it was only then that the smell hit me, and again this is something I should have noted sooner.

Rotten meat. Faeces, urine, and the stench of fouled bodies. Jared Kumar was present, along with his good lady wife and their two children, one boy and one girl, and all of them infected. Red eyes clawed hands, and upon seeing me did they utter their first growls, but by then, they had already commenced their charge, and it was backwards out of the room I went while frantically trying to find the blasted trigger for the assault rifle.

I tripped, fell on my arse and was thinking this is it, I'm done for at the first hurdle when finally, my index finger found the trigger, and in my panic, I emptied the whole magazine straight into them. I sprayed without aiming, and although at the time the noise, the deafening retort of the weapon seemed to go *on forever, it was over within seconds. Cordite hung in the air, my ears were (and still are) ringing. The infected family who waited so long for a bite to eat, and who came so close to ending my crusade, were ripped apart with chunks of flesh and meat taken out of them. Skulls were imploded and exploded with bits of cranium and brain matter splattered here there and everywhere. Only the youngest girl was still alive as it appeared, she had taken only body shots. Shot to ribbons and bleeding heavily but still, she made an effort to crawl at me, and her ragged, course breathing is a sound I will never forget. I crabbed away in utter fright with my finger still held down on the trigger. I thought she was in her final seconds and would surely die, but alas she did not and in fine spirits, she clawed and crawled her way across the landing to nip and gnash at my feet which were cycling away in terror.*

It was only when the back of my head struck the wall and I screamed in panic, did I remember the pistol, and had to make a conscious effort to remove my hand from the rifle, draw my pistol, flick the safety, take aim and fire. I missed the first two shots from my shaking hand, but the rest struck home, with direct shots to the face that removed the back of her head, and she slumped down to rest her now dead remains on my feet and I can still see, in alarming detail, the strands of her black hair fanning out across my tan coloured trousers.

Tears flowed thick and fast as the adrenalin abated and left me shaking with almost uncontrollable tremors. It took my precious minutes to get the courage to drag my legs from under her head and ease myself away, and I just made it outside into the fresh air before the retching started and those lovely juicy blackberries popped back out.

With the contents of my stomach heaved up, I made it to Jess who, thankfully, had stayed where she was left, climbed aboard and urged her away. She responded with a toss of her mane, and led me quickly away from my first killing, and it was upon her warm, solid and reassuringly alive neck that I sobbed and cried until slowly my wits returned, and I was able to make this brief stop.

I HAVE MADE MY FIRST KILLS OF THE INFECTED. FOUR MOWN DOWN WITHIN seconds and done merely by the motion of one finger. Four lives taken forever, but truly I can place my hand upon my heart, and say I had no other choice.

NB

'Someone got here before us then,' Clarence says with a forced lightness. Late in the day, and maybe an hour or so before nightfall, and we made good progress getting here. Thundering through any built-up areas and maintaining a solid path ahead.

Clarence knew the area, but Roy seems to have a built-in GPS system in his head and soon, had us on the right approach road. In fact, this has been the easiest day so far in terms of getting things done. Four bloody doctors. Seriously, you couldn't make that shit up. We've struggled to find one, but now we've got four.

Anyway, we made it. Cookey got a bit over-excited and despite having everyone in stitches, Dave did eventually tell him to calm down, but that was only because we were getting closer.

I'm not sure what I was expecting, but certainly not this. I think maybe in my mind's eye I was expecting a huge fortress style bastion of high concrete walls, barbed wire fences, attack dogs and machine-gun turrets when in fact, the area looks like any other industrial style zone with manicured grounds laid to lawn and a modern built building that looks more executive than factory. No barbed wire fence, no boundary wall, nothing. Even the sign just gives the name of the company, BAE

Systems. That's it, but then I guess this is the best way. I could drive past this place every day and have no idea what it was or what they made.

A new notice, printed, laminated and fixed smartly to the big sign-board tells us someone got here before us.

WARNING
THIS BUILDING IS OCCUPIED.
YOU WILL BE FIRED UPON.
APPROACH SLOWLY AND WAIT.
DO NOT ATTEMPT TO GAIN ENTRY.

'WELL,' I SAY WITH A SIGH, 'THEY AREN'T SAYING WE CAN'T APPROACH…JUST that we've got to do it slowly.'

'Yep,' Clarence nods slowly, 'sign is professional, and someone has taken the time and effort to put it on there.'

'No bodies either,' I remark looking around at the grounds, 'the power station had them all stacked up.'

'Yeah,' he says quietly while conducting his own scan of the area.

'Dave, you see anything mate?'

'Nothing, Mr Howie.'

'Right, guess we'll approach then,' I edge the Saxon forward until we're level with the sign then pause and wait to see for reaction. The approaching road to the modern-looking building is long, but mostly straight so the view is clear. No movement, so I ease forward again, and keep the speed low. Still no movement so we proceed, scanning the front of the building, and as we get closer, I realise the windows are all two-way darkened glass with no view into the interior. There could be hundreds of people watching us now, and we'd never know.

'They have guns here?' I ask out loud.

'Fixed firing points for testing,' Clarence explains, 'they could have rigged something up or have access to firearms, but…looks empty,' he glances over at me.

'Nah,' shaking my head I can feel we're being watched through those windows. I stop a good hundred metres from the building, and wait for a few seconds with the engine running, 'anyone got a white flag on a stick we can poke up through the turret hole?'

'Blowers can use his pants,' Cookey quips.

'Anything, just let them know we're coming in peace.' Mutters and rustling as they go through kit bags and lockers to find anything suitable.

'Nothing here, does it have to be white?' Nick asks, 'we got loads of black tops and stuff.'

'I dunno, does it have to be white?' I ask Clarence who shrugs, 'it's always a white flag,' he replies.

'We must have something,' twisting around, I watch them going through bags and searching the vehicle until Paula yanks something out of her bag, 'got this,' she announces.

'A bra?' I ask.

'It's white,' she replies.

'A bra? You want us to wave a bra at them?'

'What? It's bloody white...and it's a sports bra, you know, not like a lacy thing or...'

'Oh, that's good then, god forbid we wave a lacy bra at them instead of a sports bra.'

'Got any knickers?' Cookey asks.

'Alex!' Dave glares at him.

'No...no, I mean they won't see they are knickers from there...'

'Fucking pervert,' Blowers shakes his head slowly while Nick tuts.

'No white knickers,' Paula replies, 'sorry, it's the bra or nothing.'

'I've got a white sports bra too,' Lani announces, 'we could put them together.'

'Two bras? What the fuck we trying to say to them? *Hello, we're an army truck full of horny women with no bras on?*'

'Not a bad idea,' Clarence says, 'bet they bloody open up then.'

'Okay, do it,' I nod down to Paula and Lani now holding the white sports bras.

'Um,' Paula looks round, 'we got a stick then?'

'Stick?'

'For the flag,' she looks at me, 'we need a stick.'

'Does it have to be a stick?' Blowers asks, 'tie them on the top of a rifle.'

'We can't wave bras tied into an assault rifle,' I reply, 'they'll think we're fucking nuts.'

'We are nuts,' Lani says, 'who else would drive ten people and a dog in an old army thing to a bullet factory waving a sports bra?'

'Good point, so, we don't have anything else we can use?'

'Not long enough to poke up there,' Blowers motions towards the turret hole.

'Shitting hell,' I groan and rub my face, 'here, give me those bras.'

'What for?' Lani asks with a look of worry.

'I'll go out with them.'

'Carrying bras? That's even worse.'

'What's that?' Mo Mo looks down as Jagger rifles through his bag.

'Nuffin,' Jagger snaps.

'What was it?' Mo Mo presses, 'Jag, what was it?'

'Nuffin, leave off.'

'Was it white?' I ask and spot the poker face settle on Mo Mo, 'lads, Jagger…you got something white? Mo Mo, you see something white?'

He shakes his head and looks away, silent and sullen.

'Yeah, but…' Jagger goes to say something, stops then looks back around at everyone with a defiant glare, 'my nan gave it me, like…so…'

'What is it?'

'Handkerchief, but like she put my name on it and…fuck off taking the piss,' he glares at Mo Mo.

'Didn't say nuffin, bruv,' Mo Mo recoils quickly.

'I don't wanna lose it,' Jagger says quietly, 'she gave it me before she died like and…' his face drops and the young boy shines through so clearly that it brings us to silence.

'Don't worry mate,' I say calmly, 'I'm happy to take the bras out.'

'I'll do it,' Clarence offers.

'Yeah, cos that will look even better with a giant carrying two bras,' I chuckle.

'Nah, here like…you's can use it,' Jagger starts opening his bag again as I motion for the bras to be handed over.

'It's alright mate, got these…wait here…' door open and I'm dropping down onto the concrete ground then stepping away from the Saxon with a white bra held in each hand away from my body, and feeling like a complete and utter tool. I stand there for some minutes with nothing happening, Clarence stretches across the seats to lean his head near the driver's door, 'anything?' He asks.

'Nope, I'll go a bit closer.'

Holding the underwear out from my body, I slowly approach the building then curse as I remember the pistol on my belt and the knife too. I stop, glance down and start heading back the way I came with a look of apology towards the building and feeling even more of a complete dick.

'What's up?' Clarence calls out.

'Still got my pistol on me,' I get back, and slip the gun and knife out before once more walking back towards the building with my bras held out.

I stop about twenty metres shy of the front, standing directly in front of the big double glass doors that are also two way and darkened. Scanning the front but nothing, no movement, no noise.

Minutes tick by, nothing happens. My arms ache so the bras get lowered down to my sides, and I start shuffling about in boredom wishing I had a cigarette, then I start thinking about how much I want a coffee and a cigarette which makes me think about wanting things, and then I'm thinking that we still need to find Marcy, and how my mood has been up and down like a yo yo today.

'Hello.'

The voice snaps me out of self-induced daze to stare about with wide eyes as I start thinking I imagined the voice as there is no one here. I shake my head as though to clear my mind, and the voice calls out again, 'Hello?'

Perfect clarity and a normal adult male voice, but no one is here. I'm going crazy, hearing things. Maybe it's Dave but then Dave wouldn't say hello if he got in my head, he would just stand there waiting.

'ARE YOU ENGLISH?'

The voice comes out again, and I stare at the doors in front of me, then up at the windows and along both sides of the brick-built building.

'ER...WHAT...DO...YOU...WANT?' The voice speaks slow and clear in a typical way that English people speak to foreigners.

'Er...where are you?' I ask out loud.

'At the intercom,' the voice says with a sigh, 'here...next to the front door...see it? Big shiny metal thing with buttons on it...yes! There you go, well done!'

'Huh, sorry,' I say sheepishly, 'didn't see it.'

'Which is not the least bit worrying considering you were staring right at it.'

'I wasn't staring at it; I was just staring but without looking...'

'How can you stare without looking?'

'You know, like when your mind drifts off, and you just stare...er... vacant stare, I think they call it.'

'Oh, yes, yes I've heard of that. Bit of a weird time to drift off, isn't it?'

'I didn't think anyone was here,' I reply defensively.

'Why stand there then?'

'Waiting.'

'What for?'

'For someone to come out.'

'But you just said you didn't think anyone was here.'

'Er...dunno really, just sort got thinking about coffee and cigarettes, and then...anyway, er...so who are you?'

'Me? I'm the person inside this massive building that you can't get into.'

'Doesn't look that strong really.'

'Appearances can be deceptive. Do you know where you are?'

'I'm here.'

'Do you know where here is?'

'Yeah, it's here,' shit, I sound like Dave.

'What do you want?'

'Er, ammunition please...is this the ammunition factory?'

'I don't know...is it?'

'Um, you're kind of inside? So, like...you should know that...'

'Who are you?'

'I'm Howie and er...'

'Howie?'

Oh, not again, 'yeah, Howie, and my mates are back in that vehicle... we ran out of bullets yesterday, and we need some more.'

'Bullets for what?'

'Eh? For our guns.'

'Yes, thank you,' the sarcastic tone comes clearly through the speaker, 'what type of bullets?'

'Oh, right, yeah, we've got 9mm pistols and er...army assault rifles the er...SA80 and a GPMG and a shit load of police machine guns, and other bits and bobs....er....' silence from the intercom, 'are you still there?'

'Yes.'

'Oh, okay...er...did you hear what I said?'

'I did, sorry I thought you were still talking.'

'Oh, no, my mistake, no, I had finished...should have made them clearer.'

'No problem, I wasn't paying attention properly er...yeah, we can do that.'

'Do what?'

'We could give you ammunition for all of those.'

'Really?'

'Er, yeah,' the intercom says in that tone lifting manner I cannot fucking stand, 'we are a munitions factory, you know.'

'Right, so...er...how do we get them?'

'Ah, now I said we could, I never said we would.'

Taking a deep breath, I close my eyes, and force my tone to remain neutral, 'okay...so...can we get the ammunition from you?'

'You could...but...'

'But what?'

'What's in it for us?'

'Er...I dunno,' I shrug, 'we don't really have anything.'

'You must have something to trade.'

'Er…not really.'

'What about that Army vehicle?'

'No way.'

'We can't just give you ammunition for free.'

'You can't have the Saxon, we need it.'

'We can give you a van.'

'Sorry, mate. Can't trade the Saxon. What you like for weapons in there?'

'Er…' that annoying teenage *er* comes back, infuriating as hell, 'we are a munitions factory…we have weapons.'

'You have bullets, but where did the weapons come from?'

'How do you think we tested the bullets?'

'You've got fixed firing points.'

'Correction. We *had* fixed firing points, they are no longer fixed anywhere, plus we've got assault rifles and all sorts of things.'

'Hmmm, okay…I was thinking we could trade some guns but…'

'What guns?'

'You said you had guns.'

'We do, but what guns did you have in mind?'

'What guns do you need?'

'What have you got spare?'

'Er…none reall,y but…what are you missing then?'

'Missing?'

'Yeah, like what haven't you got?'

'Oh, right…er…we need some…er…hang on,' the dull thump comes out which I figure is his hand clamping over the microphone or mouth-piece, 'you still there?'

'No, I've gone.'

'We don't *actually* need anything, but er…more guns are always good.'

'Hmmm, I think you are lying.'

'Pardon?'

'You don't have any guns do you.'

'We have, we've got lots of guns.'

'So, why do you need more?'

'So, we can trade.'

'You've probably got a couple of machines that can fire the bullets in simulation of assault rifles or whatever else you make, but I bet you don't have any actual guns.'

'We do have guns. This facility was armed...I mean it had armed police posted here.'

'Yeah, and they would have gone when the shit started, and took their guns with them.'

'No, they stayed here, and their guns...we have their guns.'

'Why did you have armed police?'

'Pardon?'

'Why have armed police here? Is your building not secure?'

'It is, it's very secure...a tank wouldn't get in here.'

'So, why have armed police?'

'Deterrent.'

'Against what?'

'Attack.'

'From who?'

'The terrorists.'

'Oh, *the* terrorists....not any terrorists but *the* terrorists...look mate, you are tucked up cosy in your building which is great, but we're out here killing zombies, and we've run out of bullets...you can stay in your fortress, but give us the bullets and we'll kill the zombies...'

'No need to be like that about it.'

'What? Like what?'

'Like you're the ones doing all the work.'

'Have you been out killing zombies?'

'That's not the point.'

'Have you been in there since it began?'

'Yeah, but...we *could* be attacked by zombies at any time so...'

'How they gonna get in?'

'Well, they won't but...'

'So, you can stay inside all safe, and we're out here doing all the hard work.'

'No, hang on a minute…it's not easy staying here you know.'

'Have you got food and water?'

'Yes, but that's not the point…'

'Power?'

'Generators, but listen…'

'So, you've got a fortress, with bullets, food, water and no need to go outside while we have shotguns and bloody axes…'

'Yes, but…right…this really isn't fair you know.'

'Okay then, you take the Saxon and the weapons, and we'll have the nice big fortress with the food and water and power…'

'What? No way.'

'Go on, you do a week out here then we'll swap over.'

'We're not doing that!'

'Then give us some bloody bullets so we can do it.'

'…'

'You still there?' I ask when he doesn't reply.

'I'm thinking.'

'Thinking? In your nice dry safe fortress with your food and….'

'Alright! You've made your point…you killed many then?'

'Many? We've killed thousands… like shit, maybe two hundred thousand in total.'

'How many? How?'

'We got guns from an army base, and took all their ammo, then we got more from a navy supply ship in the Solent and…'

'Two hundred thousand? Are there any left?'

'Are there any left he asks! Population of over fifty million, and he asks if there are any left while inside his big safe fortress…'

'Alright, alright, don't start that again…you must have used a lot of bullets.'

'We did, and we used our hands too…while running around in the heat, and the rain and the storm and…'

'Enough about the safe dry fortress!'

'Then, give us some sodding bullets then!'

'We can't just give them away. We need something in return.'

'In return?' I stare at the intercom with my eyes wide from the anger starting to bubble inside me, 'in return? We're out here running about like fucking idiots, and you're in there with ALL THE FUCKING BULLETS...'

'Don't shout please, it's really not necessary.'

'I WILL FUCKING SHOUT...'

'Please don't, you're amplified on this system and your voice distorts.'

My breath hisses out between clenched teeth, nostrils flaring, 'mate, I don't have fucking time for this...I'll ask nicely...please, can we please have some bullets...please...'

'And I said yes, yes you can have some bullets, but only when we've worked out the terms of our agreement.'

'Listen, fuckhead,' I snap, 'you can't sit inside the fucking bullet factory while the world goes to shit...that isn't fair...it's...it's...'

'It's what?' Condescending and goading.

'It's not British is what it's not...not bloody British...you've got the bullets; we've got the guns and there are millions of zombies that need killing...'

'Britain was built on trade so...'

'Britain was built on a sense of fair play and doing the right thing...'

'Apart from the slavery, yeah?'

'Slavery? What a million fucking years ago! We abolished slavery before most of the world did.'

'We still colonised everywhere which effectively rendered their countries as slave states against our imperial ruling.'

'We did colonise, but we gave them back...and that was in the Victorian times and...'

'Nineteen forty-seven...that's when we gave India back.'

'That was post-war, but we still gave it back.'

'Even the yanks had to fight for their independence from us so don't come here giving me all this British sense of fair play nonsense...look what happened to Lady Di...'

'What!'

'That was a conspiracy you know, where was the fair play then?'

'It wasn't a conspiracy; it was a fucking car accident.'

'Yes, it was a car accident, but who caused it? Eh? Who caused the accident?'

'The driver…who was pissed…the pissed driver…'

'And Iraq.'

'Oh, my god…look can we please have some…'

'Weapons of mass destruction? Yeah, what weapons…they had oil is what they had.'

'Yes, okay fair point…but the country reacted when we all realised, we had been duped and lied too….so *that was* the sense of fair play…'

'Yes, yes, I'll agree to that one, yes, we did react…but nonetheless the British sense of fair play was brought about as a way of suppressing the masses.'

'Mate, are you a communist or something? How did a communist get a job in a munitions factory?'

'I'm not a communist, I am not an anything ist…I'm a realist…but yeah, I was the secretary of the union and…'

'That's an ist…Realist is an ist…look, I'm sorry, but we are really busy and we're desperate for some bullets…'

'Busy doing what?' Light of tone and pitch, and the more he speaks the more I realise this bloke must be permanently like this with some notion in his head that it's his role in life to play devil's advocate to any perceived authority.

'Killing FUCKING ZOMBIES, YOU TWAT…'

'Don't shout into the intercom…stand back a bit if you…'

'Mate,' I press my mouth to the grill, 'if you don't give me some fucking bullets I will come in there and fucking take them…'

'How?'

'Trust me…'

'You won't get in here…'

'We will…WE FUCKING WILL…WE HAVE A DAVE…'

'A what?'

'A FUCKING DAVE …WE HAVE A DAVE AND A CLARENCE… RIGHT…I GAVE YOU A CHANCE…'

'Where are you going?'

'I'M GOING TO GET OUR DAVE AND CLARENCE AND

THEN….AND THEN…' I turn to point at the intercom…'where's the camera?'

'What camera?'

'Am I on camera?'

The voice sighs, 'yes you are on camera…it's in the intercom…'

'Ha! Right,' I switch my pointing finger to the intercom, 'I'm getting Dave and Clarence, and then you'll be bloody sorry…'

'Come back! We were talking about conspiracy theories…'

'I'M GETTING DAVE AND CLARENCE AND THEN WE'RE COMING INSIDE AND…AND…AND WHEN WE DO…' I waggle my finger at the intercom while walking away, 'AND WHEN WE DO… YOU'LL BE SORRY…YES…SORRY…BECAUSE…BECAUSE I'LL PUNCH YOU IN THE FACE.'

'I can't hear you, you're too far away now.'

I race back to the intercom, 'I SAID YOU'LL BE SORRY…WHEN I GET DAVE AND CLARENCE AND AND… AND PUNCH YOU IN THE FACE!'

'Good luck with that,' the sneering voice laughs, 'you can't get in and if by some remote magical chance, you do get inside…we'll bloody cream the floor with you.'

'Wipe the floor, you bloody idiot.'

'What?'

'It's wipe the floor, not cream the floor.'

'Oh, is it? Hang on,' the dull thump comes back as he seeks clarification from those around him, 'split decision.'

'What is?'

'Creaming the floor, we've got a split decision on the correct terminology.'

'Think it through,' I reply, 'cream the floor? What image does that conjure up? Wiping the floor denotes that firstly you will beat us down to the extent *we are on the floor* and then use as rags to *wipe the floor…*'

'He's got a valid point there,' he says to whoever is with him, 'I'm not disagreeing with you, Bob…I'm just saying the lad has a valid point…no, no, it's not about taking sides, Bob…I'm just playing devil's advocate here so…'

'Right…we're coming in and we're gonna punch you all in the face, including Bob and…and then, we'll just take the bullets!' The words are out of my mouth before I realise what I'm saying.

'You can't punch Bob,' the voice says indignantly, 'he's a lovely old fella, been here donkey years…'

'Oh, has he,' a flood of guilt rushes through me, 'okay, not Bob then, tell him I'm sorry and I didn't mean it.'

'Bob, he said sorry and he didn't mean it…'

'Hullo?' A different voice, older and clearly not used to speaking into the strange magical metal thing, 'hullo? Can you hear me? Can he hear me, can he?'

'I can hear you, is that Bob?'

'Yes, over…this is Bob…over…'

'You don't have to say *over*, Bob,' the first voice says in the background.

'Yeah, I can hear you, sorry about that, Bob…I didn't mean you would get punched in the face.'

'Nah, it's alright nipper, you probably running about out there getting all worked up ain't ya.'

'Yes, yes something like that…listen, we just need some bullets.'

'He wants some bullets,' Bob says to someone else, 'does he have to have the requisitions sheets? You got the requisitions sheets there, nipper?'

'Er, no Bob…we don't as er…kind of like seeing as how the er… world has sort of ended?'

'Oh, right, ended has it, he says the world has ended, does he still need the requisitions sheets? Hullo nipper, I'm being told you don't need the requisitions sheets now.'

'Great,' I say with forced lightness, 'can we get some bullets then, please.'

'Ah, now that's a common mistake,' Bob replies with an obvious smile, 'you don't *get* the bullets you see, we gives them to you…so you *have* the bullets, like when you order food in a café like you don't actually *get* it yourself, do you…'

'Sean Lock said that,' I say scratching my chin thoughtfully.

'Sean who? He works here, does he? We got a Sean working here now? I think this nipper knows him.'

'No, Sean...Sean Lock...he's a comedian...he did a joke about ordering coffee in Starbucks or something, and did the whole *get* and *have* routine.'

'Oh, did he? Funny, is he?'

'Er, yeah...very funny...'

'Probably one of them modern ones that swears all the time. We had Bob Monkhouse back in my day, he made me laugh he did...oh, I got to hand you back over to Derek, nice talking to you nipper, and I'll say hello to Sean if I see him, over and out.'

'I'm back,' Derek announces, 'that was Bob you were talking to.'

'Yes, I er...I figured that one out. Er, Derek...can we *have* some bullets please...we probably got off on the wrong foot back there, but er...we,' I glance back at the Saxon, make a decision and hope for the best, 'it's just that our..er...battalion is scattered all over place and er... HQ are demanding that we clear our sector er...before we can er...go to...er...the next sector?'

'Battallion? What battalion you with? Which outfit you with? Who is the commanding officer then?'

Shit. Think...'Er...it's the newly formed one, Derek...under the command of...' who was that bloke we met at Salisbury? The annoying officer?' 'Er...Gibbs, we're under Galloway-Gibbs, he was from the intelligence service er arm of the er...Royal Logistics but really you know, I shouldn't be passing that information on.'

'You think that's going to work? Pretending to be from the military? Not a chance,'

'Fine, then just give us some bullets, and we'll sod off.'

'Fair enough,' he says with an air of indifference, 'what you got then?'

'Been through this, Derek, we don't have anything.'

'You said you had guns.'

'Changed my mind. We need them.'

'What use are your guns without rounds?'

'What use are your rounds without guns?'

'We already have guns.'

'Then, you don't need ours. Derek, I'm running out of time here, mate…please, I'm asking you nicely, we've been through hell out here, but we've survived, and we've got people to look after…'

'Your problem, should have found a secure place like we did.'

'You didn't find it! I bet you already worked there…what were you? The night shift or something?'

'Doesn't matter what we were, only that we're here and you ain't… and no trade means no bullets.'

'Derek?'

'What?'

'Do you have women and children in there?'

'Is that a threat?'

'No mate, but I suggest you put them somewhere in the back where they won't get hurt because we are coming in and we are taking the bullets.'

'You will not get inside this facility, and any attempt will result in you being fired upon.'

'We don't want that, we don't want anyone getting hurt at all…but we need ammunition, we'll back up and you can pop some outside these doors for us…'

'We can do that, once you've worked out what you can trade for them.'

'We don't bloody have anything!'

'We need alcohol. Go into the local town and get some booze for us, decent stuff mind. Scotch, Brandy…get some wine too…in fact, bring back as much as you can carry.'

'We're not going to do that, Derek.'

'And the lads asked for some adult magazines too, you know…the top-shelf stuff…bloody internet has gone down and…'

'You want to get pissed and have a wank? While we're out here…I saw my sister being killed in front of my eyes…I saw my friends taken and infected then, had to kill them…we've all had to do those things but…'

'And we've all had to make sacrifices.'

. . .

I STOMP BACK TOWARDS THE SAXON WITH A FACE LIKE THUNDER, 'DAVE...
where are you?'

'In here...where I was before...'

'We need to get inside.'

'Okay,' he jumps down from the Saxon and watches me approach
then switches his gaze to take in the building. He thinks for a moment,
stares at the building line then traces his gaze down to the front
doors...'ram those doors, Mr Howie.'

'That your plan, is it?'

'Yes, Mr Howie.'

'Awesome plan, Dave.'

'Thanks.'

'I was being sarcastic...right...everyone out we're going to ram the
doors...'

'Er boss,' Clarence interjects, 'I think everyone should stay in...in
case they fire at us...'

'Right, everyone stay in the Saxon,' I shout as I clamber up into the
driver's seat, 'and bloody hang onto something. I'm gonna punch that
man in the face...right in the chops...and like really hard too.'

'What man?' Clarence asks.

'The man!' I shout back as I start reversing the Saxon back to get a
good run-up, 'the man on the intercom...I'm gonna punch him...no...
actually, Blowers!'

'Yes, Mr Howie...'

'You're good at punching...you are going to punch the man in the
face.'

'Okay, Mr Howie...what for?'

'Mr Howie does not have to explain why he wants someone punched
in the face, Simon.'

'Sorry, Dave...okay Mr Howie, er...will you point him out? Or er...
do I just punch anyone?'

'Punch anyone...but not women...or kids...punch any men...unless
they're old or disabled or like...wearing glasses...any able-bodied men,
punch any able-bodied men.'

'Can we all punch the able-bodied men?' Nick asks.

'Yep, everyone find an able-bodied man and punch him. But not Bob.'

'Who's Bob?' Clarence asks.

'Lovely old fella, worked there for donkeys' years.'

'What about able-bodied women?' Lani asks.

'Yes…er…Lani and Paula, punch the able-bodied women and everyone else find an able-bodied man…apart from Clarence…'

'Huh? Why?'

'You're too big.'

'I'll punch soft.'

'Right, everyone braced…fucking gonna get inside and…oh fuck it! FUCK IT…Not a word…not a word from anyone…Cookey!…Not a word…'

'I didn't say anything, Mr Howie.'

'Anyone can stall a vehicle…it happens all the time…right we braced? Good…'

I press my foot down and stare at the doors, the engine roars, screams, shouts and curses as it gains momentum and speed. I don't hammer it as we don't need great speed, just power and enough to punch through. I hold my middle finger up facing towards the intercom as we get, closer and the solid line of the building suddenly looks very big, and very tough and we're going very fast…shit…shit…this was a bad idea.

A cacophony of screams as we all slightly panic at the second before impact. Clarence holds on dearly, everyone holds on, screaming and yelling, apart from Dave who just hangs on and gives one of his big grins at the prospect of something being broken and smashed.

The impact is monumental. The doors give instantly as we plough through, glass smashing, metal framework screeching and twisting, bricks thudding down onto the Saxon, and the big wheels churn us further into the reception area as we smash into sofas, reception desks, computers and chairs. Grinding, smashing noises, and the big vehicle judders and shakes as we skid and slide across the polished floor to slam into the end wall where we come to rest in a dust cloud of debris spewing out everywhere. The engine cuts out, and gradually we regain some composure as the noises trickle down to the odd thump of bricks and masonry falling, and glass tinkling on the ground.

'Shit...' I groan and shake my head, 'bit fast...sorry...'

'A bit?' Clarence glares at me, 'fucking hell, boss...we almost went right through...'

Still groaning, I go to push my door open and realise we're wedged in against the far wall, I don't say anything but a motion for Clarence to scoot out so I can clamber over. He does and drops down to shake his head and look around at the trail of destruction behind us.

'Actually,' I say mildly, 'that was easier than I thought it would be, I really thought we might bounce off.'

'Why did you do it then?' Lani asks, 'no, don't answer...just...just don't answer.'

Clarence stares around then fixes his eyes on a set of double doors at the end. Kicking broken furniture aside, he threads a route over and starts feeling the doors before banging on them a few times, 'metal,' he calls back, 'the reception wasn't reinforced, this is the reinforced bit.'

'Oh...oh, shit...so...we've still got to get through there? Are they solid?'

'Very solid,' he bangs again, a dull thud which is clearly from solid metal with no sign of any hollow sections.

'Bollocks, Dave...we need to get inside those doors.'

'The doors are the strongest point,' he remarks, 'we need to go for the weakest point.'

'Which is?'

'Windows.'

'Won't they be toughened?'

'Yes, but still weaker than the wall or that door,' he replies dully.

'And they'll be on the other side waiting to shoot us,' Clarence adds helpfully.

'Right, Saxon it is then,' I head back and get through the passenger side into my driver's seat and then, commence a long drawn out million point turn as I try and get the huge vehicle away from the wall and turned to face the doors. Eventually, and with everyone watching with interest, I get the front of the Saxon up and touching the doors with

Clarence guiding me in, he gives a thumbs up and shouts, 'try now, hard forward.'

Foot down, engine screams, and the big wheels spin on the tiled floor. We don't go anywhere.

'Back up and ram,' Clarence shouts.

So, I do. Back up that is. I reverse until the back of the Saxon hits the end wall with a nice big bang and some winces from the faces watching, forward gear, foot down and I go for it. Several tons of metal against several tons of metal, and the noise is a resounding boom, but little else happens other than I almost smash my face into the steering wheel.

'Try the wall,' the big man motions me to pull back then points at the section of a wall right next to the door. The back of the Saxon hits the wall again, more winces, forward gear, and I surge the vehicle across the once pretty reception area that is slowly getting completely ruined. The boom is less than before, more of a grinding wallop than anything, but the wall does shake as the front-end gauges nice big chunks of plaster away from the render. Backing up, and Clarence, Roy and the lads all crowd in to stare, point and poke at the damaged wall. Much shaking of heads, some sucking of teeth and Roy even puts his hands on his hips, all he needs is a pencil behind his ear.

'Reinforced,' Clarence shouts, 'it'll go but it'll take some doing.'

'Fair enough, mind out then,' I try again, ramming the front of the vehicle into the wall then, reversing back until I collide with the other wall. Back and forth until the reception room fills up with acrid diesel fumes, and the tiles become black from tyre rubber. It does strike me that the poor Saxon is probably wondering what she's done to deserve having her head repeatedly smashed into a solid concrete wall.

Seven or eight times, and Clarence once again waves me to stop while the general builders gather around to inspect the works and get ready for the quote. They pick bits of broken concrete out from the hole forming, inspecting it, pointing at it, turning it over in their hands, nodding, shaking heads before I get the go ahead to try again.

Another few times back and forth, and my head starts hurting from the fumes building up in the enclosed space, the noise and the constant jolts. The concrete is smashed away in huge spots only to expose steel rods running through the wall. These get inspected by the builders, and I notice there are much less nods this time and far more shaking of heads. I jump down and head over.

'No good,' Roy turns as I approach, 'these rods are too thick...only way through would be by cutting them with a torch.'

'Bollocks, how about a digger or something? If we got one of those... would that work?'

'Eventually,' he nods, 'but it won't be a quick process.'

The frustration builds again, delay after delay. One step forward and ten steps back. We can't afford these delays, and it's alright for everyone to fucking stand about waiting for me to make a decision. Let Mr Howie figure it out. Let Mr Howie work out how to get inside. Let Mr Howie talk to the fuckwit through the intercom and negotiate.

Irritation escalates straight past annoyance, ignores anger, and goes straight for fury, pure bloody fury. Fury at having to deal with everything and being the one who decides everything. Fury at knowing we have to find Marcy to work out our next step but having to deal with Lani and everyone else. Fury at being seen as the bad guy for making everyone run a few miles today and having to say no to Maddox to going back for a meal and a rest. A fucking rest! Yeah, let's sit around and talk about how well we've all done finding four doctors.

'I want in that building,' muttering to myself, the darkness in my eyes again, 'I want in that building...' The others turn slowly in ones and twos to watch me muttering to myself, 'I want in...I want in...'

'Mr Howie?' Paula says with real concern in her voice, 'are you okay?'

'I want in.'

'Howie,' Lani starts towards me, 'we'll get in, just take it easy.'

'I want in,' I say it louder.

'And we will,' she says soothingly.

'NOW...I want in that fucking building NOW!'

'Hey,' she says softly, 'take it easy.'

'No. I want inside that fucking building...fucking pricks sat in there drinking tea, and wanking off in the toilets while we're out here getting the shit beaten out of us...'

'Howie,' urgency in her voice as she reaches out to grasp my hand which I pull away harshly.

'Fucking...fucking...Sarah died right in front of me...Chris...Ted... remember Ted?'

'Of course, yes, of course, Howie.'

'Remember Ted and the others? Remember them? They died...THEY FUCKING DIED WHILE THAT LOT SAT IN THERE TALKING ABOUT FUCKING CONSPIRACY THEORY...THEY'VE GOT THE BULLETS...'

'Boss,' Clarence strides towards me with an alarmed expression, 'calm down.'

'Calm down! Fucking calm down...I'll fucking calm down when I get inside, and smash that cunts face in...'

'Hey!' Lani says sharply, 'you don't say that word.'

'What cunts? They are cunts...YOU HEAR ME? YOU FUCKING HEAR ME, YOU **CUNTS**.'

'Stop it, stop it right now, and come with me,' she starts pulling me away, dragging me towards the smashed in wall we drove through.

'CUNTS...FUCKING CUNTS...I'LL GET IN THERE AND RIP YOUR FUCKING FACES OFF...I'LL FUCKING END YOU PRICKS...'

'Dave! Get him outside now,' Lani snaps, 'Dave!'

'No,' he refuses bluntly.

'David! Take him outside, you're the only one he'll listen to.'

'No.'

'Dave,' Clarence growls, 'what the hell has got into you two...boss, come on...I'm taking you outside.'

'NO! I'm getting inside that fucking building...get out the way.'

'Don't touch him,' Dave warns Clarence as the big man goes to stop me striding towards the Saxon.

'Lads,' Clarence holds his hands out with the palms outwards, 'easy... take it easy...Dave, you know I'd never hurt him.

'That's right. You won't.'

'Dave...he's losing it, he needs a time out.'

'He's doing what needs to be done.'

'Dave,' Lani appeals to him while I wrench the driver's door open, 'stop him…stop him before he does something stupid.'

'Mr Howie doesn't do anything stupid,' he replies.

'Dave for fuck's sake,' Clarence starts towards the Saxon as Dave steps in front of him, 'Dave…please…move aside.'

'No.'

'GET OUT THE FUCKING WAY,' I scream, 'MOVE OR GET RUN OVER…'

'Dave, he's losing it,' Clarence pleads, 'get him out of there.'

'Dave,' Blowers moves forward followed by Nick and Cookey, 'Dave, do something.'

'MOVE!' I start the engine and grind gears while the rage spills out into my trembling hands, 'I want in…I want in…I'm getting in… FUCKING GET IN REVERSE,' screaming at the gear shift, I finally get it in and slam my foot down to pull back with a crash into the back wall.

'DAVE!' Lani shouts, 'He'll hurt himself…get him out now.'

'You are moving,' Clarence starts forward with a grim look at Dave.

'Nobody touches him,' Dave draws his pistol, pulling Clarence up short with a face of intense shock.

'Dave…Jesus Christ…put that away,' Paula shouts.

'Put that bow down,' Dave aims true and straight as Roy makes a motion to take his bow off his shoulder, 'move out the way now.'

'Dave…what are you doing?' Lani begs.

'MOVE…FUCKING MOVE,' I bellow at the top of my lungs, and stamp my foot down. The Saxon roars ahead, gathering speed as I ram the front into the wall and send the team scattering in all directions, and this time I keep my foot down, driving the power of the vehicle into the wall that grinds and splinters in protest. I push down harder, the engine screams in response, thick dirty fumes spewing from the exhaust as the wheels gain traction on the tiles now damaged and covered in debris. The wall starts to give so I back up and hammer it in again, and keep the pressure on, turning the wheel left and right to shift the front end to rake the wall. The bars start to buckle and give, centimetres are gained. I back up, slamming the back of the Saxon into the back wall and then, go for it again. Aiming for the section with the bars exposed. Movement outside, voices shouting, Clarence's deep tones, Lani screaming, Dave roaring in his parade-ground voice.

I want in. I'm getting in. I'm getting inside. The Saxon screeches in protest against the rods buried in the wall, but those rods are either not deep enough or not strong enough as the Saxon slowly eats into them with ever-increasing power and force that has them bending surely to the point they will snap and give proper. I can feel it giving, the wall is getting closer with every second I drive forward. My mind is gone. All I can visualise is getting inside and beating the shit out of every person in there who sat idly by in their fortress of bullets while everyone else watched their loved ones die.

Back I go and forward again, and this time the ramming gains me valuable centimetres, and the next time I drawback, I can see one of the bars has snapped. One bar snapped so the rest can snap so I got at it, back and forth, and grinding into that wall. I don't notice the thick fumes that fill up in the room, I don't notice I'm coughing harder with every second. All I can see is Marcy, Sarah, Ted and big Chris. All I can see is the infection never-ending to try and kill us, and a lifetime spent killing to stay alive while everyone stares and waits for me to make decisions for them.

I want in. I want in. I want in. The words become a mantra, and it's the only thing my mind can fix on. I want in. I want in.

Another rod snaps with a thunk, and suddenly the vehicle shoots forward another few inches, and my eyes go wide with fervent glee. I want in. I want in. I want in.

I back up and ignore the waving figures in the reception so desperate for my attention, forward again and another foot is gained. A whole foot in one go, and another rod pings as it breaks. I want in. I want in. I'm getting in. I'm getting in. My lips twitch as the words are formed and spill from my mouth to be lost in the outrageous sound all about me and of which I am oblivious.

Got to find Marcy. Got to get ammunition. Got to get in here. Got to find Marcy. Got to get ammunition. Got to get inside here. Got to find Sarah. Got to get ammunition. Got to get in. Got to find my sister. Got to find her. Sarah.

Tears are streaming down my face. The diesel fumes choke my throat, but I refuse to yield. This wall is the infection. This wall was put by those people inside and they put all the walls up. I only ever wanted to find Sarah and get to the fort. I didn't ask for this. I should have stayed with her and kept her safe. If I had been there, they wouldn't have taken her. I'm Howie and they fear me, but I left, and she died only to be reborn and die again, and now she's with Paco and their baby.

Oh, god. I'm losing it. I'm deep inside myself staring in horror at the beast that screams in hysteria as he drives the poor Saxon into the wall so desperate to get at the people within. Dave fights and threatens with his almighty misplaced sense of loyalty to me. He'd kill the lot of them without hesitation if he thought they threatened me. I've got to stop. Stop now. But I've got to find Marcy and get ammunition so I must get in. I want in. That's it. That's what I have to do. I have to get in and get the bullets.

One last reverse. One last surge forward, and I know this will be it. This one will punch me through, but those fucking rods hold strong, snagging and bending and breaking, but too slowly. I pull back again, but I can see a gap. A gap big enough to get through.

I'm out of the Saxon and running across the floor. The machine stalls in my haste and in the silence, I can see Lani sobbing with tears running down her face as she screams my name. Clarence roars at Dave to back down, Cookey cries while Nick and Blowers plead for him to move out the way. Roy and Paula shocked to the core, but I can get through that gap. I want in and I can get in.

At the wall, I start to push my head through, then my shoulders that snag, and get cut from the metal rods and sharp bits of concrete and plaster that graze every bit of exposed skin. I can do it. I can get through here.

'Howie stop,' Lani screams at me, 'don't Howie...'

'Mr Howie,' Cookey yells, other voices shouting my name, and I glance back to see Dave right on my heels nodding at me. I grin at him and my mouth is wet, so I wipe it with the back of my hand which comes away bloodied.

'Stop,' another voice this time, a voice from inside, the same voice from the intercom, 'please...stop...we're unarmed...'

'FUCK YOU,' I rage and twist and buck as Dave pushes and shoves me to get through.

'Please...we're not armed...please, take the bullets, you can have what you want but please...'

'I'M COMING...MR FUCKING HOWIE IS COMING...'

'Screams from women and children, men shouting, and someone appears at the gap. A big man that tries pushing me back through the hole, so I lash out with spittle and rage tearing through my body. He reels back from a hard punch to the face, and other men rush to pull him away. Lots of them, women crying and sobbing, men holding sticks and knives but no guns. I don't care. I want in. I'm almost in.

With a final howling heave, I wrench my torn body through the gap, and fall down the other side to flare upright and scream in victory. Blood drips from the cuts on my arms, hands and face. There they are. They stayed in here safe while we fought and died. They hid with all the bullets while my sister died. They did it. They killed Sarah. I am Howie, son of Howard and I bring vengeance upon you.

I charge forward with hell in my eyes. The men push the women and children to run and scatter, but in their haste, they run towards me, around me, near me, and I attack anything I can reach. The braver ones try to block my path and intercept me, but the first one goes down with a broken nose from the headbutt I smash into him.

A woman screams, but they are the screams of the undead who killed Sarah, so I grab her hair and launch her flying off to one side as a man tries to swipe at me with a long wooden handle from a shovel. I take the blow on my arm, and the fact that I don't flicker nor flinch terrifies him to the spot so I wrench the weapon from his hands, and use it to beat him down onto the ground, but the weapon is too cold, too impersonal and I want to use my hands. I break away from the poor man cowering and bleeding on the floor and launch at two more men coming to attack me. They go straight for a full-on charge, clearly hoping to use their combined body weight to take me down except I jump into them, and so doing I disrupt the momentum they have gained, and quickly set about whacking hard fists into faces and heads. I break noses, jaws, and I hear the satisfying crack of an arm fracturing at the elbow as I ram my knee into the back of a joint while pulling backwards on the wrist. Men. Women. Children. I attack without care for I have to be ruthless and driven, as ruthless and driven as the infection for these people are the infection. They caused it. They made it. They killed Sarah and all the people I loved.

The faces of the screaming innocents become the drawn faces of the hissing undead. Eyes that weep real tears become red and bloodshot. All I see are the undead and so I hurt them.

LANI WATCHED AS HOWIE TURNED FROM ANGRY, TO FURIOUS, TO FILLED with a wild and demented rage. His normally soft eyes grew darker and hooded. The reason within him, that reason that kept him apart from all others…that reason was gone. Howie was gone, eaten away by a growing desperation that swept his rationale aside. She saw this. She watched all day as he struggled with his impatience and made them fight, run and flee. She cursed herself inwardly at the bitterly jealous words that spilled from her mouth when he talked about Marcy. She is in his team and loyal beyond question, but she is also in love with the man and to see him act like that, to say things like that invoked a response that she could barely control. As the day wore on, she watched him closely, always vigilant and constantly exchanging quiet silent messages with Clarence and the lads. Even Paula and Roy could see the change, so they all stayed close, ready to react, ready to do what was needed.

But this, seeing Howie become this was extraordinary and far worse than they could ever imagine. Urging him to stop, pleading, shouting, demanding, crying but nothing would get through to him, and then Dave stepped in and they knew Dave would kill them without hesitation if they so much as tried to touch Howie.

Dave is Howie's sentinel, the ever-present bodyguard that feels no fear, no remorse and is blinded by his utter devotion to his leader.

Lani tried, Clarence tried, Blowers, Cookey, Nick…they all tried, but

Dave showed them what would happen. The face he presents to his targets was now presented to them. The eyes, so quick and watchful, the fluidity of his movements, the way his head cocked as he tracked and calculated. The way he always knows exactly where Howie is.

With Howie and Dave through the gap, Lani is the first one through after them, pausing only to stare aghast at the terrible sight within. Unarmed men, women and children being attacked by two men now so deadly in their skills. Dave watched Howie, watched how he punched kicked and lashed out, so he did the same, brawling rather than killing and for that, Lani offered a quick thanks to the Gods.

Through the gap and into the melee, desperately trying to disarm those who have taken up hand weapons, desperately trying to protect Howie while also trying to stop him. The others get through, and one by one they rush in to do the same. Fist fighting, brawling, shouting and screaming.

SOMEONE GRABS ME FROM THE SIDE, THEN AN ARM AROUND MY NECK. Hands go for my pistol on my belt while they shout and plead for me to stop, but I can't, I can't stop, I'll never stop. So, I thrash and buck and punch and kick while I dig my chin under the arm around my throat and dig my teeth into the soft flesh. Howls of pain screams of agony, and I break free.

Someone punches me hard to the side of the head, so hard it sends me flying off. Dave is out and rushing in, Lani behind him, Nick and Blowers, Cookey too. They're all here to punch and fight with me and give vengeance to these bastards that stayed in here and killed my sister. Another punch, then another and my lips split. I hit out and keep punching, lashing out with hard fists that connect and break bones. I bite and screech, kick and smash into anything and anyone that comes near me.

More of their side rush in and a big man comes at me only to be taken out by Blowers charging forward with a dive at his legs. Cookey fends two off with wild punches, more men pile in from their side and women too. Everyone is screaming and shouting, people crying, sobbing *stop...please stop...take what you want...stop him...stop Howie...stop Howie...get Howie...*

'Dave! They're trying to kill us, Dave! Fight Dave...fight Dave...' He turns to glance at me, his face looks different now, 'Dave...they killed Sarah...kill 'em Dave...kill 'em all...' He doesn't move but stares with wide eyes, 'Dave...with me...you're with me, Dave...kill 'em...'

He turns his body to face me, and his face is a mask of pure pain. I see hurt in his eyes, deep hurt and a tear spills from his eye to roll down his cheek. He looks around as though seeing things differently.

'Dave...why aren't you killing...KILL 'EM DAVE...KILL...KILL... THEY KILLED SARAH...'

'Dave for the love of god,' Lani screams...his head snaps around to stare at her as she fights against a man armed with a stick, deftly turning as he swipes to pluck it from his hands and throw it aside, 'Dave, listen to me...if you love Howie...if you love him...stop him...stop him now...'

Dave nods as the tears spill down faster and harder. He turns to look at me.

'TRAITOR...DAVE YOU TRAITOR...KILL THEM...I'M HOWIE AND...' fuck this, they're all against me, they all want to kill me, and they all killed Sarah. I'll shoot the lot of them. I go for my pistol, but even at my fastest, I can't hope to be quick enough to stop Dave crossing that ground. As I tug it free, he is on me, sweeping my legs out and plucking the pistol from my grip.

'CUNT...YOU FUCKING CUNT...DAVE NO...'

'Hold him,' Clarence bellows, 'everyone stop...stop...'

'Dave, keep him down...'

'DAVE...GET OFF ME...THEY KILLED SARAH...THEY...THEY KILLED HER...DAVE...They killed Sarah...she's dead, Dave...my sister is dead...they...they killed her...'

'They didn't, Mr Howie,' he mutters softly, 'they didn't.'

'They did...Dave...my sister is dead.'

'She is,' he nods, and the tears from his eyes fall on my face to join mine that rolls fat and fast down my cheeks.

I reach up, gripping his shoulders, 'Sarah is dead...my sister...I'll never...I'll never see her again...'

'I know, Mr Howie,' his red eyes fill with fresh tears. Lani rushes in, free from whatever fight she was in.

'It's okay,' she's in my ear, soft words from a soft voice, 'it's okay, Howie.'

'Sarah...my sister...'

'It's okay...'

'I can't...I can't do it anymore...Lani...Dave...I can't...I want her back...'

'Oh, Howie,' she cries as I weep, and I pull them both into me, burying my head in their bodies where I want to suffocate in their warmth and love.

Someone presses in behind me, a deep voice, and two huge arms that envelop us all, 'easy, boss...easy now.'

'She's gone...they're all gone...oh, god...I can't go on...I can't...it's too much now, too much...please...'

'Easy, boss, come on, it's okay.'

'Howie, we're here...we're all here,' Lani so close to my ear.

'I'm sorry,' Dave cries and his voice breaks.

'Mr Howie,' Cookey is there, his own voice breaking with emotion, and he cries and weeps as I do, 'don't cry, Mr Howie.'

'Form a line in front,' Blowers snaps at the rest of the team, 'Jagger, Mo Mo...in front of the boss now, Nick...get them disarmed.'

'Everyone stay calm,' Nick's voice, strong and confident, 'drop your weapons and move back. We're good people and will take care of this, but drop your weapons now...please...please, everyone, stay calm now...no one will get hurt...'

'It's okay,' Paula joins him, 'he's our leader...'

'Please,' Nick repeats, 'he kept us alive since it started...please...just stay calm...we'll take care of this I promise.'

'Give us space,' Paula commands, 'let us take care of this, please... nothing bad will happen...'

'We're good people,' Nick urges them, 'we do things the right way, and this...this is not our way, this is not Mr Howie's way...he's a good man, the best man you could ever meet...let us take care of our own... we won't hurt anyone or do anything, I promise you...'

'Sort him out,' A rough voice shouts, 'fucking lunatic.'

'YOU WILL MOVE BACK,' Nick orders as the remaining team turn as one to fix on the now brave man shouting his thoughts from the back, 'we've been out there fighting for two weeks and we will take care of this, but one more word like that and...'

'Okay,' a female voice calls out, 'okay...just...just please keep him down.'

'We will,' Nick replies.

Noises of people murmuring, but they recede and drift away, children crying, men sounding angry, but I don't care. As night falls and the darkness arrives, all I can do is weep.

S he holds him close. Her arms wrapped protectively around his neck as she keeps his head pressed to her chest, her own tears of sadness and despondency roll freely down her cheeks as she feels Howie sobbing with a harshness, she never thought possible. That he clings so tight shows her the man she loves is still inside.

He reaches for Dave, a subconscious act to re-assure himself that Dave is close, and Dave is always close. Lani looks over Howie's head at the small man, both hating him more than she has ever hated anyone, but also loving his dedication, and knowing that nothing could ever hurt Howie as long as Dave was drawing breath.

Clarence finally gets through the hole, his big hands torn and bleeding from having to wrench plaster and bricks away to make a gap big enough. As he runs towards Howie, intent on taking him down from behind, so Dave crosses the ground and Clarence watches the most tender, gentle take-down he has ever seen as Dave sweeps Howie's legs and deftly plucks the pistol from his grip. Howie down, and Dave pins him and the look of pain on Dave's face tells Clarence the danger is over. So, Clarence drops to his knees and stretches those huge arms around to envelop them all, his group, his team, and he holds them close. Howie reaches a handout and grips Clarence's wrist as the big man lets his own tears break free.

Blowers, on seeing the seniors swept up, takes command. Sliding effortlessly into his role as corporal, he orders the rest into position.

They all feel it. Roy, so new to the group, and so amazed at the carnage erupting around him suddenly feels that tremendous pulse of electricity as Howie goes down. The leader has fallen, the leader needs protecting. He moves into position, taking a flank to cover with his bow ready, and his deadly eyes fixed on the jostling and panicking crowd. Paula moves through them with Nick, pistols up and aimed they pluck sticks and knives from trembling hands to throw them safely aside, both of them giving clear yet confident commands with a sense of purpose and authority that soon settles the wild energy of those attacked.

As Howie falls, so the team take the strain, and gather close together to stare into the darkness of the night.

35

The bay sweeps around, longer and deeper than it was. The reclamation of land during the storm has made it grander and far more pleasurable to the eye.

In the distance, a dark building juts up into the night sky. Lights flicker and twinkle here and there, ones and twos then more until the fort is illuminated and stands bright and real in the ruined landscape.

People within that fort. People who have survived, and now work tirelessly under the watchful eye of a young Polish woman and a young black man.

The only light to see. The only sign of humanity in a night lit only by the moon and stars.

'It's beautiful.'

'If you like that kind of thing.'

'I do.'

'Good and er…well, far be it from me to pass comment but, well, it's very nice to finally see you up and about. Really, I was very fretful at the amount of time you stayed locked away in that room, and I truly did not know what to do.'

'I'm fine now.'

'Well, that's good, and you look better, far better. More colour in your cheeks...which is strange considering what we are...'

'I feel better...calmer...'

'Calm is good! Very good. We like calm...we like calm and peace... yes, calm and peace, far underrated in my opinion...what we need is a long period of calm and peace.'

'He's coming.'

'Who is? Oh, no...please, not that again! Please...we need calm and peace, lots of calm and peace...In fact, I was just thinking earlier that perhaps we could move away from this wretched area. Find a lovely little cottage somewhere er...calm and peaceful, yes...that's what we shall do.'

'He's coming, he'll be here soon.'

'Right. I see. And er, if I may be so bold...you know this how?'

'I know.'

'You know. Right, yes...you know, do you? I worry, oh, you know how I worry and I fret, yes I worry and I fret, and I cannot stand to see you so upset and really, really I think we should just go far, far away from here. I mean...you've been locked in that room for days now, actual days of being stuck in a room with me worrying and fretting all day and all night. Not a word from you, nothing other than hearing you crying and weeping, and what could I do? Nothing. I couldn't do anything.'

'You'd worry, no matter what.'

'Yes, yes, you are right. I must confess that I am predisposed to be of a worrying nature but really, someone has to worry about you.'

'I'm fine now.'

'Fine she says, fine she says! I don't think you are fine, yes, you look fine, you look very fine, and oh, gosh don't look at me like that, I did not mean in any manner of being inappropriate, I merely meant that you look well, and healthy. Yes! Well and healthy.'

'Reggie, you are funny.'

'Marcy, my name is Reginald, and I am not funny and really, really we should go, go far away.'

'No. He's coming, Reggie. He's coming, and we're waiting.'

'Oh, dear…oh, dear, oh, dear…this won't end well, mark my words…'

ALSO BY RR HAYWOOD

A Town Called Discovery

The #1 Amazon Time Travel Thriller

A man falls from the sky. He has no memory.

What lies ahead are a series of tests. Each more brutal than the last, and if he gets through them all, he might just reach A Town Called Discovery.

*

EXTRACTED SERIES

EXTRACTED

EXECUTED

EXTINCT

Blockbuster Time-Travel

#1 Amazon US

#1 Amazon UK

#1 Audible US & UK

Washington Post & WSJ Best-seller

In 2061, a young scientist invents a time machine to fix a tragedy in his past. But his good intentions turn catastrophic when an early test reveals something unexpected: the end of the world.

A desperate plan is formed. Recruit three heroes, ordinary humans capable of extraordinary things, and change the future.

Safa Patel is an elite police officer, on duty when Downing Street comes under terrorist attack. As armed men storm through the breach, she dispatches them all.

'Mad' Harry Madden is a legend of the Second World War. Not only did he complete an

impossible mission—to plant charges on a heavily defended submarine base—but he also escaped with his life.

Ben Ryder is just an insurance investigator. But as a young man he witnessed a gang assaulting a woman and her child. He went to their rescue, and killed all five.

Can these three heroes, extracted from their timelines at the point of death, save the world?

*

THE WORLDSHIP HUMILITY

#1 Audible bestselling smash hit narrated by Colin Morgan, star of Merlin & Humans.

#1 Amazon bestselling Science-Fiction

"A rollicking, action packed space adventure…"

"Best read of the year!"

"An original and exceptionally entertaining book."

"A beautifully written and humorous adventure."

Sam, an airlock operative, is bored. Living in space should be full of adventure, except it isn't, and he fills his time hacking 3-D movie posters.

Petty thief Yasmine Dufont grew up in the lawless lower levels of the ship, surrounded by violence and squalor, and now she wants out. She wants to escape to the luxury of the Ab-Spa, where they eat real food instead of rats and synth cubes.

Meanwhile, the sleek-hulled, unmanned Gagarin has come back from the ever-continuing search for a new home. Nearly all hope is lost that a new planet will ever be found, until the Gagarin returns with a code of information that suggests a habitable planet has been found. This news should be shared with the whole fleet, but a few rogue captains want to colonise it for themselves.

When Yasmine inadvertently steals the code, she and Sam become caught up in a dangerous game of murder, corruption, political wrangling and...porridge, with sex-addicted Detective Zhang Woo hot on their heels, his own life at risk if he fails to get the code back.

*

THE UNDEAD SERIES

THE UK's #1 Horror Series

Available on Amazon & Audible

"The Best Series Ever…"

The Undead. The First Seven Days
The Undead. The Second Week.
The Undead Day Fifteen.
The Undead Day Sixteen.
The Undead Day Seventeen
The Undead Day Eighteen
The Undead Day Nineteen
The Undead Day Twenty
The Undead Day Twenty-One
The Undead Twenty-Two
The Undead Twenty-Three: The Fort
The Undead Twenty-Four: Equilibrium

Blood on the Floor
An Undead novel

Blood at the Premiere
An Undead novel

The Camping Shop
An Undead novella

www.rrhaywood.com

Find me on Facebook:

https://www.facebook.com/RRHaywood/

Find me on Twitter:

https://twitter.com/RRHaywood

Printed in Great Britain
by Amazon